Praise for
The Professors' Wives' Club

"As an NYU alum, I enjoyed the behind-the-scenes escapades at the fictional Manhattan U in *The Professors' Wives' Club*. Joanne Rendell has created a quick, fun read about a wonderful group of friends."

—Kate Jacobs, *New York Times* bestselling author of
The Friday Night Knitting Club

"Joanne Rendell's irresistible debut novel is a captivating look at an ivory tower Peyton Place filled with intrigue, heartbreak, and hope."

—Michelle Yu and Blossom Kan, authors of *China Dolls*

"The four women in *The Professors' Wives' Club* who risk it all in pursuit of life, love, and green space in New York City are smart, funny, and real—friends you'd want for life. Rendell doesn't shy away from tough issues, but her light touch and readable prose make this charming first novel a delight."

—Christina Baker Kline, author of *The Way Life Should Be*

"As a self-absorbed undergrad I never realized that the really juicy stuff was going on outside of the frat parties and late nights at the library! The women of *The Professors' Wives' Club* are a force with which to be reckoned. Joanne Rendell's debut novel is smart and suspenseful with an intriguing Edgar Allan Poe backstory. I cannot wait for Joanne's second novel."

—Robin Kall, host of "Reading with Robin"

Written by today's freshest new talents and selected by New American Library, NAL Accent novels touch on subjects close to a woman's heart, from friendship to family to finding our place in the world. The Conversation Guides included in each book are intended to enrich the individual reading experience, as well as encourage us to explore these topics together—because books, and life, are meant for sharing.

Visit us online at www.penguin.com.

THE PROFESSORS' WIVES' CLUB

WIVES' CLUB

Joanne Rendell

NAL Accent
Published by New American Library, a division of
Penguin Group (USA) Inc., 375 Hudson Street,
New York, New York 10014, USA
Penguin Group (Canada), 90 Eglinton Avenue East, Suite 700, Toronto,
Ontario M4P 2Y3, Canada (a division of Pearson Penguin Canada Inc.)
Penguin Books Ltd., 80 Strand, London WC2R 0RL, England
Penguin Ireland, 25 St. Stephen's Green, Dublin 2,
Ireland (a division of Penguin Books Ltd.)
Penguin Group (Australia), 250 Camberwell Road, Camberwell, Victoria 3124,
Australia (a division of Pearson Australia Group Pty. Ltd.)
Penguin Books India Pvt. Ltd., 11 Community Centre, Panchsheel Park,
New Delhi - 110 017, India
Penguin Group (NZ), 67 Apollo Drive, Rosedale, North Shore 0632,
New Zealand (a division of Pearson New Zealand Ltd.)
Penguin Books (South Africa) (Pty.) Ltd., 24 Sturdee Avenue,
Rosebank, Johannesburg 2196, South Africa

Penguin Books Ltd., Registered Offices:
80 Strand, London WC2R 0RL, England

First published by NAL Accent, an imprint of New American Library,
a division of Penguin Group (USA) Inc.

First Printing, September 2008
10 9 8 7 6 5 4 3 2 1

 REGISTERED TRADEMARK—MARCA REGISTRADA

LIBRARY OF CONGRESS CATALOGING-IN-PUBLICATION DATA:

Rendell, Joanne.
   The Professors' Wives' Club/Joanne Rendell.
     p. cm.
   ISBN 978-0-451-22491-0
   1. College teachers' spouses—Fiction. 2. Female friendship—Fiction. 3. Gardens—Conservation and
restoration—Fiction. 4. Poe, Edgar Allan, 1809–1849—Fiction. 5. Manuscripts—Fiction. 6. Manhattan (New
York, N.Y.)—Fiction. I. Title.
   PS3618.E5747P76 2008
   813'6—dc22   2007048911

Set in Fairfield
Designed by Alissa Amell

Printed in the United States of America

For Brad, my professor

Acknowledgments

This book wouldn't have been possible without many people, and therefore I offer my infinite thanks to the following:

My agent, Claudia Cross, for believing in this project from its very inception and for her fine readership and encouragement. Anne Bohner, who is the kindest and smartest editor any writer could ask for, and whose editorial suggestions—every one of them—were spot on. The curator of the Poe Museum in Richmond, Chris Semtner, whom I have never met face-to-face but who gave me invaluable information about Edgar Allan Poe and "The Raven." Yvette Manessis Corporon, Jay Fisher, Dina Jordan, and Jean Railla, my fabulous writing companions and first readers, who cheered and advised me as I wrote *The Professors' Wives' Club*. Also, thanks to Bonnie Bernstein, Amanda Darrach, Beth Feldman, Luke LaCroix, Vanessa Manko, and the East Village Baby Crew, who supported and encouraged me in all kinds of ways. My online writing pals, including the wonderful Amanda Ashby and Jenny Gardiner. Melanie Feakins and Kate Dorney, my best friends in the world, who over the years have shown me the fun and importance of sisterhood and friendship (the same sisterhood and friendship that inspired this book). All my family, particularly my mum, Kate Matthews, who always believed I would be a published author, and Jana Lewis, my mother-in-law, who was the first person to finish the earliest draft of the novel. My son, Benny, for his deliciously long naps and for being one sweet kid. And finally Brad Lewis, my love, my life, my inspiration, and the best professor in academia! *The Professors' Wives' Club* is, of course, for you.

"Quoth the Raven, 'Nevermore.'"

—Edgar Allan Poe, "The Raven"
(First published January 29, 1845,
in New York's *Evening Mirror* from a copy
prepared for *The American Review*)

THE PROFESSORS'
WIVES' CLUB

One

Mary

Even though the sky was heavy with rain clouds and an eerie morning gloom hung over the city, Mary didn't take off her dark glasses. It was bad enough that Sandra, their cleaner, had caught a glimpse of her swollen eye; she couldn't risk anyone else seeing it. As if to make doubly sure the puffed and purple mess remained concealed, Mary pushed the glasses farther up her nose and winced as the plastic pressed into her tender skin.

Squinting upward through her one good eye, she could just make out the Empire State Building and the twinkling tip of the Chrysler peeking above the university's library. On either side of the garden where she sat, two apartment buildings jutted thirty floors into the sky. Although each building housed hundreds of Manhattan U's faculty, each with their own window looking down on the garden below, Mary found this place strangely secluded and anonymous. Perhaps it had something to do with the high fence and the garden's heavy iron gate with its large, menacing lock. Only people who lived in the two towers had keys to the garden, and when it was gloomy like today only a few of those people actually used them.

She would miss the garden. After she was gone, that was. Back when her daughter was young, they spent almost every summer afternoon out here. It was their small oasis in the heart of the dirty and rambunctious city. The trees around the garden were always thick with leaves, and the blooming honeysuckle that weaved its way through the steel struts of the fence made it impossible to see bustling Bleecker Street only a few feet away. She knew her daughter was safe in this garden, and on shady spots in the diligently mowed grass the two of them would play and skip and stretch out for hours, drawing, reading, and napping. Back in those days Mary would sometimes even pull out a battered leather-bound notebook and write.

Today, however, with the trees still bare from winter and a sharp spring breeze whipping Mary's long black and silver hair across her face, the garden was not so inviting. But it was the only place she could think to come. The only place where she wouldn't have to explain the dark glasses, and the only place she wouldn't see *him*.

It was ironic that Mary came to the garden on days like this one; particularly ironic that it was the one place she would miss when she left New York. After all, Mary was the wife of Dean Jack Havemeyer, and it was none other than Dean Jack Havemeyer who wanted the garden demolished and replaced with a parking lot. Although it hadn't been given the final go-ahead, Jack's campaign was gathering steam. As ever, Jack was outspoken about his cause, and Mary knew he would get his way in the end. The garden was a drain on university resources, Jack argued passionately to anyone who'd listen, whereas a parking lot would require little maintenance and would be highly lucrative. What he didn't make so public was that the parking lot plans included reserved spots for deans and other university management like himself.

If Jack was obsessed with one day becoming president of Manhattan U, he was even more obsessed with his prized metallic blue Ford Explorer.

"If it was parked out there," he'd often say, gesticulating out of their thirtieth-floor apartment window with a tumbler of whiskey lodged in his hand, "I'd be able to keep my eye on it. Make sure no punks are scratching it up."

Mary would merely nod. She couldn't care less about the car. They rarely used it, and it sat in a cramped garage in the West Village, eating up hundreds of dollars each month. She just couldn't understand why he loved it so much. A long time ago, when he was a lowly professor in the history department, his passions were simple: his writing, his research on the American Revolution, his students, and his Rolling Stones albums.

But then he began to move up Manhattan U's management ladder, and everything changed. He suddenly started wanting things, grasping things, needing things. All kinds of things that he'd never been interested in before. Not only did he demand a bigger and higher apartment in faculty housing with every promotion, he also started to wear hand-tailored suits, smoke expensive Cuban cigars, and import single-malt whiskeys from Scotland. Then there was the car, and the new love for golf, and the expensive holidays in Europe. To see him now, suited and swaggering, it was hard to believe he'd ever been that shaggy-haired grad student in a scuffed hand-knitted sweater and ill-fitting brown cords. The one whom she'd spied, with his intense hazel eyes and wide smile, across a smoke-filled graduate common room at Princeton three long decades ago.

The thought of Jack made Mary shiver. She buried her chin in her woolen scarf and wrapped her long arms tighter across her chest. He'd changed so much in the last few years. Some women might put up with it, stay with Jack until the grave, but she couldn't. She'd endured it long enough and it was time to go.

"Not long now," she muttered under her breath as she remembered the plane tickets and the crisp, newly signed lease hidden in her underwear drawer.

It would all be okay, she assured herself. In just a short while everything would be fine, and seeing Jack's hazel eyes every day would soon be a thing of the past. In a matter of weeks she would no longer have to hear his rants about the "imbeciles" in Manhattan U's finance office, or watch him pontificate to colleagues about the benefits of the proposed parking lot. No longer would she have to creep around the apartment as he pawed over books on Edgar Allan Poe, books that had little to do with his scholarship but, for reasons unfathomable to Mary, had consumed all his time and energy in recent months. Most of all, once she was gone, she would never feel the rage of his fist against her skin ever again.

Before she could make herself feel better with thoughts of the deep russet walls and ivory linen drapes that awaited her in a small light-filled apartment in San Francisco, the garden gate rattled noisily. She looked up with a start. Her throat tightened. It wasn't him, was it? He hadn't spotted her, had he? *Please, no,* she begged silently as she tried to see who was coming in. The last thing she wanted was a round of his pathetic apologies accompanied by one of his hastily bought bouquets of lilies. (Why lilies? she wondered in anger. She'd never liked lilies, never.) She really couldn't stomach all that now. Not while her eye still throbbed ferociously behind her glasses.

As the gate clanged shut, Mary let out a small sigh of relief. It wasn't him. Instead, a woman dressed in an orange knit cap and a long dark winter coat maneuvered her way into the garden. Her coat fell open around her protruding pregnant belly, and she was holding a bottle of water in one hand and pushing a stroller with the other. Spotting Mary at the other end of the garden, the woman lifted her hand and gave a friendly wave before sitting on the bench nearest the gate. She then took a sip of her water, shook open a newspaper, and lifted a foot onto a chunky plastic wheel and began wobbling the stroller back and forth. From where Mary was sitting, the child inside was just a pair of pink cheeks poking out from a rainbow-covered fleece blanket.

Mary had seen this woman in the garden before. Last summer when the little girl was just beginning to walk, Mary had watched the two of them giggling and squealing together under the shade of the large maple. When they finally got breathless from their game of raspberries, both mother and daughter lay on their backs and smiled happily at the fluttering leaves above them.

There were other women who came to the garden regularly. The beautiful young woman with the bright red hair who sometimes painted on an old wooden easel. The woman always dressed in the immaculate work suits who would sit on the bench, throw her head back, and stare peacefully up at the sky. Like Mary, they all came alone and left alone. None of them knew one another, as far as Mary could tell. Years ago Mary had nicknamed this place the Widow's Garden. And even now, with these women passing anonymously in and out, the garden still seemed like a refuge for sad, lonely wives waiting for husbands who would never return.

Looking at the pregnant woman across the garden, Mary smiled to herself. The women she saw here weren't really sad or lonely widows. These women were probably more like Sarah, her own strong, successful, and independent daughter. No doubt they had good lives, happy lives, fulfilled lives. They just came to the garden for a little peace and quiet. They came for a break in their busy, bright days.

Sucking in a long, slow, but determined breath, Mary reached down and gathered up her old briefcase, which was overflowing with dog-eared term papers. Soon she would be like those women, she assured herself. No longer scared and sad, wishing she were somewhere else and living some other life. Soon she'd be happy too.

But, for the time being, she had a job to do. Unlike hotshot Dean Jack Havemeyer, Professor Mary Havemeyer still had classes to teach, and at this very moment a group of sophomores would be clogging the corridor outside Seminar Room D. Thinking about their wide-eyed young faces, Mary felt an unexpected warmth tingle in her chest. It was a long, long time since she'd won the Pulitzer for her novel, and now she was just some fiftysomething professor who taught creative writing and was tough on time wasters. However, her classes were always oversubscribed. The kids had probably never read her prizewinning novel, *Casey's Echoes.* Yet they seemed to like her; they seemed genuinely interested in what she had to say, and in spite of everything, that made her feel good on this chilly April morning.

As she stood up, she tentatively touched the cheek below her throbbing eye. She had no idea how she would explain the glasses to the students, or why she, a stickler for timekeeping, was over ten minutes late. But one thing was clear: She was going to get through today. And through tomorrow. And the rest of week. And the rest of the month. She was going to make it through to June, when Sarah, her daughter, would get married.

After that she would be free. She would be out of here and away from Jack. At long last.

Two

Hannah

"Would you cheat on him?" Hannah had seen the question just a few days ago, as she'd flicked idly through a glossy magazine in her dentist's waiting room. Her eyes had scanned the words and article below, and she'd thought about Michael and whether she could ever cheat on him. Under her breath, she'd found herself muttering, "Never, never, never."

But only a few days later, as Hannah rolled over in bed, reached out, and smoothed the crinkled sheet where Michael had been sleeping until just an hour ago, her stomach lurched and a burn of nausea radiated in her chest. Last night, she'd done exactly what she only just vowed she'd never do. She'd cheated on Michael, and now she was feeling ill, hopelessly ill, with guilt. Hannah knew she wouldn't be able to tell her husband what she'd done. It would kill him. But keeping it from him forever? Keeping her guilt bottled up? It would kill her.

After fingering each crease in the soft green sheet, Hannah propped herself up on her elbow and stared out of the window next to the bed. Plump raindrops clung to the windowpane, and, even though the rain that had fallen in the night had now stopped, heavy clouds sat in the air like fleshy Buddhas. When she'd left the building the evening before it had been warm, slightly fresh, with a sky that was vivid blue. It was the kind of sky that still amazed Hannah. Before she moved to the city ten years ago, she'd imagined New York skies as a giant cocktail of car fumes and swirling dust. Instead she was surprised to find that on so many days—winter, summer, spring, or fall—the city would bustle beneath a dazzling blue ceiling. Hannah would often stop and stare at the blueness that peeked through the tall buildings and reflected in their windows. On numerous occasions she'd tried to reproduce the color on her canvases. But the paints she bought or mixed never quite captured it. It was too impossibly blue.

Looking out at the dreary sky, she sighed. The weather was telling her something. She was sure of it. It was reminding her how bad she'd been.

How could you do it? the wind seemed to demand as it beat noisily against the window. *How could you?*

Inching herself farther up on her elbow, Hannah pressed her nose against the glass and looked down at the garden below. She was surprised to see some people. Although they were just tiny from way up here on the twenty-ninth floor, she could make out a stroller at one end of the garden's rectangle of grass and at the other end a person, probably a woman, slowly creeping away from the long wooden bench. She had a sudden urge to be out there with them, alone but together with these solitary figures haunting the Manhattan U garden.

But then another wave of guilt hit her and she slumped back on the pillow. *Why did I do it?* she thought. *Why?* What kind of person would cheat on Michael? Solid, smart, nice-guy Michael. Her husband for over five years. The guy who'd been such a breath of fresh and intelligent air after all the rogues and sleazeballs Hannah encountered when she used to be a model; the same sleazeballs whom Hannah had too often gotten involved with. By comparison, Michael was gifted, trustworthy, kind, and hardworking.

Michael was also the person who'd kept a roof over Hannah's head when she quit modeling, and it was thanks to his job at the university that Hannah was now enrolled in the prestigious and expensive MFA program at Manhattan U—with a generous fee waiver. The master's program was everything she'd ever dreamed of. Michael wasn't quite so enthusiastic, however. Even though he and his job allowed her to do the MFA in the first place, he often made it clear what he thought about her degree.

"Why do you need some master's certificate to tell you that you're an artist?" Michael would ask from time to time. "You've sold some paintings. You have a studio. Isn't that enough?"

This from the guy who had two MAs and a PhD. The same guy who was the new star of MU's computer science department, and the same guy who, despite being a baby among his gray-haired peers, had recently been lured away from Columbia to Manhattan U by the promise of a handsome salary and a much-coveted twenty-ninth-floor apartment.

Michael hadn't liked it when Hannah gave up modeling, and getting his rational, computer science brain around Hannah's passion for art was too much. Yet, after much cajoling and heated late-night discussions, he'd finally agreed to support her through her MFA, and sometimes, when he wasn't tired or tapping on his computer, he would ask her halfhearted questions about her classes.

Thinking about Michael, Hannah sighed again. Her eyes wandered over to the clock. Ten thirty. She had to get up. She had class in a couple of hours, and she wanted to get some painting done before that. She didn't have time to get to her studio in Brooklyn, but she could squeeze in a couple of hours in the garden. It was gloomy out there, but dry, and the garden—its neutrality and its privacy—was just what she needed right now.

Fighting her tiredness, she swung her long legs out from under the covers and slowly sat up. She rubbed her eyes, stretched out her arms, and then gasped as she caught a glimpse of herself in the mirror on the opposite wall. Her eyelids were puffy, her skin translucent. Her big, dark eyes were underlined by brooding circles, and her full lips, which had always been her signature, were dry and pale. Without even really thinking, Hannah let her eyes slip over to the black-and-white photograph hanging to the left of the mirror. Her own eyes stared back at her. It was a photograph of Hannah that La Perla had used for a raunchy ad campaign in *Vogue* more than five years ago. Michael loved this shot and still insisted it should be hung in their bedroom. Meanwhile, Hannah tried not to look at it much these days. It just reminded her of the life that she didn't really care for anymore.

Today, though, she couldn't help studying the picture. Her smooth skin, her bright eyes, her moist lips, her long hair lapping seductively across her heart-shaped face. It was like seeing another person after the one she'd just glimpsed in the mirror. Indeed, that was how Hannah felt these days. Like another person. Since she'd started taking her art seriously and enrolled in the MFA program, the dread, insecurities, anxiety, and hunger that went along with being a model had evaporated. Concerns about when the next job would come, whether she'd posed well on a shoot, walked right on the catwalk, spoken to a designer in suitably reverent tones, or whether her skin was clear and her body slim enough—all these worries were gone. Now Hannah woke every morning, exuberant and happy, itching to be among her canvases and paints.

Except this morning, of course. Hannah's belly gave another roll of guilt, and her eyes flicked back to the mirror. She reached up and touched her short bangs, which were plastered to her forehead. She'd recently dyed her hair fire-truck red and cut it into an elfin crop. Michael had nicknamed it "the MFA 'do." He'd meant to be lighthearted, but there was bitterness in his tone. He missed her honey waves and long wispy bangs, and made it very clear from the moment she'd walked into their apartment with her dramatic new hairstyle that he didn't approve.

Sneaking another look at herself, Hannah gave a small laugh. "A living Picasso," she murmured.

She pulled herself to her feet and headed toward the dresser. She needed to find her favorite pair of paint-splattered combat pants. With those on, Hannah assured herself, she'd feel better and ready to work. As she yanked at one of the drawers, two candlesticks and a pot of loose change wobbled precariously on top of the dresser. She yanked a little harder. This time two old postcards fluttered to the floor, revealing a photo in a wooden frame.

Smiling up at Hannah were Michael, Michael's mom and dad, and Hannah herself. The photo had been taken nearly two years ago when they were in Italy on vacation. The four of them were standing in Piazza della Signoria in Florence, their arms linked and saying goofily at the camera, *"Formaggio."*

"Oh, God," Hannah puffed out, as she stared down at the picture.

Suddenly grabbing her stomach, she ran to the bathroom and was sick.

Hannah lifted her head and let the cold breeze sting her face as she crunched along the gravel path toward the garden. It felt good, an odd but perfect antidote to the gnawing emptiness in her stomach. If she could just make herself eat the bagel that she'd grabbed from the kitchen on the way out and stuffed into her backpack, Hannah was convinced she'd soon feel better. Seeing the gate in front of her, Hannah rummaged for the key in the deep pocket of her parka. The wooden easel gripped under her arm began to slip, and as she fumbled to catch it, the canvas under her other arm clattered to the ground.

"Shit," she hissed, urgently trying to stop the painting—and two weeks' work—from falling facedown on the wet gravel.

"Excuse me," snapped a male voice behind her.

Amid her tangle of easel and canvas, Hannah twisted clumsily around. In a long black overcoat and charcoal gray fedora, a man loomed in the path behind her. Two other men stood a few paces behind him wearing glowing yellow jackets and carrying clipboards.

"Oh, sorry," she began, realizing they wanted to pass.

But before she had time to gather up her things and move aside, the three men stalked onward, picking their way over her canvas and easel as they went. In the dull light, under the gray skies, the jackets of the two men were blinding. WILKINS CONSTRUCTION, it read in blue writing across their broad backs. Reaching the gate to the garden, the man in the fedora looked back. For the briefest moment his narrowed eyes snaked over Hannah, and his eyebrows knitted together under the rim of his hat.

"You need a key to use this garden," he barked at her.

"I have one," she shot back, annoyed by his arrogant tone.

As he took a haughty sniff and turned toward the gate, it dawned on Hannah. She'd seen this man before. Perhaps a month ago Hannah had been stepping into the elevator in the lobby of her building and someone behind her had bellowed, *"Hold it!"* She'd gripped the door, in fright more than anything, and turned to see a tall, barrel-chested man with a flock of gray hair swish into the elevator beside her. When she finally let the doors slide closed, she'd reached across to push the button for her floor. But before she reached the panel her arm was violently jolted out of the way as the guy pushed her aside and jabbed at the thirty button. Hannah looked up, shocked. But instead of apologizing, the man kept his cool and indifferent eyes fixed on the elevator's display panel and said nothing. Hannah was too stunned and flustered to reproach the man about his rudeness, and so they made the long ride to her floor in silence.

Now, as she watched his fedora disappear into the garden, Hannah seethed. But a second later she let out a bitter laugh and shook her head.

"He's the last of my worries right now," she muttered under her breath.

Finally reaching the garden, Hannah wrestled with the lock, and then, with her canvas and easel under her arms once again, she pushed open the heavy gate with her hip. As she shuffled inward, she noticed the stroller that she'd seen earlier from the window. It was parked in front of a pregnant woman reading a newspaper on a nearby bench. Hannah didn't want the gate's noisy clang to wake the sleeping child, so she carefully eased it shut behind her.

Passing the woman, she nodded hello and realized she knew her. Like Hannah, this woman used the garden a lot, but they'd never really talked, nothing more than brief exchanges about the weather or the garden.

Today the woman caught Hannah's eye, sat upright, and dropped her newspaper into her lap. "Hey," she said, giving a warm smile and folding her arms on top of her big pregnant belly.

"Hey," Hannah replied, sounding terser than she meant to.

"I've seen you painting here before, haven't I?" the woman asked. "I'm Sofia, by the way."

Hannah couldn't help warming to the woman's kind and candid manner. "I'm Hannah." She gave a small wave. "This is a great place to work. When it's not raining, that is."

Both women looked up at the gray, heavy sky.

Finally Sofia sat forward and asked in a whisper, "Have you heard?" She then nodded to the three men who were now at the other end of the garden stretching out tape measures and making notes on their clipboards.

Hannah shook her head. "Heard what?"

"Old Dean Havemeyer over there"—she nodded again in their direction—"the one who thinks he's Dick Tracy in that ridiculous hat. He wants this place gone."

"What do you mean, gone?"

"Demolished. Kaput. Replaced with a parking lot."

"You're kidding." Hannah was genuinely shocked.

Sofia shook her head. "And it looks like it's going to happen soon." She trailed off as she stared over at the men, who were now huddled together and pointing at the old maple tree in the far corner of the garden.

As Hannah's gaze returned from the men to Sofia, she was suddenly struck by her incredible wide, honey-colored eyes. Those eyes, coupled with her olive skin and dark hair (sprinkled with the occasional strand of gray), made her seem enigmatic yet also curiously open and innocent. She had a beautiful, paradoxical face that Hannah would love to paint.

"That sucks," Hannah whispered.

"Especially for you, right?" Sofia's honey eyes slipped from Hannah down to her easel and canvas.

Hannah nodded. "I have a studio, though. Luckily."

"Yeah?" Sofia seemed genuinely interested. "Where?"

"Over in Brooklyn." And then, unsure why, she found herself adding with a nervous laugh, "In my in-laws' attic."

Sofia smiled. "That's a sweet setup."

Hannah knew all too well what a sweet setup it was. In a city and an art world where an artist's studio—its whereabouts, its size, its price, and its light—was more fretted over and talked about than his or her artwork, Hannah's studio was a sparkling gem. It was as precious as the *Mona Lisa*. Although drafty and undecorated, the attic was huge, quiet, and bathed in light from four big windows. Not only that, it was free and *all* hers.

"They must be cool in-laws," Sofia then added.

"They are," Hannah said with a wistful nod and a lump rising in her throat.

She couldn't get the photograph from their Italian vacation out of her head. Diane, Michael's mom, looked animated and vibrant, as she always did. Her mass of wild silver hair was tousled by a breeze, and her mouth was wide and laughing. Bill, Michael's dad, stood beside her looking a little more reserved, and with his dark eyes and white beard sparkling in the Italian sun. And then there was Michael, whose intense chocolate brown eyes were exactly like his dad's. He was smiling his broad, good-looking smile, and his neat chestnut bangs had blown upward, revealing a tanned forehead.

"Are you okay?" Sofia was looking at Hannah, concerned.

"Yes," croaked Hannah.

But she wasn't okay at all. Suddenly her body felt like lead, and, unable to do anything else, she slumped down on the bench next to Sofia. Tears pricked in her eyes.

"I cheated on my husband," she found herself blurting out.

Sofia's dark eyebrows shot up, but then she reached over and wordlessly squeezed Hannah's hand. Before Hannah knew it, she was telling this woman, this stranger, everything. She rambled on and on, unable to stop, and Sofia looked over at her with wide but sympathetic eyes. Hannah told her about what had happened last night. She told her about her marriage.

"He just doesn't get me anymore," Hannah whispered, shaking her head. "My husband, I mean. He doesn't understand why I love my art so much. He's only ever been up to my studio in his parents' house twice. Twice. Can you believe that?" Not waiting for an answer from Sofia, she carried on: "A while ago I overheard him joking with a friend, saying that an MFA was an expensive 'little hobby' for a wife to have. And then there was another time I caught him using one of my sketches as a coaster for his coffee." Hannah shook her head again. "It sounds so clichéd, though, doesn't it? Saying your husband doesn't get you. Using it as some lame excuse to justify cheating on him . . ." She trailed off.

Sofia spoke up finally. "It's not lame. And it's only clichéd because it's so common. There are lots of husbands out there who don't *get* their wives, who don't really understand their passions or ambitions. Even guys of our generation, who think they're sensitive and supportive, they can be like that too."

"Perhaps I'm just a bitch. Perhaps I'm asking too much," Hannah carried on, not really convinced by Sofia's words.

"I don't think it's asking that much to want your husband to understand you and to see what makes you tick and what gives you happiness," Sofia retorted. "I'm lucky. My husband does see that I'm a person as well as a wife, which means he goes along with all my crazy ideas and whims." She laughed and added, "Including quitting my fantastic and lucrative job as a talent agent to become a stay-at-home mom."

Hannah's eyes widened. "You did?"

Sofia sighed. "It's a long story," she said, and then added with a chuckle, "And if my husband hadn't been so understanding and supportive, right now I might be whooping it up at some movie screening or other. Instead, I'm here." She waved toward her belly and the stroller. "Not that I regret it, of course," she muttered to herself more than to Hannah.

"When I was still modeling, Michael was supersupportive too," Hannah said. "He used to come on shoots, carry my bags, and paw over test shots with producers and photographers. Everyone loved him, and my friends in the business used to say how lucky I was to have Michael. He wasn't like the guys so many models date—like the ones I dated before Michael. He wasn't in it just for the parties and the chance of being photographed with some hot chick on his arm. Michael was encouraging and interested and fun to have along for the ride."

"But then you quit modeling?" Sofia prompted.

Hannah nodded. "Then I quit modeling, and Michael seemed to lose interest in me." She gave a bitter snort of laughter. "He certainly doesn't offer to carry my palette and easel, if you get what I mean. These days he works *all* the time, and when we are together we talk about the bills that have to be paid and that's about it. He doesn't even tell me about his research like he used to." Hannah plopped her head into her hands and groaned. "But it's no excuse. It's really no excuse. And his parents—oh, God, if they found out . . ." she began, but then stopped as another big lump of sadness gathered in her throat.

"You adore them, don't you?"

"They're not just in-laws," Hannah explained, sitting back up and twiddling the strap of her backpack between her thumb and forefinger. "They're my best friends."

Clever, fun, and extraordinarily kind, Michael's parents were psychotherapists who ran a private practice out of the basement of their rambling Brooklyn brownstone. When they weren't seeing patients, they loved to drink wine, sing old Dylan songs, and hang out with their countless friends. Every Sunday night they'd cook Thai curry for Michael and Hannah, and every summer they'd take them on vacation.

Hannah adored them, just as Sofia had guessed. They weren't just wonderful people and great friends; they were surrogate parents too. Hannah's own father had left when she was four. One night he packed his bags and without a word left their modest bungalow in small-town Virginia. Hannah's mother lived in a state of bewilderment and loneliness for the next twenty years. She died one brisk spring day when Hannah was in Paris. She'd been there for two years working for a French modeling agency, her days spent tripping between photo shoots, parties, rambunctious Parisian restaurants, and back to photo shoots again. Hannah had flown home straightaway when the news came, and was told by a gray-haired doctor (with sullen eyes, Hannah would never forget) that her mother had had a congenital heart defect that no one had ever picked up on. When the doctor left, Hannah sat in the sterile waiting area outside the morgue, clutching her mother's old blue leather purse to her chest, a single tear trickling down her cheek. The doctor could call it a congenital heart defect, but Hannah knew it was a broken heart that had killed her mother. It was during that painful and wretched moment that Hannah had vowed never to let anyone break her own heart. She didn't want the life of loneliness that her own mother had endured.

But Hannah had been lonely too, even if she hadn't realized it. In her early twenties, she had no parents, no brothers or sisters to lean on, and thanks to her modeling career, which took her all over the world and never let her stay anywhere too long, she didn't have many decent friends either. And so when kind and smart Michael came into her life, bringing his adoring and beautiful parents with him, Hannah was hooked. His family became her family, and although Michael loved his mom and dad, it was Hannah who was passionate about them. It was Hannah who would drag Michael to their house every Sunday, and it was Hannah who would sit for hours with Bill and Diane, pawing over maps of Europe or North Carolina or California, helping plan their annual trip.

"Hannah," Michael would sometimes say, "we're going to have to quit going to Brooklyn every Sunday for dinner."

"Why?" Hannah would ask, a sharp panic rising in her chest.

"I have too much work," he'd reply in his perfunctory way.

Unlike his parents, who loved to talk, Michael was a man of few words. At least, these days he was. He'd say what was needed to be said and that was that. No further explication or elucidation. To an emotional and erratic person, as Hannah saw herself, Michael's composed and measured way of talking had always been appealing. Lately, though, composed and measured had turned into sparse and silent. Hannah often struggled to engage Michael in even the smallest of conversations.

"I think someone wants you."

Hannah was so caught up in these thoughts about Michael, she'd barely noticed that Sofia was now tapping her arm.

"Huh?" Hannah said, looking up and seeing that Sofia was pointing toward the end of the garden.

"I think someone wants you."

Hannah followed Sofia's outstretched arm. At first she saw nothing but a knot of bare trees, the old fence, and the blur of cars hurrying past on the street outside. But then she caught an unfamiliar movement. Someone on the other side of the fence was waving. At her.

She sat up and gasped. It was him. It was him!

As she scrambled to her feet, she looked briefly at Sofia. Sofia looked back. From her eyes Hannah could tell she understood. She knew that this was the guy—the guy whom Hannah had just confessed everything about in this damp, chilly garden. But there was no judgment in Sofia's eyes, only understanding.

With her legs tingling and a dizzy feeling in her head, Hannah padded across the grass. Her heart pounded in her chest and her mouth turned to sandpaper as she drew closer to the fence. When she was just a few feet away, her eyes settled on his pale green ones. He was smiling that slightly off-center smile of his. The laugh lines around his eyes, deep and long, and the silver streaks that snaked through his dark curly hair seemed to shine even in this gloomy light. Taking in his lanky frame and his familiar woolen jacket with its collar turned up against the wind, Hannah remembered everything. The warmth of his lips on hers. The smoothness of his chest under her touch. His hot breath on her neck. Her naked legs twisted around his.

"Hello," Patrick said as Hannah reached the fence.

She felt herself shiver. She loved the way British vowels rolled off his tongue.

"Hey," was all she could think to say back.

Digging deep in his pocket, Patrick said quietly, "You forgot this." He pulled out her cell phone. "I saw you. From my window."

He waved toward his fifth-floor apartment in the building opposite Hannah's. "I thought I would just nip down and give it to you. You're probably missing it."

Hannah blushed. He'd seen her from the window. Had he been looking for her?

As she took the phone, her fingers grazed his. "Thanks," she said in an awkward mumble.

"Well . . ." Patrick looked awkward too. "I have a class to prepare for . . ." He trailed off, and Hannah blushed again.

Of course he had a class to prepare for. It was her class. The art theory class he would be teaching in just a few hours, and the same class she would be sitting in as one of his students.

Looking down and still smiling, Patrick began to move. Hannah didn't want him to leave. But she didn't want him to stay either. So she stood silently, watching him as he backed up a few paces. Just when she thought he was going to turn and leave, he stopped and smiled. "Thank you, Hannah. For last night." He then tipped his head, gave a small wave, and walked away.

Hannah was left staring at the space on the sidewalk where he'd been standing. Her eyes pricked with shameful tears, while her pulse raced with paradoxical excitement. *What have I done?* she wondered as she looked back toward the garden. The men were now gone, and Sofia was reading her newspaper once again. Hannah's canvas was still propped against the bench, billowing vaguely in the wind.

Unsure what to do next, Hannah flipped open her cell, which was still warm from Patrick's pocket. There was a message. On autopilot, she jabbed at the small silver buttons and held the phone close her ear.

"Hey, Hannah." She drew in a sharp breath at the sound of the voice. It was Diane, Michael's mom. "I just realized that it's your fifth wedding anniversary coming up. Bill and I would love to throw a party for you guys. What do you think? Call me."

Three

Sofia

Gracie had been napping under a pile of blankets, but her hands and cheeks were still cold from the garden. After wheeling her into the apartment, Sofia blew on her daughter's small fingers, softly rubbed her round cheeks, and then hoisted the now awake Gracie out of the stroller and onto her hip. They probably should have come home earlier, Sofia thought. But then that artist woman showed up and, out of nowhere, started telling Sofia everything she was going through. She'd seemed so confused, haunted by guilt, and Sofia found she couldn't leave her.

If Sofia was honest, she didn't want to leave the woman, either. It had been so long since someone had confided in Sofia like that. Back when she was still working as a talent agent in Hollywood, it happened all the time. Clients would pour out their Versace-clad hearts to her every day. Movie producers would pull Sofia aside and whisper about monies they'd embezzled or Porsches they'd bought on borrowed cash. Casting directors would jam up her phone lines as they admitted their addiction to Vicodin or whatever other drug was du jour in the movie world.

For reasons Sofia still couldn't really fathom, she had always been a magnet for people's confessions and woes. It had seemed so exhausting then, but now she missed it. Talking to a toddler for the better part of most of her days was fun, though not really the same. Sofia entertained so many fantasies about life as a full-time mom, and she'd given up her career hoping to live those fantasies out. But the reality of life at home with Gracie was very different. It was hard and challenging and mundane in ways she'd never imagined, and yearning to hear the sorrowful stories of her Hollywood clients was something she definitely hadn't envisaged.

"Baba?" Gracie was tugging on Sofia's hair, shaking her from her thoughts.

"Yes." Sofia laughed at her daughter's predictability. "You can take a bath."

At two and a half, Gracie was just like Sofia: She hated to be cold, and a warm bath was what she always instinctively asked for when she was chilled. In spite of being a New York–born child, Gracie seemed to share Sofia's own Californian aversion to the cold. It was one of the many things about her daughter that both surprised Sofia and didn't surprise her, all at the same time.

Once Gracie was settled in the bath, surrounded by plastic toys, puffy bath books, and brightly colored foam letters, Sofia shimmied down the bathroom wall and eased her eight-and-a-half-month-pregnant body onto the cold tiles. Gracie looked over the edge of the bath and clapped her hands in delight. Her small head was covered in bubbles, and she was sucking hard on the beak of a rubber duck.

Sofia waggled her finger playfully at her daughter. "When the time comes, *you* have to help me up."

Gracie looked at Sofia blankly for a second. Dropping Duckie from her mouth into the soapy water, she then let out a deafening squeal, followed by, "Up, up, up, help, Mama, up, up," singsonged at the top of her lungs.

Although Sofia was uncomfortable on the hard floor, she couldn't help laughing. Bath time was always such a delicious time for Sofia. The warm, steamed-up bathroom, Gracie's beautiful gleaming skin, the echoing sounds of her joyful singing.

Plus, the jumbled pile of celebrity magazines by the bathroom sink.

Back in California, when Sofia was still one of the senior agents at Venture, LA's leading talent agency, she'd always been so scathing about celebrity magazines. They were a constant source of anxiety for her clients and therefore a continual headache for Sofia. A paparazzi shot of a client with no makeup or carrying a few extra pounds would be enough to send even the most levelheaded on her list into hiding for weeks. At the same time, if no pictures of a client appeared on the pages of *Us* or *People* for more than a month, Sofia would be plagued by frenzied phone calls from her client wondering if she or he were on their way out.

As inexplicable as it was, though, Sofia just couldn't kick this new habit. The high of a crisp, newly bought copy of *Life & Style* was too much to resist. And, seeing as it started early on in her pregnancy with Gracie, she figured she had full license to blame it entirely on her hormones.

"Some women eat chalk; others howl at the moon. I read celebrity magazines," she explained on numerous occasions to Tom, her husband.

She knew he was baffled by the slow infiltration of these glossy magazines into their once entirely book-filled home. Even though it was Tom who was the English professor, she used to devour fiction as much as he did, and their apartment was always crawling with well-thumbed paperbacks, and hardbacks that had long since lost their dustcovers.

Today, as Gracie's singing reverberated around the bathroom, Sofia fought the urge to pick up the magazine on top of the nearby pile, in spite of its very tempting headline, *Courteney Cox Goes Commando*. Impressed with her own resolve, Sofia smiled and reached instead for the red plastic cup floating in the bathtub.

"Okay, Britney Spears." She chuckled. "Let's rinse your hair."

Sofia gently trickled the water onto Gracie's head as she smoothed back her unruly curls. Gracie wriggled a little at first, but after a while seemed to relax under Sofia's touch. When nearly all the suds were gone, Sofia looked down at Gracie's face. Her daughter's eyes, which were the exact same color as her own, looked back at her with a mix of worry, concentration, and surprise.

"What . . . ?" began Sofia.

But there was no need to finish. She knew exactly what was going on; she knew that face. She knew it all too well. It could mean only one thing.

"Gracie," she asked in an urgent whisper, "are you pooping?"

Gracie didn't reply. Instead she lowered her eyes, was silent for a moment, and then made a small grunting sound. Sofia's gaze dropped from her daughter to the bathwater. She sighed. There it was, perfectly formed, circling dangerously close to Gracie like an alligator in a bayou.

"Honey," Sofia whispered, trying hard not to sound exasperated, "you should tell Mommy if you need to go potty."

Gracie looked up, her eyes turning glassy with tears. "No potty." She started to sob.

Immediately feeling terrible, Sofia reached over and cupped Gracie's cheeks in her hands. "Oh, sweetie, it's okay," she soothed.

She then quickly heaved Gracie from the tub, perched her on top of her belly, and wrapped her in a fluffy pink towel. With Gracie's wet hair pressed against her cheek, Sofia hugged her daughter close and sang "Baby Beluga" in a soft murmur until the sobs began to fade.

"Tubbies?" Gracie finally asked in a small whisper.

Sofia replied, "Sure. You can watch *Teletubbies*."

Gracie sprang off Sofia as if nothing had ever happened and padded out of the bathroom, her naked behind pink and wiggling.

Sofia took a deep breath and then half sang, half puffed, "Up, up, up," as she grabbed the side of the bathtub and the corner of the sink and heaved herself to her feet.

When Gracie was snuggled in her favorite spot on the sofa, clutching ragged Mrs. Bunny under her arm, Sofia headed across the living room back to the bathroom. She scanned the room for the phone as she went. The place, she noticed, was in disarray. Piles of books fought with Gracie's toys for space on the floor. The shelves were a jigsaw of old newspapers, more books, more toys, and clusters of Christmas cards, although it was now April. She felt a sudden rush of nostalgia for the sparse, breezy, lily white condo she had once owned in West Hollywood, and the cleaner she used to be able to afford who would come twice a week and keep the condo pristine.

Even though Sofia had had a beautiful apartment and a great career in LA, she always knew she would give it all up when she started a family. It baffled Tom, of course, because he knew how much she loved her work and her life in California. It baffled everyone, in fact. But Sofia was resolute. Her own mom had always worked full-time, and Sofia didn't want her kids to have the same latchkey childhood she'd had. She wanted a close and engaged relationship with her children, unlike the distant and strained relationship that, to this day, she had with her mother.

Being a stay-at-home mom would be wonderful, Sofia had argued to anyone who'd questioned her decision (and many people did, at the time). She'd spend her days running from mommy groups to Baby and Me yoga to postnatal fitness classes at the Y. At home, she would flit around the apartment with a feather duster in hand, a floral apron adorning her middle, and a big smile plastered across her face. Her happy and pretty children would coo up at her from an immaculate play rug on the floor, and she would while away the afternoons cooking beautiful dinners for the family.

"So deluded," Sofia muttered as she shook her head and rifled through some of the junk piled on the couch.

Tom had always teased Sofia about her overactive imagination, and these days it seemed all her old fantasies about stay-at-home motherhood were exactly that: fantasies. Sofia had never in her entire life enjoyed housework. She'd never been particularly maternal either. The only domestic thing she was any good at was cooking.

"Deluded." Sofia sighed again, and this time she added, "And hormonal."

Like her obsession for celebrity magazines, Sofia now put all these overblown fantasies about motherhood down to prenatal hormones.

Feeling very hormonal and awkward, Sofia lumbered across the cluttered room still searching for the phone. She was about to give up but decided to try one more place: Gracie's toy box. There, under a beat-up copy of *Green Eggs and Ham* and a Talking Elmo doll, she found what she was looking for. Sofia grabbed up the receiver and punched in Tom's number, then paced into the bathroom and examined the unwanted visitor in the tub.

"Hey, hon." Tom knew it was her; he always did. He didn't need caller ID; he just knew.

Her husband's low, gravelly voice still made her chest flutter and her mouth tweak into a smile. "I'm about to embark on dangerous military operations," she said. "I thought I should call to wish my final farewells."

"What is it this time? Toddlers on the offensive? Shock and awe at storytime?"

"USS *Bath Poo* has resurfaced."

Tom gave a knowing laugh, and then after a pause added quickly, "Sweets, just leave it. I'll clean up when I get there. Go put your feet up."

But Sofia was already kneeling at the side of the bath chasing the fortunately pretty solid poop around in the warm water with one of Gracie's plastic buckets.

"It's an easy one," she replied. "How was class?"

"The usual. None of them had done the reading. They sat there, bleary eyed and morose."

"Barely alive after spring break, no doubt."

She heard Tom grunt in agreement. "Anyway, what did you and Gracie-girl get up to?" he asked.

"Not much. Park, then the garden. Oh, and this woman told me her life story."

Sofia paused for a moment. The poop was edging near the faucet, and she nearly had it in the bucket. As she fought to catch it, she thought about Hannah out in the garden. She was so beautiful, with those amazing catlike eyes, plump lips, and her endless, svelte body. It just showed that even the gorgeous and the stunning could be confused and heartbroken. Hannah's story also reminded Sofia how lucky she was. Even if Sofia didn't have the razzle and dazzle of her Hollywood life anymore—or a clean, minimalist white apartment, for that matter—at least she had her happy marriage with Tom and their beautiful daughter.

"Sofia?" Tom's voice interrupted her thoughts.

As she opened her mouth to answer, the poop disappeared into the bucket and so she gave out a whoop of delight. But then her elbow slipped on the side of the bath and she lunged forward.

"Ouuccch," she cried.

"Sofia?" The panic was clear in Tom's voice. "What's going on?"

Sofia dropped the bucket and sat back on her heels. "I'm fine." She laughed, rubbing her elbow where it had jarred against the tub.

"Jeez, I thought you were in labor."

A thought flashed in Sofia's head. "If I *do* go into labor, will that excuse me from the dreaded dinner party?"

"No, it won't." Tom laughed. "We can*not* disappoint the Havemeyers."

"Oh, of course not, no. We couldn't let down our *great* friends the Havemeyers. God forbid." Sofia's tone was heavy with sarcasm. She then added, "Our great friend Dean Havemeyer, who didn't even recognize me this morning, by the way."

"You saw him?"

"In the garden. He was starting work on his new parking lot."

Tom snorted with disapproval.

"I just don't see why you agreed for us to go. After everything *he* did," Sofia blurted out.

"I'm up for tenure this year," Tom said, clearly bored with having to go over this again. "If the dean asks us for dinner, we say yes. Anyhow, I like Mary," he added.

God knows why, thought Sofia. Mary was the dean's wife and also happened to be one of Tom's colleagues in the English department. Sofia had never met her, but she suspected she wouldn't like her if she did.

"She can't be all there," Sofia muttered under her breath. "Married to Demolition Jack? Insane. The guy's evil."

Demolition Jack was Sofia's nickname for the dean, not only because of his current scheme to destroy the garden, but also because a few years back he'd been central in approving Manhattan U's infamous Third Street development project. In order for the business school to have a state-of-the-art lecture theater and computer center, Manhattan U management decided that a group of buildings on Third Street had to go. One of the old tenement houses to be destroyed happened to be the place where Edgar Allan Poe had once lived and worked. But this didn't stop the dean and his cronies, and when the New York Poe Foundation tried to protest the development, he found all kinds of ways to malign their cause and quash their campaigns.

As it happened, Tom had been the chair of the foundation. Tom was a rising star in Poe scholarship (not that he would ever blow his own horn about such a thing), and he'd written two books on the famous writer. His third was forthcoming. Tom loved all things Poe, including the house where he'd lived and the foundation that fought to save it.

When Dean Havemeyer finally worked out that one of his own faculty was chair of the group, he started to play hardball. First he ran an article in *Manhattan U News* that painted Tom as an incompetent, Poe-obsessed radical. Then he called Tom to his office and informed him, in no uncertain terms, that it was the Poe Foundation or his job. Sofia and Tom had only just had Gracie. They couldn't afford to risk everything, and so Tom was forced to step down at the foundation. The development went ahead soon after, and the only concession to Poe fans was to incorporate an imitation facade of the old house into the front of the new building and to preserve an old staircase within.

Although she knew his name all too well, Sofia had met the dean for the first time only recently. They were at a book launch in the West Village when Tom had nudged her, jerked his head to the right, and whispered, "There he is. Demolition Jack."

"I want to meet him," Sofia whispered back as soon as she set eyes on the gray-haired dean.

Sofia always loved a challenge. She wanted to make this pompous dean squirm. After all he'd put Tom through, she had to do something. She wasn't scared either. Sofia was used to dealing with big egos—superstar egos, in fact—and she figured this guy was probably a kitty cat compared to some of the Hollywood stars, movie directors, and profit-hungry publicists she used to deal with all day, every day.

But before she could make off in the dean's direction, Tom's hand shot up and gripped her bare elbow.

"Remember, honey," he hissed, "Havemeyer's the big cheese. Don't upset him or we'll be kissing my academic career good-bye."

Sofia was undeterred. "Don't be so dramatic," she teased, kissing Tom's long, familiar cheek. Gently peeling his fingers from her arm, she added with a wink, "I'm just going to introduce myself."

Swishing toward the dean, she caught his hooded eyes sliding over her. It wasn't a look of lust. God forbid. She was seven months pregnant, after all. It was a look of disgust, and it made Sofia falter slightly. The antipathy in his eyes surprised her. Like a missile on a collision course, however, she carried on.

"Dean Havemeyer." She smiled with confidence, sticking out her hand. "I'm Sofia. Tom Burgess's wife. He's on faculty in the English department."

Havemeyer looked at her hand as if it were mangled roadkill and then slowly took it into his.

"I *know* who Tom is," he snapped, and then as his face cracked into a pained smile, he said, "Pleasure to meet you, Mrs. Burgess."

She was about to correct him and say that she still went by Muñoz, her family name, when the professor started to move, saying, "Well, I must—"

But Sofia wasn't going to let him get away that easily. So she reached out, touched his forearm, and said, "How's your wife, Dean Havemeyer? Is she still writing? *Casey's Echoes* is still a favorite of mine."

This was a lie. Sofia had never read Mary Havemeyer's novel, although she'd always meant to. However, she knew all too well how men like Dean Havemeyer hated to be trumped by their wives. Praise for Mary would undoubtedly displease Jack Havemeyer.

Sofia was right.

"She doesn't write anymore," the dean muttered, wincing a little, as if it pained him to talk of his wife.

"And what about your daughter?" Sofia went on, maintaining her sweet tone and plastic smile. "I hear she's doing well as a curator at the Whitney; is that right?"

"She is," was the dean's terse and reluctant reply.

Sofia was really beginning to enjoy herself. The dean's neck was growing red, and his irritation was clear. Just as she was about to ask him another question, however, he interrupted.

"Should you really be drinking in your state?" he barked.

At first she didn't know what he was talking about, but then she followed his gaze down to the glass of red wine in her hand.

"Pregnant women can drink the occasional glass of wine," she began to protest, but it was already too late. He'd won. He'd found a way to get out of their conversation. He'd already moved a few paces away and was saying with a grimace, "Now if you'll excuse me, Mrs. Burgess."

Sofia had had to tense every muscle in her body to stop herself from hurling her very small glass of wine at his retreating silvery gray head.

"I should have done it," muttered Sofia into the phone, which was still lodged under her cheek as she held the side of the bath.

"What?" Tom asked.

"Oh, nothing." Sofia's eyes drifted back to the tub and the still-circling poop. "So why does Demo Jack want us to come for dinner, anyway? Have we figured that out yet? He's never invited us before."

"Apparently he has some questions about Poe," said Tom.

"Poe?" scoffed Sofia. "That's rich. The guy who mowed down the Poe house wants to talk to you about Poe. What on earth does he want to know? If there are any other houses he can pull down?"

"That's what this dinner's all about, I suppose. For us to find out."

Sofia sighed. "Couldn't he just send an e-mail?"

Tom didn't bother to answer. He rarely got worked up like Sofia did about these things. Instead he changed the subject.

"Speaking of e-mails," he said, "Hayden wrote this morning. He's coming into town."

Sofia groaned. "First Jack Havemeyer and now your brother. What a week." She slumped back on her heels and leaned her head against the tub. "Which boob-jobbed nineteen-year-old is Hayden chasing this time?"

"He didn't say," Tom said, his tone flat.

"We all know that Hayden only ever leaves Hollywood and that Malibu mansion of his when there's a new piece of skirt to be chased."

Tom never rose to the bait. He knew that defending Hayden wasn't an option. Nevertheless, he was loyal to his brother and refused to criticize him—although Hayden's behavior over the years had certainly warranted it. Sometimes it was hard to believe they were brothers at all. Hayden was a glitzy, fast-living movie star, and even though he never mentioned it, Sofia was convinced that his idea of a good time was snorting lines of coke off naked, surgically enhanced breasts. On the other hand, Tom was a diligent, nerdy academic who loved nothing more than sitting in a sleepy coffee shop, sipping a cappuccino, and reading "The Pit and Pendulum" for the thousandth time.

The only thing Hayden and Tom shared was their looks. Although where Tom's pale blue eyes were usually hidden behind a pair of smudged wire-rimmed glasses, Hayden's exact same eyes were generally found splashed across movie screens and billboards. And where Tom's thick blond hair dangled in ruffled abandon around his ears, Hayden's was perfectly coiffed and blown by the most expensive stylist in LA.

Just as she always did when she found herself stewing about Hayden, Sofia reminded herself that if it hadn't been for Hayden, she'd never have met Tom. The chances of a Hollywood agent hooking up with a nerdy but cute English professor were very slim. Much as it pained her to admit it, she did have one thing to thank her annoying brother-in-law for.

"Hey," she said with a yawn, "maybe Hayden could go to the Havemeyers' dinner party instead. He and Demo Jack would make great buddies."

"Hon?" Tom sounded concerned again. "You sound tired. Go take a nap."

The contractions caught her by surprise. One minute Sofia was snuggled on the couch with Gracie, idly watching *The Teletubbies* and brooding about her pain-in-the-ass brother-in-law; the next minute she was doubled over on the floor, writhing in pain. In one of the brief pain-free spells, she'd managed to crawl to the bathroom and find the phone, which she'd abandoned earlier next to the tub. Unfortunately, after crumpling onto the white bathroom tiles as she groaned through another contraction, she'd discovered the phone's battery was dead.

Since she had no idea where her cell could be, the only thing she could think to do was crawl to the apartment's front door.

"Hell-lllp! . . . Helllp!"

Sofia had managed to unlock the door's heavy bolts and was now shouting down the corridor between low groans of pain. Gracie was standing behind her, looking down with a curious gaze and sucking her thumb.

"It's okay." Sofia panted, reaching out to touch her daughter's hand and trying to remember her breathing techniques from prenatal yoga. "Everything's okay." *Pant, puff* . . . "Mommy's okay."

But then the next contraction hit and Sofia slumped with her forehead to the floor, moaning loudly as she went. The pain consumed her like a huge wave, slowly carrying her up to its peak and then crashing her down again on the other side.

After what felt like minutes—hours, even—the pain began to subside, and Sofia heard a voice from the hallway.

"Are you okay?" a woman called out. "Oh, my, is the baby coming?"

Sofia raised her head to see a pair of neat black pumps heading toward her. As the woman stopped in the doorway and Sofia began to look up, she saw sheer stockings, a charcoal gray skirt, matching suit jacket, and finally a familiar, pretty, but worried face. It was the young woman who lived a couple of doors down. What was her name?

"Ashleigh!" Sofia cried out, suddenly remembering.

"Yes." Ashleigh crouched down next to her and gently put her arm under Sofia's and helped her sit up. "I'm Ashleigh. You're Sofia, aren't you?" Then she smiled over at Gracie, who still seemed unfazed by the commotion. "And you're Gracie."

"Can you help? My . . . my phone's dead," Sofia stammered, feeling the first twinges of the next contraction.

"Of course." Ashleigh reached in her pocket for her cell. "Who shall I call?"

Sofia hissed through gritted teeth, "Tom. My husband."

A flicker of panic crossed Ashleigh's face. But then, pushing back a loose strand of her otherwise immaculately pinned-up blond hair, she slipped straight into a businesslike mode befitting her clothes. As Sofia huffed out numbers amid moans of pain, Ashleigh punched them with a calm precision into her phone.

While Ashleigh spoke to Tom, Sofia crawled back into the apartment, knelt by the couch, and slumped into its soft velour cushions. She rocked back and forth; whispering, crying, mumbling, groaning. She'd forgotten just how painful this was. Her body felt as if it were being pulled apart, compressed in on itself, twisted, extended, crushed, all at the same time. It was too much. It hurt too damn much.

Once again the contraction ebbed away, and she could hear Ashleigh telling her Tom was on his way. He'd be there in five minutes, and the taxi would wait in front of the lobby.

"Mama?" Gracie was tapping on Sofia's shoulder. "Bay-bee?"

"Yes, sweets." She managed to turn, rest her cheek on the sofa cushion, and smile at Gracie. "The baby's coming."

Looking into Gracie's eyes, she felt a stab of guilt. It wasn't supposed to happen like this. The baby wasn't due for another two weeks. They'd had the whole thing so well planned. Gracie was going to stay with friends. Tom would be here. They'd make their way calmly to the birthing center at the hospital. Everything would be ready. Her bag would be ready.

"The DVD!" she shouted. "I need the DVD."

Ashleigh was already at her side, one hand on Sofia's back and the other wrapped around Gracie's small waist.

"Which DVD, Sofia?" she soothed.

"Term . . . Terminator."

Ashleigh's eyebrows shot up. *"The Terminator?"*

"Yesssss," Sofia cried. "I need Arnold Schwarzenegger."

The contractions were coming so fast. Last time with Gracie it had all been so slow. So painfully slow. But now her body felt like a steam train careening out of control.

"Tom," she groaned through her fog of pain. "Tom. Hurry. Please."

Four

Ashleigh

Ashleigh had been frightened. She'd never seen someone in so much pain, and it would be a long time before she forgot that fearful look in Sofia's eyes. Although Ashleigh tried not to show it, from the moment she had found her neighbor balled up in the open doorway, she was terrified. Her heart pounded in her chest, and her mind raced with panicked questions: What if the husband doesn't get home in time? What if she starts giving birth? What should I do with the little girl? Should I call 911? As a young attorney in a busy New York law firm, Ashleigh thought she was used to stress and drama and having to think on her feet. But birth was a whole different ball game.

Fortunately, Sofia's husband thundered down the hallway and burst into the apartment just as Ashleigh was gathering together coats and bags and the *Terminator* DVD that Sofia was demanding with such tenacity. He looked flustered and breathless, yet he instantly knew what to do, and Ashleigh felt the knot of panic in her chest loosen. As Tom half guided, half carried his wife out to the elevator, Ashleigh trotted behind, clutching Gracie in her arms.

"Let me help," she called to him. "I could come with you. Look after Gracie."

He turned and looked at her, his blue eyes flickering with surprise and gratitude. "Would you?"

"Of course." She nodded as Sofia, who was now gripping her husband's chest, let out a long, low, guttural moan.

At the birthing center, Ashleigh hadn't had to stay long. Within an hour Gracie's regular babysitter showed up, and Ashleigh was soon in a cab back downtown to her apartment. Once home, she flew into the shower, pulled on a dress, and was back out of the house in less than twenty minutes. In spite of her hurry, however, she still showed up over an hour and a half late for her cousin Gina's engagement party. Not that Ashleigh particularly cared.

Despite all the glitz of the Waldorf, the free-flowing champagne, and the mile-long buffet, Gina's engagement party was the last place Ashleigh wanted to be. Ashleigh found her cousin tiresome. She couldn't stand Gina's creepy fiancé, Davey; and Gina's mother, Ashleigh's aunt Gaynor, was a throbbing pain in Ashleigh's head. The only person in the family she liked was her uncle Ray, Gina's father. He was sweet and kind, but he was also her boss. Ray, together with her father, had founded the law firm where Ashleigh worked, and so these days she saw her favorite uncle every day.

Ashleigh had come tonight only because her parents were too busy to make the trip. Although they couldn't drive the three hours from their home in DC, they'd let Ashleigh know that she must attend.

"We don't want to let the family down, do we?" her dad had said in that chipper yet knife-edged tone he often used with his daughter.

Once, when Ashleigh accidentally caught a glimpse of her father on CNN, she'd noticed that he used the exact same tone when he was sparring with a Democrat on the Senate floor. Since leaving the family law firm years ago, her father had worked his way up the political ladder and quickly became a senator for Ohio—a state where he'd lived as a boy, where Ashleigh's parents owned a large summer house, and where Ashleigh had spent every summer as a child and teenager. Her father had proved to be a slick and persuasive politician and was now serving his second term in office.

Senator Chad Rocksbury did not leave his rhetorical skills and biting tones on Capitol Hill. He employed them at home with his family too. Even though Ashleigh was now a confident and successful attorney, she was no match for her father. He could intimidate and outpersuade at every turn, and in any confrontation between the two of them, Ashleigh would always end up conceding, agreeing, or simply whining.

The other night on the phone had been no different.

"Da-ad!" she'd pleaded, sounding unnervingly like her teenage self. "I have a *really* big presentation the morning after the party." Then, in the most serious and businesslike tone she could muster, she added, "Uncle Ray said this might be the biggest contract of the year. We have to do a good job."

Ashleigh was sure this would clinch it. If Ashleigh was determined not to follow her father into politics, then the next-best thing she could do was be a great lawyer and one day take up her father's vacated seat as a partner at Rocksbury, Chatham, and Wise. Since she'd stepped out of Georgetown Law School a few years ago and into the offices of the small but highly respected New York law firm, that was all Ashleigh's family had talked about.

"Ashleigh," chimed her mom, who as always was listening on the other line, "I'm sure the party won't run *too* late, and Gina would so love to see you."

"I suppose." Ashleigh sighed, feeling outnumbered and defeated, as she always did when she talked to her parents.

A while ago Sam had nicknamed them "the UFCF": The United Front of Chad and Frances. Not that Sam had ever met them, of course. Although she and Sam had been living together for nearly six months now in their Manhattan U apartment, Ashleigh hadn't told her parents. They still thought Ashleigh was sharing a cramped two-bedroom in Battery Park City with her old Georgetown roommate. By redirecting her mail and insisting her parents talk to her only at work or on her cell phone, she'd successfully managed to keep up the ruse. In fact, Chad and Frances hadn't suspected a thing, and as much as Ashleigh hated having to represent the family at Gina's party, she was relieved they hadn't made the trip to the city. There was no way she'd have been able to keep up the pretense if they had.

Now, as she stood alone and awkward in one of the Waldorf's ornate ballrooms dressed in a pink silk Calypso dress that was way too cheap for this crowd, Ashleigh was suddenly brightened by this thought. Maybe coming tonight wasn't so bad after all. *Let's face it,* she told herself, *arriving late means I have to stay only a little while longer.* All she had to do was smile a few more smiles, shake a few hands, avoid her aunt Gaynor, and say her good-byes. She could then disappear and go home to Sam.

Ashleigh smiled to herself at the thought of her wonderful, funny, intelligent Sam, who, right now, was probably sitting up in bed, sipping a steaming mug of cocoa, surrounded by student papers or a stack of books and articles. *My Sweet Professor.* Ashleigh's skin tingled as she thought of the nickname she used for Sam when she felt particularly giddy and loving.

The fuzzy feeling skittered away, however, as she heard a familiar squawking voice behind her.

"Here you are!"

She turned to find Gina tottering toward her, a flute of champagne in her hand.

"Mwaauu, mwauu." Gina air-kissed Ashleigh, and then wagged her finger. "Where have you been?" she demanded.

"Helping a neighbor give birth," Ashleigh said, her face deadpan.

Gina looked at her blankly for a second, and then her heavily made-up face cracked into a wide, toothy smile.

"Oh, Ashleigh, you are to die for!" she squealed.

Ashleigh looked on as Gina proceeded to giggle and hiccup on a mouthful of champagne. A huge diamond glinted on her tiny finger, and on her equally tiny body Gina wore a dress made of layers of expensive silk, hand-stitched with hundreds of pearls and sequins. No doubt the dress alone cost a ridiculous amount of money. Four figures, at least, perhaps even five. Although for Gina and her vast trust fund (bequeathed by her mother's family), such money was small change.

"So, Gina," Ashleigh began, "congratulations! You must be so happy. And the party? It's been wonderful. But I have an early morning, so I'm afraid I'm going to leave in a little while."

Gina's eyes grew wide. "No, no, no," she shrieked. "You can't go yet, Ashey." Ashleigh hated it when Gina called her that. "No, no, no. Don't go yet," Gina continued, leaning across and gripping Ashleigh's arm. "I have someone for you to meet. He's divine."

Ashleigh's heart sank. Gina was always doing this to her, trying to set her up with guys who turned out to be stupidly rich, dumb, and obnoxious. It didn't matter how hard Ashleigh protested, Gina always tried it. Of course, if Ashleigh told Gina she was living with someone, Gina's excruciating setups would end. But if Ashleigh told Gina, Gina would tell her mother. And if Aunt Gaynor knew, soon enough Ashleigh's parents would be told. Uncle Ray would be told too, and although he was generally a discreet man, Ashleigh suspected that it wouldn't be long before all her colleagues at the law firm were plaguing her with questions or curious glances.

"I really have to go," Ashleigh pleaded one more time.

It was already too late. Gina started pulling Ashleigh through the crowd. People swarmed around Gina, offering their congratulations and cooing over her ring. All the while Gina's grip on Ashleigh's arm never loosened, and she continued to drag her cousin onward. Only when they reached a group of guys dressed in identical black tuxedos standing at the bar did Gina let her hand drop. She tapped one of the men on the shoulder.

"Josh," she said as he turned to face them, "this is Ashleigh. My cousin. The one I was telling you about." She puffed out her chest proudly. "You know, Senator Rocksbury's daughter."

Josh was broad shouldered, tall, and as catalog-model handsome as they came. He gave Ashleigh a slow, lingering once-over as he chewed idly on a bread stick. He then turned and did the same to Gina. When his eyes finally landed on her perky breasts, they remained there for a while, and he grinned.

Gina giggled, clearly enjoying his shameless gaze. "Well, I'll leave you guys to it."

With that, she flicked her long, shiny dark hair over her shoulder, blew Josh a kiss, and turned to talk to some people clamoring behind her.

Meanwhile, Ashleigh began to formulate her escape plan. But as she turned to Josh, she found him ogling Gina's small behind and couldn't help barking out, "Oh, for God's sake."

"What?" Josh looked up at her, his languid brown eyes vaguely surprised.

"You're staring at the bride-to-be's ass."

"So?" he scoffed, biting at his bread stick. "Not jealous, are you?"

This one is the king of jerks, Ashleigh thought. She couldn't wait to laugh about him with Sam when she got home. Just as she was about to walk away, Josh put out his arm to stop her.

"Not so fast, sweetie," he drawled, his voice thick with alcohol. "Don't sweat it. You're pretty too."

Before she knew what was happening, he began to run his partially chewed breadstick along her bare shoulder and then under the strap of her dress.

Ashleigh tensed and shuddered, and then a weird burning feeling rose from her bosom. She spun around, grabbed the bread stick, snapped it barely an inch from Josh's face, and then nudged one soggy end into his forehead.

"Look, you asshole," she hissed, "I don't give a damn what you think about me. You are just some overprivileged, small-dicked, whiny frat boy. A cockroach has a higher IQ and greater sex appeal than you do."

She pushed the bread stick harder into his forehead and glared into his stunned eyes. Her heart thumped in her chest. She'd never, *ever* done anything like this in her life. Usually she'd politely talk with whoever it was Gina was trying to set her up with. She'd endure their indifferent flirtations, where they'd desperately try to make her want them, but at the same time they didn't really want her at all. She'd then wait for the right moment and slip away, praying she would never see the guy again.

But this time something had snapped, and here she was skewering some trust-fund frat boy with a bread stick while the crowd around them descended into a hushed, enthralled silence.

"Ooh, you got a live one there, Josh," sniggered one of the other tuxedoed guys, setting off a ripple of giggles and whispers.

Ashleigh fought a burning desire to take the other piece of bread stick and ram it into his forehead too. Or better still, ram it somewhere where it would really hurt. She knew it was time to stop and go home, though. She'd made enough of a spectacle for one evening. So, dropping her bread sticks onto Josh's alligator shoes, she smiled at him sweetly, said nothing more, and walked away.

She might have gotten out of the party scot-free if she hadn't stopped at the abundant dessert table near the door. The desserts looked heavenly, and Ashleigh couldn't help pausing to take a quick look. Her eyes scanned whipped creams, colored fondants, and chocolate sponges, and finally she spotted a mini-cheesecake decorated with glazed cherries. She reached out and grabbed for it, knowing the tiny dessert would be Sam's favorite. But just after she wrapped it in a napkin, and when she was delicately trying to position it in her purse so it wouldn't get squashed, a voice behind her shouted, "Ashleigh, what was all that about?"

She turned to find Gina, pink-cheeked and breathless.

Ashleigh gave a nonchalant wave. "Just some friendly bread-stick jousting."

Gina looked angry. "Josh is a nice guy. Don't you see that?"

"Gina," Ashleigh said, "I don't want to be set up with Josh. I don't want to be set up with anyone." Then, exhausted by the evening and suddenly tired of lying to her family about Sam, she added, "I'm seeing someone."

"*What?* Why didn't you say?" As Gina spoke, Davey, her reptilian fiancé, appeared from nowhere and snaked one of his long arms around Gina's shoulders. "Why didn't you bring him?" her cousin demanded.

Ashleigh immediately regretted bringing up Sam. "I—" she began, but she stopped as Gina's mother emerged from the crowd wearing a ruffled jade green dress two sizes too tight for her and an ornate diamond necklace that glinted and sparkled under the lights from the ballroom's chandeliers. Moving forward to stand by her daughter, she gazed at Ashleigh with a saccharine, questioning smile.

"Because, you know," Gina twittered on, "the invitation said 'plus one.' You should have brought him."

"Who's *him*?" Aunt Gaynor squawked with glee, sounding just like her daughter.

Ashleigh felt a slight sweat break out in the palm of her hands. She opened her mouth to speak but was halted by Davey's loud, jockish laugh.

"There's no *him*." He guffawed, pointing an intrusive finger at Ashleigh. "She's dating a woman." He then paused, giving everyone time to gawp and gasp, and added with a flourish, "A *black* woman."

The rain that had soaked the city as she'd left for the party earlier that evening lay in vast puddles on the sidewalks and roads. However, the sky was now completely clear. Ashleigh looked up and saw a shining crescent moon and even a few stars, a rare sight in Manhattan. There was a slight chill in the air, but it was surprisingly mild. Perhaps spring had finally decided to arrive.

Standing outside her apartment building watching the taxi swerve away from the curb and off down Bleecker Street, Ashleigh didn't move. Only an hour ago she had wanted nothing more than to be in Sam's arms. But now she needed time—time to herself. It wasn't that Sam wouldn't understand. She always understood. It amazed Ashleigh, in fact, how understanding Sam always was. She never pressured Ashleigh to come out and tell her parents about their relationship. She didn't get upset when Ashleigh wouldn't take her to family events like tonight's.

In spite of all this, though, Ashleigh needed to be on her own for a while. It was late and she had to be in the office early in the morning, yet she had to think about all that had happened. And all that was about to happen. She had to figure out what she was going to do when the earthquake hit. Whether it was from Gina or Gaynor, her parents were going to find out very soon. The press might find out even sooner. She could see the trashy headlines now. *Republican Senator's Daughter Has Black Lesbian Lover,* they would read. It made her wince to think about it.

Fiddling with her key in the near darkness, Ashleigh finally felt the lock click and then loosen. She pushed hard on the heavy gate. She'd never been in the garden this late, but she did come on the weekends or sometimes the occasional morning before work. Sam's apartment—their apartment—was so small, and Ashleigh liked the space of the garden, but also its seclusion. It was the only place in the city she knew that felt wide-open yet enclosed all at the same time. The garden was also the perfect antidote to the goldfish-bowl law offices where she spent so many hours of her week, with their bright lights, low-slung partitions, and constantly circling colleagues.

Now, as she turned in to the garden and her eyes adjusted to the darkness, Ashleigh was surprised to find she wasn't alone here either. Someone was huddled on the nearby bench, buried deep in a fur-lined parka. At the sound of the gate shutting, the stranger looked up. Ashleigh instantly recognized her. It was the beautiful red-haired woman whom Ashleigh often saw out in the garden painting. Even though she couldn't make out her red hair in the gloom, Ashleigh knew those amazing eyes. It was definitely her.

Ashleigh wavered for a second. It seemed strange to go sit somewhere else and not say a word, the two of them alone in the darkness not even acknowledging each other. But it didn't really seem the right time to make small talk either.

"Hey," the woman said, pulling down her hood and smiling at Ashleigh. She'd clearly been thinking the same thing.

"Hey," Ashleigh said, moving toward the bench.

"Beautiful night, isn't it?"

"Uh-huh," Ashleigh replied, and, warmed by the woman's friendly tone, sat down beside her. "I'm Ashleigh."

"Hannah," the woman replied. And then with a smile, she asked, "Can't you sleep either?"

Ashleigh sighed. "Something like that."

They sat for a few seconds, saying nothing.

"Have you heard that some dean wants to bulldoze this place?" Hannah finally whispered.

"What?" Ashleigh said. "The garden? Really?"

Hannah nodded beside her and whispered, "Yep."

Ashleigh shook her head in disbelief. "When?"

Her question went unanswered, because as she uttered it, there was a loud rattling at the gate. Both women looked over. After a few more rattles and a hefty clang, a woman emerged wrapped in a long raincoat and wearing, strangely for this midnight hour, a pair of heavy, dark glasses.

Seeing Ashleigh and Hannah on the bench, the woman faltered and looked as if she were going to turn and leave. Thinking better of it, she changed her mind, stepped forward, and asked in a hushed whisper, "What are you night owls doing here?"

"Thinking," replied Hannah.

"Me too." Ashleigh smiled.

The woman half laughed and half sighed. "Well, that makes three of us."

As she drew close, Ashleigh blinked with surprise. Wasn't this Mary Havemeyer? *Casey's Echoes* was one of Ashleigh's all-time favorite books. She'd never seen Mary Havemeyer in person, only a photo on the dustcover of Ashleigh's lovingly battered copy of *Casey's*. But she knew that Mary taught at Manhattan U, and in spite of the darkness and the glasses hiding the woman's eyes, she was now convinced this was her. The striking cheekbones were unmistakable, and except for some silver streaks around her face, time hadn't altered her raven black shoulder-length hair.

As if reading Ashleigh's mind, the woman smiled and said simply, "Mary." She then added, "Can I join you?"

Introducing themselves, Hannah and Ashleigh shuffled along the bench, allowing Mary to sit between them. As she lowered herself onto the seat, Ashleigh noticed a dark shadow peeking below Mary's glasses on her left cheek. Ashleigh wondered if it was a bruise; a bruise might explain the dark glasses. She sneaked another quick look out the corner of her eye. No, perhaps it was just the light. It was gloomy out here, and shadows clung to everything.

Ashleigh pulled her jacket around her and settled back against the wooden bench. In the silence that followed, she and her two companions sat motionless, lost in their thoughts, staring up at the clear navy sky.

Five

Sofia

Sofia stared out at the starry night with her elbows propped on the windowsill and her nose pressed against the clammy glass. Just ten minutes earlier she'd been writhing on the pink carpeting in the birthing suite, but then as suddenly as her contractions had started, they'd stopped. The same thing had happened when she was in labor with Gracie, so Sofia wasn't worried. In fact, she was relieved to have a moment to breathe normally again and towel off her sweaty, tired body.

She was concerned about only one thing.

"When are they going to bring that damn TV?" Sofia muttered, her breath steaming the window in front of her. "They promised it would be here as soon as we checked in. It's been an hour already."

"They'll get it, hon; don't worry."

She turned and looked at Tom, who was slumped in a low arm-chair near the Jacuzzi. His brow glistened with sweat, and his eyes looked red and tired.

"But what if they don't?" Sofia pleaded. "I can't do this with-out it."

Tom pushed himself to his feet and came toward her. As he reached the window, he rested one hand on the small of her back.

"You're doing great," he said in a soothing whisper. "It's going to be fine."

Sofia flopped her head against Tom's chest, and she sighed as he encircled her in his long arms. At least they'd gotten to the birthing center in time, she thought. With the speed at which her contractions were coming earlier, she'd been convinced she was going to give birth in the back of the taxi.

"Still nothing?" a cheery voice shouted behind them.

They turned to see Joan, their midwife, smiling in the open doorway.

"Not a peep," Tom said.

"Playing hard to get, this little one." She laughed, radiating the kind of calm that only someone who'd been delivering babies for thirty years could radiate.

Joan moved off, chuckling loudly, her heels clacking along the corridor outside.

"Do you want me to go ask her?" Tom said, sensing Sofia's anxiety about the television.

Clutching her fingers around his wrist, Sofia half laughed, half hissed, "You. Are. Not. Going. Anywhere! What if the contrac—"

Sofia didn't finish. As if hearing their cue, her contractions returned with a mighty vengeance. Sofia was thrown to the floor as the first contraction slammed through her body. She let out a long, low yowl and then grabbed hold of Tom's legs and clung to them as she tried to ride out the pain.

No sooner had the first contraction finished than the second started its inescapable crescendo.

"Ahhhhh," she cried. "Oohhhhh." And then, as she felt Tom trying to peel her arms off his legs, she shrieked out, "No, no, no!"

As the contraction began to ebb away, she realized it wasn't Tom pulling at her arms, but Joan. She must have heard Sofia's cries from the hallway.

"Come on, sweetie," whispered the midwife. "Tom needs his legs so he can help you. Let's get you somewhere more comfortable. You want to try the tub?"

Sofia thought for a second about the warm water and the soothing bubbles and was about to loosen her grip when the next contraction hit. She immediately refastened her grasp on Tom's legs and drove her head between his knees.

"The television. She needs the television."

Sofia could hear Tom's panicked voice swimming around above her. "Yes," she cried out in agreement. "The movie. I need my . . . my . . . *movie*."

The television did not arrive, and as the fourth, fifth, tenth, and fifteenth contractions came and went, Sofia remained glued to her spot on the floor. Her knees ached, and she could vaguely sense Tom's legs weakening under her intense grip. Yet she couldn't let go. His legs were her lifeline; they were the ship's mast in a squalling ocean of pain.

"Sofia, sweetie"—Joan was talking again—"you might be ready to push. Can I check you?"

For Joan to check how far her cervix had dilated, Sofia would have to get up. At the very least, she'd have to unfurl herself and move into a more cooperative position. She knew she should do it, but she just couldn't let go of Tom. She felt like she might die of the pain if she let go. Thus, Sofia continued to kneel and clutch and moan, and in the brief moments between each contraction her mind swam with thoughts of drugs and epidurals and C-sections.

"Why?" she whispered through a fog of her own panting breaths. "Why, why am I doing this?"

It had been exactly the same with Gracie. At the moment when the contractions began to slam into one another, pounding her already exhausted body, she'd started to regret her decision to give birth naturally. She loved her midwife, Joan, and the cozy suite in the birthing center, with its plush carpets, soft lights, and bubbling Jacuzzi. Moreover, since an operation to remove her tonsils when she was four, the smell of antiseptic, the glimmer of shining surgical instruments, and the bleeping of hospital machines was enough to send Sofia's heart racing and her stomach turning somersaults. But as she'd writhed in pain during her first labor, her fear of hospitals rapidly receded, and she'd been about to demand to be taken to the nearby ER to have the baby removed by any medical means possible.

In the end, however, Gracie was born in the birthing center with no drugs and no knives, just as Sofia had planned. And it was all thanks to *The Terminator*. For some reason, in the midst of her contractions, Sofia had become fixated on a bundle of unreturned DVDs lurking somewhere in her purse. Between her groans and cries, she demanded that Tom find a TV and start playing one of the movies.

As he fumbled with the disks and tried to read her the titles, she barked, "It doesn't matter which one. Just play a goddamn movie!"

Whether it was delirium that stirred her to make this bizarre request or some sort of primitive insight that only a birthing woman intuitively understood, Sofia never knew. Whatever it was, it worked. Within a few minutes Arnold Schwarzenegger's *The Terminator* flickered onto the screen of the hastily found television, and, in spite of the pain, Sofia became focused, calm, and serenely hypnotized.

Movies were Sofia's passion, and the passion that took her to Hollywood and the film business ten years earlier, after she'd graduated college. Representing needy actors wasn't exactly what she'd imagined herself doing in "the business," but it was good enough. And action movies were her favorites. Her very *secret* favorites. Among her colleagues at the Venture Talent Agency—which prided itself on its long list of "edgy" and serious actors—Sofia had to wax lyrical about the indies and scoff at the likes of *Die Hard* or *Mission: Impossible* or *Kill Bill*. For Sofia, though, it was all pretense. She liked some indies, but give her car chases, sword fights, and kung fu any day.

And so, as one of her all-time favorite action movies played on the TV, Sofia rode a torrent of contractions, pushed for twenty minutes, and finally gave birth to a wrinkled pink baby girl whom they would soon name Gracie. Sofia's labor became infamous among the midwives at the birthing center, and Sofia loved to tell anyone who'd listen her amusing "birthing with *The Terminator*" tale. One thing she could never quite explain, however, was exactly how the movie had helped.

"It just did," she would tell people. "And you know what?"

she'd add with a chuckle. "If I have another one, I'm going to do the same thing all over again."

Yet now, as she labored for the second time with no television or *Terminator* in sight, Sofia was beginning to drown. The contractions were unceasing and excruciating, and she felt as if she were being dragged down and down in a whirlpool of pain. No encouraging words from her midwife or Tom were helping. She just wanted this baby out.

Sofia finally said the words she never thought she'd say.

"Take me," she groaned, her knuckles turning white as she clutched harder at Tom's calves. "The hospital. Now." Then, in a low murmur, she repeated, "Hospital. Now. Hospital. Now."

"You might not have time, sweetie," the midwife said in a kind whisper as she pulled back Sofia's hair and then stroked her back. "The contractions are coming so fast, you're nearly there. I can tell."

Sofia didn't listen. She couldn't listen. Instead she continued to moan and plead for the hospital, and soon the midwife, realizing there was nothing else to be done, started to make arrangements for her transferral.

However, just as the wheelchair arrived to take Sofia down the long corridors toward the adjoining hospital, an orderly arrived with a large TV propped on a rickety trolley.

"Great timing," Tom huffed.

Meanwhile, Joan told the orderly, "We won't be needing the television."

They were both silenced when Sofia let out a loud yelp, unhooked herself from Tom's legs, and started to crawl toward the DVD lying on a nearby table.

"Put it on!" she begged, grabbing the case and waving it furiously in the air.

Tom took the movie. "But, honey—" he began.

"*On!*" Sofia screamed.

The room became a whirlwind of action. The television was hooked up, the wheelchair removed, and Tom flicked through the DVD menu with fumbling haste. As soon as the movie began to run, Sofia looked up at the screen and suddenly remembered what she'd forgotten since Gracie's birth. She remembered, in that instant, why the movie had been so perfect. Its intensity and noise and furor were part of it. For Sofia, it seemed much more fitting to be surrounded by noise and commotion while she grunted and screeched through her contractions. All that tranquillity and scented-candles stuff she'd read about in birthing books just seemed ridiculous. Who needed whale songs and the smell of rose petals when you were trying to get a seven-pound baby out of a very small hole?

But it was more than just the movie's riotous sound track. There was also something about the Terminator himself. The way he was constantly getting shot and maimed and crushed but then rising up again and again, with his red eyes glowing. It was kind of how she felt as each and every contraction swept her up and then dumped her out on the other side. She and Schwarzenegger, she realized, were one. They were unlikely soul mates, compadres, brothers in arms.

With this revelation, Sofia shouted up at Tom, "Forward to the chase scene. Forward to the chase scene."

While Tom did what he was told, Sofia heaved herself up, perched on the edge of the low table, and spread her legs wide. It was time; she knew it. It was time to get this baby out.

Sofia stared fixedly at the screen and clutched the table with all her might. Sounds of gun fire and screeching wheels blared out from the television and echoed around the birthing suite. While Sarah Connor fought with the relentless Terminator on the screen, Sofia panted and groaned her way through her last furious contractions. And just as the credits began to roll, Sofia finally pushed her new baby into the world.

Later, after Sofia was guided into bed, her midwife's familiar chuckle rang out.

"Let me tell you," Joan said as she placed the newborn baby boy onto Sofia's chest, "you're one feisty *Terminator* mama!"

*   *   *

Sofia's eyes blinked open. It was still dark, but gloomy morning light was beginning to creep in through the window. Sofia had been moved from the birthing suite to her own room, where she'd fallen into a deep and exhausted sleep under the deliciously crisp sheets.

"What time is it?" she croaked, seeing Tom in the chair next to her bed.

He was awake and holding the baby high up against his chest. "A little after six," he whispered.

Sofia inched herself up against the pillows. Every muscle in her body ached, even ones in her face and neck. Looking over at Tom again, she desperately wanted to take her new son in her arms but was scared to wake the baby. So instead she and Tom sat in silence, staring down at their sleeping child.

"Wow," she muttered.

Even though she'd been through this once before, Sofia was still struck by how amazing yet weird the whole childbirth thing was. Only yesterday she'd been big and pregnant, fishing for Gracie's poo in the tub, and out in the garden listening to that woman's sorry tale. Now here she was, her body exhausted and deflated and her tiny son asleep beside her. Who could believe that after all that exertion and trauma she'd produced *this*? This serene and defenseless being whose long, dark eyelashes fluttered as he slept.

"He looks like an Edgar," Tom said, interrupting her thoughts.

Sofia grimaced a little, but then smiled. "I hate to admit it," she whispered, "but you might be right."

The new baby's name had been a sticking point. A big sticking point. From the moment they'd found out Sofia was pregnant again, Tom had lobbied relentlessly for Edgar if it was a boy, and Eddie if it was a girl.

"We are not naming our child Edgar, honey," Sofia would say. "Or Allan or Poe."

It was bad enough that she had to live with every book ever published on the author, including all kinds of rare editions they were allowed to touch only with cotton gloves. The last thing she wanted was a little Edgar running around the house. But when Tom offered to bid for a limited-edition boxed set of Schwarzenegger movies on eBay in exchange for full baby-naming rights, Sofia had buckled. Her Internet abilities were severely lacking, and the intricacies of eBay auctioning were unfathomable. Plus, she really wanted the boxed set.

"So"—Tom grinned, looking up from Edgar—"we can call him that? Seriously?"

Sofia nodded. It wasn't so bad, she supposed. If she was honest, it was pretty cute, and not unlike the other old-men names she'd have picked for her son, like Henry or Benny or Lenny. She'd make sure he got some decent middle name, in any case. As a teenager, Edgar would undoubtedly hate all things Poe and would need another option.

Sofia wondered what that name could be while Tom gently shifted the baby, reached across, and squeezed her hand. "You did so good, hon." He smiled.

A peaceful quiet followed, until the door slammed open and a gigantic bouquet of flowers entered the room. The rainbow of lilies and ribbons was flanked by a pair of flushed-looking nurses.

"I'm sorry," the shorter nurse said, blushing and giggling and waving toward the flowers. "We told him he shouldn't come in here. But he was *so* persuasive."

Sofia immediately groaned. There was only one person who could be "*so* persuasive," and only one person who could get pretty young women this pink and giggly at six in the morning. She looked from the vast and lush bouquet downward. The Chip & Pepper jeans and immaculate Prada sneakers confirmed her suspicions. It was him, all right.

"Hayden," she muttered, slumping back against the pillow.

Hayden lowered the flowers and, peeking over a large blooming lily, grinned.

"Hey, guys!" he boomed. "Surprise!"

The grin was instantly wiped off his tanned face as everyone in the room, including his two new fans, urgently shushed him and pointed toward the baby. But it was too late. Little Edgar was already blinking his eyes, arching his back, and opening his lungs for one of his first all-out wails. Glaring at Hayden, Sofia quickly beckoned for the baby.

"Good one, bro," Tom shouted above the din, as he handed Edgar over.

"Oops," Hayden said with a sheepish smile.

Oops indeed, Sofia thought. But she chose to ignore her brother-in-law and instead tugged at her nightshirt and tried to encourage the screaming baby toward her breast.

"Man, I didn't mean to wake him," she heard Hayden explaining to Tom, who'd now jumped up and was giving his little brother a welcoming hug. "I was just so excited to see my nephew."

How did he know it was a boy? Sofia fumed. He'd probably smooched one of the gooey-eyed nurses who'd just left the room to get that little tidbit of information. Sofia tutted and tried for the second time to get the wailing baby to latch on as Tom and Hayden laughed together at the foot of her bed.

"Kick-ass *Terminator* mama strikes again." Hayden was guffawing.

"Tom," Sofia snapped, interrupting the hilarity, "can you take your brother for breakfast or something? I—*we*—need some peace and quiet."

Like a pair of scolded pups, the two brothers looked at Sofia with their matching pale blue eyes and together muttered, "Sorry."

For a brief second she wanted to laugh. She couldn't help thinking of the time, years ago, when she'd caught Tom and Hayden stuffing frozen shrimp into the gilded curtain rail in their stepfather's study. Even though she didn't like their stepfather much, she'd demanded they return the shrimp to the freezer. The old man was a cantankerous ass, but even he didn't deserve the smell of rotting shellfish stinking up his house.

Sofia smiled a little with thoughts of the old days and found herself relaxing into the pillows. Edgar sensed her new calm, and, as his sobs subsided, he found her nipple and began to suckle.

"Okay, honey," Tom said, tiptoeing toward her. "I have to go pick up Gracie, and I'll take this one"—he jerked his thumb toward Hayden—"with me."

"How is our Gracie-girl?" Sofia asked.

"The sitter said she was amazing. Slept the whole night through."

Sofia smiled again. Gracie had only just mastered sleeping all night, and Sofia was glad to hear that yesterday's events hadn't disrupted this achievement. However, as she looked down at Edgar nursing, Sofia was reminded that sleepless nights awaited her once more. When she was still working at the agency in LA, Sofia had been used to the late nights that a Hollywood life entailed. In fact, she had thrived on them, and all it would take to keep her fresh was a grande cappuccino picked up on her morning drive to work. But when she moved to New York and Gracie arrived, bringing her colic and then her countless ear infections, Sofia had been consumed with a tiredness like nothing else. No cappuccino in the world could fix her exhaustion or elevate her from "the perpetual state of yawn," as she sometimes called it.

Sofia just hoped Edgar would be different. She prayed he would be one of those dream babies she'd only heard about from friends, who slept through the night from the moment they popped out of the womb. She needed sleep if she was going to stay sane and look after two kids under the age of three—not to mention be a fun and loving wife who might occasionally feel like having sex.

"I wanted to give you this." Hayden interrupted Sofia's thoughts and tiptoed forward. "I thought you deserved something nice after your latest motherhood ordeal."

Putting aside the bouquet, Hayden produced a box from a cloth Barneys bag slung over his shoulder. He set it down on the bed beside her when he remembered Sofia's hands were full with Edgar, and began to unwrap it.

"Voilà." He smiled as he pulled back some pink tissue paper and unfurled a dusky red silk robe.

She gasped in spite of herself. It was beautiful, completely beautiful. She shifted the baby so she could reach out and touch the fabric. Exquisite, she thought. It probably cost a small fortune. Indeed, she could see the Barneys price tag still attached to the robe's belt loop, and it *had* cost a fortune.

"Hayden," she murmured, "you shouldn't have."

A satisfied smirk crept across his face. "It was nothing."

"No," Sofia snapped, "I mean, you really shouldn't have. This is ridiculously expensive," she hissed, flicking at the price tag. "I could have covered a month's rent with that kind of money."

Hayden looked crestfallen, and Sofia felt a kick of guilt for being so peevish. Perhaps she was being a little hard on him. Whatever crappy things he'd done in the past, she couldn't deny his persistent generosity. She had to hand it to him: Not many people would buy gorgeous silk gowns for women who'd just given birth, not even their own husbands. Usually all the gifts and lavish packages went to the baby.

So instead of demanding he take the robe back, she drew it to her cheek and gave a little laugh. "But I suppose I'll keep it," she whispered.

Hayden grinned, knowing he'd been forgiven, and then added tentatively, "And I have some news." He looked from Sofia to Tom and back again. "I've dropped Lori."

Sofia stiffened at the sound of the name.

She eyed him suspiciously. "You dropped Lori? You're kidding."

He raised his right hand. "It's true."

Sofia eyed him again, and after a few beats decided he must be telling the truth. Sofia felt her mouth twitching into a smile. After four years he'd finally fired Lori Spiegler—the bitch of all bitches.

"Why?" she asked, trying to disguise her pleasure.

"She just wasn't getting me the movies I wanted."

"She was getting you the big bucks you wanted," Sofia blurted out.

"But, Sofe, you know I get bored just doing all those cheesy movies. I want more interesting stuff, challenging stuff. You know . . ."

Hayden trailed off. He was dreading her "I told you so" speech; she could tell. But, boy, he deserved it. When Lori Spiegler had first come sniffing around Hayden, Sofia had warned him. Sure, Lori could get him big deals, but as much as Hayden liked the Hollywood lifestyle, the money, and the fame, he was also a smart guy who loved doing intriguing movies and roles that stretched him. Lori, on the other hand, had no taste, no intuition, and saw only dollar signs when she read scripts.

But Hayden didn't listen and ended up dropping Sofia, his first and most devoted agent, not to mention his sister-in-law. Then he ran off to Lori, lured by her promises. It was true that Lori had come through with some seven-figure movie deals for Hayden, but it didn't excuse the fact that she was a backstabbing, client-poaching bitch. And it didn't excuse the fact that Hayden had dropped Sofia for that woman.

Sofia was too tired today to make her speech. She'd save it for later, when she could enjoy it more fully.

"So, who's your new agent then?" Sofia yawned. "Anyone I know?"

Hayden's eyes darted from Sofia to Tom and then back again. He gave a nervous cough. "Well," he started, "there's something I want to ask you, Sofia."

"Uh-huh," Sofia said with a distracted nod as she moved Edgar to her other breast.

"How would you like to be my agent again?"

Sofia almost dropped the baby into her lap. On the other side of the room Tom was spluttering on a mouthful of water.

"What?" Sofia barked, causing the baby to let out a brief wail before he nuzzled back into her chest.

Hayden waved his hands frantically as he spotted Sofia's narrowed eyes and flaring nostrils.

"Look, I know, I know," he stammered. "You might want to think about this. But I want you to be my agent again, Sofe. You used to get me great roles. You knew what I liked doing. You knew what I was good at. The money wasn't great, but—"

Sofia grabbed the silk robe with her spare hand and flung it into her brother-in-law's face.

"I don't need to think about anything, Hayden," she hissed. "Now take your *kind gift* and get out!"

Hayden tried to protest, but Tom, who knew his wife's fiery temper and ability to hold grudges all too well, was already guiding Hayden away from Sofia and out of the room.

As the door shut, Sofia looked down at her newborn son and mumbled angrily, "Who does your uncle think he is?"

Six

Mary

Mary's bruise lingered for a good while. Two weeks after Jack had done the damage, a small purple line remained under her right eye. Her dark glasses were no longer necessary, and she could disguise what was left of the bruise with a little concealer and a touch of foundation. So before leaving the apartment for her one-o'clock class, Mary stood in the bathroom and fished around in her small makeup bag, looking for an old tube of foundation that she rarely used.

Once she'd covered the dark line and dusted her face with powder, she smoothed down her blouse, took one last look at her eye, and then headed out the bathroom. In the hallway she picked up her briefcase but then faltered for a second. She had to pass by Jack's study to get to the front door, and she really didn't want to be heard. The last thing she wanted was a conversation with him. He'd been trying to be nice for two weeks now, and even brought her a morning coffee in bed a couple of times. But she couldn't stomach it: his fake smiles, his phony politeness. It all made her so sick.

Only a few more weeks to go, she thought as she crept slowly along the hallway, holding her breath as she approached Jack's study. Her daughter's wedding was just twenty-eight days away, and in twenty-nine days Mary would be gone—out of this apartment and out of Jack's life.

Just as she was about to pass in front of Jack's door, she heard an ominous click, then a creak. Mary froze.

"Are you going?" Jack chimed in a weird chirpy voice as he opened the door.

"Yes," she muttered, refusing to look at him. "I have a class at one."

Mary tried to carry on toward the front door, but Jack stepped out of his office and blocked her path. She was forced to stop just inches away from him.

"Of course, yes." Jack chuckled, laying a hand on her upper arm. "Not long to the end of the semester," he said. "Then you'll be a woman of leisure for three months."

Mary stiffened. She hated his hand on her arm. Even worse, she despised this patronizing tone of his. As she looked briefly into his eyes, what she really wanted to do was shout, *I won't be a woman of leisure, Jack. I'll be something so much better. I'll be a woman free of you!*

She knew better than that, though. She couldn't screw everything up, not now, after coming so far. All her plans were set, and Jack knew nothing, absolutely nothing, about them—and it had to stay that way. If he had any idea about what she intended to do, it would be the end. He'd find some way to mess it all up for her. Jack knew people. He knew people who knew people, and there wasn't much he couldn't do through his connections. In fact, Mary was surprised he hadn't already found out about her new appointment at Golden Gate College. She'd asked her new department to keep things under wraps until she got there, but the academic world was a gossip tree, and it was only a matter of time before someone leaked the fact that Pulitzer Prize winner Mary Havemeyer was going to join the creative writing faculty at San Francisco's most famous liberal arts college.

In the breeziest voice she could muster, Mary said, "I must get going."

But Jack's hand stopped her as she tried to move past him. This time he took hold of her forearm with a firm pinch and pulled her close to him. As he did so, she felt a familiar lurch in the pit of her stomach and the bubble of fear in her chest. There was nothing she'd said this time that could have made him angry, Mary thought amid her rising panic. What did he want?

Looking up, however, she found he was still smiling. There wasn't a trace of fury in his hazel eyes.

"I was just thinking," he began. "Let's invite Tom Burgess and his wife for dinner again. Next week, perhaps?"

Mary's eyebrows shot up. *"What?"*

"It was a shame they couldn't make it last time, don't you think?"

Mary couldn't help letting out a puff of laughter. "They couldn't make it, Jack, because Tom's wife gave birth to their second child three days before." She paused and then added, "And I don't suppose dinner parties are going to be high on their agenda for quite some time."

Jack seemed unfazed by Mary's incredulous tone. "It won't hurt to ask."

Mary shook her head, but decided not to argue. It was when she questioned him or talked back at him that he got so angry. Anyhow, it wasn't worth it. In these last few weeks living with him, she was better off keeping her head down.

"Okay," she muttered. "I'll ask Tom today, if I see him."

As she tried once again to move past Jack, he stopped her.

"Why don't you go and see his wife?" Jack said, and as Mary looked at him for the second time with her eyebrows raised, he added, "You could take them a gift for the new baby. Then you could ask them for dinner."

A million questions popped into Mary's head. Why was he so desperate to have dinner with this couple? What could he possibly want with an assistant professor of English? Usually Jack socialized only with his golfing buddies or with university deans and provosts. What was he up to?

Figuring there was no point asking, she simply sighed and said, "And what kind of gift do you suggest?"

Jack beamed, shouted, "Hold on," and made off into his study.

Mary watched him as Jack opened drawers and ferreted in his filing cabinets. It had been a long time since Mary had looked into his office, and an even longer time since she'd actually set foot inside. Jack's office was his kingdom, and Mary had absolutely no desire to enter. Even so, she immediately sensed something was different. She gazed about as Jack continued to hunt for whatever it was he was looking for. Finally, Mary worked out what had changed. Over the desk, which was stacked high with books, a poster she'd never seen before was tacked to the wall. The poster showed a man with dark hair and mustache, sketched in black ink. Above the man's head hovered an ominous black bird. Mary narrowed her eyes and stared harder at the poster. That was Edgar Allan Poe, wasn't it? And the bird? Wasn't that a raven? As Mary pondered this, her eyes dropped down to the tower of books on Jack's desk. Every one of them had the words *Poe* or *The Raven* on its spine. She'd seen him looking at books on Poe before, but she had no idea he'd amassed so many.

What was this new obsession with Poe about, anyway? she wondered as she continued to scan his desk, waiting for Jack to finish ferreting around his cluttered office. Jack was a history professor whose area of expertise was the American Revolution. The handful of books he'd published over the years looked very specifically at the battles of Lexington and Concord. To Mary's knowledge, Jack had never been interested in literature, and during their long marriage she'd rarely seen him pick up a novel, and certainly never a poem. Up until a few months ago, only dry-looking history books would be found on Jack's bedside table. Or sometimes a nonfiction blockbuster by the latest acclaimed journalist. Jack was a "facts" man, and definitely not a man to enjoy imaginary worlds or flowery words.

"Aha," Jack suddenly cried, making Mary jump and snap her eyes toward him. "Here it is!" He beamed.

On the end of his finger he was waggling a powder blue gift bag decorated with a large silver ribbon. A stork twinkled on the bag's gift tag.

Mary eyed the bag. "What is it?"

"A gift. For Tom's baby." He prodded the bag toward Mary and said, "Pajamas, I think. My secretary picked it out. Here, take it. Perhaps you can go see her today."

Mary reluctantly took the bag. "I'll try," she said, as she squashed it into her briefcase.

Finally Jack let her pass, and she moved along the hallway and out of the apartment. As she closed the door behind her, Mary's neck prickled with rage. This was so typical of Jack, she fumed. He was always up to something, and he always wanted someone else doing his dirty work. She didn't have a clue what this new plan with Tom and his wife was all about, but she was damn sure it wasn't simply about being friendly to a young faculty member. There had to be an ulterior motive.

She pressed the button for the elevator and took some long, slow breaths. One. Two. Three. Okay, she thought, finally beginning to feel her anger subside, she would do this. But it was the last thing she would do for him—the last thing ever.

When Mary reached the seminar room, the students had already arrived. Greeting them with a smile and a nod, she sat down at the long oak table. The sounds of scraping chairs, papers rustling, and the familiar chalky aroma that lingered in these old basement rooms made her breathe a sigh of relief. For the first time that day, she felt peaceful. She loved the classroom. The classroom for Mary was like the ocean for a penguin: an element where she felt most at ease and where, like the penguin, she could be her most elegant and unhindered and free.

Smiling to herself, she pulled out three student compositions from her briefcase. She arranged them carefully in front of her and quickly scanned the names to remind herself whose pieces they were discussing today. *Ella Bernstein, Peter Coulthard,* she read. Then as she got to the final paper, her chest tightened. *Chrissie Nouvelle.* Today they were discussing Chrissie's story. How could she have forgotten?

Mary's earlier calm began to ebb away, and sweat gathered in her palms. She couldn't do this today, not this piece, not now. It was a few weeks since Jack had hit her, and Chrissie's story about a family with a violent father was just too raw and sad and, for Mary, too close to the bone.

She looked again at the printed pages in front of her. No, she thought, silently chastising herself, she had to go through with it. Chrissie was one of her favorite and most gifted students. She'd finished this story weeks ago, and Mary knew the girl was itching to hear what she and the class thought. Anyway, Mary *could* do this. The classroom was where she was strong; this was her space. Jack, or thoughts of Jack, should not and could not stop her.

"Professor Havemeyer?"

A whisper close to her ear shook Mary from her thoughts. She looked up to see Chrissie bending down beside her.

"Yes, Chrissie?"

"I know we usually do it alphabetically, but is it okay if we work-shop my story first? I'm so nervous, I don't know if I can wait."

Mary noticed that Chrissie's hands were shaking, and she felt a stab of pity. She'd been like Chrissie once too. In the early days, when she was just twenty-four and writing fiction for the first time, she was so excited about her work, but she also brimmed with anxiety. She had desperately wanted people to read the first drafts of *Casey's Echoes*. Yet when friends, family, and eventually agents and editors would sit with her and tell her what they thought, her heart raced, her mouth turned dry, and she froze in fearful anticipation.

In a way, Mary was still just like Chrissie. In spite of all the ac-claim *Casey's Echoes* had received, fears about what others would think continued to plague her. Her dread of the words *a disap-pointing second novel from the former Pulitzer winner* meant that Mary had never written another book. When her daughter was young Mary made some halfhearted attempts—a few chapters here and there—but the chapters never turned into books, not even short stories. And then when she took the job at Manhattan U, her own writing took a backseat. In the classroom she spent her days telling students to do exactly what she herself didn't do: "Just keep writing," she'd say, waving a stern finger in the air. "Don't write for other people or write what you think they'll like. Just keep writing."

Mary was resolved, however. San Francisco was going to be a

fresh start. Her teaching load at Golden Gate College was going to be light, and there would be no Jack. She imagined endless sunny afternoons writing and writing at her small, neat desk in front of an open window. The drapes would flap quietly in the breeze beside her, gulls would circle and caw outside, and the San Francisco Bay would twinkle in the distance. She'd be happy and light and free. She'd be an author again.

"Will that be okay?" Chrissie whispered, still at Mary's side.

"Of course," Mary said, waving Chrissie to sit down.

As Chrissie skulked to the back of the room, Mary turned to the rest of the class. Twelve pairs of wide, youthful eyes looked back at her. The exhilaration that she felt so often when she taught began to surge in her chest.

"Let's start with Chrissie's piece," she began. "I'm sure everyone has a lot to say. You all know the routine. Clockwise around the room, starting with positive comments about Chrissie's story."

Ben, a small, bearded student to Mary's left, cleared his throat and began. "I liked the descriptions of the suburb where the family lives. I hate to admit it, but this is the place where I grew up. You know, cookie-cutter lawns, Little League, SUVs in the driveway." Ben chuckled and then paused for a moment as he flicked through his copy of the story. "Although I don't buy the whole abuse stuff. I mean, you know, the dad is too much of regular guy. There's no way he'd be doing all this violent stuff."

"Ben," Mary interjected in a firm tone, "let's keep to what we like about the piece first. Remember, I want examples from the text. *Which* descriptions of the suburbs do you like, and why do you think they work?"

As Ben began to search Chrissie's piece, Mary relaxed into her seat. *I can do this,* she thought. The subject matter was difficult, for her at least, but she could do this; she had to—for Chrissie's sake, as much as her own.

After Ben was finished, it was Ella's turn to speak. With a confident flick of her long blond hair, Ella sat forward and said, "I liked the way the mom and daughter talked to each other. It was,

I don't know, really believable. I was just like that with my mom when I was thirteen. You know, all sass and kinda like 'screw you, Mom. . . .' "

Ella trailed off as the rest of the group laughed. Only Chrissie remained silent.

Mary sat forward and asked Ella, "Could you point us to a particular piece of dialogue and tell us why you think it works?"

Ella found her example and began to talk. Mary looked over at Chrissie. She was hunched forward, her long bangs flopped in her eyes, scribbling furiously on a yellow notepad. Mary couldn't tell if she was really taking notes or if she was just trying to distract herself.

Chrissie remained like that as every student in the class offered their feedback.

"Ben," Mary said after the final student was finished, "would you now like to offer your *constructive* comments to Chrissie?"

As she spoke, Mary sensed a change of mood in the room. The students shifted in their chairs, straightened their backs, and stared more intently at the papers in front of them. Like a group of lions who'd been lying in wait, they were rearing up for the attack. Meanwhile Chrissie, the lone gazelle, sank lower into her seat.

"Like I said," Ben started, "I'm not sure I buy the abuse angle. I know this stuff happens, but, well, the dad is supposed to be a successful banker or something, and his wife is this big-deal ex–tennis player. I don't know; I just can't imagine him beating up on her like he does."

Just as Mary was about to speak up, Ella jumped in: "Yeah, I agree. It would be like my dad hitting my mom." She stopped and laughed. "She would hit him right back."

"I don't think you could hide that kind of thing," the student to Mary's right chimed in. "Not in the suburbs."

Mary leaned forward in her seat and tapped the table with an angry finger. "So, where does domestic abuse happen? You think women are abused only in trailer parks or in the projects?"

The students stared at her, not saying a word.

Breaking the silence, Ben finally said, "It's just, well, I just don't get why this guy is so mad. He's got everything. He's not a drinker. So why's he doing this to his wife?"

"They don't have to be unshaven, foulmouthed alcoholics to beat their wives." Mary could feel anger flushing her cheeks.

If only you knew, she thought, as she glared at the students in front of her. Jack Havemeyer, a dean at their very own university, had everything, but that didn't stop him from lashing out at his wife. He had a good job, nice clothes, a healthy daughter. He didn't have a drinking problem. In his neat suits and polished shoes he looked like a regular, upstanding guy. Yet he was a man who could get angry—really, frighteningly angry—and he'd hurt Mary too many times in the midst of his rages.

Jack hadn't always been that way. It all started five years ago, after his father got sick and died. Before the old man's illness, Jack didn't have much to do with him. Although they were both Princeton alumni with PhDs in history, their similarities ended with their degrees. Jack's father was a world-renowned historian who'd written a slew of influential books and even, at one point, had his own TV series about the Civil War. At home, however, he was a cold and aloof father and a mean and unavailable husband. Meanwhile Jack doted on his daughter and Mary, and he was content being a hardworking but far from world-renowned professor. In the old days, living in the shadow of his father's fame never bothered Jack. His illustrious but standoffish dad was more often the butt of his jokes than an object of his affections or jealousies.

But then his father got sick and everything changed. Suddenly Jack wanted to connect with the old man, and thus for five months he spent every spare minute in Princeton, where his father had lived and taught for forty years. Mary joined him on weekends, and it broke her heart to see how the old man's iciness toward his son never thawed. He would bark orders and humiliate Jack at every turn. Yet Jack kept at it, tending and caring for the cantankerous old professor. When his father finally died, something altered in Jack forever. It was as if the sparkle in his once lively eyes was snuffed out and replaced by a steely glare. In time, this glare was coupled with a new all-consuming yearning for status and success.

Mary never understood the change in Jack, but what she quickly came to understand was that this new burning ambition was not good for her husband. And it certainly wasn't good for her or their marriage. He began to aggressively claw his way up the university management ladder, and as he did so he became hard and aloof, just like his father. On those days when things didn't go right for him, he'd come home in a thunderous mood. He'd pick and needle and fuss at Mary, and soon they would become embroiled in a full-scale row. More often than not, Mary would say something that would throw Jack over the edge, and he'd send a right hook or kick or a hard object in her direction.

Two weeks ago Jack had been brooding about a standoff the administration was having with the graduate students' union. Storming around their apartment, he barked incessant questions at Mary: "Where are my cigars?" "Can you please move these trashy books from my sight?" "Did you talk to the damn neighbors about that squeaking ceiling fan?"

She'd tried to ignore him at first. As always, though, she found herself being sucked in.

"For Christ's sake, Jack," she'd said finally, exasperated after an hour of this, "stop barking at me."

Coming toward her as she stood over the kitchen counter chopping an onion, Jack leaned in close and bellowed, "I can bark at whomever I please."

Mary's eardrums vibrated. She chose to remain calm, however. Slowly setting down the knife, she turned to Jack. "What is the matter with you?" she asked quietly.

"What's wrong?" he bellowed again. "I work hard and I come home to this"—he waved his hand around—"this pigsty and you." He prodded her shoulder. "You give me *no* respect."

That was when Mary made the fatal mistake: She laughed. Standing next to her with his eyes blazing and the blood vessels in his forehead pulsating, he seemed to Mary so adolescent—so stupidly, amusingly adolescent. She couldn't help laughing. But before another chuckle could rise in her throat, a punch slammed into her shoulder and she was thrown face-first into the overhead cabinets. A sharp pain shot through her eye as her cheekbone and eyebrow hit the wooden frame.

In the classroom, still glaring at the students around the table, Mary couldn't help flushing with anger again at the memory.

"But why doesn't she just leave?" one of the students asked in a hushed voice. "It's not like she's poor. She could totally leave."

"It's not as easy as that," Mary said, this time softening her tone. "Women have commitments, jobs, families. It's hard to just up and leave, even if there is abuse going on."

Mary thought of all the times she swore to herself she was going to leave and then didn't. Somehow it always seemed easier to stay. She had friends in the city. She loved her job, her students, her colleagues, and money was never a problem. And then there was Sarah, her daughter. It was only after Sarah left home that Jack changed and became so angry. Sarah knew nothing about how her father had hurt Mary over the last few years. Mary's pride, coupled with a maternal desire to protect her daughter from everything ill in the world, stopped her from confessing everything to Sarah.

It was only after a particularly bad evening a couple of months ago, when Jack lashed out and left Mary winded and with a large, angry bruise on her rib cage, that she finally began making real plans to leave.

"Leaving is tough," Mary continued, looking around at the class. "Finding a new job, a new place to live, a new community. It all takes time and"—she blinked for a second—"courage."

As she said the words, a warmth tingled over Mary. She hadn't left Jack yet, and she was holding on a little while longer for her daughter's sake, but soon she would be gone. Soon she would be brave and strong, and she would pick up her luggage and finally walk out the door.

Feeling a renewed wave of confidence, Mary cleared her throat and began, "If you all look back at the story, you'll see that Chrissie *does* capture these difficulties and contradictions, and her depiction of the abuse is, in fact, very believable. For instance, if we turn to page three . . ."

The students filed out of the room while Mary scooped up her bag from the floor. Wiggling her stack of papers inside, her hand grazed the gift bag. Jack's package should have reignited Mary's anger, but she was glowing from a great class, and her thoughts about leaving had left her buoyant and excited, as they always did. She smiled to herself. *Perhaps I will go see Tom's baby today,* she thought. After all, she liked Tom, and it had been years since she'd held a newborn in her arms.

After spending the rest of the afternoon in her office, sending e-mails, seeing students, and reading assignments, Mary collected together some books and headed toward home. Tom and his family, according to the faculty list, lived in the apartment building opposite her own. It was raining outside and getting murky and dark, and Mary had to hunch under her flimsy umbrella as she zigzagged among the sea of puddles and shoppers on Broadway.

When she reached the Burgesses' front door, she pressed the buzzer and waited. For over a minute she heard nothing. She was beginning to think no one was home when suddenly the heavy gray door swung open and in front of her stood a tall, attractive woman with tousled hair and large caramel eyes underlined by dark circles. Mary recognized her straightaway as the woman from the garden. The one whom she'd seen a few weeks back, out there with her young daughter and pregnant belly.

"Hi." The woman looked at Mary, her expression friendly but also a little bemused.

"Hi," Mary replied. "I don't think we've ever met. I'm Mary. Mary Havemeyer. I'm a colleague of Tom's."

"Of course, yes." Sofia nodded, still looking baffled and now slightly awkward too. "I'm Sofia, his wife." Then, as her eyes darted from Mary to the floor, she added, "I'm so sorry we didn't make it to dinner."

Mary laughed and pointed toward a baby carriage parked in the hallway. "You've been busy. I forgive you."

Sofia's face at last cracked into a smile. "Busy? I thought I was busy when I was a career girl. But this is a whole new ball game of busy."

"It's a long time ago for me, but I remember those days with a newborn like they were yesterday." Mary chuckled and then she added, "But you have a little girl too, don't you? That must make it doubly exhausting."

"A million times more exhausting." Sofia groaned as she opened the door wide and waved Mary inside.

"You poor thing," Mary whispered as she stepped inside. "You look like you need a good, long sleep."

Sofia simply nodded.

The baby was taking a nap in a bouncy chair in the living room, and so the two women tiptoed quietly to the nearby couch, where they sat down and began talking in hushed whispers. They smiled over at tiny Edgar every now and then.

"One time"—Mary giggled, thinking back more than twenty years—"I tried to breast-feed Sarah as I stood in line at a local deli. She'd been screaming and screaming, and I knew it was a hunger cry. But I was desperate for a bar of Hershey's, and even if it meant balancing a baby in my arms and exposing my breast to all the other deli shoppers, I had to buy that candy. You should have seen the looks I got. It was the seventies, and breast-feeding was still something you had to do under wraps—and definitely not in grimy Manhattan delis."

Sofia laughed and then held her stomach and winced. "Oh, man, do you remember the postpartum aches and pains? I'm certain it's worse the second time around. My body feels like it's just been run over by a dump truck and then put through a cement mixer. I can barely lift a diaper, let alone twenty-nine-pound Gracie."

Mary shook her head. "Torture."

Laughing and groaning, they traded more stories, and only when Edgar began to stir in his seat and blink his tiny eyes did Sofia finally ask, "So, Mary, did you want to talk to Tom?"

"No, no," Mary rushed in. "I came to bring you a gift for the baby."

She pulled the crumpled gift bag from her briefcase and handed it to Sofia.

As she unfurled a small, fleecy sleep suit from the bag, Sofia's eyes sparkled with surprise. "It's beautiful. This is so kind and so, well, so unexpected."

Mary couldn't help blushing. She'd had no part in buying this gift and now, she realized, she had to propose this dinner idea too. Sofia was going to think her completely mad, blustering into her house with gifts and dinner invites and the two of them never having met until now.

Nevertheless, Mary knew she had to do it. So she sucked in a breath and said, "Jack . . . I mean, Jack *and I* were hoping that we could reschedule dinner."

Sofia blinked at her. "Oh." She paused. "Sure."

"Next week, perhaps?" Mary said tentatively.

"Next week?" Sofia's eyebrows shot up.

Mary quickly interjected, "We'll completely understand if you can't make it."

"Next week might be hard," Sofia began. But then, as she leaned forward to scoop Edgar from his seat, she paused for a second. When she looked back toward Mary, her expression had changed. "You know what?" she said, her eyes twinkling again. "Why don't you guys come and have dinner here?"

Mary was thrown. "Really?" She looked around at the cluttered living room strewn with books, toys, and baby clothes, and thought throwing a dinner party would be the last thing Sofia would feel like doing.

Sofia laughed as she followed Mary's gaze. "I'll tidy up, of course."

"No, no, I didn't mean—"

"Mary, listen." Sofia patted Mary's knee. "I love to cook. It'll be fine. Plus," she said with what seemed like a mischievous chuckle, "your husband would love to meet our kids, wouldn't he?"

"Oh, yes." Mary squirmed, thinking how kids and babies were the last people Jack would want to dine with these days.

Fortunately the door buzzer saved her.

"Do you mind?" Sofia held out Edgar for Mary to hold. "I'll go get that."

While Sofia answered the door, Mary clutched the squirming, blinking Edgar in her arms. He was so beautiful and new, she was transfixed. She couldn't wait until she had grandchildren of her own. It would probably be some time before she did, though. Sarah might be getting married in a month, but as far as Mary knew her daughter wasn't in a rush to start a family. Sarah adored her work as an assistant curator at the Whitney, and she was eager to become a full curator in the next couple of years. Her fiancé, Greg, was trying to make partner at his architecture firm and thus worked long and grueling hours. A baby was the last thing on either of their minds, and Mary would no doubt have to wait awhile for her first grandchild.

A clattering noise and a squeal shook Mary from her thoughts. She looked up to see Sofia's little girl skipping into the apartment, dragging a plastic dog on wheels behind her on a string. Seeing Mary, Gracie stopped dead in her tracks.

"Who you?" she shouted.

Mary couldn't help laughing. "Mary." She smiled. "And who are you?"

With her dark curls bobbing, Gracie skipped around in a circle and announced, "Graay-seee!"

As Mary continued to laugh, she heard Sofia saying, "Mary, this is Ashleigh. Ashleigh, this is Mary."

Looking up, Mary realized another familiar face was now in the apartment.

"Oh, hi," both women said, recognizing each other straightaway.

"You know each other?" Sofia asked, as she chased Gracie around the room trying to unzip her jacket.

"From the garden," Mary said, and then, remembering their late-night meeting, she added, "We were on the night shift."

Sofia didn't seem to hear because of Gracie's squeals, but Ashleigh moved forward and smiled. "It was strange, wasn't it? The three of us all out there in the middle of the night."

Mary really didn't want to get into the reasons she had been in the garden that night, so she simply nodded and then changed the subject. "So, you babysit Gracie? Is that a full-time job?"

"Oh, no." Ashleigh waved her hands. "I wish it were. It would make a sweet change from being an attorney." She let out a small chuckle. "No, I'm just helping Sofia out for a couple of days."

"She's been my savior," Sofia bellowed from down the hallway, where she was still pursuing her daughter. "And I've only known her a few weeks."

Mary and Ashleigh smiled at each other again, and then, as each of them looked down at the baby, Ashleigh lowered herself onto the sofa.

"You're Mary Havemeyer, aren't you?" Ashleigh asked with a sheepish smile.

Mary nodded.

"I have to tell you," Ashleigh went on, "I love *Casey's Echoes*. It's one of my all-time favorite novels."

Mary stared at Ashleigh. "You've read it?"

"Of course." Ashleigh bobbed her head up and down.

Shifting the baby in her arms, Mary sighed. "It's been a long time since anybody said that to me. That they read and liked it, I mean."

"Really?" Ashleigh looked shocked. "I thought Pulitzer Prize winners would be fighting off admirers all the time."

Mary laughed and shrugged. "Not me. I suppose some of us get forgotten sooner than others."

While they talked, Sofia swept back into the room with Gracie's yellow jacket over one arm and a pair of small red sneakers tucked under the other.

"Did I hear you say you met in the garden?" Sofia asked, and when Mary and Ashleigh nodded, she added, "I can't believe they're going to destroy that place."

As if suddenly hearing what she'd just said, Sofia then slapped her hand to her mouth and darted a worried look at Mary. Meanwhile, Ashleigh looked at the floor. It was clear to Mary that both women knew that demolishing the garden was all Jack's idea.

She could feel the heat rising in her cheeks, and before she could stop herself she blurted out, "I told him it was a ridiculous idea, but he didn't listen. He never listens to me. Not these days."

Ashleigh and Sofia exchanged glances. Sofia then lowered herself into the armchair opposite and, as she did so, her eyes began to flicker with excitement.

"Well, maybe he'd listen to us." She waved around at the three of them. "All of us. Perhaps we could *all* get your husband to listen. We could start a petition or"—Sofia leaned forward, her smile wide and animated—"we could organize a protest!"

On the short walk home, Mary bubbled with excitement—and nerves. She'd just agreed to help organize a protest: a protest against her own husband. Was she crazy? This went against all her plans to keep her head down before she left. Jack hated it when she disagreed with him even in the privacy of their own home. More often than not it was when Mary disagreed with him that he got violent. Even the smallest of things would set him off. If he saw her waving banners in a public protest against his parking lot scheme, he'd go ballistic.

But something told her she had to go through with this. The garden was a beautiful place; it had meant so much to her too. Moreover, these women whom she really liked, they loved the garden and would need it after she'd gone. She had to help them fight for it. She just had to.

Entering the foyer of her own building and taking the elevator to the top floor, she steadily convinced herself she was doing the right thing. After all, by the time the protest happened, she'd be almost out the door and out of Jack's life. He wouldn't be able to touch her then or meddle with her plans.

As she opened the door to the apartment, Mary's heart sank a little as she heard music playing and the clink of glasses. Jack was home. She'd hoped he'd be gone to some dinner or meeting and she'd have the rest of the evening to herself. Unable to see him in the living room, Mary quietly set her bag down and tried to tiptoe toward her bedroom. But just as she passed the kitchen, Jack's voice rang out, "Mary! Come join us. We're celebrating."

Mary peered through the kitchen to the dining room beyond and saw Jack hovering by the table. A man in a dark suit, sucking on a cigar, stood beside him.

"This is Alan Wilkins," Jack continued. "We've just signed the construction contract for the parking lot. It's ready to roll ASAP!" He grinned and held out a champagne flute. "Here. We've opened some Clicquot. Come help us celebrate."

Mary was silent for a second, and then, with her heart thumping in her chest, she called out, "I'll be with you in a second."

Seven

Hannah

On Saturday evening, Hannah and Michael whisked along Prince Street holding hands. Their anniversary party at Michael's parents' house in Brooklyn was due to start in twenty minutes, and they still hadn't reached the subway. As they swept down the busy SoHo sidewalk, Hannah looked down briefly at their linked fingers. She was struck by how familiar this felt. With her hand in his, it was like wearing an old glove. A very tight glove, admittedly. Michael always gripped her hand as he pulled her with his usual purposeful gusto in the direction he wanted to go. But it was familiar and comforting, all the same.

They neared the entrance to the subway, and Hannah wondered for a second what it would be like to walk with Patrick, holding hands. She imagined his long fingers laced around her own. They would go slowly, she was sure of it, dancing idly among other pedestrians and stopping now and again to point out ornate cornices on buildings or to marvel at vivid-colored fabrics in shop windows. His hand would be warm but gentle.

"Hannah?" Michael's voice blasted in her ear as he shouted over the din of an incoming train. They'd descended into the subway station, and Michael was now pointing toward the ticket machine. "I need to refill my MetroCard."

He released her hand from his grip and stalked off in the direction of the machines. Meanwhile, with his hand gone, Hannah stood lifeless, unable to move. She watched Michael as he fed his card into the slot and punched the nearby screen, and she told herself she had to stop thinking like this about Patrick. These daydreams were killing her. They'd pop into her head—it didn't matter where or when or whom she was with—and they were always followed by a gut-wrenching wave of guilt.

What is wrong with me? she thought as people jostled around her. *I'm on my way to my fifth wedding anniversary party and all I can do is think about a man who isn't my husband.* She gave a heavy blink and flicked her head slightly, as if to shake out the image of Patrick and her holding hands. This had to stop, she scolded herself. They were history. It was a mistake, one small mistake, never to be repeated.

"Hi. It's Hannah, isn't it?" a female voice broke into her thoughts.

She turned to see Ashleigh, one of the women she'd met in the garden a couple of weeks ago, standing in front of her. She was wearing a dark green pantsuit and carrying a heavy-looking briefcase. Even though she was smiling, her blond hair, which was pinned up in a barrette, looked ruffled, and her eyes were tired and bloodshot. It looked like she'd just been busting a gut at an office someplace.

"Hey, Ashleigh." Hannah smiled back.

The two women stood for a moment in awkward silence.

"I'm glad I ran into you," Ashleigh said finally. "I was going to ask . . ." But she didn't get to her question, because Michael returned and hovered beside them, jiggling from foot to foot.

Hannah introduced the two of them, and, even though she knew Michael was itching to get on the train, she turned to Ashleigh and said, "What were you going to ask?"

"Right, yes, I was wondering whether you"—Ashleigh looked from Hannah to Michael—"and your husband, of course, might want to be involved with a protest we're organizing."

Michael narrowed his eyes and looked at Ashleigh. "Protest?"

Ashleigh gave a nervous laugh. "Well, maybe *protest* is a strong word. But basically, some of us who live in faculty housing want to try to save the garden, and I know . . . well, I know you use the garden a lot, Hannah, so I was wondering if you might be interested."

Michael rolled his eyes. Hannah had been ranting about the garden's demolition since she'd found out about it a while ago, and it was obvious he was sick of hearing about it. But that was no excuse to be rude to Ashleigh, Hannah thought, and she shot him a warning glare.

Grabbing a pen and a scrap of paper from her purse, Hannah scrawled down her cell number. "I'd love to help out," she said with a defiant smile inching across her face. "Here's my number."

Ashleigh folded the piece of paper. "A few of us are going to meet in the garden tomorrow." She patted her pocket where she slid the number. "I'll let you know the time."

When they said their good-byes, Michael gripped Hannah's hand again and hurried her through the turnstiles. Being late was not Michael's style.

Once on the train, squashed amid a gaggle of excited teenage girls, Michael leaned close to Hannah and said, "You shouldn't get involved in that protest."

"What?" Hannah swiveled on the seat and looked at her husband. "Why not?"

"Oh, come on, Hann," Michael went on. "Do you think it's really necessary? I mean, if Dean Havemeyer has his way, which he always does, the garden is going to be demolished. A little protest isn't going to do a lot to change that."

Hannah's cheeks flamed. "But we should at least try, shouldn't we?"

"I just don't think"—he gave Hannah a small smile—"*you* should get involved."

"Why not *me*?"

"Because you're too beautiful," he replied.

Hannah rolled her eyes. "*What* are you talking about?"

Michael held up his hands. "All I'm saying is, if you get involved and any press turn up, you know what will happen." He flicked his fingers like quotation marks. " 'Ex–*Vogue* Model Turned Eco-Activist.' "

Hannah shook her head in disbelief. "That's ridiculous. Who'd even remember I was a model, anyway?" She looked at him out of the corner of her eye and said, "It's only you who ever seems to remember that."

Michael's eyes turned sulky and his tone serious. "I just don't want any of this jeopardizing my reputation, that's all." He then snapped his lips closed.

"That's ridiculous," she retorted again as she scanned his face.

She wanted to argue with him, tell him that he was being selfish as well as absurd, but she knew the conversation was over. This was what Michael did best: start a conversation, say his piece, and then close down. It drove her insane. So, deciding it was best just to leave it be, she slumped back against the hard plastic subway seat and brooded.

Silences between Michael and Hannah, like the one they were having on the clattering train, happened more and more these days. When Michael wasn't working—which wasn't often—and he and Hannah were in the apartment together, they could often be found orbiting each other in silence. It hadn't always been like this. When they met nearly seven years ago, it seemed like Michael and Hannah would never run out of things to say. It felt like they would never be snappish or brooding with each other.

Hannah and Michael had met at the party of a mutual friend in a tiny apartment in the West Village. With his neat haircut, dark, thoughtful eyes, and quiet manner, Michael was a complete novelty for Hannah. In her years as a model, she'd been surrounded by and dated a whole string of sexy, bad-boy photographers and beautiful, egotistical male models. Many of them were unshaven; with manes of designer-rumpled hair. They smoked cigarettes, talked loudly about themselves, and oozed sex appeal. Many of them were penniless. Some had even taken money from Hannah's purse on occasion. She never allowed herself to fall in love with any of them, however. Like her father had left her mother, deep down Hannah knew these shallow and self-centered men would leave her the moment she offered them her heart. Just by looking at him, Hannah could tell Michael was everything these guys weren't: polite, clean-cut, seemingly dependable, handsome but not dangerously handsome.

At the party Michael and Hannah had ended up accidentally squashed together on a small red velvet couch. Hannah felt a little shy and awkward at first, being so close to someone who seemed so smart, so refined, so well mannered. But when he began to make conversation, she found herself hypnotized by his intense brown eyes and their distinctive gaze. Back in her modeling days a lot of guys would stare at her; it went with the job. But there was something different about the way Michael looked at Hannah. He didn't seem be just gazing at the surface of her. He seemed to be searching much deeper; studying her soul. Or so she thought.

She'd also found herself enraptured by the precise way Michael spoke and the intelligence and authority he exuded. He was so un-like those fickle, shallow, and ultimately pretty screwed-up men Hannah had always mixed with before. He might not be a sexy bad boy, but he radiated an assurance and intellect that Hannah found attractive. As the two of them sat on the couch with their bodies gradually relaxing more and more into each other, Michael asked her questions about who she was, and what she did, and what it felt like to be a model. He seemed so interested, so genuinely fas-cinated with her and her modeling life. And then when it was his turn to talk, he explained his research in a precise, matter-of-fact way. Not once did he stop to ask if she understood. In spite of her pretty face and model credentials, he just assumed she did. A burn of desire began to rise in Hannah's chest as they had talked, and after a while, when she couldn't fight it any longer, she reached over, took his surprised face into her hands, and kissed him.

Two days after they met, Michael took Hannah to his parents' house. As she sat in their cluttered and cozy kitchen in Brooklyn watching Michael talk with Bill and Diane, something surprising had dawned on Hannah: She was in love.

"Right on time!" Diane beamed as she threw open the heavy green front door. "Everyone's here."

She bustled Hannah and Michael inside, hugging and kissing them as they went. The three of them moved through the hallway, and as they reached the large, high-ceilinged living room, a big crowd greeted them with clapping and cheering. A banner over the fireplace read, FIVE YEARS TODAY, and the sound of popping champagne corks came from the adjoining dining room.

"Congratulations, you two," Bill said, emerging from the crowd with two champagne flutes in his hands and with his white hair and beard in their usual disarray. "Five whole years."

In a whirl of hugging, kissing, and congratulating, Hannah and Michael moved through the room greeting everyone who'd turned up for the party. Most of them, Hannah realized as she smiled her way around, were really Diane and Bill's friends. Therapists, old college friends, neighbors. But she'd known these people from years of parties and dinners with Michael's parents and, if she was honest, they were probably among the best friends she herself had. She'd long ago removed herself from her modeling friends—if you could really give the label *friend* to people who made sly comments about an extra ounce of weight you might be carrying; or who pointed out skin blemishes in your most recent shot in *Marie Claire*; or who slept with your boyfriend because he was a photographer who might get them somewhere. Even though Hannah was getting to know people in her MFA program, being a married woman older than most of her classmates meant it was hard to make any real friends there either. Except for Patrick, of course.

She blinked her eyes and flicked her head again. *No,* she scolded herself, *not here, and definitely not now.*

"Why do you keep doing that weird blinking thing?"

Hannah spun around to see Michael beside her, his eyes quizzical. She hadn't realized he was standing there.

"What blinking thing?" She tried to sound dismissive as she took a sip of champagne.

Meanwhile she was panicking. He'd noticed the way she kept trying to shake Patrick from her thoughts. What would he notice next? Would he start getting suspicious? After all, she had been acting odd and guilty in the last few weeks. She couldn't help it, but she was hoping it had passed him by.

"You keep doing this." Michael was smiling as he tried to imitate her head shake, but then his eyes turned serious. "It makes you look weird, wobbling your head and screwing up your eyes like that."

Hannah sighed. Typical Michael, she thought. There she was worrying he might be onto her, when in fact all he was worrying about was how she looked.

In the early days she'd thought Michael was different. With his intense gaze and patient and listening ear, she'd thought he was seeing and hearing her in a way no one had ever done before. Unlike other guys she'd dated, he listened to her dreams and seemed genuinely interested in who she was. But as the years passed, she began to realize her looks were in fact a big preoccupation for Michael—much bigger than she'd ever expected from a big-brained computer science professor. When she was still modeling, Michael would take time out from his busy days at the university to join her on shoots. Sometimes he even advised photographers on angles and lights to achieve the best shots of Hannah. Usually photographers with big egos would never have listened to some boyfriend of a model. Yet Michael was forceful and tenacious, but always in the most disarmingly smart and calm way. Even the best-known photographers in the industry weren't immune to Michael's persuasive demeanor and would often listen to the advice he had to offer. So too did Hannah's agent, who called from time to time to consult Michael about Hannah's portfolio.

Back when modeling and her looks were big concerns for Hannah too, this was all fine. Wonderful, in fact. Not many models had such supportive, engaged, and astute husbands. But as the fashion world got tiring and Hannah turned more to her art, Michael's lingering preoccupation with her looks began to bother her. She'd hoped he would get over it once she was out of the business, but he didn't. He could joke about it now, but when she had cut and dyed her hair into her current bright red crop, Michael brooded for days. And only a few weeks ago, after a few bottles of wine with a couple of his colleagues, Michael did his dumb mirror trick.

Whipping out a small rectangular mirror, he'd pushed it at right angles into Hannah's nose.

"See," he said, turning to his friends and beaming. "Look, perfectly symmetrical. The cameras love this kind of symmetry."

When his two male colleagues looked at him, completely baffled, Michael continued, "C'mon, look. If I put the mirror like this against my face"—he moved the mirror to his own nose and pressed it into the bridge of his glasses—"it looks weird, doesn't it?"

His friends were still bemused.

"You see," Michael persisted, "my face isn't symmetrical. So when the mirror makes it look symmetrical, it looks odd. But do the same thing to her." He waved toward Hannah. "It looks fine because her face is symmetrical."

Before she could stop him, the mirror was once again thrust onto Hannah's nose. The two guests nodded, finally understanding what Michael was trying to explain.

"If you're this symmetrical," Michael went on, "you can be photographed from every angle."

The mirror thing was an old party trick of Michael's. Hannah used to find it amusing, flattering almost. Recently, however, it was just plain irritating, and that night, when their dinner guests had left, Hannah and Michael fought into the night, Michael insisting that he was just joking around and Hannah arguing that that wasn't the point.

Standing among the guests at their anniversary party, Hannah felt her skin prickle at the memory, and she had a sudden urge to be away from him. Waggling her empty champagne flute, she said with fake cheeriness, "Time for a top-off."

Hannah walked toward the dining room. Her chest felt tight. She needed to breathe, to think, to be alone, if only for a minute. But just as she'd poured her drink and was looking for somewhere quiet to escape, Diane appeared at her side.

"Hannah," Diane almost squeaked, "what's the big news?"

Diane's face was flushed. A pair of large bronze zigzag earrings bobbed under her silver hair as she nodded her head excitedly.

"News?" Hannah had no idea what her mother-in-law was talking about, but she couldn't help smiling. Diane always had that effect on her.

"The news—you know, the news Michael's going to announce later." Her earrings bobbed again. "Oh, come on, Hannah, you know I can't wait. I rely on you for all the gossip."

It was true. Hannah and Diane were more like girlfriends than in-laws. Every few days, when Hannah was using the studio in Michael and Diane's attic, she'd find herself lured down to their big kitchen to read the arts section of the *New York Times* and sip fresh coffee. Usually her break would coincide with Diane's, whose snug office was in the basement, and the two of them would sit at the huge old oak table, tracing its scuffed surfaces with their fingertips, and talk. They'd talk about anything and everything: politics, family, Brad and Angelina, the weather, work. There wasn't much they didn't share.

"Di," Hannah laughed, still baffled. "I haven't a clue what you're talking about."

Diane clutched Hannah's arm. "Ooh, this must be juicy news if *you're* keeping zipped too."

"Honestly," Hannah pleaded, "I don't know." She trailed off as she noticed that Diane's expression had changed, and her eyes, instead of twinkling into Hannah's, were now fixed intensely on Hannah's belly.

"Oh, my God." Diane's clutch on Hannah's arm tightened. "You're not? Are you?"

Hannah looked down. Above her black Chloé skirt, a leftover from her fashion-shoot days, she was wearing a yellow blouse. She rarely dressed so femininely anymore, and it was strange to see her body in something other than her paint-splattered work clothes. She'd also put on a few pounds recently, so the clothes fit a little tighter than they used to.

As she studied the way her belly pooched out above the skirt's waistband, she suddenly realized what Diane was getting at.

"No, no, no." Hannah waved her hand frantically. "No, Di, I'm *not* pregnant."

No sooner had the words come out of her mouth than a pang of panic hit her. *Could I be pregnant?* For a second she couldn't focus. Her heart began to race, sweat beaded at her temples, and the taste of champagne clawed bitterly on her tongue. *No, no.* She panicked. *That can't be right. When was my last period? When? April? Perhaps, but no, wait.*

"Hannah?" Diane's voice swam into her thoughts. "Hannah? Are you okay?" Hannah looked up to see Diane's concerned eyes searching her own. "I'm sorry," Diane continued, "I didn't really think you were preg—"

Not wanting to hear the word again, Hannah interrupted. "It's fine." She then forced a laugh and patted her belly. "This is just too many Magnolia Bakery cupcakes for you."

"There's not an ounce of fat on you, Ms. Beautiful! You could probably eat anything and it would never stick." Diane chuckled, but she was having a hard time disguising her disappointment. All three of her kids were now in their thirties, and Hannah knew she was desperate for a grandchild.

"Speaking of food," Hannah said, "I'm starving. I must grab something from that amazing buffet over there."

When Hannah escaped Diane and reached the table, she didn't feel one bit like eating. She stood with her plate and napkin in hand, staring at the dips and crackers and breads and cheeses while her mind raced. *When was my last period?* she thought again and again. *When?* She remembered having cramps one day after class. But when was that? It felt like just a few weeks ago, but it was such a cold, rainy day, maybe it was a few months ago.

Hannah started to grip and ungrip her paper plate until it crumpled pathetically in her sweating hand. She looked from the plate around the crowded room. *Okay,* she thought, trying to calm herself, *I must find somewhere quiet. If I just think for a minute, I*

*can work this out. When I've calmed down, I'll realize that there is
no way I can be pregnant.*

A couple of minutes later, as she huddled on the front steps of
Diane and Bill's brownstone, she still couldn't figure it out. In fact,
the more she tried to remember her last period, the longer ago it
seemed. Panic ebbed and flowed in her chest. One moment she'd
convince herself she must be pregnant; the next minute she'd convince herself that that was the dumbest idea she'd ever had.

Staring out at the quiet street, she let her hand drift to her belly.
As she felt the soft flesh, fear gripped her again. If she was pregnant, could the father possibly be . . . ? She stopped the thought
there. If she was pregnant it had to be Michael's. Of course it
would be Michael's. Her night with Patrick was only a few weeks
ago; it couldn't be his. Hannah had put on this weight a long time
before that night.

She continued to panic, however. Michael and she were always
so careful. She wasn't on the pill, but they were diligent about con-
traception. They had discussed it a million times and wanted to try
for kids only when her grad school was done and when Michael's
big research project was complete. He was working too hard to be
an engaged father, and she wanted to establish herself in the art
world before thinking about a family.

With Patrick, though, it was a different story; they hadn't been
so careful. The whole thing had happened so unexpectedly, so
quickly and so passionately, they'd been careless. Stupidly, stupidly careless.

"Shit, shit, shit," she whispered under her breath, as memories
of that night crowded into her head.

Hannah had never meant for it to happen. She was married,
after all, and Patrick was her professor. Although she had thought
about it happening many times, and every time she saw Patrick,
spoke to him, or heard his soft British accent echoing in the hall-
ways of the art department, she couldn't help thinking about all
the things she'd like to do with his long, sinewy body. But she
never seriously thought that she would do these things.

Even when he invited her to the surrealism lecture at MoMA, she still didn't think it was anything more than a professor being kind to his most enthusiastic student, who liked to stay behind after class and talk art theory. Sitting side by side, listening intently to the gray-haired woman at the lectern, Hannah had felt his arm keep grazing hers, sending an irrepressible shiver up and down her spine. But she figured it was just the way the hard plastic seats in MoMA's lecture hall were crowded against one another. He wasn't doing it on purpose—no way.

Only when they'd stumbled out of the museum, giddy with ideas and thoughts about the lecture they'd just heard, did she begin to feel things turning between them. A wind had whipped up on bustling Fifty-third Street, and the hand-dyed scarf Hannah was wearing blew across her face. Laughing, Patrick reached up and pulled it down, his finger lightly tracing her cheek.

An awkward silence followed, which was broken only when Patrick asked with a sheepish smile, "Do you fancy a glass of wine?"

Hannah knew that Michael would be out late tonight having drinks with his colleagues, so, looking up into his green eyes, she whispered softly, "That would be nice."

Later, they found themselves sipping wine and nestled at a small table in a tiny, antique-strewn bistro on West Fifty-fifth. Candlelight flickered across Patrick's long, handsome face as they talked about Hannah's final paper for his class.

"I've decided to write about Dalí's *William Tell*," she said, turning the stem of her wineglass between her thumb and forefinger, "and the Oedipus complex."

His eyes twinkled and he clapped his hands. "Excellent. Wonderful." Then, as a thought struck him, he raised his finger and added, "Wait a minute."

After rooting around in his briefcase, which was squeezed between them on the floor, he pulled out a copy of Sigmund Freud's *The Interpretation of Dreams* with a flourish.

"Ta da!" He laughed. "You can borrow it if you like."

Without missing a beat, she laughed too, and after scrabbling around in her tote bag, she pulled out her own hardback copy. "I'll stick with mine." She giggled. "It's bigger and harder."

Her own flirtatiousness shocked her. But as Patrick threw his head back laughing, she smiled. There was no doubt about it: Something deeper, richer, and more dangerous was happening between them.

Two hours and a couple of glasses of wine later, they stood outside the restaurant. She knew it was time to head home, but Patrick seemed to be exerting a kind of gravitational pull. Since the Freud joke, his arms, hands, and legs had been gently brushing hers and now, as they stood dangerously close on the sidewalk, she knew those brief touches had been intentional.

"Thank you," she began.

She never finished. Patrick had already moved closer. "I shouldn't do this," he whispered, his gaze burning into hers. "I never do this kind of thing. . . ."

He didn't finish either. Before she could come to her senses and stop what was going to happen, they were kissing. Deep, soft, long, passionate kisses. The world seemed to stand still around them. Hannah could hear nothing but Patrick's light breaths and her own thudding heart. After what felt like an eternity, they pulled away from each other and moved like one being toward the edge of the sidewalk. Patrick hailed a taxi, and before she knew it they were entering his apartment building, which lay only a short block from her own.

Still sitting clutching her knees on the front stoop of her in-laws' home, Hannah whispered for the second time, "Shit, shit, shit."

Whenever she thought of that night, a wave of desire and longing for Patrick would hit her. After that wave peaked, as she remembered Patrick's touch, his kisses, his soft whispers, and his face so near hers, it would be closely followed by waves of guilt and regret. He was her professor, for God's sake. She was a married woman; she shouldn't have done it. She'd been out of her mind to be so foolish.

And now, out here on the tree-lined Brooklyn street, she was experiencing a whole new wave: a wave of fear. Could she really be pregnant? By Patrick? There was a chance. They hadn't used a condom, after all. But he hadn't come inside her. That was no guarantee, though; she knew that. For some reason it hadn't occurred to her to worry about it until today, and as she touched her belly again her throat tightened.

"Hann?" Michael had emerged from the house behind her. "What are you doing?"

She looked up at him, slightly dazed. In the evening light his face seemed a little drawn and tired.

"Everyone's waiting," he continued, a testy edge in his tone. "We're going to make some toasts, and there's something I want to tell everyone."

In her panic she'd completely forgotten about his mysterious announcement. The thought of whatever it might be made the hairs on her neck bristle. Michael had this habit of springing things on her. Like the time he announced at a dinner party that he'd booked them tickets to fly to Florence—the next day. Or the time he stood up in a packed bar in Midtown, grabbed a microphone, and proposed to her. In the old days she'd loved his spontaneity. Especially as it seemed so at odds with his measured academic demeanor. But now being kept in the dark and then publicly surprised irritated her.

Knowing there was nothing she could do to avoid it tonight, however, she dragged herself to her feet and followed Michael back into the house. As she watched him move through the crowd—his neat brown hair, his purposeful stride—something startling occurred to her. *If I'm pregnant,* she thought, *I don't want it to be Michael's.*

"Thanks so much for coming, everyone."

As Bill and Diane took turns thanking the guests and then congratulating Michael and Hannah on their five "glorious years of marriage," Hannah stood beside them, a tight smile frozen on her face.

". . . and now, I believe Michael has something to say," Hannah heard Diane say.

Next to her, Michael hugged his parents and then cleared his throat to speak.

"Yeah, thanks, folks. Thanks for coming, and thanks, Mom and Dad, for a great party. Hannah and I really appreciate it." Michael then puffed his chest out a little. "I also want you all to be the first to hear some exciting news." His eyes darted momentarily toward Hannah to make sure he had her full attention. "I've been offered a one-year research fellowship at Stanford working on the Athena Artificial Intelligence project." Beaming at the faces in front of them, he added, "You've probably read about it in the press."

There were claps and whistles, and a few people stepped forward to pump Michael's hand. Although they patted him on the back, Michael's parents looked a little shell-shocked, and Diane, with a glint of worry in her eyes, snatched a quick glimpse at Hannah. She was no doubt asking some of the same questions that, at that moment, were racing through Hannah's mind. What did this mean? Was Hannah meant to go with Michael to California? Was she going to have to give up her MFA? Her studio? The New York art galleries? Her life?

Unable to speak a word or move a limb, Hannah found herself swept up into a hug by Diane. As she was trapped in her arms and looking over at Michael, another thought occurred to Hannah. *I don't want to move to California with him,* she thought.

"I feel sick," was all she could say, before she escaped Diane's grasp and ran to the bathroom.

Eight

Ashleigh

Ashleigh arrived first for the meeting. Hannah and Sofia were due to get to the garden at four, so she had just a few minutes to wait. The afternoon was beautiful. Newly budding trees were fluttering in the warm breeze, and, thanks to the strangely quiet street outside, Ashleigh could even hear birds chirruping. It was sometimes hard to believe that this garden was in the heart of Manhattan. Adjoined to some secluded English mansion seemed more fitting—if you ignored the surrounding tower blocks and distant sounds of the city, that was.

They had to save this place, Ashleigh thought as she lowered herself onto one of the garden's benches. She loved it here; it was so different from the law offices of Rocksbury, Chatham, and Wise, where she spent most of her waking hours. Ashleigh worked late nearly every night of the week, and spent every day hurrying between meetings, tapping on her laptop, and bent over the mountains of files, contracts, and letters cluttered on her desk. She rarely saw natural light, let alone swaying trees and budding green leaves. Being the niece of one of the partners, and the daughter of an ex-founder, meant Ashleigh worked hard. Really hard. When she came to the firm she had never wanted nor expected an easy ride just because she was family. Ashleigh put in more hours than any of the other twelve associate attorneys at the firm, because she was determined not to have accusations of nepotism thrown her way. When she one day made partner, she wanted it to be because of her own hard work and her sterling reputation as a lawyer, not because her uncle was the boss.

During the last couple of weeks, though, things had been different. After Gina's engagement party and Davey's announcement to her family about Sam, Ashleigh did something she had never done before: She played hooky. It still shocked her that she'd done it. After all, before two weeks ago Ashleigh had never been late, never taken an hour off for a dentist appointment, and never once called in sick. Usually Ashleigh thrived on her fast-paced, work-horse life. She loved what she did, and even if it meant getting home late to Sam most evenings, she was happy.

But after the party Ashleigh just couldn't face going into work. She was sure that news of her and Sam would spread through her family like a brushfire, and pretty soon all her colleagues at Rocksbury, Chatham, and Wise would know too. So the morning after the party she rolled over in bed, dialed the number for the office, and told her assistant, Charlotte, she was sick.

Over the days that followed, Ashleigh continued to call in sick. She just couldn't face the knowing glances of her colleagues, who no doubt already knew her secret, and she dreaded being pulled into her uncle's office for "a small chat." She was also beginning to feel despondent about work in general. Whereas she used to wake up every morning keen to pull on her suit and head downtown, Ashleigh now woke up tired and uninspired. Even the thought of looking at a contract or attending a meeting or calming the nerves of some frazzled client made her yawn and scurry back under the covers.

Sam was right, of course. Ashleigh couldn't keep up the sick excuse forever. People, including her uncle, were going to start asking questions. Sam was also right that if Ashleigh just faced up to her parents, got it over with, and told them the truth, everything would get better. At the very least it would be all out in the open and Ashleigh could move on.

"I'm not saying you *have* to tell them, Ashleigh," Sam had said after Ashleigh's sixth day playing hooky. The two of them sat at either end of the old yellow couch in the apartment with their feet entwined. "I just want you to be happy. Hiding out at home, baby-sitting the neighbor's kid, not returning your parents' calls—it's not like you." She paused and looked intently at Ashleigh. "In the end, when your parents know, I think you'll be a whole lot happier. You'll be able to get back to work, back in the swing of things."

"I know, I know." Ashleigh shook her head and then stared down into the hot chocolate clasped in her hands. They'd been over this a million times. She knew Sam was only trying to help, but Ashleigh really didn't want to hear it. She just wanted to forget about the whole thing and keep her head in the sand.

In a lame voice, Ashleigh finally said, "As soon as Dad's done working on this big Senate hearing, I'll go down to DC and tell them. And"—she gulped some of the warm, sweet drink—"I'll go back to work tomorrow. I promise."

"You don't have to promise me anything, sweetie." Sam smiled, her beautiful dark skin crinkling a little at the corners of her hazel eyes. "Like I said, I just want you to be happy."

Despite being scared, Ashleigh had gone back to work the next day, just as she said she would. What confronted her was a nightmare. There was so much catching up to do that she'd been working until eleven p.m. every day since—including this weekend. Worse still, she had returned to work to find ten voice-mail messages and five e-mails from her parents. These messages were just like the ones they'd left on her cell phone and gave no clue whether the news about Ashleigh and her girlfriend had reached them. All they said, in increasingly exasperated tones, was that Ashleigh must call home soon.

There was one small blessing: Since she'd returned to work, Ashleigh hadn't seen her uncle. He'd been away on a conference, followed by a long weekend golfing trip to Florida. She loved her uncle—he was probably one of her favorite people in her entire family—yet she was pleased that she didn't have to face him. His wife and daughter had no doubt told him the news about her and Sam, and Ashleigh really had no idea how he would react. He was a kind man, but he was old-fashioned in his values. He was also a man of honesty, and one thing she was pretty sure of was that Uncle Ray would insist she tell her parents.

Sitting in the garden, wearing a navy pantsuit from another

Sunday spent in the office, Ashleigh gripped the bench. Every time she thought of her parents and the idea that she was going to have to confront them, a pulse of panic would ripple through her body. She'd try to calm herself by remembering Sam's joking words: "Since Dick Cheney, lesbian daughters are all the rage among Republicans." But the calm wouldn't last. The memory of Sam's words would be quickly followed by an image of herself sitting in her parents' plush Georgetown living room, watching their appalled faces as she told them she was in a relationship with a woman. Her dad wasn't Dick Cheney. One of the main platforms he ran on in his home state, Ohio, was opposing gay marriage. Embracing his dyke daughter on the next campaign trail wasn't likely.

But before the sunny afternoon could be ruined by a full-scale panic attack, she heard a familiar high-pitched squeal coming from the garden gate.

"Ash-leeee!"

She looked over to see Gracie's small, smiling face squished up against the gate's iron bars. Leaning over her excited daughter, Sofia was trying to open the gate. As she fingered the lock Sofia jiggled up and down, trying to soothe the whimpering baby that was strapped to her chest in a sling. Ashleigh immediately jumped up to help, and she couldn't help smiling as Gracie continued to singsong her name through the gate.

"Hey, Gracie." Ashleigh laughed after they'd opened the gate and the little girl swooped toward her legs and clamped herself on like a limpet.

Following Gracie into the garden, Sofia nodded down at her and said to Ashleigh, "She's been so excited about seeing you; she's been talking about you all day. Ashee this. Ashee that."

"You should have called. We could have met earlier and I could have watched her for a while," Ashleigh said, unwinding Gracie's arms and pulling her up onto her hip. "I needed an excuse to leave the office."

Sofia waved her free hand. "Ashleigh, you're so sweet." Then she moved closer and gave Ashleigh's elbow a soft squeeze. "But you have a life. I can't take up all your time."

Ashleigh said nothing. She pushed back a lock of Gracie's wild curly hair and then plopped her down on the grass so she could chase a nearby butterfly. Ashleigh never told Sofia much about why she'd played hooky that week. She simply said she needed a break and was taking a few days off. Sofia seemed to buy it.

"Did Mary call?" asked Sofia, who now sat on the bench, unfurling the sling and shushing the whimpering baby.

Ashleigh shook her head. "I left another message, but she still hasn't returned it. Perhaps she's out of town."

"Or lost her nerve." Sofia raised her eyebrows. "I was astounded when she said she wanted to help us organize this protest. I mean, for God's sake, she's married to the guy who's trying to bulldoze the garden."

"Poor woman." Ashleigh sighed. "Imagine being married to him."

"You know Havemeyer?" Sofia looked surprised.

"Know *of* him. Sam, my . . ." The word jarred in Ashleigh's throat. "My girlfriend," she finally said, "she's a professor in the anthropology department, and she's told me about him. He was a real jerk to her once at some big humanities and social sciences meeting."

"He's a jerk to a lot of people." Sofia shook her head. "His wife included, I imagine."

"Why's the guy so mean, anyhow?"

Sofia started to gently rock Edgar in her arms. "I don't know. But I intend to find out." She flashed a grin at Ashleigh and added, "The two of them are coming for dinner on Wednesday."

"They *are*?" Ashleigh couldn't help laughing.

"I know, crazy. As if I have time for dinner parties." Sofia chuckled. "It's a long story. I figured the dean would choose to pull out his own teeth rather than come to dinner at my place. Turns out I was wrong. Apparently he e-mailed Tom to say he's looking forward to it. I—"

Their conversation was interrupted as the gate swung open

and Hannah walked in. She looked as beautiful as ever, Ashleigh thought, in her low-slung Levi's and frayed Manhattan U hoodie. But there seemed an air of sadness following her. Her shoulders were slumped, her eyes dark and tired.

"Hey," she said quietly as she paced toward the bench.

"Hannah, you made it." Ashleigh smiled and then waved toward Sofia. "Do you guys know each other?"

Hannah let out an embarrassed laugh. "We do. I sobbed my heart out to Sofia a few weeks ago. She probably knows me much more than she really wants to."

Sofia pointed toward Gracie, who was now rolling and giggling in the grass. "Believe me, hearing grown-ups talk about grown-up things is heaven." She then looked up at Hannah. "How's all that going, by the way?"

Hannah frowned, puffed out her cheeks, and sat down beside Sofia. "It looks like Michael and I are headed to Stanford. I suppose that resolves everything." Then, clearly wanting to change the subject, she leaned over and peered at Edgar. "Congratulations, by the way. Last time I saw you this one was just a bump. And now look. He's . . ." She paused. "He's a *he,* right?" Sofia nodded. "He's beautiful."

"He may be beautiful, but he's making my arms sore." Sofia sighed. "Could you hold him for a second?"

"Oh." Hannah sprang back against the bench. "Oh, no, I'm not good with babies. They always cry."

Sofia looked a little surprised, but didn't say anything. Instead she handed Edgar to Ashleigh and then, reaching into her crowded diaper bag, pulled out a notepad and pen.

"Okay, girls." Her eyes sparkled. "Let's get to work. We have a protest to organize."

Half an hour later the three women hadn't gotten very far. They'd started off well, agreeing that the protest could be some sort of garden sit-in. But then, in the glow of the late-afternoon sun, with Gracie flitting playfully in front of them, the mood turned lighthearted. As they dug into Sofia's bag of Pepperidge Farm cookies, they imagined themselves chained to bulldozers, getting arrested, and instigating uprisings in New York City jails. Sofia's suggestion they should protest wearing Uma Thurman *Kill Bill* jumpsuits had them giggling uncontrollably for at least five minutes. And when she persuaded little Gracie to do her Uma Thurman kung fu kicks, the three of them were helpless.

Somewhere amid all the merriment, they moved from the bench to the grass. Sprawled on their backs under the shade of a maple tree, the three women wiped tears of laughter from their cheeks. Edgar gurgled happily on a soft red blanket beside them, and Gracie lay with her head on Ashleigh's belly and murmured some unrecognizable song. She was pooped out and sweaty from her earlier Uma Thurman impersonations.

"Perhaps we should agree on a date?" suggested Hannah when they finally stopped giggling.

Sofia coughed back a laugh. "Okay, yes, the date." She sat up and retrieved a small journal from her bag.

Hannah propped herself up on her elbows. "Do we know when construction is going to start?"

"Soon." Sofia frowned, tapping on her journal with a pen. "I heard from Tom, via his department chair, that the contract has been signed and the construction company will start work this summer. Although I don't know the exact date."

Ashleigh propped herself up too. "The department of buildings publishes the construction permits they grant online. I could run a check."

"That would be gre—" Sofia began, but she was interrupted by Hannah.

"Wilkins!" Hannah exclaimed, with a finger raised in the air. "I think the construction company is called Wilkins." She then looked over at Sofia. "You remember the day we met in the garden? When we saw the dean?" Sofia nodded, and so Hannah went on. "The other two men were wearing those construction jackets, you know, the bright yellow kind? Both said 'Wilkins' across the back."

"Good memory." Sofia grinned and nodded.

Meanwhile, as she tried not to disturb Gracie, who was still propped on her belly, Ashleigh rifled in her nearby purse for a pen and paper and scribbled down the name Wilkins. "I'll check online later, and tomorrow I'll make a couple of calls."

Hannah leaned forward. "We really should have the protest in the next few weeks, whether or not the construction is starting that soon. Semester ends in less than a month and as soon as summer comes"—she nodded toward the two Manhattan U towers—"everyone here will be gone. Including me." The last words she said with a grimace.

"So you're moving to Stanford?" Ashleigh asked, as she twiddled Gracie's hair in her fingers.

Hannah sighed and plopped her head back on the grass. "Michael, my husband, he's just gotten this big-deal fellowship out there. It's one of those once-in-a-lifetime opportunities. Or so he says. He's going to work on the Athena project."

Sofia's head shot around. "*Really?* You mean the whole 'computers with feelings' project?"

"Something like that," Hannah muttered with clear disinterest.

Sofia was excited, though. She turned to Ashleigh and said, "Have you heard about it? These Athena guys are making computers that are, like, happy or stressed or depressed. Crazy, huh?" She laughed and added, "It would make a great movie."

Even though Gracie was still leaning on her stomach singing, Ashleigh heard Hannah let out a quiet sigh. Turning her head to look at Hannah, she ventured the question, "And you don't want to go?"

"No. I'm in the middle of my MFA, and nothing can beat the art world here. Or my studio."

"Or your sexy art professor!" Sofia laughed before she slapped her hand over her mouth and said in a hurried whisper, "Oh, God, sorry, Hannah. I didn't mean to bring that up."

Hannah sat up. "It's okay," she said, waving a hand. "I apologize for unloading my whole sorry story onto you that day. But it had all just happened, and keeping it—*him*—a secret was killing me. It's still killing me," she added with a frown.

"Tell me about it," Ashleigh blurted out, before she could stop herself.

Hannah and Sofia looked over at her, and immediately Ashleigh's cheeks burned. Yet, in spite of her embarrassment, she found herself talking.

"I . . . well," she began, "my parents don't know about me and Sam. They don't know"—she reached down and covered Gracie's ears—"that I'm a lesbian."

Sofia swiped Ashleigh's hands away from her daughter and smiled. "Gracie is very progressive. Don't you worry about her."

At the sound of her name Gracie sprang up, squealed, "Pogess-is," and then skipped away from the three women, down the garden.

Meanwhile, Hannah sat up, crossed her long legs, and looked down at Ashleigh. "Wow," she hissed. "How long's it been?"

"I had a few *sort of* flings at college. With girls, I mean." Ashleigh felt herself blushing again, but still she carried on. "I thought it was just, you know, a phase or something. But then I met Sam. Nearly a year ago."

In fact, the anniversary of Sam and Ashleigh's first meeting was just a few weeks away. The thought made Ashleigh smile. One whole year, she could hardly believe it.

"Where did you guys meet?" Sofia asked, putting down her journal and reaching to hoist tiny Edgar into her lap.

Ashleigh sat up. "The big deli on Fourth Street." She beamed. "We both reached for the same pint of Cherry Garcia."

Hannah and Sofia laughed, and then Sofia said, "You found your soul mate, then."

Ashleigh grinned and nodded. "I did," she said, before leaning back on her hands and telling her two smiling listeners the whole story.

A year ago, Ashleigh had visited an old school friend in the Village for the evening. Before hopping on the subway home to Battery Park, she was lured into a nearby deli by a battered Ben & Jerry's sign. In what she thought was an empty store, she lingered in front of the freezers contemplating her options: Phish Food or Cherry Garcia? Cherry Garcia or Phish Food? It was only when she reached toward the ice cream and another outstretched hand did the same that Ashleigh realized someone was beside her. Confusion followed as the two women laughed nervously, each of them trying to force the other to take the pint of ice cream. Finally the Cherry Garcia dropped to the floor, split open with a loud thudding noise, and spewed onto the deli's ceramic tiles. Ashleigh and Sam babbled their embarrassed apologies to the deli owner, offered him money for the spilled ice cream, and then hustled out of the store, each with a fresh Cherry Garcia under her arm.

"Sometimes I sit over there," Sam said as they stood on the sidewalk and she waved toward a deserted stoop overlooking Washington Square Park. "To eat my ice cream, I mean."

Looking up at the heavy, dark sky, Ashleigh laughed and asked, "Even at night, in drizzling rain?"

"Even at night, in drizzling rain," Sam said with a smile. "Want to join me?"

Only a short while ealier, Ashleigh had been itching to be home and get ready for bed. Another early morning at work awaited her. But just as the Ben & Jerry's sign had lured her, so did Sam's twinkling eyes, wide smile, and soft, kind voice.

"I'd love to," she replied as she shook open her flimsy umbrella.

At first they sat side by side on the stoop in silence, opening their ice creams and staring out over the gloomy park. But as soon as they found a rhythm—digging at their Cherry Garcias with white plastic spoons and then trading Ashleigh's umbrella between them—they began to talk. And then, just as effortlessly as they worked together in their ice cream–umbrella dance, so words, stories, even secrets began to spill from the two of them.

"My ex-girlfriend couldn't stand Cherry Garcia," Sam confessed, sometime into their conversation. "She was more of a Super Fudge Chunk kind of girl. It's no wonder we split up."

Ashleigh laughed and then asked shyly, "When was that?"

With a mouthful of ice cream, Sam waved her spoon and said, "Over a year ago. We're still friends, though."

Ashleigh smiled, not really because of what Sam was saying but more because of her own reaction. Up to this moment she'd always feared meeting or talking to what she considered a *real* lesbian. She'd never been friends with any women who were officially "out." The girls she'd had one-night flings with at college eschewed the "dyke" label with all their might. They were just college girls having some fun, or so they said. For Ashleigh, then, the idea of being close to a *real* lesbian was terrifying. She figured someone like that would know. They would be able to read her mind and see all those thoughts and desires she'd had since she was a teenager—those same thoughts she'd tried to shut out for so long about women, their beauty, their soft voices and bodies. Ashleigh knew deep down that she wasn't just having fun or experimenting, like the other girls in college, and she was scared a real lesbian would know that too.

But as she sat on the cold stoop clutching her small umbrella and her Cherry Garcia, Ashleigh didn't feel at all scared or uncomfortable. On the contrary, there was something magical about being with Sam. Though they were strangers, they seemed so in sync, and Ashleigh couldn't deny the pulse of attraction beginning to beat hard in her chest. Sitting there with her cropped hair, her elegant velvet scarf, her high cheekbones, and those dazzling eyes, Sam was stunning. And although Ashleigh's fingers were chilled from the ice cream and her legs were numb from the cold stoop, she couldn't bring herself to stop staring, let alone leave.

"To save our frozen asses, I invited her back to my place!" The voice laughed above Ashleigh, Sofia, and Hannah.

She was so wrapped up telling the others their story, Ashleigh hadn't even heard the gate open and Sam approach. She felt herself redden, but then, as she looked up at Sam, Ashleigh grinned. Sam always had a way of surprising her and making her smile and laugh and feel good about who she was, and who *they* were.

"You *bad* girls." Sofia winked at Sam. "Sleeping together on your first date!"

"Very bad." Sam winked back.

After introducing everyone to Sam, Ashleigh patted the grass beside her.

"Hey, babe," Sam whispered as she sat down and looped her arm through Ashleigh's.

Ashleigh leaned over and softly kissed Sam's cheek, and in that second, with her lips grazing Sam's warm skin, she knew the time had come. No more procrastinating, she thought. Her parents had to be told, and she was going to do it tonight. How could she keep this person—this wonderful, beautiful person—a secret any longer?

"Okay, so, Hannah, you're doing the flyers," Sofia said an hour or so later as she consulted her notepad. "Ashleigh and Sam, you're going to distribute them, and I'm in charge of press. Does that sound right?"

The others nodded, and Ashleigh asked, "Do you really think the *Manhattan U News* will agree to advertise the sit-in?"

Sofia waved her hand and said, "I have my contacts. Or, at least, Tom does." She then added, "And we're all sure that next Saturday works? It doesn't give us much time. But, like Hannah said, we need to do this ASAP."

Everyone made noises of agreement.

"If the protest starts at two, perhaps we should all get to the garden at one," Hannah suggested. "We can put up ribbons, posters, and banners. I can organize all that if you guys can help me decorate."

Ashleigh's hand shot up. "I'll work on refreshments. That will guarantee a crowd."

"Go easy on the Cherry Garcia, though." Sofia giggled. "We don't want this protest turning into a love-in!"

As all the women laughed, they began to gather together their belongings and get to their feet. The tips of the trees were bathed in a pinkish glow from the setting sun, and long shadows lay across the grass. Edgar had fallen asleep in Sofia's arms and was now being bundled into his sling. Gracie was on the nearby bench, swishing her small feet to and fro. It was a perfect evening, Ashleigh thought. And as she looked at the women around her, she felt happy. Telling her parents wasn't going to be so bad, she figured. They might disown her, or at least get very, very mad. But when she had all this—she looked at the garden, at Sam, at the other women and Gracie—it didn't matter. She could handle what her parents were going to throw at her; she was sure of it.

But when the four women were letting themselves out of the gate, still laughing and sharing last-minute ideas for the protest, Ashleigh came to a sudden halt. Tottering along the adjacent sidewalk in a hot pink sundress and dangerously high silver sandals came Gina. She was waving one manicured hand high in the air and calling, "Ashleigh! Ash-leigh!"

"Oh, no," Ashleigh muttered under her breath, but before she could try to hide behind the others or pretend she hadn't seen her cousin, Gina lollopped across the street toward them.

"Ashleigh," she shrieked breathlessly, "I found you! I've been looking everywhere. I've left a *zillion* messages. Where have you been?"

"I, um—" Ashleigh began.

"Your mom told me to find you," Gina carried on, seemingly oblivious to the other women who stood beside Ashleigh. "It's your dad. He's sick." She licked her lips and paused dramatically. "It's his heart."

Nine

Sofia

Lying in bed late on Tuesday night, Sofia was wide-awake. She couldn't blame the insomnia on her newborn baby, however. Compared to Gracie, who'd had night and day mixed up for the first month of her life, Edgar was proving to be a great sleeper. From the moment they brought him home from the birthing center he'd slept peacefully every night, waking only once or twice to nurse. Sofia knew it wouldn't last, of course. Having been through all this before, she knew that boasting about a child's sleeping habits would just come back to her haunt her, because sooner or later a good sleeper would turn into a colicky, screaming, awake-all-night monster. She'd learned that fast about babies: Just when you thought you had them figured out, they transformed into something completely different.

Sofia turned on her side and stared out the window at the glimmering lights of the city. Edgar might not be keeping her awake, but her own whirring mind was proving to be as sleep-depriving as a fussy newborn. The upcoming protest was one source of preoccupation. With Ashleigh now gone, it was down to Hannah and herself to get everything organized before Saturday. Sofia had spent today flying around campus with the kids in tow, tacking up posters. Hannah, meanwhile, stood outside the library pressing flyers into students' hands. Neither Hannah nor Sofia had any idea whether their last-minute, slapdash advertising would bring people to the protest, but they were determined to try.

Tomorrow's dinner party with the Havemeyers was another reason for Sofia's restless mind. Only this evening, Tom had tried to persuade her to rethink the whole idea.

"Sofia, honey," he'd said as they emptied the dishwasher together, "aren't you taking on too much? I mean, Edgar's just two weeks old, your body's still recovering, and you're organizing a protest?" He shook his head. "*And* this dinner party with the Havemeyers tomorrow night. Can you really manage it?"

"Tom," Sofia replied with a sigh, "the dinner is all under control. I'm going to pick up salmon and all the sides from Whole Foods." She smiled halfheartedly and added, "I won't even lift a finger, let alone go in the kitchen."

"Why don't we postpone?" Tom persisted. "I'm sure they would understand."

Sofia was sure they would, and, if she were honest, she'd considered postponing too. A dinner party with Dean Havemeyer wasn't exactly her idea of a thrilling evening. In fact, she'd initially hoped inviting them to their place would put Jack off the whole dinner party idea. Moreover, Sofia was now organizing this protest against the dean's plans to demolish the garden. He didn't know yet that she was behind the posters and flyers fluttering around campus, but he was sure to find out soon enough. Sofia was fully aware of the irony of inviting the enemy to dinner a few days before the protest. Indeed, the irony secretly delighted her, and that, in the end, was exactly why she was resolved to go through with the dinner party.

Sofia also wanted the party to happen so she could see Mary. She hadn't heard anything from the dean's wife in the past few days. They'd left messages about the protest on her cell, but she hadn't returned any of their calls. Even if Mary had lost her nerve, Sofia was surprised she hadn't left some sort of polite, apologetic message.

"I hope he hasn't murdered her and buried her under his parking lot," Sofia scoffed to herself.

Tom, who had been reaching to place some plates in an overhead cabinet, turned and stared at his wife. "Huh?"

"Nothing," she said.

She was too exhausted to explain her worries about the dean's wife. Tom would just say it was her Hollywood imagination running rampant again, and that Mary seemed fine. But he'd never been good at reading people—except people in his beloved Poe books. Sofia, on the other hand, always prided herself on her good intuition.

"So why don't you take on Hayden too?" Tom asked after the dishes were done.

It was now Sofia's turn to say, "Huh?"

Tom flashed Sofia a smile. "Why not represent Hayden too? You're taking on all this other stuff, so why not Hayden as well? At least you'd make some money. A whole lot of money, in fact," he added with a wink.

Tom was probably joking, but Sofia wasn't in the mood for jokes. "I am *never, ever* representing that low-life brother of yours again," she snapped.

"He's not a lowlife, Sofe," Tom countered, his expression now serious.

Sofia was taken aback. Tom very rarely defended his brother. He loved Hayden, but he knew more than anybody how flighty, inconsistent, and demanding Hayden could be. Tom also knew how hurt Sofia had been when Hayden had dropped her as his agent.

"Well, if he's not a lowlife, what is he?" Sofia snapped back, angered and annoyed by Tom's sudden turnaround.

Tom waved a hand. "He's my brother, Sofia. And all I'm saying is, maybe he's not that bad, and just maybe you should consider taking him on again."

Sofia's eyebrows shot up. "You're serious, aren't you?" she blurted out, her voice strained and appalled.

"You miss the old life, Sofia; anyone can see that."

"I do not," she shouted back, and then, after a pause, she added, "And even if I did, I still wouldn't take on your good-for-nothing brother."

Tom looked at Sofia with tired eyes. The demands of the new baby, together with all the usual end-of-semester madness in his department, were clearly taking their toll. "Stop it, Sofe," he growled. "Give Hayden a break."

A full-scale row erupted after that. It was unusual for Tom and Sofia to fight, but they'd been doing it a lot more lately, and every time they fought Sofia would huff off to bed on her own, and Tom would fall asleep on the couch in front of *The Daily Show*. Sofia hated being alone at night; she hated not hearing Tom's low, peaceful breaths beside her; but she was always too stubborn to go into the living room and make up.

Their latest row was playing on her mind and was probably the biggest reason for tonight's wakefulness. Every time Sofia would feel the emptiness of the bed beside her, she'd think about the heated words she and Tom had exchanged. Was she too hard on Hayden? she'd wonder. Her thoughts would then turn to her old life as Hayden's agent in LA. She'd think about the highs and lows, the exhilarations and disappointments, and as she tossed and turned she remembered the cocktail parties, the extravagant dresses, red carpets, and flashing bulbs, the frantic phone calls, and the anger she felt when a producer would turn Hayden down for some role or other. Most of all she'd think about the movie shoots. They were so exciting and tense, but also technical and mundane. She loved every part of them.

It had been on a movie shoot that she'd first met Hayden. On a scorching July day almost ten years ago, Sofia was standing outside a trailer on a shadeless sidewalk in Venice Beach waiting for one of her notoriously unreliable clients to show up. She was hot, frustrated, and about to throw in the towel and return to her office when she heard a rumble behind her, followed by a shout, and before she knew what was happening she was slammed to the ground and something cold and wet slipped over her entire body.

"Eeee-uuuk!" she shouted as she lay sprawled on the burning tarmac.

When she recovered enough look up, Sofia found herself squinting into the palest pair of blue eyes she'd ever seen.

"What the . . . ?" she began.

"Jeez!" Blue Eyes whistled as he knelt down beside her. "I'm so sorry. I couldn't stop." He pointed to his Rollerblades jutting out from under a pair of battered Levi's. "I'm a rookie," he explained.

"Well, rookie," Sofia barked from the floor, "do you plan to help me up?"

Blue Eyes quickly reached for her elbow and gently began to pull her up. When she was finally on her feet, Sofia looked down at her once–pale green suit. It was soaked, stained brown, and dappled with tiny ice crystals.

"What *is* this?" she demanded, shaking the dress between her thumb and forefinger.

"Iced tea," the guy offered, looking curiously unfazed by the whole incident. "It's for the director." He then paused and looked down at the crumpled plastic cup on the sidewalk. "He's going to be pretty mad."

"And what about me?" snapped Sofia. "I'm pretty mad too."

"The director, Mr. Reiner," continued Blue Eyes, as if Sofia hadn't spoken, "he's very demanding."

Sofia saw the side of his mouth twitch and found herself interjecting loudly, "What are you laughing at?"

His eyebrows shot up, and he said with one hand waving, "I wasn't laughing at you. Honestly. I was just thinking about how loud Reiner is going to shout at me this time."

Sofia made a huffing sound and started to dab at her dress with a napkin she'd found in her purse. Out of the corner of her eye she looked at the rookie Rollerblader. For the first time she noticed that his pale eyes were coupled with a thick avalanche of blond hair, vast square shoulders, and a wide, luscious mouth. He was beautiful. Not her type, of course. She liked her guys quirky and interesting, and definitely not Rollerblading in butt-hugging Levi's and a 69ers tee. Nevertheless, she was fully aware that this guy in front of her was gorgeous. At her agency they called this kind "HAB": Hollywood A-list Beautiful.

"So," Sofia said after she'd cleaned off the worst of the mess, "what's a rookie Rollerblader doing fetching coffee for Reiner? You his assistant?"

Blue Eyes nodded and then gave a wry smile. "And a wannabe actor, of course."

"Of course." Sofia smiled in spite of herself. She'd guessed as much.

Something about his honesty was endearing. She looked him over again, this time more slowly. Too many of these beautiful guys were deprived of talent; they couldn't act if Laurence Olivier were pulling their strings. But there was something about this one. It wasn't just his good looks. There was a certain poise about him; he seemed so easy in his skin. She was convinced it would work on-screen. In fact, she was sure of it. The camera would love him.

After glancing at him one more time, she said what she rarely said to wannabes: "Do you have an agent?" He shook his head, and so she asked, "What's your name?"

"Hayden." He smiled. "Hayden Burgess."

Perfect, thought Sofia, *perfect.* Elegant, aristocratic-sounding, but also sexy: Hayden Burgess.

As he looked at her more closely, Hayden's pale eyes began to glitter. "Are you an agent?" he asked, cocking his head to one side.

She nodded and then flicked a business card into his hand. "Call me," she said, before turning on her heel and strutting away.

He did call her, and it turned out all Sofia's intuitions were right. He could act—pretty damn well, in fact—and the camera adored his glossy hair, pale eyes, and unflinching composure. Sofia was soon booking him small roles here and there, then bigger roles, and after just a couple of years he was playing some big roles in serious big-budget movies. He fast became her highest-grossing client, and both their careers rocketed into the fast lane. Not a week went past when she wasn't going to a fancy gala or meeting some high-powered studio executive or chasing around boutiques on Rodeo Drive while Hayden tried on tuxedos.

There was never a dull moment with Hayden, but as the fame and dollars mounted, he soon became a royal pain in the ass too.

Not all the time, but he definitely had his moments. One time he pleaded with Sofia to fly to Hawaii and bring a pair of sunglasses he'd forgotten to pack. On a crackling phone line from Maui he'd implored, "I need them, Sofe. You know they're my lucky ones; you know how much I need them and you also know I don't trust FedEx." Hayden was due to meet a big director the next day and was beside himself with panic that he'd lose the role if he didn't have the lucky sunglasses with him. And so, even though her schedule was hectic, Sofia booked herself on the next flight, and Hayden and his sunglasses were reunited within twenty-four hours.

After a number of requests like this, Sofia hired Hayden a personal assistant, but it didn't help much. He always wanted Sofia's advice and assistance, and no one else's would do. Scared to lose her number one client, Sofia too often found herself doing the crazy things he demanded. She'd been right about his poise and self-possession and, indeed, his honesty. He was deep down a kind and charismatic guy. However, what she hadn't bargained for that first day they met was what a prima donna he would turn out to be, and how, after all her loyalty and hard work, he would drop her like a stone the moment some hotshot, sweet-talking agent came along.

That was why it was such a surprise when Sofia finally met Tom, after three years of being Hayden's agent. Hayden had talked about his brother a lot, and always called him with a loving chuckle, "My egghead bro." The two brothers didn't get together much, though. Hayden's new Hollywood life was frantic, and according to Hayden, Tom was permanently buried under a dusty pile of books at Penn finishing up a PhD in literature.

Before they met, Sofia had expected Tom to be one of those stiff, arrogant academic types. She imagined him just like the snooty young professor who had taught her film theory as a junior at Berkeley; the same professor who'd given her all B-minuses—driving down her otherwise stellar GPA—and who constantly rolled out words like *poststructuralism* or *Hitchcock-esque* in a painfully fake British accent. With a brother as self-absorbed as Hayden, Sofia was convinced that Tom would be the same kind of pompous, overeducated asshole.

But then she met Tom, and everything she'd expected turned out to be wrong. At a Christmas party at Hayden's place in Santa Monica (before he took on Lori as his agent and moved out to his pad in Malibu), Sofia was hovering by the abundant buffet trying to decide between a slice of ham or another sweet potato when she heard Hayden behind her.

"Yo, Sofia," he bellowed, "come meet the Egghead."

She turned to see Hayden with his arm looped around a guy in glasses and a rumpled brown jacket. As Sofia moved toward them across the shining marble floor, she found herself staring into Tom's pale blue eyes, which glimmered out at her from behind a pair of thumb-printed wire-rimmed specs. Quite unexpectedly something kicked in her stomach, and her mouth went dry.

"Hi, Egghead," she said with a smile as she offered her hand. "Great to finally meet you."

Tom grinned. "Hey, Ballbuster. Likewise."

Sofia threw back her head and laughed. "That's what he calls me, eh?" She jerked her thumb toward Hayden, who was waving his hands and shooting exaggerated warning glares at his brother. "How original," she scoffed.

"He was never very good at name-calling." Tom laughed, a deep, low chuckle. "He was always more your pinch-bite-and-pull-hair kind of guy."

"How manly." Sofia laughed again.

As the two brothers pretended to punch and wrestle, Sofia couldn't stop staring at Tom. Although he had the same eyes and hair as his brother, the same wide shoulders, he wore it all so differently. He stooped a little, unlike Hayden, and his hair was disheveled. His movements were jerky and bashful. Yet his eyes shone with an intensity completely different from Hayden's. They seemed so deep and wise and thoughtful, but funny and ironic all at the same time.

From that first moment Sofia was hooked, and, as it turned out, Tom was too. They spent the rest of the party sitting close together on Hayden's leather couch, quietly laughing at other party guests fumbling kisses under some nearby mistletoe. Late into the evening they sneaked off to the ocean and spent the rest of the night wandering on the sand, throwing tiny pebbles into the waves, all the while laughing and talking. It was only as the sun began to rise over the city that they finally kissed and headed together to Sofia's apartment.

Dating was hard, with Sofia in LA and Tom in Philadelphia and eventually New York. Nevertheless, not a weekend passed when they weren't flying cross-country to see each other. Even after they married—in a beautiful ceremony on a windswept cliff in Big Sur—they continued to commute back and forth. It was only when Sofia got pregnant with Gracie that they finally moved in together. Tom offered to move out to LA and look for any academic position he could find, but Sofia was insistent. Now that she was pregnant, she would give up her job and move to New York. Of course, she knew she'd miss her work and California, but since she was a little girl she had promised herself she'd never be a working mom. She knew it was her right to be one, and she was thankful to feminism, and all those career moms before her, for giving her that option. But she just didn't want to take it.

"Why not?" Tom asked her a million times.

"Because I don't want my kids to grow up without a mom around." Sofia would sigh, exasperated at having to repeat herself. "My mom was *always* working, and sometimes it felt like I didn't have a mom at all."

Tom would knit his eyebrows. "Come on, Sofe, it wasn't that bad. Sure, your mom worked a lot, but she tried to be there as much as she could, didn't she?"

"If my mom had been home more," Sofia would snap, "perhaps we would get on better now. I don't want my kids and me to have the same kind of relationship."

Whenever Tom and Sofia ended up talking about her mom,

Sofia always came away feeling irritated. Tom just didn't get it. He tried to argue that Sofia and her mom were just different and that the fact they didn't get on had nothing to do with how her mom had worked full-time as a tax accountant throughout Sofia's childhood. But Sofia was convinced that things would have been different between them if her mom had been there when she'd cut her knee on that sharp metal fence, or when that nasty kid from down the street had lopped off one of her long black curls with a pocketknife, or when her debate team won the regional finals in tenth grade. If her mom had been at home more, Sofia was sure they would have a better relationship. They'd be friends, even.

As it was, Sofia and her mom had a strained relationship, which only got worse when Sofia's dad died suddenly of a heart attack when Sofia was just twenty-one. Her mom still lived in San Diego, where Sofia grew up, and even though Sofia lived relatively close by in LA, for over ten years she only ever went home once a year for Christmas, when she'd stay just for a few days. Her mom's silent judgments, the little sneering looks she'd give Sofia's clothes, or the scoffing comments she'd make about her "glitzy" career would soon drive Sofia crazy. When she'd finally escape the miasma of her mom's white stucco home, with its manicured lawns and uniform palm trees, Sofia would turn onto the highway north breathing long, slow sighs of relief.

Still wide-awake in bed, Sofia thought of those trips home and sighed all over again. She then looked over at the clock. Five a.m., it read. She was never going to sleep, she realized; her mind was just too fretful. And so, after hauling herself out of bed, she pulled on her nightgown and padded out to the kitchen. Since she'd had Gracie and given up her job, cooking had become Sofia's passion—and her therapy. The feeling of warm dough in her hands, the smell of fresh herbs on her fingers, the sound of a sharp knife cutting through an onion could clear her mind in an instant. She hadn't been in the kitchen since Edgar's arrival, and now, staring at the glinting steel saucepans that hung from the ceiling, she wanted nothing more than to be chopping and blanching and stirring and sautéing.

Reaching for the refrigerator door, she whispered into the kitchen's gloom, "It looks like the Havemeyers will get some home-cooked food, after all."

Sofia pulled the leg of lamb from the oven. The air filled with the scent of orange, white wine, and rosemary as the marinade sizzled and gleamed. Although she was sweating from the heat, she smiled. The meat was cooked to perfection: golden but not too brown, crisp but not burned. It was a perfect follow-up to the appetizers she'd made in the middle of the night. Having found two eggplants in the bottom of the refrigerator, Sofia had baked them and blended them with chilies, lemon juice, basil, and fresh mint to make moutabel, her favorite Middle Eastern dip. Then, even though the sun was rising, sending shafts of red light into the kitchen, she had set about draining a can of vine leaves and mixing dill and parsley and freshly cooked rice for their stuffing. The hours slipped away, and before she knew it Gracie was at her feet asking for breakfast.

Now it was evening; the kids had crashed early and were in their beds. As Sofia slid the hot roasting tray onto the work surface, she heard Dean Havemeyer's voice ring out from the living room.

"Mary, pass me that napkin," he ordered.

In the kitchen Sofia shook her head. Jack and Mary had been in the apartment only a short while, and already Sofia wanted them gone. At least, she wanted Jack gone. When she'd answered the door earlier, Jack had given her the briefest of nods as a greeting and then blustered past her to pump Tom's hand. Once inside, Jack snatched up the glass of Bordeaux he was offered and then plonked himself down on the couch. Before anyone else was settled in their seats, he looked up at Tom, who was hovering nervously in the center of the room, and barked out, "Tell me,

Thomas, which poems did Edgar Allan Poe write while living on Third Street?"

Sofia saw Tom's eyebrows flicker. He was trying not to show it, but he was shocked that Jack would bring up Poe's Greenwich Village house. After all, it was Dean Havemeyer who had ordered the demolition of the old house to make way for Manhattan U's business school. On top of that, it was Jack who'd publicly chastised Tom for opposing the plans, and Jack who'd told Tom he'd lose his job if he didn't give up his chairmanship of the New York Poe Foundation.

"Obviously that's a matter of some debate," Tom began, running a hand through his thick hair.

"Am I right in thinking that 'The Raven' was written *before* Poe took up residence there?" Jack demanded as he leaned forward and propped his elbows on his knees.

"Correct," Tom said. "The poem was published in the *American Review* in early 1845, six months prior to Poe's living at the Third Street address." He paused and then added, "But Poe did revise 'The Raven,' and virtually all of his major poetic works, while living there."

Jack nodded, his face unsurprised and composed, as if he knew all this already. He then asked, "Do any early versions of the poem still exist?"

"An original manuscript of 'The Raven,' you mean? Written by Poe?"

Jack nodded again.

"The Free Library in Philadelphia owns a copy of the poem, which Poe wrote in 1848," Tom said as his eyes began to get that excited, glassy twinkle they always got when he talked about Poe. "But the Free Library's copy is a later version of 'The Raven,' and it contains a number of changes from the original, which was first published in the *American Review* three years earlier."

"So," Jack said with a small laugh, "would a copy of the earlier version be a kind of holy grail for Poe scholars and collectors?"

Tom smiled. "Now that so many of Poe's manuscripts are off the market, it would be immensely valuable. It's hard to say whether it would be the ultimate Poe artifact, but it would attract a great deal of attention." Tom chuckled. "If you lay your hands on one, let me know."

The dean raised his glass of wine and chuckled too. "Of course."

Sofia, who'd been watching and listening to all this from her seat by the dinner table, couldn't help flinching with annoyance. The dean's smiles and chuckles were bad enough, but the way Tom was rolling over like a puppy dog—grinning, laughing, and happily feeding Jack answers to his questions—was much worse. Had Tom forgotten how cruel and manipulative Jack had been to him a few years ago?

As the two men carried on talking, Sofia decided to offset her anger by talking to Mary, who sat stiffly in a neighboring chair, grasping her wine in her lap.

"So, Mary." Sofia smiled. "Are you writing anything at the moment?"

Mary's eyes darted across to her husband. "Oh, no, no," she said quietly, shaking her head. "I don't get the time these days."

"That's a shame," Sofia said politely. "Well, how's teaching?"

Mary's eyes once again flitted in Jack's direction. "Fine, thank you. Just fine."

"Great, that's great," Sofia said, beginning to feel a little exasperated. Trying another tack, she asked, "Have you been out in the garden recently?"

This time Mary's head whipped upward, and she looked at Sofia with wide eyes and tight lips. She seemed to be begging Sofia to keep quiet.

"Oh," Sofia murmured, "sorry."

Not knowing what else to do, Sofia stood up, passed around the appetizers, and then escaped to the sanctuary of the kitchen.

Now, with her brow glistening and the pot of couscous bubbling next to her, Sofia carefully carved the sweet-smelling lamb.

She tried to ignore the dean's voice coming from the other room and concentrate on cutting perfect slices of the succulent, pinkish-brown meat. She couldn't help noticing Mary's silence, though. Did she ever speak when that bully of a husband was around? Sofia wondered. Mary was so different when she had come by and brought Edgar's gift. That day she seemed so loose, confident, wise, and smiling. Today she was another woman: haunted and scared, with those big circles under her eyes and her knuckles white from clutching her wine. With a shiver, Sofia wondered if Jack had ever hurt her. You never could tell, but he certainly seemed mean enough.

"Do you need a hand, Sofia?"

Mary's soft voice made Sofia jump. She looked up to see Mary in the doorway.

"Oh, no," Sofia said, a little flustered, as if Mary had heard her thoughts. "Thanks, but I'm nearly done."

Mary shifted slightly from foot to foot, her eyes skirting over the room. It was clear she didn't want to go back into the other room, so Sofia finally said, "You know what? Could you serve that"—she waved to the couscous—"in that over there?" She nodded to a large green platter at the end of the counter.

Mary smiled and walked toward the stove to pick up the hot saucepan. "This looks amazing, Sofia," she said, scanning the meat and other side dishes Sofia had prepared. "You're some cook!"

Sofia snorted with laughter. "I try."

The two women worked side by side, Sofia still carving and Mary ladling couscous onto the platter. When Mary was finished Sofia handed her the olive oil, and Mary carefully drizzled it into the steaming couscous without stopping once to ask for direction. Sofia then handed over pepper, salt, and parsley, and Mary sprinkled them in lightly and then fluffed the whole mixture with a fork. For a brief second the two women looked up and smiled at each other. Sofia wanted to ask Mary a million questions. She wanted to ask why Mary seemed so scared of her husband, and if he ever hurt her. She wanted to know if Mary was planning—daring?—to come to the protest on Saturday. In the end, Sofia reasoned that if Mary was too scared to speak when her husband was in the same room, she probably wouldn't say much when he was just next door either. So Sofia worked on in silence, keeping her questions to herself.

When everything was ready, Sofia and Mary began loading platters and bowls onto two large trays.

"You're amazing, Sofia"—Mary shook her head—"doing all this with a newborn and a toddler in the house."

"I am, aren't I?" Sofia joked.

The two women chuckled and picked up the trays.

All through the main course, Jack's incessant questions about Poe continued. Not once did he stop to praise Sofia on the tender meat, or the crispy, citrusy green beans, or the delicately fragrant couscous. Although Tom complimented his wife once or twice, he was also preoccupied. Having someone share his passion for Poe was proving to be too alluring, and as fast as Jack was firing questions, Tom was happily answering them with excited monologues about his favorite author. Meanwhile, back in her husband's presence, Mary said very little except a few comments here and there about the food. A couple of times Sofia tried to engage her in conversation, but each time Mary would retract further into her shell.

By the time everyone was tucking into dessert—small squares of cinnamon halvah, sprinkled with almonds—the discussion between Jack and Tom had turned to Poe's drinking.

"I don't know if I would label him an alcoholic," Tom was saying. "That seems too modern a term. But there are certainly many records of Poe's drunken sprees."

Jack clattered his spoon into his empty bowl and wiped his mouth with a napkin. "Are there any records of such sprees while he lived on Third Street?"

Tom thought for a second and then raised his finger. "You know what? That reminds me. I read something a while ago that . . ."

He didn't finish. He was already springing to his feet and moving toward the bookshelves. Without having to scan more than two shelves, he found the book he was looking for.

"This is it," he exclaimed with a grin, pulling the book into his hands.

Sitting back down at the table, he flicked through the pages.

"Here," he said, tapping the hardcover book. "Here it is." He then scooted his chair closer to Jack and held the book for them both to see. "Look. This letter was written in the summer of 1845 by someone who knew Poe. It talks about Poe being 'frequently carried home in a wretched condition,' and it also says"—Tom began to read from the book—"'He was to have delivered a poem before the societies of the Manhattan U, a few weeks since, but drunkenness prevented him.'"

Jack immediately grabbed the book. "Let me see that," he barked, and after his eyes scanned the words Tom just read, he gave a loud puff of laughter. "Well, I'll be damned. Poe was going to deliver a poem at our very own Manhattan U but was too drunk to show up!"

Tom nodded and grinned. "He was definitely a character!" He then added, "Poe moved to Third Street in the summer of 1845, so this might have happened while he was living there, or possibly a short while before, when he was in the West Village."

Jack was grinning now too. "I wonder which poem he was going to read. 'The Raven,' perhaps?"

Tom looked again at the book. "It doesn't say. But maybe. After all, 'The Raven' was published only a few months earlier and was getting a lot of attention."

A silence followed as both men studied the book in front of them. Sofia looked on, annoyed and suspicious. She was sick and tired of the way Jack was dominating conversation. Yet at the same time her mind whirred with questions. Why the hell was Jack so excited about Poe and Poe's drinking habits? Sofia knew why this kind of thing excited Tom. Anything Poe-related excited Tom. But wasn't Jack some sort of American Revolution scholar? Shouldn't he be off getting excited in an old Virginia town somewhere? Sofia glared over at the dean. He must be up to something. He had to be. She could just feel it in her gut. She'd met men like Havemeyer before. There were so many sharks like him in the Hollywood waters, she could spot them a mile off. They would be all toothy smiles and pats on the back one minute, but they'd eat you alive the next. Sofia's eyes flicked over to her husband as concern suddenly clutched in her chest. She hoped Tom wouldn't be the dean's next meal.

Tom's cell phone jingled on the nearby coffee table, breaking the silence that had descended around the dinner table. Tom automatically lunged for it, not wanting the loud rings to wake the children.

"Hey," he said, as he flipped the small cell open and waved an apologetic finger at Jack. "Oh, hey."

Tom smiled for a few seconds as he listened. But then his expression turned quickly to a frown.

"Um," he said, looking at Sofia and then Jack and Mary, "this isn't really a good time."

Whoever was on the line interrupted him and then hung up. Tom was left looking down, his eyebrows knitted, at the silent phone in his hand.

Finally he said to Sofia, "That was Hayden." And before she could say anything, he added, "He's on his way up."

"Jeez," she groaned, and forgetting they had company, she spat out, "What does he want?"

Tom shrugged. "He wanted to swing by and see the kids."

"At this time of night?!" Sofia half laughed, half shouted. "What does he think? They're up enjoying a glass of wine or watching *Charlie Rose*?"

Before she could instruct Tom to call his ridiculous brother back and tell him to stay away, the door gave a noisy buzz.

Tom scooted around the table and headed for the small hallway, apologizing to Jack and Mary as he went. The door clicked open and Sofia heard Hayden's familiar cry of, "Yo, Egghead." She couldn't help frowning. Then, when Hayden's laughter and talk filled the hallway, followed by a long, warbling wail from Edgar in the nearby bedroom, Sofia's face crumpled into a deadly scowl.

"You idiot," she muttered as Hayden walked in and she blustered past him out of the room.

When Sofia reached the bedroom, Edgar's wails were deafening. She immediately scooped him up, sat gently in the rocker by his crib, and with her free hand pulled up her blouse and fiddled with her nursing bra. Edgar didn't usually wake for his first nightly feed until midnight, but Sofia knew that there would be no getting him back to sleep without one, especially with her noisy brother-in-law in the apartment. So she sank back in the chair and pulled Edgar up to her breast. She couldn't fully relax, though. Jack's presence and now Hayden's had her feeling wired and annoyed. Tom's stupidity at letting Hayden come up made her even more agitated. To top things off, Edgar was clearly sensing Sofia's tension and wouldn't settle. With his little arms flailing, he fussed and cried and refused to latch on.

Five minutes later Edgar was still thrashing, mewing, and letting out intermittent wails, and Sofia was having no success getting him to feed. It seemed that the two of them were making each other more and more tense. Finally, pulling down her blouse, Sofia decided it was time to change tack. She'd take Edgar back out with her to the living room and perhaps the light and the distraction of other people would soothe him.

As it turned out, she was right. The moment she stepped back into the busy living room, Edgar relaxed in her arms and fell silent. Scared that his wails might resume, though, Sofia continued to stand, holding him high in her arms, swaying from side to side.

"Can I do anything to help?" Mary whispered as she stood up and moved close to Sofia.

No, Sofia mouthed, and, seeing the kindness and concern in Mary's eyes, she smiled and added, "But thanks."

On the other side of the room, Tom, Hayden, and Jack were in animated conversation.

"Sofe!" Tom said, finally spotting his wife. "How's he doing?" he asked, nodding toward the baby.

"Fine," she muttered, and then, shooting a stare in Hayden's direction, she said, "*Now* he's doing fine."

Hayden flashed her a doleful look with his pale eyes and said in a sheepish whisper, "Sorry, Sofia."

Sofia simply raised an eyebrow and said nothing.

Tom moved toward Sofia, a grin plastered across his face. "Guess what?" he sang out. "Jack has just let us in on some fantastic news. This fall, Manhattan U will be launching an Edgar Allan Poe research institute. It will be the first and *only* one in the country."

Sofia did the silent eyebrow raise again.

"Jack's already got the go-ahead from the president and secured monies for two full-time staff and four research fellows."

Although Tom was bubbling with enthusiasm, Sofia couldn't raise a smile. She couldn't let go of her suspicions about the dean. He had to be up to something; she could just feel it. And although it might all look wonderful and rosy for Tom now, Sofia was scared that whatever the dean was up to was going to backfire—probably in Tom's face.

Now it was Jack's turn to speak up. "Your brother-in-law, here," Jack said, thumping Hayden on the back, "has just said he will donate five hundred thousand dollars to the project."

"He did, did he?" Sofia hiccuped with shocked laughter.

Hayden puffed out his chest. "I did." He grinned. "The institute sounds great, and I want to help."

"Since when have you been interested in Edgar Allan Poe, Hayden?" Sofia inquired. Her incredulity was thinly disguised.

"I like Poe," he shot back defensively. Then he grinned and added, "My egghead bro digs him, so I dig him too."

"You *dig* him?" Sofia asked, cocking her head to one side. "Is that so?"

The dean, who'd clearly been ignoring this exchange between Sofia and Hayden, was now talking loudly to Tom.

"With your brother's donation, the Poe Research Institute can now be housed in offices on Third Street." He then added, "A Poe research institute could be nowhere else!"

Sofia's eyes snapped over to Jack. Did she just hear him right? Did the man who pulled down Poe's old house on Third Street just say what she thought he'd said? She looked from the dean around at the others. They were all smiling. Except Mary, though. Her face bore not a trace of a smile. Instead she glared over at her husband, her dark eyes fizzling with shock and consternation. As she looked at Mary, Sofia realized she wasn't the only one with suspicions. Jack's own wife had no idea what he was up to either, and she, like Sofia, looked highly skeptical about Jack's big announcement.

Sofia knew this was no time to make a scene or ask any probing questions, though. For one thing, she now had a sleeping baby in her arms to deal with.

In the end, she simply looked at Jack and said in a quiet voice, "It's a shame the old Poe house on Third Street was demolished. That really would have been the perfect place for your new institute."

With that, she turned on her heel and headed back to the bedroom.

Ten

Mary

While Mary sat on a small leather ottoman, her daughter, Sarah, twirled in front of her. Layers of ivory silk and tulle danced around Sarah's ankles as the sequins on the gown's bodice twinkled under the boutique's soft lights. A small veil embroidered with pearls and tiny silk flowers was clipped to Sarah's glossy dark hair and fluttered upward as she moved.

Mary sucked in a breath. "You look beautiful, honey, beautiful."

It was Saturday morning, and this was Sarah's final dress fitting before her wedding next month. Even though Mary had heard all about it, this was the first time she'd seen her daughter wearing her gown. As she watched Sarah twirl, shimmer, and smile, Mary couldn't stop the prick of happy tears in her eyes. She was so glad she'd stood up to Jack when the matter of Sarah's gown had come up a few months ago. Although Jack and Mary had more than enough money these days, and even though Sarah's wedding was going to be a very modest affair, Jack had tried to argue that Sarah's choice of gown was too expensive and that Sarah should pay half. Mary had dug her heels in, though. She knew she was risking one of Jack's tirades, but she did it anyway. Fortunately, Jack was preoccupied with some altercation he was having with Manhattan U's finance office, and in the end he backed down without too much of a fight. Since then, Mary had not mentioned the dress or the fittings. If he was reminded, Mary had no doubt Jack would find renewed energy to fight her on the issue.

"Beautiful? You really think so?" Sarah was now laughing. She'd come to a stop in front of the long silver mirror.

"Of course." Mary laughed too.

Sarah was just like her mother: jet-black hair, tall, wide shouldered, with a distinguished, angular jaw. She often complained
she looked like a man, and Mary knew exactly how she felt. When
she was Sarah's age she'd thought the same about her own height
and brooding dark face. As she got older and saw the same features flowering on her daughter, Mary came to realize how beautiful the look was, and how stupid she'd been, all those years, to see
herself as ugly and cumbersome.

But today, standing in front of the mirror, Mary saw Sarah's
eyes flicker with happiness, and she knew that at last her daughter
was seeing her own strong, dark beauty.

"Gorgeous," Mary whispered, standing up.

She moved forward and pressed her cheek to Sarah's, and,
with their same dark eyes staring into the mirror, the two of them
giggled.

They broke away from each other only when the boutique assistant moved toward them and asked Sarah, "How does it feel
here?" and tugged lightly at the waist of the bodice.

"Perfect." She glowed.

The woman frowned a little. "Are you sure? It's not a little
tight, is it?"

All three women looked down. Mary noticed that the silk was
straining just a little across Sarah's middle. She didn't say anything, remembering that the last thing a bride wanted to hear was
that she'd put on weight before her upcoming wedding.

"Perhaps I didn't let it out enough?" the assistant was now
saying.

Mary looked up at the woman, then at Sarah, her brow knitted
with confusion. Had they taken the dress out already? Sarah had
filled her mom in on every other detail about her dress fittings—
the fabrics that were swapped, the extra beads sewn on, the loose
button that had to be fixed. Yet she'd never mentioned that the
dress size had been altered.

Seeing her mother's inquisitive expression, Sarah blushed.
"Brenda, here"—she waved a flustered hand at the assistant—

"she's had to do a little work to the bodice. I think I've put on a few extra pounds recently. The excitement about the wedding makes me pig out," she added with a nervous giggle.

Mary found her eyes wandering back down Sarah's body. Perhaps she had gained some weight. But Sarah's figure was like Mary's, tall and straight, and thus it was hard to tell.

"But I think it will be fine," Sarah was now saying, as she sucked in her middle and looked at the dress in the mirror once again.

Brenda snapped the tape measure from around her neck and began winding it around her fingers. "Well, if you're sure it's okay, then it looks like we're done. Do you want to take the dress home today?"

Sarah looked sheepishly at her mother. "Can we?"

"Of course," Mary said with a grin. "Let me get my purse and we'll pay for it right now."

She walked back toward the ottoman, picked up her soft leather purse, and began rifling through it for her credit cards. As her fingers brushed against old receipts, tubes of lipstick, a Metro-Card, and two tampons, she found no wallet. Her heart sank. How could she have forgotten it? She suddenly had an image of her own mother bent over the enormous purse she used to carry, her wild red hair falling across her wrinkled yet beautiful face, and tutting over whatever it was she couldn't find. *I'm getting that old,* Mary thought with a frown.

It was her age—or perhaps it had more to do with Jack. As each day passed, as each hour and minute went by, he was getting under Mary's skin more and more. He hadn't hurt her again, but everything he did and said annoyed her. His smoking, his whiskey glass clinking, the smell of his aftershave, his books on Poe hogging the hallway table, his pompous behavior at Tom and Sofia's place the other night. Even the sight of his recently used toothbrush was enough to make her feel edgy and irritable. And the more Jack got under her skin, the more flustered, distracted, and scattered Mary felt. She wasn't just forgetting her wallet, like today; she was forgetting to e-mail colleagues, hunting for books that she'd already returned to the library, and showing up for her office hours on the wrong afternoon. Even if Jack was not nearby, his presence in her life made her flustered and anxious. She couldn't help yearning for the day, in just a few weeks, when she would leave New York. She'd be sad to leave behind Sarah and her fiancé, Greg, but in San Francisco Mary was convinced she'd be able to think properly, see properly, and be a whole person once again.

"Honey," Mary said, shaking her head and looking from her purse to Sarah, "it looks like I've forgotten my wallet."

"Don't worry, Mrs. Havemeyer," the assistant interjected. "You can settle up later."

"No, no." Mary waved her hand. "I live just a few blocks away. I'll run home now; it won't take a second."

"Mom. It's fine. We'll come back another day."

Mary shook her head, adamantly this time. "No, I want you to take your dress today, Sarah. Finish your champagne while I'm gone," she said, nodding to the flutes of champagne they'd barely touched.

Before Sarah could protest any more, Mary was out onto the SoHo sidewalk, trotting up Mercer Street toward home.

To save time, Mary decided to take the shortcut that ran between the two Manhattan U apartment buildings and alongside the garden. As she rounded the corner and saw the familiar red maple tree looming over the garden fence, she heard loud voices and the sound of a drum beating. She stopped abruptly on the gravel path. The protest. Today was the day of the protest. A lump rose in her throat. She didn't want to go past. Sofia would see her—they would all see her—and what if they asked her to join them? She'd want to, of course, but Jack was around today—unusually for a Saturday he wasn't on a golf course—and what if he saw her?

Then there was Sarah. She couldn't leave her standing and waiting in the bridal boutique. Mary raised her wrist and looked at her watch. She'd been gone only five minutes, and if she hurried, she still had time to go the long way around to the front of her apartment building. So, turning on her heel, she began to jog back the way she came.

"Excuse me." A male voice brought Mary to a halt again.

She looked up to see a tall man with a close-cut gray beard and even grayer eyes a few paces in front of her.

"I'm sorry," he went on. "I'm looking for the garden."

Mary jerked her thumb over her shoulder and said, "Just there."

She was about to move off again when the man's gray eyes flickered with recognition. "Are you"—he blinked—"are you Mary Havemeyer?"

Mary was thrown for a second. "Yes," she finally replied.

"I'm a fan," he explained. "*Casey's Echoes*. I love it."

Mary thanked him, and the man flashed a warm smile, the laugh lines around his eyes deepening into long arcs. He then peered over Mary's shoulder toward the garden and said, "Perhaps I'm in the wrong place. There's supposed to be a protest here, but I can't see anyone."

Mary turned to look. He was right. Through the fence they could see the garden, but it was empty.

"They're probably meeting at the gate," she said. "Follow this path around to the right."

"Thanks," he replied. Then, after a brief pause, his light eyes twinkled. "You're not going then? To the protest?"

Mary opened her mouth to answer, but the man interjected.

"We could fight the power together." He chuckled as he gave a playful wiggle of his eyebrows.

Something about the man—his kind demeanor, his pale eyes, his lighthearted smile—something about him was disarming, and before Mary knew it she found herself rambling on about Sarah, the wedding dress, her credit cards. As she chattered on, she felt slightly giddy and girlish, and for some reason she even confessed to the stranger that her husband wasn't happy about the price tag on Sarah's gown.

"But I support it. The protest, I mean," Mary muttered finally, realizing she was making a fool of herself and needing to change the subject.

The man was looking at her with an intense gaze, saying nothing. Mary couldn't help noticing how his shirt, which lay open over the V-neck of his dark cashmere sweater, was the exact same shade as his eyes. She also noticed his elegant hands, one of which was holding a battered leather journal. He could be a professor, she supposed. But then again he seemed too stylish, too self-possessed, and so unlike the middle-aged professors she worked with, who were more like sacks of neuroses wrapped up in corduroy and tweed. As she looked at him again, quite unexpectedly something tingled at the nape of Mary's neck, and she could feel herself beginning to blush under his gaze.

"What's your interest in the protest?" she asked, trying to snap herself out of whatever it was she was feeling. "Are you on the faculty?"

The man blinked. "No." He laughed. "No, no. I'm way too dumb to be a professor. No, I'm covering the protest for the *New York Mail*."

Mary's heart leaped to her throat, and her palms pricked with panic. This was all she needed. There she was thinking how kind and composed and—yes, she had to admit it—how attractive this man was. But it was all a ruse. He was just some hack from a tabloid newspaper out for a story. Mary shuddered a little. He knew who she was, and no doubt he knew who Jack was too. It would all make such a great headline: *University Dean and Wife at War over Garden*, or something like that.

Nudging her purse higher onto her shoulder, Mary gave a tight smile. "I must get going. My daughter's waiting."

The man's forehead furrowed for a second, but then he quickly followed up with a polite nod. "Yes, of course."

Mary nodded back, muttered a terse, "Good-bye," and resumed her hurried journey along the gravel path.

She didn't look back, but she knew the man's eyes were upon her.

When she reached the apartment, Mary was still flustered. She grappled clumsily with her door keys and ended up dropping them twice onto the hallway floor. As she leaned over to pick them up the second time, the front door clicked and creaked open.

"What *are* you doing?" Jack's voice blustered out above her.

"What does it look like I'm doing?" she snapped.

As the words escaped her she immediately regretted them. Even though Jack had been getting under her skin, she'd been doing well at not rising to his bait, at keeping a low profile, at living like a silent shadow in her own apartment. It was paying off. She and Jack were saying very little to each other, and when they did it was polite and restrained. He had no inkling, she was sure, of her plans to leave, and she wanted it to remain that way until the moment she walked out the door.

There had been moments when it was excruciatingly hard to stay calm in Jack's presence. Like the other night at Sofia and Tom's place, when Jack was so overbearing, dominating every conversation and not stopping once to commend Sofia on her exquisite food. Mary had squirmed with embarrassment and silent fury all night long. She felt guilty and cowardly too. She wanted to say something to Jack, to tell him to shut up, and to apologize to Sofia for his awful behavior. If it had been one of her students behaving so impolitely, or her daughter (not that Sarah ever would), Mary would have pounced. Because it was Jack, because Mary was desperate not to incite his fury, she just sat there all evening, frozen and speechless.

"What did you say?"

Mary heard a familiar crackle of anger in Jack's question, and right away her heart began to thud.

"Nothing," she mumbled as she straightened up and began moving past him into the apartment.

Once inside she scurried toward the bedroom. Behind her Jack closed the front door with a bang and made a loud tutting sound. It was clear he was gearing up for a fight. Mary kept walking, though.

She figured that if she could just collect her wallet from the top of her dresser and quickly leave the house, the situation would defuse. She would come home later and his anger would be forgotten. It was only the times when she stood up to him, the times she argued her point, that he got really mad and then violent.

But as she reached her bedroom, she heard Jack's thudding footsteps behind her. He wasn't going to make this easy. He was going to try to force her into a confrontation; she could feel it. What was it today? she wondered. What was making him so mad? Then she remembered the protest. He must know about it, she thought, feeling her chest swelling with panic. Perhaps he knew she'd spoken to the other women about it. Did he think she'd engineered the whole thing? He'd been gloating for weeks about how his parking lot plans were going ahead. This protest and Mary's involvement with the organizers, however brief, were going to make him mad as hell.

Mary moved quickly toward her dresser, and, reaching out for her small leather purse, her hands shook with fear and rage. She was scared about the confrontation that was about to happen, but mostly she was angry: angry because she wanted to fight it out with him and tell him what a mean, egotistical, power-hungry, and violent man he had turned out to be. She wanted to yell into his face, *You have become your father!* If she wanted to slip out of his life without him interfering, though, she had to keep her cool.

"Mary," Jack barked from the doorway.

The phone trilled out from the living room.

"Damn it," hissed Jack, and after a short pause, as he considered whether to answer or let the phone ring, he turned and left the bedroom.

With her hand clasped around the wallet and her mouth dry, Mary stood motionless. She listened as Jack picked up the jangling phone.

"Hello," he snapped, and after a few beats he chuckled. "David. Hi." His tone was now bright and breezy; all traces of anger had evaporated.

Mary breathed out slowly. The storm had passed. She was safe. David was dean of Manhattan U's medical school, and Jack's golfing buddy. He was also just about the only person who could make Jack smile these days.

As Mary began tiptoeing out the bedroom, she stuffed her wallet into her purse.

"No, no," she heard Jack saying. "No, it's just some lame-ass protest. Uh-huh. A bunch of women."

Mary stopped.

"No." He laughed. "They're not faculty. Just some wives, some pissy wives."

Holding her breath, Mary peeked through to the living room. Jack was standing in front of the large picture window letting out peals of crowing laughter and peering outside—at the garden thirty floors below, no doubt. Every hair on Mary's body prickled as she watched his shoulders heave up and down.

"Don't worry." Jack chuckled on. "I had the locks changed; they can't get in. Nope. Yes. I have the new key."

Just as Jack uttered the words, Mary's eyes drifted to the small table next to the front door. In the glow of a nearby lamp a clutch of keys glinted on the polished tabletop. Breaking into a tiptoeing trot, Mary scooted forward, grabbed the keys, and slipped out the door.

Marching to the elevator, she flicked through the keys. A silver dead-bolt key shone out among the others. That must be it, she thought; it had to be. She bundled the keys into her other hand, delved into her purse, and pulled out her cell. Quickly she scrolled down to Sarah's number and pressed call.

"Honey," she said when Sarah picked up, "there's been a change of plans."

Eleven

Hannah

Hannah stood next to Sofia as Sofia jostled and tugged at the garden gate.

"I can't believe this," Sofia was saying over and over, her knuckles turning white on the metal handle.

"Try my key again," Hannah offered.

Sofia huffed, snatched the key from Hannah's palm, and plunged it into the lock. Just like the last time they tried, it did nothing.

"The lock's been changed," Sofia growled. "Havemeyer did this; I'm sure of it."

"You think?" Hannah said as Sofia began shaking the gate again.

"No doubt about it." Sofia grimaced.

After a couple more clanking rattles, Hannah laid her hand on Sofia's arm. "Come on," she coaxed. "It doesn't matter. We'll just protest outside instead."

"But we're supposed to be having a sit-in," Sofia hissed angrily. "How can we sit in with no place to sit?"

Hannah moved her hand to Sofia's shoulder and gently pulled her around. "Look," she said, waving toward the path in front of the garden. "Look how many people have shown up."

The two of them scanned the assembled crowd. People were squeezed along the pathway, packed against nearby shrubs, and even spilling out onto the sidewalk beyond. There was a hum of laughter and chattering voices. A couple with matching gray hair clasped homemade banners that read, SAVE OUR GARDEN and TREES NOT CARS, and a young woman dressed in a flowing tie-dyed blouse sat cross-legged on the gravel, beating gaily on a small clay drum.

Taking in the scene, Hannah sucked in a quick breath. She couldn't believe their last-minute flyer and poster campaign and the small announcement in the campus newspaper had attracted so many people. She sneaked a look at Sofia and was pleased to see her recently raging eyes were now wide and twinkling.

"You're right," Sofia said, catching Hannah's glance, "we'll do it here. In fact"—she waved her hands in excitement—"we should march around the garden, you know, like a procession."

Hannah began to nod, but Sofia had already raised her hand to her mouth and was shouting to the people in front of her.

"Okay, folks," she bellowed, "looks like we've been locked out." The crowd booed and jeered. "But that won't stop us!" Sofia added, punching the air with her fist. "The protest must go on."

This was met with whooping and cheering, and the girl with the drum shouted, "We shall overcome," causing a ripple of laughter.

After the crowd had laughed, cheered, and chanted some more, Sofia informed everyone of her new plan.

"We'll circle the garden," she explained, "until we can't walk anymore."

After encouraging everyone to sign the petition that was being handed around, Sofia plowed through the crowd to lead the procession. Hannah followed a few paces behind. As she watched Sofia maneuvering her way along the path with her upright stride, head held high, and her dark curls flying up in the breeze, Hannah wished she could be more like her. If she had even just one ounce of Sofia's gusto and spirit, Hannah was sure she wouldn't be on her way to California in a few weeks. She wouldn't be giving up the city she loved and the MFA and studio that were her whole life.

Jostled amongst the crowd that was now swarming behind Sofia, Hannah felt a pulse of frustration beat in her temples. Why had she agreed to go to California? Why? She hadn't agreed straightaway, of course. After the anniversary party at Bill and Diane's, Hannah and Michael had fought all the way home on the subway in hissed whispers. When they got to their apartment, the argument continued long into the night at a much louder volume.

"But what about my MFA?" Hannah remembered shouting, her voice ringing in her own ears.

She had sat on their couch, her arms crossed tightly over her chest. Michael stood by the window, looking out at the night sky and rubbing the bridge of his nose with his thumb and forefinger.

"You can pick it up again when we get back," Michael snapped, frustrated that the argument was still continuing. "This fellowship is just a year, Hann. Just a year." Then, with a heavy sigh, he said what he'd been repeating over and over since their fight began: "It's an amazing opportunity, Hannah. I thought you'd be more supportive."

Shaking her head, Hannah asked, "Why didn't you tell me, Michael? Why didn't you tell me you were applying? Isn't this something we should decide on together? From the start?"

Michael's forehead furrowed and his brown eyes took on a steely glare. "Do I have to run everything past you?"

"No, of course not," Hannah replied. "I just like to be kept in the loop sometimes. These days you are always working, always tapping away on that computer of yours. I hear you typing more than I hear you talk."

"I'm busy, Hannah," Michael barked, his eyes still flinty and annoyed. "You probably don't know what busy means. Swanning about painting pictures all day? That isn't *busy*."

His words were like a punch in Hannah's gut. She'd always suspected that this was what he thought, but he'd never actually said it.

"So that's what you think of me, is it?" she asked, her voice strangled and breathless. "I'm a time-wasting, dallying-about art student, is that it?"

Michael was now shaking his head. "I didn't mean it like that. I just meant you don't understand how busy I am. You don't understand my work, so there is no point keeping you 'in the loop.'" He flicked his fingers in quotation signs as he echoed Hannah's words.

"Oh, so now I don't understand your work either?" Hannah

lobbed back, her cheeks flaming. "Perhaps if you talked to me sometimes, told me what you're up to, like you used to in the old days, perhaps I would."

Michael was shaking his head again. "You're overreacting." He sighed. "The ins and outs of the grants and scholarships I apply for would take a lot of explaining. You wouldn't want to hear it, and I haven't got the time to go through it."

"It wouldn't take two seconds to ask me, 'Hey, do you mind if we go California for a year?'" Hannah blurted out.

Michael was silent for a second, and then he held up his hands and muttered, "Okay, okay, I'm sorry I didn't run it past you. But, Hannah, this is an amazing project." His eyes began to glint with excitement. "I have to go. I have to."

"If you *have* to go," Hannah sneered, "then I suppose that's that."

But as the words escaped her, it suddenly struck Hannah how bitchy and snippy she was sounding, and a feeling of doubt began to grow in her chest. Perhaps she *was* overreacting. Perhaps Michael *had* just wanted to surprise her, and perhaps he'd thought it was something she would be pleased about. Hannah snapped her mouth closed and looked over at her husband. His face—a handsome and haunting mix of his dad's dark eyes and his mom's wide mouth—looked back at her. Decent and generous Michael, she thought. He could be distant and unthinking at times, and he didn't really understand her like she once thought he might, but he was good to her. He supported her, he made it possible for her to pursue her degree, and his parents were angels. Was she being unfair to be so hard on him? After all, she was the one who'd cheated and lied and broken their wedding vows, not Michael.

Feeling a surge of guilt, Hannah looked down, and as she did so she glimpsed her belly pooching above her skirt. After Michael announced his news earlier and their argument began, Hannah forgot her pregnancy worries. But in an instant they'd returned, and another wave of guilt shuddered through her. Could she really be pregnant? And was there really any chance the baby could be Patrick's? She blinked heavily and continued to gaze down at her middle. No, she thought, if she was pregnant it had to be Michael's. It had to be.

As she and Michael sat in silence, her mind kept swirling. If it was Michael's, she wondered, perhaps it wouldn't be so bad. He would be a good dad; there was no question about that. Plus, she'd always wanted kids, and it was probably time to think about having her first. She'd be thirty-five in a couple of years, and wasn't that when women's fertility dropped by half? Hannah's mind then jumped to thoughts of California. As Michael said, it would be for only a year, and then they would be back in New York. She could finish grad school, and if it did turn out she was going to have a baby, she could work in her studio at those times Michael's parents weren't seeing patients and could babysit downstairs.

The thought of having a child terrified her, but the accompanying thought of Bill and Diane as doting grandparents gave her a small kick of pleasure, and a smile flashed across her face.

"What is it?" Michael asked, seeing her change of expression.

Hannah took a deep breath. "You're right," she whispered. "It's a great opportunity for you, and it's only for a year."

But as Michael gave a satisfied nod, clearly pleased that their argument had come to an end, a memory of Patrick fluttered through Hannah's mind. For a brief second she saw him in his dark linen shirt, sitting across the bistro's candlelit table, his head cocked slightly and his thoughtful brow furrowed as he carefully listened to her talk. Her spine tingled momentarily, but as she looked again at Michael, the tingle was swiftly replaced by a gnawing sadness in the bottom of her stomach.

Now, a week later, as she walked among the happy, chanting protestors outside the garden, the gnawing feeling persisted. In fact, during the week it had gotten worse, and was now coupled with the throb in her temples. At first she'd tried to convince herself that California was the only good and right thing to do, and she'd told Michael she was okay with the plan, so she couldn't back out. As the hours and days passed, though, Hannah's uncertainty and sadness grew.

None of this was helped by the fact that Hannah's period still hadn't come. Every morning she was convinced she could feel the twinges in her abdomen that always signaled her period, but then nothing happened. She was too scared to do a pregnancy test, however, and an unopened Clearblue box had loitered at the bottom of her purse all week. She'd made a promise to herself that she would do it today, the day of the protest, but as she ambled among the crowd, watching Sofia's bobbing curls leading the procession ahead of her, she doubted she would. The thought of seeing two blue lines shimmering into focus in the plastic wand's small window was too frightening.

"What's going on?" a voice nearby demanded.

Startled, Hannah turned to see a short woman looking up at her. The woman was pointing ahead of them, and she clearly wanted to know why the impromptu procession had ground to a halt.

"Wait a second," Hannah said as she moved forward, pushing her way through the gaggle of protestors in front of her.

As she approached Sofia, she could hear her shouting.

"You have to be kidding." Sofia stood with her hands on her hips in front of two Manhattan U security guards. Flames of anger were flashing in her eyes once again.

"Sofia?" Hannah whispered urgently. "What is it?"

Continuing to glare at the uniformed men, Sofia barked, "Apparently, we're not allowed to proceed along this path. Apparently," she spat again, "we are *contravening* fire codes."

Hannah looked from Sofia to the two guys. Now it was her turn to lose her cool. *"What?"* she hissed.

"Ma'am?" The taller of the two guards looked at Hannah and waved his hands in the air, gesturing for calm. "They're the rules. I'm just telling it like it is." He then folded his arms across his large chest and planted his feet wide in the pathway.

Unfazed by the guard's defiant pose, Sofia stepped closer and whispered near his ear, "Where do you suggest we go, *sir*?"

"Not our problem, ladies," said the shorter guy, overhearing Sofia's question.

Angered by his patronizing tone, Hannah moved forward. Just as she was about to open her mouth, however, she felt a hand on her shoulder. She whirled around, expecting to see another security guard, or perhaps Dean Havemeyer himself—no doubt he'd sent these guards—but instead she came face-to-face with the dean's wife, Mary. Although Hannah had met her only once, that dark night in the garden, she knew it was her. But Hannah had no idea what Mary was doing here. Had Jack sent her?

While Hannah was temporarily lost for words, Mary smiled.

"Hi, Hannah," she said, effortlessly remembering Hannah's name. Mary then turned to Sofia and jingled a set of keys on her outstretched finger. "These might help." She grinned.

Moving away from the security guards, who were eyeing Mary suspiciously, Sofia looked both surprised and confused.

"Your keys?" she said, tentatively taking them into her hands.

"One of those—that shiny silver one"—she nodded—"will get you into the garden." She then gave a mischievous wink and added, "I mean, it will get *us* into the garden."

Sofia's eyes scanned the keys and then Mary's face. "For real?" She beamed.

"Yup." Mary grinned back.

Letting out a delighted whoop, Sofia threw her arms around Mary and then Hannah. "Come on, *ladies,*" she cried, giving a quick sideways glare at the two guards. "Let's get this party started."

Hannah looked at the two smiling women in front of her and smiled too. For a second all her worries were forgotten.

It was a perfect afternoon. The low gray clouds that hung over the city earlier had been replaced by one of the dazzling blue New York skies that Hannah loved so much. The garden was now bathed in golden sunshine, and strung to the fence, the paper banners that Hannah had painted the day before fluttered in a warm breeze. Across the grass people sat on blankets, sprawled on their backs, or stood in small groups shielding their eyes from the sun. A small white dog chased its tail under the shade of the red maple tree.

Sofia's family had arrived, and from where Hannah sat on a bench she could see Sofia jiggling the baby in her arms. Nearby, her husband lay in the grass lifting Gracie with his feet into the air. "Ai-plane, ai-plane," Gracie squealed. On an adjacent bench Mary sat with Sam, Ashleigh's girlfriend, who'd brought boxes and boxes of pizza, which had already been devoured by the hungry protesters. Over empty paper plates the two women were in deep conversation and nodded gravely from time to time. An older man with a distinguished gray beard hovered to the left of them, scanning the garden and scribbling notes in a small spiral-bound pad.

Hannah's eyes drifted over to the gate. Michael said he'd come, and it surprised her that he hadn't arrived yet. He didn't give a damn about the protest; that was for sure. But he did give a damn about Hannah being there. She knew he was still worried that her involvement in the protest would reflect badly on him, and he wanted to keep tabs on her, or at least keep tabs on the hordes of paparazzi that he imagined showing up. Hannah let out an amused snort and glanced over at the guy with the notebook. He could be press, she supposed. But the protest wasn't exactly the news event of the century. She hadn't seen one camera, let alone a news van.

She looked back toward the gate. People had been wandering in all afternoon, and now a woman carrying a sun chair under her arm ambled into the garden. Just as the woman was about to close the gate, she stopped and held it for someone behind her. Hannah shifted forward and squinted through the sunlight to see if it was Michael. As a familiar figure bobbed into sight, Hannah's stomach kicked and somersaulted.

It wasn't Michael. It was Patrick.

As he walked into the garden he scanned the scene. At first he didn't see Hannah, but as he walked a few more paces his eyes found hers. She wanted to run and hide, but at the same time she didn't want to be anywhere else but under Patrick's gaze.

The first time Hannah's own eyes had found Patrick, she was

captivated. He had breezed into Hannah's classroom, his black shirt undone, his wavy hair peppered with gray tucked behind his ears, and his green eyes shining. He had a handsomeness she'd never encountered before. He wasn't clean-cut or wholesomely attractive like Michael. He didn't have the brooding eyes or the striking chiseled features of the pretty boys she used to date in her modeling days, either. There was something inquisitive, mature, and sparkling about Patrick's good looks, something enchanting and unique. When Patrick introduced himself to the class and Hannah heard his soft British accent for the first time, something shifted and thudded inside her. She was overwhelmed with a strange mixture of nausea, dread, and excitement. This man, she knew instantly, would cause her to lie awake at night fantasizing and wondering. He'd drive her to the library for endless hours as she tried to write art theory papers that would please him, excite him, even. As Hannah gazed at Patrick's long fingers as he scrawled his name on the whiteboard, she knew that even though she was now a married woman, she was on the verge of the second big crush of her life. Her first crush had been when she was fifteen, and started when Mr. Norman, a dashing young history teacher, strolled into her classroom and chalked his name on the board just as Patrick had done.

All her initial intuitions were right. After her very first class with Patrick she couldn't stop looking at him, thinking about him, daydreaming about him. In class she loved to study his soft green eyes and hear his gentle, long vowels as he spoke. She'd watch and smile as he pushed back his thick hair when he got passionate about a topic. Most of all, though, it was what Patrick said that enthralled her. Everything he said about art and theory and the world rang true with Hannah. In fact, she didn't have to labor too hard over her papers for his class because she and Patrick seemed to be coming from the same place. Her papers flowed effortlessly, and Patrick loved them, awarding them As every time. Often after class he'd pull her to one side and, leaning on the desk in front of the chalkboard, they would talk about what she'd written or the comments she'd made in class. Their conversations were peppered with words like *surrealism, psychoanalysis, formalism,* and *Marx*—words that Hannah never imagined herself using with such unself-conscious ease. And when she spoke, Patrick would nod and listen intently to every word.

Now, as he walked across the garden toward her, the afternoon sun twinkling in those familiar green eyes, every part of Hannah ached for him. She wanted to talk to him, listen to him, touch him, be held by him. It filled her with guilt, but she couldn't help it. She'd never been drawn to anyone like this before, not even Michael.

"Hello," Patrick said, his familiar gentle vowels coupled with his even gentler smile.

Hannah stood up from the bench. "Hey," she whispered.

For an awkward second neither of them knew what to say or do. Hannah moved forward as it occurred to her she should greet him properly, with a hug or perhaps a kiss on the cheek. But then she caught herself, remembering who he was and where they were. She couldn't kiss her professor, not now and especially not here.

Seeing Hannah falter, Patrick looked down at his shoes and then out toward the bustling garden. "I, um," he began and then, turning back to look at Hannah, he continued, "I'm glad I saw you."

"I'm sorry I haven't made it to class. It's been kind of crazy," she blurted, but realizing how much she sounded like some kid who'd cut eighth-grade math, she snapped her mouth shut and blushed.

"I understand. Not a problem." Hannah looked up to see Patrick smiling again. "It's just . . . there's something I want to ask you," he added.

Hannah tensed. What was he going to ask? Was he going to ask her to see him again? For a date, perhaps? But he knew she was married; would he really do that? Her pulse raced with dread—and excitement.

"I'm putting together a panel for this fall's College Art Association conference. It's going to be here in New York." He nodded toward the skyline. "I was wondering if you'd like to submit a paper. I think your piece on the Impressionists would be a great fit."

Hannah couldn't speak. She was immensely flattered. Giving a paper at the College Art Association's conference was a big deal. Some of the world's top art academics gave keynote papers, and only a few grad students ever got seats on the CAA's prestigious panels. Yet Hannah was at the same time crushed. All traces of intimacy seemed to have disappeared between them, and she realized, as Patrick spoke, that they were back to being professor and student again, nothing more.

Aware of her hesitation, Patrick nodded and said, "I'm sure you need to think it over."

She wanted to jump in and say she would do it. But she remained silent. *Don't be absurd,* she thought. *In the fall I'm going to be in California and possibly pregnant.* There was no way she could come back to New York and give a conference paper, not like that. And having to keep up this "we're just colleagues" shtick would kill her.

So, instead, Hannah glanced up at Patrick, trying not to look at the black curl that had fallen across his eye, and said with strained politeness, "Thank you. Thank you so much for considering me, Patrick, but"—she had to look away as she said the next part—"I'm not going to be here in the fall. I . . . we . . . Michael and I, we're moving to Stanford."

"Oh," said Patrick, his eyebrows knitting together. "What about your MFA? Are you transferring?"

Hannah waggled her head. "I'm just taking a break for a year."

"Right. I see," he said, not looking like he understood at all.

Once again an awkwardness hung between them. Silently Hannah begged Patrick to say something, to tell her she shouldn't go, to plead with her, to ask her to leave Michael and be with him. But he didn't. He just looked at her with his pale green eyes and said nothing.

Only when a voice close to Hannah's ear said, "Hey," did the silence break.

Hannah spun around and came face-to-face with Michael. "Hi," Hannah barked out, shocked and flustered by his sudden arrival.

She was silent for a second, and then she nervously jabbered, "Michael, this is Patrick, one of my professors. And, Patrick, this is Michael, my husband." The last word caught in her throat, and she covered her stumble with a small cough.

"Pleased to meet you," Patrick said as the two men shook hands. He seemed calm, but Hannah could tell by an almost imperceptible pulse in his jaw that he was as tense as she was.

"What's it like having Hannah here in your class?" Michael smirked, his eyes amused.

Hannah raised her eyebrows and glanced curiously at Michael. She rarely saw him look so playful these days.

"She's a very talented student," Patrick was saying, with a slight flush coloring his cheeks.

"I bet all the other students want to paint her." Michael grinned.

Hannah blushed and gave Michael a sharp nudge in his ribs. Patrick looked bemused.

"Sorry?" he asked.

Michael ignored Hannah's glare and went on. "Hannah used to be a very talented model, and very successful, as you probably know."

"I didn't know," Patrick said quietly, his baffled eyes shifting from Michael to Hannah.

"You might want to use her skills in your classes." Michael chuckled. "She could pose. No nude stuff, though," he added with a wag of his finger.

"Patrick is an art theory professor," snapped Hannah, her cheeks now on fire. "No one *poses* in his class."

Then, desperately trying to think of a way this awful encounter could be brought to an end, she snatched a brief but meaningful look at Patrick and asked, "Have you signed the petition yet?"

"Ah, yes, I must pop over and do that." Patrick nodded, immediately picking up on his cue. "Lovely to meet you, Michael, and see you soon, Hannah." He then ducked his head and moved off into the garden.

As soon as he was out of earshot, Hannah turned on Michael. "Why did you bring that up?" she demanded. "Why did you have to talk about me being a model?"

Michael's eyes were off scanning the garden. "Why not?" he said with a distracted shrug. Then, glancing back at Hannah, he added, "You should be proud of who you are, Hann. You shouldn't hide it."

"But that's not who I am anymore, Michael." Hannah hated her angry tone, especially on such a beautiful day, but she couldn't help it.

Michael wasn't listening, though. "There he is," he said with a grin, as his arm shot in the air and he waved to someone on the other side of the garden.

"Hey, Charlie," he shouted as he started to bound off across the grass.

A short while later the sun was setting, throwing long streaks of orange and gold across the garden. The crowd had thinned out, but there was still a gentle buzz of laughter and voices. Hannah was cross-legged on the grass with Gracie in her lap. Together they were picking tiny blades of grass and blowing them up into the air with their cheeks puffed out and lips pursed. Gracie whooped and squealed as the specks of green fluttered down onto her eyelids and nose.

With the little girl in her lap and the warmth of the late sun on her shoulders, Hannah felt happier, even though Michael stood nearby laughing and chatting with Charlie, one of his colleagues from the computer science department. She still couldn't believe he'd said what he'd said to Patrick. As the moment passed, however, she reminded herself that it was she who was in the wrong, not Michael. He might have brought up her modeling and embarrassed her, but she was the one who'd been unfaithful. She really had no right to be mad at him.

From time to time the wind would change or the noise in the garden would hit a lull, and Hannah would hear a snippet of Michael and Charlie's conversation.

"You're the bomb," she heard Charlie saying as he jabbed at Michael's arm. "I still can't believe it, man. The Athena project? That's awesome," he added, shaking his head and then whistling.

"I'm telling you, dude." Michael beamed. "I'm psyched."

Hannah frowned a little. Michael and Charlie always did this when they got together, talked like a pair of surf buddies hanging out on Laguna Beach. The reality, of course, was that they were a pair of big-brained academics who'd probably never touched a surfboard in their lives, let alone ridden a wave.

Hannah didn't quite catch what Charlie said next, but the words *babes* and *beach* were audible. She frowned again as she remembered why she'd never really liked Charlie. Whenever she got stuck talking to him at faculty mixers or dinners with Michael's colleagues, which seemed to happen a lot, Charlie's eyes never focused on her face. Instead they wandered down to her chest, hips, and legs, and as they lingered there he'd make jokes about Hannah's model friends and whether she could give him their numbers. Hannah was used to this kind of creepiness from guys, but she was disappointed to find it at the university, especially coming from one of Michael's favorite colleagues.

As Hannah felt her mood dipping again, she noticed that Michael and Charlie had begun talking in animated whispers. They grinned and raised their eyebrows at each other. Hannah hadn't seen Michael look this amused in months. She kept watching and noticed that every now and then Michael would shoot a look in Hannah's direction, as if making sure she wasn't listening. Of course, this spiked Hannah's curiosity, and she tried harder to hear what was being said. With Gracie burbling and giggling in her lap, it was difficult. Although, she did catch Charlie asking, "Did you get the last one I sent?" and when Michael nodded, Charlie said something about Russians being the best, and how "they are so stunning it hurts, man."

On the other side of the garden the girl with the drum started up again, and Michael and Charlie's conversation was lost among the thumping beat and the accompanying cheers and shouts from the gathered crowd. At the same moment a shadow loomed over Hannah, and she sensed someone standing near her. She looked up, squinting into the evening sun. The man with the gray beard, the one she'd seen earlier scribbling in a notepad, was smiling down at her.

"Sorry to disturb you," he said, continuing to smile his sparkly smile. "But I was told by, um"—he consulted his notepad—"by Sofia that you helped organize the protest."

Hannah gave a hesitant nod. After Michael's worrying about Hannah's involvement, she couldn't help feeling a little nervous about speaking to someone who was clearly a reporter. However, if Sofia had already talked to him, then perhaps it was okay, she reasoned.

The man crouched down beside Hannah, and, after saying a sweet hello to Gracie, he asked Hannah, "Could I ask you a couple of questions? I'm writing a story for the *New York Mail*. My name's Jerry Milo, by the way."

Hannah looked from Jerry over at Michael, who was still whispering and chuckling with Charlie. Seeing Michael being so jovial, not like he ever was with her nowadays, she felt an unexpected kick of annoyance and so turned back to the reporter and said, "Sure."

Rearranging himself into a cross-legged position on the grass beside her, Jerry asked a few questions about why Hannah had gotten involved with this afternoon's protest. She told him about how she often painted in the garden and how she loved its tranquillity. Then the two of them talked about the disappearance of gardens like this one in New York City.

"Back in the eighties," Jerry told her with a nostalgic grin, "I spent a lot of time in the East Village protesting against the real estate developments that were eating up the urban gardens."

Hannah smiled and said, "So you're an old hat at this game then."

"Kind of." He chuckled.

As she played with one of Gracie's wayward curls, Hannah chuckled too and said absently, "Was it the evil Dean Havemeyer pulling down those gardens too?"

Jerry sat upright. "Dean who?"

Hannah immediately regretted what she'd said. She'd assumed Sofia would have already talked about the dean, but clearly she hadn't.

"Did you say Dean Havemeyer?" Jerry persisted.

"Um, yes," Hannah replied in a nervous murmur. "He's not really evil," she backpedaled, thinking about Michael's precious job. "It's just that he's the one who's been in charge of this whole parking lot project."

Jerry's eyebrows were raised. "I see. And his name is Have . . ."

Luckily Gracie chose this moment to get fidgety. She'd moved sideways in Hannah's lap and was now pinching a short lock of Hannah's cropped hair in her small fingers.

"Red 'air," she said, a smile spreading across her pretty face.

"You like it?" Hannah asked, relieved to have the distraction and not to have to answer Jerry's questions.

Gracie gave a furious nod. "Like it."

As Hannah laughed and pulled the toddler in for a hug, Jerry clearly sensed that Hannah no longer wanted to talk. Their conversation was over.

"Thanks so much, Hannah," he said, beginning to get to his feet. "You've been a great help."

Over Gracie's dark curls, Hannah watched him stride off across the garden. Her heart fluttered a little as she wondered whether she'd said too much. She was soon distracted, though, as her eyes settled on Patrick standing by the garden's open gate. He'd been drifting around talking to people since he'd arrived. Although he now had his back to her, she could see that he was laughing with a pretty woman in a yellow sundress. Jealousy bolted through Hannah, and immediately she pulled her eyes away. She couldn't watch; it was too painful. Instead she looked down at Gracie and then up at Michael and tried to remind herself that *this* was her husband, the man she loved, the man she might even have a child with soon. But as she studied him further, he seemed more and more like a stranger, and more and more like someone she used to know and used to love.

Before long, the gnawing feeling returned to the pit of Hannah's stomach.

Twelve

Ashleigh

Four hours away in DC, Ashleigh stood at the window of her childhood bedroom and looked out at the setting sun. She couldn't stop staring even though it was burning hazy red spots onto her retinas. It was so beautiful, teetering above the neighbor's pine trees and glowing like a Christmas bauble. But it was kind of sad too. There was something mournful about its golden rays and the dappled pink clouds. Tears pricked in Ashleigh's eyes, and she blinked hard to stop herself from crying. She'd done too much crying already this week, and it was time to stop. Her father had been out of the hospital for three days now, and although he was weak, he was definitely out of danger. In fact, just today, when Ashleigh was preparing lunch in the kitchen with her mother, they heard his raised voice coming from the living room. He wasn't calling for them, but instead he was yelling at the TV, just like his healthier old self. Hearing him boom out, "Oh, shut up, you idiot liberal," Ashleigh and her mother exchanged knowing glances: He was definitely getting better.

But when Ashleigh had cried this past week—alone in the narrow bed of her old bedroom—she wasn't crying for her father. She was crying for herself, and for Sam, and for the secret that she had to go on keeping. Before Gina brought news of her father's heart attack, Ashleigh really believed she was going to tell her parents everything about Sam. For that brief time she'd felt so liberated, so free. But then, whisking down to DC and seeing her father's gray face against the plump white hospital pillows, and her mother's dark, worried eyes scanning over him, Ashleigh's resolve ebbed away. Even when her father was discharged from the hospital, her resolve did not return. Instead, the doctor's parting words rang in Ashleigh's ears: "Most of all, Senator, lots of rest, low stress, and no excitement." Ashleigh was certain that telling her father that she was living with a woman—an African-American "liberal" professor at Manhattan U—would send him straight back to the hospital.

Since tenth grade, when she'd briefly dabbled with pink hair and a nose ring and read Simone de Beauvoir, Martin Luther King Junior, and Howard Zinn under her sheets at night, Ashleigh had sat at the other end of the political rainbow from her staunchly Republican father. Long ago, however, Ashleigh realized that fighting with him about abortion or affirmative action or gay rights was futile, and she eventually gave up trying. As fierce as she was about the things she believed in, her father was fiercer. It was his conviction and ruthless devotion to his beliefs that had gotten him his seat in the Senate.

Nowadays, Ashleigh and her father's conversations were courteous, mundane, and always mildly strained. But her father's fierce love, his obvious, almost smothering concern with Ashleigh's life, made it hard for her to reject him completely. She dutifully came home every holiday and rang her parents every weekend. And in spite of everything, there remained a nagging need to please him and to be loved by him and not to do things that would hurt him.

Still standing at the window, she felt a familiar wave of sadness and confusion rise in her chest. The whole situation was so impossible. Her love for Sam, her obligations to her father. She just couldn't get her mind around it. As she let out a small sigh, her cell phone chirped from somewhere behind her. With her eyes foggy from staring at the sunset, she stumbled over a pile of her old high school textbooks toward the bed. There she scurried around on her jumbled bedside table looking for the phone. Finding it at last under a pile of crumpled Kleenex, she flipped it open and saw Sam's name winking on the blue screen.

She punched the green button and whispered, "Hey."

"Can you talk?" came Sam's soft voice.

"I'm in my bedroom," said Ashleigh, still whispering. "He's downstairs."

"How's he doing?"

"Much better." Puffing out a small chuckle, Ashleigh went on: "He was shouting at liberals on TV today."

She could hear Sam's low laugh, and then somewhere in the background she heard loud voices and a drum beating. Suddenly Ashleigh remembered the protest.

"Oh, my God, I nearly forgot," she blurted out. But, remembering to keep her voice down so her parents wouldn't hear and ask whom she'd been talking to, she added in low murmur, "How's the protest going?"

"Great," Sam's voice sang out. "Can you hear it?"

The sounds from the protest grew louder. Sam was clearly holding her phone from her ear to capture the laughter, chatter, and music that surrounded her. As Ashleigh listened, she wandered back to her bedroom window and looked out at her parents' silent and lifeless yard, which was now shrouded in long, dark shadows.

"And these are just the stragglers. The folks who stayed late to party," Sam said, the excitement irrepressible in her voice. "Ash, you should have seen this place earlier. There were a hundred people. More, maybe."

Ashleigh whistled. "That's great. I wish I were there," she said with a sad smile.

"I wish you were too."

For a moment they said nothing. There was no need to say anything. Both of them knew the large and the small of it. They knew they missed each other like crazy, and they both wished that, instead of being four hours away, they could be together in the warm, dusky garden among the happy protesters. But they were also both aware of the cloud that loomed over them: Sam was still a secret, and she'd have to go on being a secret for some time to come.

"Are you still going to try to get back soon?" Sam finally asked in a tentative whisper.

"Yes," Ashleigh breathed, a lump rising in her throat.

What she didn't tell Sam was that she'd made another plan, a plan that Sam wouldn't like. In fact, it was a plan that Ashleigh herself didn't like, but she was determined to go through with it anyway. After a week of sadness and deliberating, Ashleigh had decided she had to move out. Just for a while—or so she kept promising herself. She figured if she moved out, gave her dad some time and space to get better, then in a slow, more considered way she could work up to telling her parents about Sam. Learning all at once that she was lesbian and living with a woman would be too much. However, she'd begun to convince herself, if she took things slowly, broached the idea with them gently, it would be better. They would never love the idea; that was certain. But this slower approach, with no more lies and false addresses, had to be a better way of coming out to them. It just had to be.

Although she wasn't saying anything now, Ashleigh was resolved to tell Sam all about this plan when she got back to New York.

"I'll meet you at Penn Station, if you like," Sam was saying, as Ashleigh wondered how she would take her news. "Just call me and let me know when you're coming in."

Ashleigh was about to respond but was stopped by an inaudible shout, followed by a crackling on the phone line. "Sam?" she asked. "Sam?"

The line was silent. Ashleigh thought they'd been disconnected, but, just as she was about to hang up, she heard booing, some more shouts, and a rhythmic swishing noise.

"Sam?" she tried again.

At last Sam answered. "Sorry, babe," she said, clearly out of breath and on the move. "Something"—she paused—"something's happening. I'm just going to see what . . ."

She didn't finish, and there was another long pause. Meanwhile, Ashleigh chewed on her bottom lip and wondered what was going on.

"I'm going to have to go," Sam said finally, sounding anxious. "The cops are here. They're ordering us out."

"*What?*"

But Ashleigh's question was lost amid Sam's cry of, "I love you," and then the click as the line went dead.

Ashleigh looked down at the silent phone. The cops? What were the cops doing there? Ashleigh's legal mind began to whir. It was a small gathering in a private garden; they couldn't order everyone out. If it was noisy, they could tell them to pipe down. Yet, from what Ashleigh could hear, it wasn't exactly a frat party. Moreover, it was still early. Who called the police with a noise complaint at seven in the evening?

"Probably that dean." Ashleigh tutted under her breath as she slipped her cell into the pocket of her jeans.

A little later Ashleigh sprawled on the long velour couch in her parents' living room. Photographs of herself—as a chubby baby, a gawky kid, a braces-wearing teenager—stared down at her from the mantelpiece above the ornate, mahogany-trimmed fireplace. The room's dark velvet curtains were already drawn, and sultry light came from a series of brass floor lamps and smaller glass lights perched on side tables. Her father sat in his leather recliner reading the newspaper, and opposite him Ashleigh's mother was perched on the edge of her own wing-back chair, staring, with a concerned frown, at her husband. Even when Ashleigh's father wasn't sick, her mother always sat like this: never relaxed, always ready to spring up and do something for him.

Looking up from the book she'd been reading, taking in her parents and this familiar scene, Ashleigh felt weary. Since her dad had gotten back from the hospital, the three of them sat like this every evening, reading books or making polite conversation about the weather, while the grandfather clock ticked monotonously in the corner. For the first couple of nights it was just about bearable. Now, though, she was tired of it, and she wanted to be gone. She wanted to be with Sam and the others, protesting with them, telling the cops and that mean dean guy where to get off.

Before coming downstairs to be with her parents, Ashleigh had tried to call Sam back a few times, but there was no reply. She'd called Sofia's and Hannah's numbers too, but got the same result: nothing. Ashleigh was desperate to know what was going on, and it made sitting here even more agonizing.

"What are you reading, darling?" Ashleigh's mother's whispery voice broke the silence in the room.

"The same as last night," Ashleigh muttered, not feeling in the mood for conversation.

It irked her how much she returned to her sullen teenage self when she was around her parents. She always vowed she'd be different. She'd promised herself that as soon as she stepped over the threshold she would embody politeness and charm. And with her father sick, this week she'd tried hard. She really had. But in the end she couldn't pull it off. It was as if something in the house always clutched hold of her, sucked all her energy and will, and spit her out as a moody, mumbling fourteen-year-old.

Luckily, before her mother could make a second attempt at conversation, as she always did, the front doorbell chimed.

Ashleigh's father looked up with a furrowed brow and crumpled his paper in his lap. "Are we expecting anyone, Frances?" he asked his wife.

Frances was already on her feet. "No," she said, hurrying to the door, looking flustered and confused.

Ashleigh pulled herself upright on the couch and smoothed down the wrinkled Georgetown Law School sweatshirt she'd been wearing all week. She suspected that it was one of her father's cronies at the door. Since her dad had left the hospital a stream of them had dropped by, bringing abundant bouquets of flowers or lavish baskets of fruit. They would come in their suits with their pearl-wearing wives and offer their get-well wishes.

A wave of even deeper weariness hit Ashleigh at the prospect of another of these visits. Another half an hour listening to Beltway gossip, and then, as the focus would turn to her, she'd find herself having to talk about work and how her uncle and the law firm were doing and, even worse, whether she had a boyfriend.

It was almost a relief when Ashleigh heard her cousin's squeal-ing hello.

Barreling into the living room, with her parents a few paces be-hind, Gina was dressed in a black Jackie O dress and a gray chiffon scarf. Ashleigh couldn't help smiling a little. Gina clearly thought this somber, funereal outfit was the suitable attire for visiting her sick uncle. She had to hand it to Gina: The girl really tried.

"How are you, Uncle Chad?" cooed Gina as she rushed toward Ashleigh's father and kissed his forehead with a flourish. "We've been so worried about you, and Daddy suggested we just get in the car and drive down."

Ashleigh's father blushed. "That's very thoughtful of you," he said with an awkward wave of his hands.

It amused Ashleigh how her ruthless and seemingly unflap-pable father got flustered by his effervescent, tactile niece. But Ashleigh's smile soon disappeared as she found herself swept up into a hug by Gina, then Aunt Gaynor and Uncle Ray, and in-stantly remembered the last time she'd seen them all. It was at Gina's engagement party, and the night Gina's serpentine fiancé announced to the world that Ashleigh was living with Sam.

Released from their breathtaking hugs, Ashleigh looked at the three of them and fear clawed in her throat. Were they going to say anything? She panicked. Were they going to tell her parents? Or would they just ask about Sam, assuming her parents already knew? Whichever it was, she was dreading it.

Luckily, though, everyone's eyes had turned from Ashleigh and back to her father.

"You gave us quite a scare, Chad. Quite a scare," Uncle Ray said as he sat beside his brother and squeezed his arm affectionately.

Ashleigh's father winced, tensed his shoulders, and said with a stiff smile, "It scared me too. But I'm feeling a lot better now."

Before her father took public office, the two brothers had worked side by side at the law firm that they founded together not long after Ashleigh was born. But Ray and Chad were very differ-ent. Ray was sweet, and tactile like his daughter. Ashleigh's dad, on the other hand, was buttoned-down, aloof, and stern—so stern that it sometimes baffled Ashleigh how he'd ever gotten people to vote for him as their senator. At the law firm the two brothers made a good team, though. It was a "good cop, bad cop" thing. Her dad was a ruthless attorney with a sharp business mind. Meanwhile, Ray had a gregarious personality that won them many connections and friends, and he was also a methodical and diligent worker. He always completed every job that confronted him, and always with a smile.

"What happened with the Smith-Evensen contract?" Ashleigh's father asked Ray.

Although no longer a partner, Ashleigh's dad still wanted to know everything going on at the firm.

Ray looked awkward for a second. "Ahh," he puffed. "Unfortunately, we lost that one."

Ashleigh's father's eyes fizzled with anger. *"What?"* he hissed. "That contract was a no-brainer. Why on earth didn't you get it?"

Ray blushed a little. "They went with Bradbury and Berkoff in the end."

The women in the room looked at one another nervously as the two men spoke. The scene was a familiar one, although it didn't usually unfold *this* fast. When Ashleigh's father had left the firm, Ray's good humor and industrious ways were not enough to keep the company at the top. It was still a very prestigious and respected law firm, but its profits and growth weren't satisfactory for Ashleigh's father, who didn't let anyone forget it, particularly Ray.

"Those guys over at Bradbury and Berkoff are clowns." Ashleigh's father was now sitting forward and waggling a finger at his brother. "Clowns!"

Ray was about to speak when Ashleigh's mother cut in. "Chad, darling, remember what Dr. Woods said: You must keep calm."

Ashleigh's father's eyes were still raging as he looked from his wife back to Ray. However, instead of ignoring his wife's pleas for calm, as he would have done in the past, he seemed to listen.

"I'm just saying," he said, lowering his voice and slumping back in the chair, "contracts like that one should be falling in your lap. You shouldn't be losing them to our competitors."

A silence hung over the room until Gina, who'd been jiggling impatiently on the couch next to Ashleigh, blurted out, "I need some water." And then, turning to Ashleigh, she added, "Come along, Ashey; let's go get everyone a nice cool glass of water."

"I was just about to fix drinks," Ashleigh's mother trilled, popping up from her seat.

Gina waved her aunt to sit back down. "No, no, Ashleigh and I can do it," she said. Jumping to her feet, she tugged at Ashleigh's arm and was soon propelling them both out of the room.

When they reached the kitchen, Gina eased the door shut and said in an excited whisper, "So was that her?!"

"*Her,* who?" Ashleigh asked as she moved toward the cabinets and pulled down six crystal tumblers.

"Your girlfriend!" yelped Gina.

Ashleigh swung around, glared at Gina, and planted an index finger on her lips. "*Shhhh.*"

"Oops, sorry." Gina grinned, but then she persisted. "Was it her? The woman you were with the day I came to find you? The black woman," she added, mouthing the word *black*.

Ashleigh hesitated but then nodded. She was reluctant to talk about Sam with Gina, but it didn't look like she had a choice.

Gina jerked her head toward the door and asked, "They still don't know?"

Ashleigh shook her head, sighed, and slumped onto one of the stools next to the kitchen counter. "No," she said flatly, "they don't."

Gina knitted her perfectly sculpted eyebrows. "It's going to be tough telling them, I guess. That's too bad."

Ashleigh was thrown for a second. Was Gina being sympathetic? Her Barbie-doll cousin seemed to be showing some understanding, which was a little hard to take in.

In the meantime, Gina chattered on. "My mom wanted to say

something to your parents. She thought Uncle Chad and Aunt Frances should know. But I was like, 'Mom, it's not our business. It's Ashleigh's business.' My dad said I was right, and—"

"So your dad knows?" Ashleigh whispered.

Gina nodded, smiling. "Yeah, and he agreed with me. Mom should keep her nose out." Gina gave a defiant flick of her hair and said, "Anyway, she's seems lovely. Your girlfriend, I mean." She opened her eyes wide. "And, omigod, so beautiful."

Ashleigh was speechless. She stared at Gina—her flawless golden highlights, her preened eyebrows, her tiny personal-trainered body—and all of a sudden she saw what she hadn't seen in a long, long time. She saw the sparkly, impish six-year-old Gina who'd once been her best friend—her sister, almost.

When they were kids, only three months apart in age, Ashleigh and Gina were inseparable. The family firm meant they were thrown together almost every day. They rarely argued, though, and would play happily and for endless hours among the make-believe dragons, knights, princesses, and castles they dreamed up together. But then Ashleigh's father left the law firm and started moving his family back and forth between DC and Ohio, his home state. Ashleigh and Gina soon lived in different cities, went to different schools, and made very different friends. In the end, they lived very different lives, and for Ashleigh their childhood comradeship was just a hazy memory.

Up until now, that was. As she stood in the kitchen looking at her cousin, it all came back to her. The goo from toffee apples on their small fingers, their damp secret hideout in Gina's Westchester garden, the neighbor's kitten that they would chase, catch, and then smother with kisses. Gina was the mischievous one, but Ashleigh would always be close behind, grinning and copying her cousin's playful antics.

As these memories rushed back to her and warmth rose in her chest, Ashleigh continued to look at Gina and began to smile. However different she'd become, with lacquered nails and blown-out hair, one thing was for sure: Gina was still that mischievous yet loving little girl. Her body was small but her heart was as big as it had always been.

"Sam *is* beautiful," Ashleigh found herself saying, her grin now long and wide.

"Bee-ootiful!" Gina giggled, and, looking down at the huge diamond winking on her finger, she added, "Davey thinks she's hot too."

Ashleigh's good mood crumbled a little at the sound of Davey's name. Since the engagement party, the question of how Gina's creepy fiancé had known about her and Sam had nagged at the back of Ashleigh's mind.

"How did Davey know about me and Sam?" Ashleigh asked, nervous but also relieved that she'd finally know the answer.

Looking at her reflection in the glass of the oven door and fluffing her hair, Gina said nonchalantly, "Oh, he saw you guys having brunch someplace in SoHo. He said he could tell by the way you were cooing over each other that you were an item."

Ashleigh let out a strangled, "He *did*?"

"Yup." Gina was now picking at her teeth, clearly growing bored with the topic.

But Ashleigh was anything but bored. Her mind was racing. Where had Davey seen them? Could they really have been "cooing," as Gina said? Ashleigh was too scared of being spotted by one of her colleagues or someone who knew her father to be overly affectionate in public. There might have been a few times when she and Sam had sneaked a brief touch of their fingers, or a quick kiss on the cheek, but she couldn't believe Davey really would have seen that.

"When did he . . . ?" she began, but was halted by a voice in the doorway.

"How are those drinks coming along, girls?" her mother said in the polite yet strained voice she always used when they had visitors.

"Fine, fine," Ashleigh muttered, busying herself with tumblers and silently praying her mother had heard nothing of the conversation that had just happened.

The three women emerged back into the living room a couple of minutes later, and Ashleigh's father and Uncle Ray were talking business once again. Uncle Ray looked reluctant, however. Unlike his older brother, he seemed to understand that this kind of conversation was no good for Chad's weak heart. But he had no choice. Ashleigh's father was persistent with his questions, and Ray was being railroaded into giving answers.

"And what about the contract for Wilkins Construction?" Ashleigh's father asked. "Has it all been signed with Manhattan U?"

Ashleigh, who'd been distributing drinks from the tray in her hands, froze in her tracks at the sound of her father's words.

"All done," Ray chirped, and then he grinned. "Invoice paid."

"Good, good." Chad nodded.

Ashleigh was still frozen to the spot. She had no idea that her law firm, her very own family law firm, was working with Wilkins Construction on the proposed parking lot. How ironic that she had helped organize a demonstration against the project, and even more ironic that, at this very moment, her girlfriend and friends were out protesting in the garden.

"Ashleigh?" Her father's voice broke into her thoughts. "Are you going to stand there all night, or are you going to pass my drink?"

Ashleigh gave a flustered nod and moved toward her father to give him his glass. She then stepped over to her uncle to pass his drink and, unable to stop herself, she asked, "So Wilkins Construction is our client?"

Her uncle smiled and nodded. "Yes. Jeremy has been working with them, mainly. But he consulted me on a few things."

Backing toward her own seat, Ashleigh inquired as nonchalantly as possible, "Do you know when construction will start?"

Ray looked a little bemused at Ashleigh's interest, but he quickly answered, "Pretty soon, I should think. In the next month. It sounds like the dean at Manhattan U, the one Jeremy has been talking with, is eager to get cracking."

"Dean Havemeyer?" Ashleigh blurted out.

"That's it." Ray nodded, but then he cocked his head and asked, "How do you know . . . ?"

He trailed off as Ashleigh made the panicked interjection, "I have a friend at the university. That's all. She, um, she knows about the parking lot project."

Ashleigh then snapped her mouth shut and sat back in her chair. She'd been an idiot. She'd let her curiosity get the better of her and nearly given too much away. Her palms began to sweat and her neck grew hot. Uncle Ray might have started asking who this "friend" was. He knew about Sam, after all. She looked over at her uncle, but his eyes were back on her father, who was firing more questions. Ashleigh gulped and then let out a tiny sigh. She might be safe this time, she told herself, but she had to be more careful from now on.

Thirteen

Mary

It was past nine o'clock, and although the police had moved everyone out of the garden a while ago, a dozen or more people were still milling by the gate talking, laughing, or raging about the abrupt end to the protest. One lone cop remained. He was leaning on his car a few yards away, and every now and then he scanned the scene to make sure no one was attempting to get back in the garden.

Mary stood alone among the chattering group. It was dark and beginning to get cold, but she was in no hurry to go home. She was sure it was Jack who had called the police department. She was also certain that by now Jack would have figured out it was she who took the key and let everyone into the garden. After all, he had eyes like a hawk. He probably spotted those missing keys and quickly worked out what Mary had done. If the protest had remained just a bunch of "pissy wives," as he called them, he would have let it slide. But with Mary going behind his back, snagging the key, and joining the protest, that would have been the last straw for Jack; she was sure of it.

Mary shivered and rubbed her bare arms as she imagined him pacing their apartment, clutching his scotch, waiting for her to get home. All the courage she'd had earlier when she marched out of the apartment with Jack's keys jangling in her hands—the same courage that had reemerged just a short while ago when she, Hannah, Sam, and Sofia stood up to the cops and tried to persuade them not to break up the protest—that courage had now ebbed away. She couldn't shake from her mind the image of Jack's angry hazel eyes.

"A penny for your thoughts."

"S-sorry," she stammered, startled by the deep voice close to her ear.

Mary turned to see the journalist she'd been trying to avoid all afternoon. She thought he'd left, but here he was, all twinkling gray eyes and smiles. She frowned straightaway.

"You looked deep in thought," he said with an apologetic wave as he took in her displeased expression. "I was just wondering . . ." He trailed off, and they stood in an awkward silence for a few seconds. "Great job with the cops," he said finally.

Mary frowned again. "We didn't achieve much," she huffed. "They still kicked us out of the garden."

The man chuckled and said, "Yeah, but you and your friends really laid it to them straight. For a second I thought they were going to put Sofia in cuffs."

Mary smiled as she remembered Sofia bellying up to a mean-looking police officer and demanding to know who'd made the noise complaint and why they were being forced from the garden without even so much as a warning. Then something occurred to her.

"You know Sofia?" She eyed the man.

He nodded his head. "I spoke to her earlier. For my piece."

Mary's nostrils flared, and anger thumped in her chest. "I guess this will all make a great story for you," she spat out.

"I'm just doing this story as a favor," he explained, looking confused by Mary's hostility. "My son's friend is an editor at the *Mail*. He needed someone last-minute to cover the story, and he knew I was in town and would be interested."

"So you're not on staff at the *New York Mail*?" Mary asked.

He shook his head and laughed. "No, no." He then added, "I used to work at the *New York Times*, but I quit when my wife died, and I moved out to California to be nearer to my kids. Now I do some freelance stuff, but mostly I work on my own books."

Mary asked, "Your own books?"

"I'm a kind of hack urban historian." He laughed again. "I've written a couple of books about New York and its history—in particular, the changing land use in the city. You know, how residential spaces have become business outlets, reclaimed land on the Hudson River, the disappearance of urban gardens, that kind of thing." He then waved a hand toward the fence behind him. "That's why I was interested in all this."

Something sparked in Mary's memory. She remembered finding a book at the library a couple of years ago about the changing face of Manhattan. On first glance she thought it might be somewhat dry, but a couple of pages in she was hooked. The writer—she couldn't remember the name—wrote such beautiful prose, and the book was peppered with intriguing anecdotes and observations about the city she'd lived in all her life. She read almost a third of the book before she even checked it out of the library.

Even though she was still a little wary, Mary cocked her head and said, "Sorry. I didn't catch your name."

"Jerry," he said with a soft smile. "Jerry Milo."

That was it. That was the book she'd read; she remembered now. She remembered *Jerry Milo* in gold font across the smooth dustcover.

"I've read one of your books." She laughed aloud.

Jerry grinned. "You did?"

Mary nodded.

"I've read yours and you've read mine," Jerry said. "Who'd have guessed it?"

As the two of them chuckled, Mary felt herself softening to the handsome Jerry Milo. Perhaps he wasn't trying to get some scoop on her and Jack. There was something so open and honest about him, and it seemed he wasn't some muckraking tabloid journo, after all.

"Are you . . . ?" Jerry began, but then he shook his head, as if he'd lost the nerve to ask whatever was on his mind.

To fill the silence that followed, Mary found herself asking him a question instead. "So you live in California?"

"Yup. San Francisco." His gray eyes sparkled once again. "It's not New York. But you know what? I like it."

Mary's heart skipped a beat. San Francisco! Soon she'd be in San Francisco too. For a brief second she wanted to tell Jerry everything. She wanted to tell him that a small apartment awaited her on Telegraph Hill. She wanted to tell him how she'd traveled out to the West Coast six weeks ago, pretending to Jack that she was going to a conference, and traipsed the steep streets of San Francisco looking for the perfect place for a new life. She wanted to tell him how she found a beautiful, light-filled, peaceful apartment only at the last minute on her final day in the city and instantly fell in love. She wanted to tell him about the novel she would soon write up there in her new place overlooking the bay.

But an unexpected gust of cold wind nipped at her arms, and she caught herself, remembering her own promise not to tell anyone—not a soul. Not even this interesting stranger with his kind pale eyes.

Instead she stuck out her hand and said, "It was nice to meet you, Jerry. Good luck with the story."

Jerry looked surprised at the sudden end to their conversation, but he continued to smile.

"It was a pleasure," he said, taking her hand gently in his. Then, as if he'd been reading her mind all along, he said in a whisper, "If you ever find yourself in San Francisco, please call me up." Jerry reached into his pocket, pulled out his wallet, and rifled through to find a card, which he then pressed into Mary's hand. "I mean it," he said, his gray eyes staring into hers. "Please call."

Mary took the card and closed her long fingers around it. "Perhaps I will." She smiled, a slight hint of pink on her cheeks.

When Mary got back to the apartment, she was met by the sound of voices and music playing. She'd expected to come home to an ominous silence, like the calm before the storm, as Jack sat awaiting her return. But as Mary stood in the hallway, the house was filled with chatter and noise, and it completely wrong-footed her.

On her short walk home, her earlier courage had begun to swell again in her chest. Perhaps it had something to do with her conversation with Jerry and the talk of San Francisco. Whatever it was, she'd decided she would confront Jack head-on. She wouldn't run to the bedroom and cower. Instead she would go straight to him and stand up to his inevitable tirade. She would let him shout and scream, but this time he wouldn't hurt her. She wouldn't let it happen, not this time and never again.

Confronted with visitors in her apartment, though, she felt her courage switch quickly to anger. The hairs on her neck prickled as she imagined Jack in the living room crowing to a couple of his cronies about how he'd broken up the protest. He loved to have these little celebrations in their apartment. Like the day his plans for the parking lot were finalized and he invited the contractor over for champagne and gloating. He knew Mary was uncomfortable with these impromptu events, and she was sure he did it on purpose. It was as if he were deliberately rubbing her face in it and punishing her for not caring about all the things he cared so much about these days: success, money, prestige.

Still standing near the door, Mary remembered the keys. She eased them out of her pocket and softly laid them back on the hall table where she had first found them. Looking down at them, she grimaced. This little party of Jack's was sure to just delay the anger he would vent later on, and now, with the wind expelled from her sails, Mary no longer felt up for the fight. It would be so much easier to walk to her bedroom, grab her tickets and the lease for the new apartment, put a few things in a suitcase, and then slip out. There would be no fight, no tears.

She wavered between walking right toward her bedroom or left toward Jack and his guests. But then a familiar voice called out from the living room.

"Was that the door? Mom! Are you there?"

Mary's head snapped around and she saw Sarah's smiling face peeking out into the hallway.

"Sarah!" Mary exclaimed, her anger seeping away instantly as she moved toward her daughter. "What are you doing here?" she asked as she hugged Sarah tight.

"Just thought we'd pay you old 'uns a visit." Sarah laughed.

Greg, Sarah's fiancé, was now at Sarah's side, and after Mary greeted and hugged him too, she turned to Sarah and laughed. "You just saw me today."

"I can see you twice in a day, can't I?" Sarah grinned.

Mary laughed again, but then, catching a glimpse of Jack over Greg's shoulder, she lowered her voice and said, "I'm sorry I left you in the boutique earlier, honey. Something"—she gave a nervous cough—"something important came up."

Sarah squeezed her mom's arm. "Don't worry, Mom. I understand," she said. "Anyway, they let me take the dress. See?"

Mary followed her daughter's gaze toward a large black carrying case hanging on the coatrack in the hallway.

"Oh, Sarah." Mary beamed. "I'm so happy for you."

Sarah always hated being the center of attention and had never wanted a huge, glitzy wedding. Instead she and Greg were planning to marry by the boating lake in Central Park and then follow with a small reception in a restaurant in Chelsea. Even though it was modest, Mary knew how much this wedding meant to Sarah and Greg. They'd been together for three years now and were such a perfect fit, both kind and hardworking and completely devoted to the other. As Mary looked over at the two of them, she realized she'd made the right choice to stick around until their wedding day. However hard it was turning out to be, it was worth it.

Mary's bubble of good feeling was soon burst, however, by Jack's grating baritone. "Where have you been, Mary?" he asked.

Mary looked past Greg and Sarah and took in Jack's face. He was smiling one of his fake "we have company" smiles, but Mary could see the bitterness in his eyes. He knew about the keys. She could read those hazel eyes like a book.

"I've been busy, Jack," she said as breezily as she could, but she was aware of the tension in her voice and hoped Sarah and Greg didn't pick up on it.

Jack began moving toward them from where he'd been standing at the window. "Sarah and Greg have been waiting for you to show up." This time Jack did nothing to disguise the disdain in his tone.

Before Mary could say anything, Sarah interjected with a light laugh. "Dad." She chuckled, patting him on the chest. "We've only been here a little while. It's not like we waited long."

Jack made a harrumphing noise but said nothing further. Meanwhile Mary tried to ignore her husband, whose glaring eyes were still burning into her, and shooed Greg and Sarah into the living room and onto the couch.

"Can I get you both a drink?" she asked as she scanned the room and noticed not one empty glass or mug in sight. It was clear Jack hadn't lifted a finger since Sarah and Greg had arrived.

Sarah wiggled a little in her seat and then grabbed Greg's hand. "Before you do that, Mom," she began, "Greg and I have some news. I was dying to tell you earlier, but"—and she looked up at her dad—"we wanted to tell you together."

Mary sank into the armchair opposite, and a small knot tightened in her stomach. She felt selfish, but she began to pray that there wasn't going to be some change in the wedding plans. Everything—all her tickets, her new lease—depended on this wedding going ahead as scheduled.

As Mary waited and Sarah and Greg beamed at each other, playfully arguing about who should break the news, the phone started to ring.

"I have to get that," Jack said brusquely, beginning to move out the room.

"Dad!" Sarah cried, looking crestfallen. "Can't you just hear our news first?"

But there was no stopping Jack. He was already heading down the hallway. "It'll just take a minute," he called before closing the door to his study.

When the phone quit ringing and they could hear Jack's inaudible mumbling coming through the wall, Mary shook her head. "I'm sorry."

Sarah shook her head too. "He's always so busy these days."

She sighed. "He never seems to have time for me anymore. And he's so distant and . . . I don't know . . . gruff." She looked over at Mary. "Don't you think, Mom? Is he like that with you?"

Mary didn't know how to answer. This was the first time Mary had ever heard Sarah say something like this about her father. She'd always been such a daddy's girl, hanging on his every word, proud of his successes, and always seeking his approval at every choice and turn she took. It seemed that in her daughter's eyes, at least, Jack could do no wrong, and in spite of everything Mary had been reticent to break the spell for Sarah. It would be like telling a four-year-old there was no Santa.

"He's very busy," Mary began, but then she stopped herself. She couldn't keep covering up for Jack and stringing Sarah along, pretending everything was normal. If she let Sarah know at least some of her problems with Jack, perhaps when Mary left him, it wouldn't be such a huge shock to Sarah—to everyone.

Mary looked Sarah straight in the eye and started again.

"Your dad," she said quietly, "he's changed. He's changed a lot in the last few years."

Sarah's eyebrows darted upward. "Really? You've noticed it too? How's he different?" she asked.

"He's, well, he's . . . ." she started. But the sound of Jack's study door opening silenced her. He was coming back, and, without saying another word, Mary, Sarah, and Greg all looked toward the hallway.

"Okay," he boomed as he blustered back into the room, smiling like he'd just been made president of Manhattan U. "What's the big news?"

As he moved toward the liquor cabinet and began pouring himself a scotch, Sarah looked guiltily at her mother. Mary knew what her daughter was thinking, because Sarah was like her in so many ways. Mary knew that Sarah was feeling bad that their conversation about Jack had been cut short.

To reassure her, Mary nodded and smiled. "Yes, come on, you

two," she said, reverting back to her earlier breezy tone. "What's your news?"

Looking relieved, Sarah smiled, and then, taking a quick glance at Greg and her father, she sucked in a deep breath. "I'm pregnant!"

Mary's heart skipped a beat, and before she knew it she was on her feet and hugging her daughter. Behind her she could hear Jack offering a cool congratulations to Greg. But her husband's lack of enthusiasm didn't stop Mary from hugging her daughter tighter and saying joyfully, "Honey, that's wonderful."

Finally peeling herself from her mother's hug, Sarah giggled and said, "And that's not all."

Mary cocked her head. "There's more news?"

"It's twins!" Greg chimed in.

Mary looked from Sarah to Greg and back again. Both of them were grinning and nodding.

"Are you serious?" Mary laughed.

"Yup." Sarah nodded again. "We just found out. We had the first ultrasound yesterday. It was kind of a shock, to say the least. And, well, getting pregnant now, before the wedding, wasn't exactly our plan. We were going to wait a few years. But it's happened and we're happy, really happy." She smiled at Greg and patted her belly.

Mary looked down at Sarah's middle and was about to laugh and tell her daughter how she'd been scared to mention the extra weight earlier when they were in the boutique. But then Mary remembered Jack's feelings about the wedding gown and kept her mouth shut.

"Two kids!" Jack was now saying with a whistle. He was smiling, but his eyes had that disdainful shimmer once again. "Two kids are going to be expensive."

"Jack," Mary tried to interrupt, but he waved her away.

"You'll need a new place, for starters," he went on. "You can't keep living in that one-bedroom apartment with two babies."

Sarah looked dismayed. "Dad," she said, "don't you think we've thought about all this? Of course we have. We know we can do it, though. We're already looking for a new place in Brooklyn."

Jack waved his hand again and, as if he hadn't heard a word Sarah said, he continued. "Your mother and I are in no place to help you out with real estate. Financially, I mean. We're just college professors, after all."

"Dad!" Sarah's face was a mix of surprise and hurt. "We don't want money from you." Her voice cracked a little. "All I'm asking is for our kids to have loving grandparents. That's all." Then, blinking a couple of times to hold back the tears glistening in her eyes, she added, "All we want is for you to babysit every now and then, take the kids to the park or something."

Mary pulled her daughter back into another hug, and, while shooting Jack an icy stare, she said quietly in her daughter's ear, "Don't listen to him. Of course these kids will have loving grandparents. We'll support them—and you—in every way we can."

As she uttered the words, however, the knot of tension returned to Mary's stomach. Was that really true? she asked herself, beginning to panic. Could she really be a doting grandmother if she were a long plane ride away in San Francisco? And twins? Sarah and Greg were going to need as many doting grandparents as they could get with two babies on the way. They would really need people nearby who could drop in if both kids were screaming and Greg and Sarah needed sleep, or if they'd run out of diapers, or if one of the babies got sick and needed to go to the doctor.

Her mind raced, and, as she pulled away from Sarah, it was her turn to blink back tears.

"Thanks, Mom." Sarah smiled, and then, looking toward her father, she asked tentatively, "Aren't you happy you're going to be a grandpa, Dad?"

Jack didn't answer. The phone was ringing again and he was already heading toward his study.

*   *   *

Half an hour later Mary was in the kitchen fixing some snacks. Jack was still locked away in his study on the phone, and Sarah and Greg were sitting on the couch looking over a family photo album. Teasing Sarah, Greg had insisted he see old baby photos so he'd have some idea of what his two future offspring might look like. Mary had gone to the closet, retrieved the old album, and thumbed through to find a picture of three-year-old Sarah standing in nothing but a pair of red panties and a blue vest with two big silver bracelets on her wrists, one of which was raised menacingly to her forehead.

"Sarah, aka Wonder Woman." Mary grinned, handing the heavy album to Greg. "Halloween 1979."

Sarah groaned and then laughed. "Thanks, Mom. He's never going to marry me now."

"Who wouldn't want to marry Wonder Woman?" Mary had laughed too.

Now, standing in the kitchen shaking bread sticks into a tall glass, Mary didn't feel much like laughing anymore. Sarah's news was beginning to hit home, and Mary was panicked and confused. She couldn't just up and leave for California with her daughter now pregnant with twins. What kind of mother would do that? Not only that, she wanted to see her grandkids. She wanted to be present in their lives. When she'd first made plans to move, Mary had mulled over this question, but she'd thought having kids was a long way off for Sarah. In the end, she figured that when that time came maybe she'd be ready to move back to New York, face her fears of Jack, and be near her daughter and her family.

Everything was different now; with two grandkids just six months away, everything had changed. San Francisco, her new job at Golden Gate College, the new apartment. It couldn't happen now. She wanted to cry again, but then a pang of guilt immediately thumped in her chest. She should be the happiest woman on earth. After all, her wonderful, happy daughter was pregnant. Mary was going to be a grandmother.

As she reached for a tray of cheese in the refrigerator, she heard someone come into the kitchen behind her. She quickly gathered her pensive face into a smile and then stood up and turned around, expecting to see Sarah or Greg. Instead she was met with Jack's smug grin. For a moment, as she clutched a cold portion of cheddar in her right hand, she fought the urge to hurl it hard into his face.

Jack stared at his wife for a second or two, and then said with a sneer crumpling his face, "So, we're going to be grandparents."

Just his presence made Mary prickle with anger, and, unable to stop herself, she blurted out, "Yes, and perhaps you could go out there and say something nice about it."

Jack moved slowly toward Mary, his sneer turning into a wry smile. Her pulse began to race and her palms moistened, but she stayed put. He wouldn't try anything now, she reassured herself, not with Sarah and Greg in the next room.

"That's rich coming from you," he hissed, his face now only an inch or so from hers. "Some grandmother you're going to be." He paused for a moment, staring hard into her eyes as his face contorted into a mocking grin. "San Francisco is a long, long way away."

Mary stopped breathing. It felt like her heart had stopped too. The cheese she'd been clutching dropped to the floor with a light thud. She was speechless.

Jack stepped back and let out a low, gravelly laugh. "You can't get anything past me, Mary. Not a thing."

Fourteen

Sofia

Early on Monday evening Sofia bustled into the empty elevator of Manhattan U's arts and humanities building and hit the button for the twelfth floor. For the first time in a few weeks she was completely unencumbered: no stroller in her hands, no diaper bag swinging from her arm, and no baby strapped to her chest. The two kids were at home with a babysitter, and without them Sofia felt free and light, but also a little strange. She couldn't shake the feeling that something was missing, that she'd forgotten something along the way.

As the doors shuddered to a close, Sofia scanned the flyers and posters stuck haphazardly to the elevator wall above the display panel. *Three Modernist Poets: Eliot, Frost, Stevens,* read one pink piece of paper, advertising an upcoming graduate seminar in the English department. Another glossy flyer screamed the words, *Respect Yourself. Protect Yourself. Use a Condom,* and tacked underneath was an outdated poster for a film series run by the French department's *Ciné-Club Du Cercle.*

Sofia smiled as her eyes darted across each advertisement. She always enjoyed coming to see Tom at work. It made her feel twenty again. All the clubs and seminars and safe-sex information. Nothing had really changed since she was a student. Not that she would turn back the clock, of course. For Sofia, unlike Tom, college had been a means to an end. She'd done her four-year stint, gotten a clutch of A grades, and moved on to Hollywood, where she had always wanted to be. However, the university still had its allure. Perhaps it was mostly about Tom. She poked fun at his obsession with Poe and his passion for research, but deep down those passions and Tom's intensity were exactly what she found attractive about him in the first place, and exactly what she found attractive about him to this day.

Of course, last week, when the Havemeyers came for dinner and Jack suckered Tom in with his questions and his promise of a new Poe institute, Sofia hadn't been so enamored with Tom's unadulterated love of all things Poe. After everyone left the apartment that night, Sofia informed Tom that he'd rolled over for Jack like some doe-eyed puppy wanting his belly scratched. She also told him that he shouldn't count his chickens when it came to the Poe institute. Havemeyer was probably up to something sinister, and Hayden's donation was highly improbable. Tom had laughed off her concerns and told her she needed to get a good night's sleep. It was true, of course—she hadn't slept well in weeks—but she didn't take kindly to having this pointed out. They ended up having a row, and Tom spent yet another night on the living room couch.

It turned out Sofia's intuitions were wrong. The very next morning Tom received a Manhattan U press release that announced the launch of the new research institute. Not only that, by Saturday, the day of the protest, Hayden was signing his big fat check and calling Jack Havemeyer to ask where it should be sent. Tom gently teased and gloated all weekend, and Sofia fumed at having to eat her words. But her bad mood didn't last long. She was too busy with the kids and the protest. And if the institute was going to happen, as it now seemed it was, Sofia couldn't help feeling pleased for Tom. The Poe Research Institute would be everything Tom had ever dreamed of. Being the only Poe scholar on faculty at Manhattan U, he would be the first choice for the institute's director, and holding such a position would really help his tenure portfolio. Not only that, but Tom would enjoy every minute running the institute. In spite of her residual suspicions that the dean was up to no good, Sofia was happy for her husband.

As soon as Tom had received the press release, he'd arranged a celebration to be held in his department, and this was the reason Sofia was currently on her way up to the twelfth floor. All Tom's colleagues and members of the New York Poe Foundation were invited to the small wine-and-cheese soiree in the faculty lounge, and Dean Havemeyer and the generous Hayden Burgess would be making their appearances too. Sofia was not excited to see either of the latter, but she wanted to support Tom. Plus, a couple of hours without the kids, drinking wine with a group of adults, was too good to miss. She'd arranged the babysitter, sought out some clean clothes, washed her hair, and was on her way to her first grown-up event in way too long.

The elevator had now reached the tenth floor and the doors pinged open. A young woman stepped in and flashed Sofia a quick smile. Sofia smiled back, and as the doors closed and the elevator rumbled back into action, she studied the pretty woman out of the corner of her eye. She seemed older than an undergraduate, Sofia thought, but she still had that glow of a twentysomething, so she was probably a grad student. Her hair was flawlessly straight and a dewy blond color. Her skin was smooth, and her hips, caught in a pair of tight, low-riding jeans, were tiny. As Sofia eyed her with a mix of jealousy and awe, she accidentally caught a glimpse of her own reflection in the elevator's mirrored walls. She instantly frowned. Her usually bouncy hair looked forlorn and disheveled, even though she'd managed to squeeze in a shower between one of Gracie's tantrums and having to nurse Edgar. The purple Indian blouse Sofia had found in the back of her closet looked washed-out under the elevator's harsh lights, and there was a tiny bleach stain on the right shoulder. Worst of all, although she thought this floaty top would cover her stodgy postbaby middle, it was in fact sticking to her skin and revealing the unflattering bulge that sat above the maternity pants she was still having to wear.

Sofia contemplated her sorry appearance and discreetly tried to flap her blouse away from her belly while the elevator shuddered to a halt at the twelfth floor. She was pleased to escape her reflection, but Sofia was then faced with something much worse: the woman stepped out of the elevator first, which meant Sofia had to follow her minuscule jeans-clad butt wiggling down the hallway.

Sofia tried not to look, yet with each step her eyes kept returning to the young woman's perfect behind and the tanned, silky snippet of skin between the top of her jeans and the hem of her T-shirt.

Sofia was feeling as forlorn as her hair by the time both women reached the faculty lounge. Back when she was an agent, Sofia was constantly surrounded by women even blonder and svelter than the one she just followed. In those days, though, it never bothered her. Sofia had always been proud of her curves and her dark, jumbled curls, and the women who walked the Hollywood boulevards beside her were just insecure, eating-disordered waifs who happened to own a bottle of peroxide. Even after Sofia had Gracie, she didn't feel self-conscious about her postpartum figure. But since Edgar, and the fresh round of sleepless nights, and her pregnancy pounds holding on more stubbornly, she felt for the first time in her life cumbersome, unsexy, and frumpy.

Sofia followed the young woman into the bustling faculty lounge with a frown creasing her forehead. Luckily she spotted Tom straightaway among the gathered crowd. He spotted her too, gave her a wink, and immediately her spirits buoyed. Just as she was about to set off toward him, however, she noticed whom he was talking to. Although his back was to her, Jack Havemeyer's thatch of gray hair was unmistakable. Sofia faltered. She definitely didn't want a conversation with Jack. He'd annoyed her enough last week at the dinner party. On top of which, he probably knew she was behind Saturday's protest and would no doubt want to upbraid her and tell her why she'd done wrong. She wasn't scared to stand up to him, but now wasn't the time or the place.

Turning on her heel, Sofia headed toward the wine table instead. She was grabbing herself a glass of red and scanning the cheeses laid out on wooden boards when a voice beside her let out a chirpy hello. She turned to see Christian, one of Tom's favorite grad students and a fellow Poe lover, standing beside her.

"Hey." She smiled down at him.

Christian was no more than five-two. His wiry Einstein hair gave him another inch, but he was still a good few inches shorter than Sofia. Usually Sofia felt nothing but affection for bubbly and zany Christian, but today she felt awkward and ungainly next to his tiny and slender frame. She stepped back a little to try to offset the disparity in their sizes.

"I'm *so* sorry I didn't make the protest," Christian was saying, shaking his head. "I totally wanted to come, but I was out of town for a conference. I heard it was a blast," he added with a grin.

Sofia smiled too. "It was a blast."

The truth was, Sofia had loved every minute of it. Seeing everyone show up, marching around the garden, and even arguing with the cops at the end, was such a trip. It gave her that same rush she used to get when she sealed a movie deal for Hayden, or when she got an "in" with a big director, or when she signed some hot new client. Of course, she'd had some highs since quitting her job. Being a mom had many amazing and beautiful moments, but they weren't the same. Motherhood was never ending; it was something you never completely wrapped up. The protest, like the contracts or connections she organized back in Hollywood, was something she'd pulled off, wrapped up, completed. Even with a few bumps in the road, nothing could beat the high of achieving something like that.

"I hate to miss a good protest." Christian was still shaking his head.

"I bet you do." Sofia laughed, remembering how Christian and a group of his buddies had dressed in black bird costumes and protested night and day outside the old Poe house on Third Street in the run up to its demolition. "What did you ravens call yourselves again?"

"The Ravenettes." Christian grinned. "I still have the costume hanging in my closet."

They chuckled for a second, but then, clearly having the same thought, Sofia and Christian let their gazes dart over toward Jack, who was still talking with Tom.

"I heard he broke up the party," Christian whispered. "As usual."

Sofia rolled her eyes. "Someone called the cops. I'm sure it was him."

Christian took a bite of his cracker, and as he chewed he waved a finger. "You know what I also heard?" he said, still talking quietly. "The university is using Wilkins Construction again for this parking lot development."

Sofia cocked her head to one side. "What do you mean, *again*?"

"Wilkins was the developer for the Third Street site," Christian explained. "Apparently they did a *really* bad job."

"They did?"

Sofia's eyebrows were now raised. She'd been past the new business school building on Third Street many times. Its modern glass windows and shining new bricks stuck out among the nearby buildings, but it seemed that Wilkins had done a reasonable enough job of integrating the facade of Poe's old town house into the new structure. Constructing an imitation facade had been the university's only concession to the Poe protestors and their call to save the house.

Christian nodded, his tousled hair bobbing. "There were all kinds of delays and mix-ups, and Wilkins charged almost three times what they originally quoted."

Although young, Christian was one of those people who knew everyone. He was on a dozen committees and a member of various clubs, as well as being the secretary for the Poe Foundation. He had friends and contacts in every department of the university, and whenever Tom needed to know something he went to Christian. It was Christian, in fact, who had managed to get Saturday's protest advertised in the *Manhattan U News*. Sofia had no doubt that what he was saying today was true.

"Why would they use them again?" she wondered aloud.

Christian shrugged just as a spoon was tinkled against a wineglass and there followed some calls for hush. Sofia looked over and saw Tom and Jack standing together at the front of the room, waiting for the chatter in the room to die down. A speech was in the air.

"Thanks, everyone," Tom said, beaming and pushing his glasses up his nose. "Thanks for coming."

Sofia smiled. Here was Tom, *her* Tom: so smart, so composed, so happy. She felt a kick of guilt about how testy and irritable she'd been lately. All the rows they'd been having were her fault—for the most part, anyway. She was just so tired these days, and she couldn't help being touchy. Sofia looked over at her husband again. Why hadn't she been nicer to him recently? The other night he'd tried to snuggle up to her in bed, like the way he always did when they were about to have sex. But she pushed him off with an angry jerk and reprimanded him for forgetting she'd given birth only a few weeks ago.

"My body is bruised and delicate," she'd barked out into the darkness.

"I just want to cuddle," Tom had huffed back as he rolled away from her, and then fell asleep.

Another pang of guilt hit as she thought of that night. Perhaps he *had* just wanted a cuddle. She certainly hadn't been giving him many of those recently.

"Jack Havemeyer, our dean who has made all this possible," Tom was now saying, "would like to say a few words."

Jack stepped forward, and Sofia tried hard not to frown too deeply. This was Tom's day, she reminded herself, and she couldn't allow Havemeyer to annoy her.

"I wouldn't exactly say I made all this possible." Jack chuckled with fake modesty. "Your generous brother"—he looked at Tom and then to the crowd—"Hayden Burgess—that's who has made the institute really possible."

Claps and whoops accompanied Hayden's name, and Sofia could see people scanning the room, hoping to catch sight of Tom's movie-star brother. Sofia was soon looking around for him too, but Hayden's coiffed blond locks were nowhere to be seen.

As if reading everyone's mind, Jack went on: "Hayden is running a little late. But he'll be here shortly."

Sofia smirked. Running a little late—how many times had she heard that in all her years working with Hayden? Her brother-in-law was renowned for his tardiness. In the early days it drove Sofia crazy, but she realized soon enough that there was nothing she could do about it. She taught herself to be mellow and not to scream at him every time he'd show up late for a screening, or when he upset a director by not being on set at the right time for a take. It sometimes amazed Sofia that Hayden had gotten so far in an industry where time meant money—often lots of money. But then she always remembered Hayden's charm, his apologetic smiles, and the way he could win over even the most prickly and precious of directors and producers.

At the front of the room, Jack was droning on about his hopes for the Poe institute, and how he imagined it was going to be a "unique" and "dynamic" research establishment that would garner large grants and scholarships from national funding committees. He talked about Manhattan U being the ideal place for the new institute because of the university's "sterling reputation for research and its copious resources." It was the logical place too, he argued, because of the obvious associations to Poe himself. He then laughed and called Poe an old neighbor of the university, and not once did he show any shame that he'd been the one to pull down this old neighbor's house. Jack then went on to tell the story Tom had related to him last week at dinner, about Poe and his aborted poetry reading at Manhattan U.

As the gathered crowd laughed and whispered little jokes about Poe's infamous drinking habit, Sofia tried not to frown at Jack. She let her eyes wander around the room instead. She spotted some familiar faces, colleagues of Tom's, friends from the Poe Foundation, and when she caught their eyes she would flash a smile. Sofia's gaze soon came back around to the front, and she spotted the young woman from the elevator. Her heart ground to a halt. Not only was the woman standing at the front, all golden and grinning and narrow hipped, as if she were running the show, she was also standing close to Tom—very close to Tom. Sofia's eyes narrowed, and as she glared over at the young woman she was horrified to see Tom smile and whisper something in her ear. After whatever it was he'd said, the woman giggled and looked up at Tom with wide and sparkling eyes and whispered something back. This whisper-smile exchange went on three or four times, and every time Sofia's stomach wrenched and twisted while her breath caught in her throat.

Sofia had never been jealous in her life, not ever. It just wasn't in her nature. She'd always taken the pragmatic view that if a guy didn't want her, if he wanted some other woman, then that was that. There was no point getting twisted up with jealousy and rage and suspicion. You just had to trust your instincts, she'd always thought, and suck it up if the man you loved ended up walking out the door.

However, as Sofia stood in the faculty lounge rendered motionless by what was happening in front of her, she realized she'd never been jealous because she'd never had any real reason to be jealous. Before Tom, Sofia had dated many guys, some of whom had dumped or cheated on her. It went with the fickle and shallow world of Hollywood, where she met most of the people she'd ever dated. But whenever her relationships ended, or when they were on the nosedive toward the end, she never spent days in bed, sniveling into disintegrating Kleenexes or eating pints of ice cream. She just picked herself up, told herself the relationship was no good anyhow, and got straight back out onto the dating carousel.

None of those guys was Tom, though. None of them had hooked her heart like Tom had, with his intelligence and wit and kindness—not to mention his pale blue eyes and the chemistry they'd always had between them. Sofia loved Tom like she'd never loved anyone before, and she also trusted him like she'd never trusted any guy in her past. There was something so open and honest about him. Not trusting Tom would be like refusing to trust Gracie or newborn Edgar.

Yet, watching this young hot grad student murmur and giggle in his ear, Sofia was gripped with panic and suspicion. *He wouldn't, would he?* she asked herself, as she continued to stare at them. Part of her mind screamed, *No, of course not. He never would. Especially not with some ditzy blond grad student.* But then another voice in her mind nagged, *Maybe? Maybe?* After all, Sofia was an exhausted, flabby grouch these days, wasn't she? No sex, rows, nights spent on the couch. Tom's married life wasn't exactly rosy at the moment.

Sofia could feel her palms beginning to sweat and her chest tighten. Tom and the student's exchange didn't last long, but Sofia hated how close they were standing. A piece of paper would have had difficulty slipping through the gap between Tom's shirtsleeve and the woman's bare, smooth elbow. Sofia tried taking a couple of deep breaths as she glared at this infinitesimal gap. But her mind continued to spiral, and her blouse clung to her increasingly clammy middle.

Sofia decided she had to leave the room. Jack was still pontificating, and thus there was no end in sight for Tom and this woman's cozy proximity. Out in the hallway, she assured herself, her head would clear and she would start thinking sensibly again. She glanced down at the wine in her hand. Perhaps it was the alcohol that had gotten her so worked up. She'd taken only a few sips from her small glass, but she was a lightweight now, thanks to pregnancy, motherhood, and breast-feeding putting an end to her life of cocktails, red carpets, and late nights. With this in mind, Sofia placed the plastic glass on the table and vowed she would grab some water in the bathroom.

"I'm just stepping out for a couple of minutes," she whispered to Christian.

Christian nodded, and Sofia began to weave her way through the party guests and toward the door as quietly and discreetly as she could. She didn't want to be spotted leaving, especially by Jack. She wouldn't put it past him to stop his rant and make some snide comment about her departure. If he wanted payback for the protest, this would be the time to get it, and in her current jittery mood, Sofia wasn't up for a fight.

She made it safely to the door, however, and breathed a quick sigh of relief as she reached for the handle. The handle, though, dipped down and out from under her grasp. Before she knew what was happening, the door was flung open and she found herself face-to-face with Hayden. He was grinning and groomed like some party entertainer's chimp.

"Yo, Sofe!" he cried out. "Leaving so soon?"

Sofia's finger jumped to her lips. "Shut up, you idiot," she hissed, her cheeks burning with anger and embarrassment.

It was too late. Behind Sofia the room had already gone quiet, with the exception of a few excited gasps and someone whispering, "He's here!" Sofia turned slowly. A sea of eyes were looking in their direction, including Jack's and Tom's and that damn grad student's.

"Hayden," Havemeyer boomed, finally breaking the awed silence. "Good to see you. And, I might add, perfect timing. Would you like to come up and say a few words?"

Hayden's eyes darted toward Sofia, and he looked at her with a pleading and flustered gaze she knew all too well. She almost grinned as the memory of Hayden's curious little secret flooded back. The little secret she'd always covered so well for him when she was his agent. Although a fine actor, a loudmouth, and a vivacious raconteur at parties, Hayden hated to give impromptu speeches. With a script he was fine. With a story he knew or a part to act he was happy. But when he was put on the spot and asked to say a few words, for some inexplicable reason he crumpled.

Hayden shot her another begging glance, and without even thinking Sofia shifted into autopilot. She nodded at Hayden and then called out to Jack, "Hayden would much prefer to talk to everyone one on one. He'd love to hear *all* your thoughts about the new institute."

Another round of excited murmurs rippled through the room.

Much to her surprise excitement rippled through Sofia too, and she realized why as she glanced over at Hayden, who was mouthing, *Thank you,* in her direction: She felt powerful again. She felt important and needed. Just like in the old days, when she and Hayden were still a team; when Hayden would go out and earn the bucks being a great, yet always late actor, and she'd follow behind covering for him and securing his next job.

Sofia grinned and found herself looking over the crowd at Jack. By the quizzical crease in his forehead, she could tell he was thrown by what she'd just said and could sense he was about to make another plea for Hayden to come join him at the front.

Quickly she said, "Dean Havemeyer, please don't let us interrupt what you were saying. I'm sure everyone would like to hear more about your wonderful ideas and visions for the institute."

The dean smiled at Sofia and nodded. He wasn't stupid, though; he could detect the irony in her tone, and his eyes flashed with antipathy.

"Thank you, Mrs. Burgess," he responded, purposely using the married name Sofia never went by. "And please don't let me keep you. I'm sure you must have pressing business to attend to with your *club*." Jack's face twisted a little as he said the last word.

Sofia had no idea what he was talking about, but she said nothing and simply smiled sweetly. She was in her work mode now, and she knew from years of practice in these situations that this was her moment to keep cool, stay put, and show complete and utter indifference. Ordinarily she'd love a showdown with an egomaniac like Jack, but she also knew when and where such showdowns should happen. This definitely wasn't the place or time.

When Sofia didn't rise to his bait, Jack turned back to the assembled audience and continued talking. Meanwhile, Hayden sidled close to Sofia and squeezed her arm.

"You rock," he whispered, and then after a pause he added, "And this is why you have to be my agent again."

Sofia prickled at his words, and the excitement of a moment ago began to seep away. "This is exactly why I should *not* be your agent," she said in a snappish murmur. "I don't want to spend my days covering your sorry ass again."

Hayden grinned. "Come on, Sofe." He chuckled. "You know you used to love it."

Hayden's knowing her so well made Sofia prickle even more, and she leaned close and shot back, "I bet Lori Spiegler loved it too."

Raising his hands and shaking his head, Hayden whispered, "Okay, okay, you can give me the 'I told you so' speech right now. Lori was a bad agent. You were right all along. Come on." He grinned again. "I'm ready for it."

"I'm not going to waste my breath. Plus, I'm listening," she lied, nodding toward Jack.

"When you're done, when you've got the speech out of your system," Hayden went on, ignoring her words, "will you *please* agree to be my agent?"

Sofia straightened her back and stuck out her chin. "Never."

Hayden ignored her denial again. "Look," he began as he started to fish around in his bag. "Just look at—"

Sofia interrupted him. "Nice purse," she scoffed, rolling her eyes at the soft leather bag slung over Hayden's shoulder. "Very manly."

"Thanks. It's Marc Jacobs," Hayden said without looking up. As he pulled out a thick stack of papers that were stapled and curling at their corners, he murmured, "Take a look at this."

Sofia didn't have to look any closer to know what it was. It was a script, and in the next moment Hayden was flourishing it right under her nose.

"Aahh," he teased, "don't you just love the smell of a fresh script?"

Sofia slapped Hayden's hand away, but not before she surreptitiously tried to read the cover page. She wasn't surreptitious enough, though, and Hayden caught her gaze and flashed a delighted grin.

He then held up the script and read in a dramatic whisper, " '*Maya*, by Norman Watts.' "

Before she could stop herself, Sofia grabbed the script and her eyes darted over the cover. "How did you get this?" she hissed. "Is it for real?"

Hayden nodded and smirked. "Yup."

Sofia stared down at the script, her hands beginning to sweat with anticipation and excitement. "But Norman Watts hasn't written anything in ten years. Are you sure this is real?"

"The great man sent it to me himself."

"Bullshit," Sofia blurted out, and as she did so a few people nearby, who'd been darting looks at Hayden and Sofia since their whispered exchange began, now turned and stared. Sofia gave an apologetic wave and ducked her head back down to look again at the script in her hands.

Hayden took another piece of paper out of his bag and thrust it in front of Sofia. She scanned the brief scribbled note. *Hayden,* it read, *Re: our phone conversation. Let me know, Norman Watts.*

As she stared at the note, Hayden said in her ear, "Tell me you don't want to be my agent."

If this note and this script were genuine, if Hayden was really being courted for a new movie written by Norman Watts—one of the most sought after, distinguished, and also elusive writers in the business—then Sofia was sorely tempted. This was a once-in-a-lifetime kind of thing. It would mean the big time for Hayden, not to mention a lot of money for Hayden and possibly Sofia too.

"Do you even need an agent?" she huffed, trying to play it cool. "If Norman Watts is sending you screenplays in the mail, why would you pay someone to hunt down good roles for you?"

Hayden laughed. "You know I need you to negotiate all the tricky contract stuff." He nodded up at Jack. "And save me from making an unscripted fool of myself."

Sofia was silent for a moment. Her eyes wandered from Hayden over to Tom. He was still standing far too close to the grad student, and both of them were still listening diligently to Jack. She'd forgotten all about the two of them since Hayden had shown up, but jealousy kicked in her chest again and she turned back to Hayden.

"I might—" she began.

Hayden had already started to speak, though. "Let's face it, Sofe: You could do with the money," he said, waggling his eyebrows.

This raised Sofia's hackles once more. "How do you know how much money I do or don't need?"

Hayden lifted his hand and began counting his fingers. "You guys haven't been on a vacation in three years. You live in a tiny apartment. You've had to borrow from Gracie's college fund."

"How do you know that?" Sofia demanded.

"Tom told me."

"He did?"

Hayden nodded, and Sofia was shocked. Tom rarely talked about that kind of thing with his brother. This also made her nervous. Had Tom been complaining about their marriage to Hayden? Was the money part just the tip of the iceberg? Perhaps he'd also complained about the lack of sex, or the rows, or Sofia's unappealing postpartum bumps and bulges.

Pressing another finger, Hayden went on. "And you guys never accept anything I offer you."

Sofia's teeth were gritted as she whispered, "We do *not* need your charity, Hayden."

"So you keep telling me." Hayden shook his head. "That's why I have to donate money to this little research institute he's cooking up," he added, nodding toward Jack.

Sofia furrowed her eyebrows. "What are you talking about?"

"If this Poe institute helps my brother get tenure, then I want to help out." Hayden shrugged.

Even though Hayden's gesture surprised and secretly impressed Sofia, she couldn't help blurting out, "Tom doesn't need your help to get tenure."

"If you keep pulling stunts that might get him fired, Tom's going to need all the help he can get," retorted Hayden.

"Fired? What are you talking about?" Sofia scoffed, figuring that Hayden was teasing.

"You and your club." He wagged a finger. "I don't think Manhattan U is going to be pleased, especially not him." He nodded at Jack again.

"Club?" Sofia now turned to look straight at Hayden, and with her voice raised well above a whisper, she asked, "Why does everyone keep talking about my *club*? What club?"

Hayden studied her face for a second, and then, realizing she had no idea what he was talking about, he said, "You haven't seen the *New York Mail* today, have you?"

"Of course not. Why would I read that trash?"

"Be-cause," Hayden singsonged, echoing Sofia's mocking tone, "there's an article about your protest."

Sofia slapped her hand to her forehead. "I completely forgot."

Hayden grinned. "Apparently you're the leader of something called the Professors' Wives' Club, and you are quite the troublemaker. You even led a poor wife into a nasty dispute with her husband." He waggled his eyebrows and then whispered, "Dean Havemeyer."

"What?" Sofia squawked, not caring now if everyone heard. "It doesn't say that."

Hayden jerked a thumb over his shoulder. "Go see for yourself. The deli on the corner still has copies. That's where I saw it."

Sofia shoved the heavy script back into Hayden's arms. "You'd better not be making this up," she hissed as she turned toward the door and lunged for the handle.

Jack and the rest of the crowded room had gone silent again, but Sofia didn't notice. She was already halfway along the hallway and heading for the elevator.

Fifteen

Hannah

Hannah sat in her bathroom with an open Clearblue box in her hands. She could hear her cell phone tinkling again in the room next door, but she didn't move. This was the third time her phone had rung, but Hannah couldn't stop now. It was after six on Monday evening, and all day Hannah had promised herself she would do the pregnancy test the minute Michael left. He was going on a four-day trip to Stanford to meet his new research team and check out his new lab. With the apartment to herself, Hannah vowed she would be brave and finally do what she'd been putting off for way too long.

Michael had left the apartment almost an hour ago, and even though Hannah had come straight to the bathroom after he disappeared out the door, she'd only just plucked up the courage to pull the plastic wrapping off the box and read the instructions. She'd sat fully clothed on the edge of the bath for the last hour listening to the tap drip and the pipes groan and wondering what she would do if she was pregnant. She would keep the baby; she knew that much. Yet the thought of being pregnant and living in California with Michael made her stomach clench and her head throb. It all seemed so impossibly far from her studio, her life, Michael's parents, the New York art galleries, her classes, and the life she loved.

Hannah's cell rang again, and she was tempted to jump up and run from the bathroom. She'd come this far, though; the wrapping to the box was finally off and the instructions read; she couldn't let her ringing phone distract her. She had to go through with this, and she had to know once and for all. So, as the phone continued to warble next door, Hannah raised the box in her hands and pulled out the plastic wand with trembling fingers. She studied it for a few seconds and almost laughed at how innocuous and toy-like it looked. The little white piece of plastic seemed so harmless, yet it held within it the secret of her future, of her happiness, of her fate. Not only that, this tiny wand had the power to make her whole body tighten and twist with fear.

Hannah took a few deep breaths and told herself to calm down and stop being so dramatic. Ever since she was a kid she'd always been too dramatic, too sensitive. At least, that was what her parents used to say, and her teachers too. In the last couple of years Michael had said the same whenever she got upset about a story on the news or angry about something she'd read. Perhaps all of them were right, Hannah thought as she stood and began unbuttoning her jeans. She had to stop overdramatizing and just mellow out and get on with it. If she was pregnant, it wasn't the worst thing in the world. She was married, she had a good and generous husband, they were comfortable, and she was healthy. What more could she ask for?

"Just do it," she muttered, moving toward the toilet and sitting down.

Once seated with the wand poised, she scanned the room. She studied every tile on the wall and every tiny crack in the ceiling. She listened once again to the tap dripping. If the test turned out to be positive, no doubt she'd remember all of this, every tile and crack and drop of water. After moments like these, big moments that changed everything, Hannah always remembered every detail, every smell and sight and sound. Like the night with Patrick. Even now every kiss, every touch, every whisper they shared was etched in her memory.

Hannah shook her head and whispered, "Not now."

She couldn't think about Patrick at this moment. She had to concentrate and get the test over with. Pushing Patrick as far back in her mind as she could, Hannah closed her eyes and waited. She concentrated hard, really hard, but found she couldn't pee. She'd drunk a ton of water in preparation for this moment, yet it was having no effect. Maybe it was just nerves, she told herself, and so she tried taking some more deep breaths and waited a little longer. Still nothing happened. Hannah continued to sit in her awkward pose with the wand poised at the ready for another few minutes. It was futile. She had absolutely no urge to go. Five minutes followed, and with each minute Hannah got more and more agitated and uncomfortable.

Finally she realized the only solution was another drink, and so reluctantly she stood up, pulled up her jeans, and moved out of the bathroom. She padded down the hallway, shaking her head and tutting as she went. When as she was about to turn into the kitchen, there was a loud rapping at the front door a few feet behind her. Hannah was startled and preoccupied, and thus lunged toward the door without really thinking. She flung open the door, and in the next instant she was face-to-face with a wild-eyed and out-of-breath Sofia.

"Have you seen this?" Sofia barked out between puffs, while waggling a newspaper in her hands.

Hannah glanced at Sofia, then at the paper, and shook her head. She was too shocked and bemused to speak.

"Page three," Sofia said, pushing the paper toward Hannah. "Take a look."

Hannah reached up to grab the paper, but then faltered. The plastic wand was still in her hand, and as she stared down at it she froze.

"Ah," was all Sofia said as her eyes followed Hannah's downward to the wand.

The two women were silent for a few beats, until Sofia glanced up at Hannah and said in a cool, commanding tone, "Okay, first things first. Have you done this yet?" She pointed toward Hannah's trembling hand.

Hannah shook her head and muttered a vague, "Nope."

Without asking another question, Sofia folded the newspaper, tucked it under her arm, and then guided Hannah by the elbow back into her apartment.

"Where's your bathroom?" she demanded.

Hannah pointed and then allowed Sofia to guide her along the hallway and gently nudge her through the bathroom door.

"I know it's terrifying," Sofia coaxed, "but once you get it over with, you'll feel a whole lot better. Whatever the results," she added.

Sofia then closed the door and left Hannah alone in the bathroom.

"I'll wait for you out here," Sofia called.

Only a couple of minutes later Hannah reemerged from the bathroom with the wand in her hand.

"I did it," she told Sofia, shaking her head in amazement.

Hannah thought that having Sofia loitering outside the door would make things worse. The last thing she really needed was an audience to this awful moment. But it was strange; Sofia's presence had the opposite effect. For the first time today Hannah relaxed a little, and as she did so she had finally managed to pee.

"How many minutes did the instructions say?" Sofia said as she took hold of Hannah once again and guided her along the hallway to the living room.

"Three," Hannah said weakly, a renewed wave of panic gathering in her chest.

In the living room, Sofia pulled Hannah down onto the couch, and when they were side by side she took Hannah's hand and held it in a tight, reassuring grip. The two of them stared down at the wand in Hannah's free hand while the seconds ticked by.

"I'm sorry I just barged in here," Sofia said. "I couldn't reach you on your cell. And I just had to vent my anger with someone." She jabbed at the open newspaper on the coffee table.

"I'm so glad you did." Hannah smiled, reaching over and squeezing Sofia's arm.

It was only an hour later, but Hannah felt like a completely different person. The test turned out to be negative. She'd insisted on doing another test just to be sure, which also turned out to be negative. Sofia had stayed with her through the whole thing, holding her hand while they stared at the test's tiny windows and waited to see if two blue lines would shimmer into focus. Both times just one line appeared. There wasn't even so much as a hint of a second.

At first Hannah couldn't quite believe it. Over the past week she'd pretty much convinced herself that she was pregnant, and it was weird to have the prospect suddenly gone. Nonetheless, Hannah soon began to feel giddy with relief, and amid this giddiness she recounted to Sofia in a garbled monologue all the worries she'd gone through in the last weeks and all the reasons she was terrified about being pregnant. Sofia listened to every word, offered her thoughts, and nodded sympathetically when Hannah spoke of her fears about moving to California, and about the way she and Michael didn't seem to connect anymore.

It was only when Sofia's cell rang and broke into their quiet intimacy that Hannah realized she'd been chattering on and on about herself for way too long. She hadn't even asked why Sofia had turned up so suddenly at her door waving a copy of *The New York Mail*. As soon as Sofia finished her brief phone conversation with Tom, Hannah finally asked. That was when Sofia placed the newspaper on Hannah's coffee table and showed her the article.

Hannah was shocked and appalled, just as Sofia had been. Under the headline *Profs' Wives' Club Fights Dirty with Stingy Dean*, the article briefly described the proposed parking lot and the reasons for Saturday's protest. For the most part, however, it talked about "Manhattan U's Professors' Wives' Club," which "engineered the protest" to help one of its members get back at her husband, Dean Havemeyer. According to the piece, the dean was refusing to pay for their daughter's wedding gown, and Mary Havemeyer, his wife, was mad as hell. The article then described the club as an "elite society founded by faculty wives Sofia Muñoz and Hannah Pattillo." Driving a final nail into the coffin, the story ended with a paragraph-long description about the protest getting out of hand. "Children were crying," it said, and the "Professors'

Wives' Club members were hysterical and shouting, so the police were called."

Hannah and Sofia read and reread the article as they sat together on the couch. Each time their tuts, sighs, and angered comments got more vigorous and more animated.

"I can't believe he wrote this," Hannah said after her fifth or sixth read. "He seemed so kind, so honest. . . ."

She trailed off but Sofia picked up where she left off. "And so smart too. I know. I thought the same. It's not often I get suckered in by a reporter. But this Jerry Milo guy really got me." Sofia's eyes were flaming, just as they had been when she first came to the door.

"And where the hell did he dream up all this Professors' Wives' Club crap?" Hannah jabbed at the words on the page. " 'An elite society that holds little protests to get back at their penny-pinching husbands'? Please."

"You couldn't dream up something so lame."

"Well, Jerry Milo clearly did," Hannah retorted, and shook her head again.

The two women were quiet for a second, and then Hannah asked, "Have you spoken to Mary? Has she seen this?"

"I tried calling, but she didn't pick up." Sofia paused. "But I just saw the dean, and he's *definitely* read it." Sofia went on to tell Hannah about the party she'd just come from in Tom's department, and how the dean had mentioned something about the club. "He looked at me like I was crap on his shoe," she added. "But that's nothing new."

Hannah laughed a little, but then she sighed. "What are we going to do?"

"I don't know," replied Sofia, sounding unusually defeated.

"This article isn't good for Tom or Michael."

Sofia shook her head. "Hopefully Manhattan U will know it's just tabloid trash."

"But even if the president and his cronies don't care," Hannah went on, "Havemeyer is no doubt mad as hell. Plus, we're never going to get any support for the garden campaign now. No one is going to listen to a group of hysterical wives."

"I know, I know." Sofia sighed. Then, snatching a look at her watch, she said, "Hannah? I've got to go. The babysitter is expecting me. But, listen, we should get together and talk. All of us."

"The Professors' Wives' Club, you mean?" Hannah said with a bitter laugh.

Sofia snorted. "Exactly."

The next afternoon Hannah sat at the back of a crowded and stuffy tutorial room in the art department. She hadn't planned to come to this modern art seminar today. It said on the flyer that Patrick would be introducing the guest speaker, and since she'd been avoiding anything where she might see Patrick, she'd scratched this event out of her diary. However, after last night and the highs and lows of the pregnancy tests and reading the article in the *Mail,* seeing Patrick no longer seemed so fraught or terrifying. The idea of having to be close to him still made her feel awkward and confused, but if she hung out at the back of the seminar, where he wouldn't see her, she figured she'd be just fine. It was silly to keep on hiding, she told herself, especially if it meant missing out on the kind of seminars and classes she'd no longer be able to attend once she moved to Palo Alto.

From her seat close to the door Hannah had a clear view of the speaker, but she was concealed from Patrick by a tall student sitting in front of her. It was the perfect spot. Of course, every now and then she would peek around the student and snatch a small glimpse of Patrick, who sat at the front, his long legs crossed and his head cocked slightly as he listened to the speaker. She couldn't help noticing how attractive he looked today. His soft sea green shirt was open at the collar, and even from way back here, Hannah could see that it made his eyes look greener than ever.

With Patrick in the room, Hannah was finding it hard to concentrate. Not only that, the speaker had a quiet, raspy monotone, and it was getting increasingly hard to follow the intricacies of his presentation. The title was "Duchamp, Dada, and Desire" and Hannah had come to the seminar expecting something intriguing and useful. She loved Marcel Duchamp and was writing about his work in a term paper for her art history class.

Yet here she was, not really listening, doodling on her notepad and sneaking peeks at Patrick. And as her mind wandered, Hannah kept thinking back to everything that had happened last night. Mostly she thought about the negative pregnancy tests and the irony that, since she'd done them, she'd been feeling dull cramps in her abdomen. In fact, as she sat in the seminar those cramps were getting more intense, and she was beginning to wonder if she should escape to the bathroom. She was reticent to leave and draw attention to herself, however, particularly Patrick's attention, so she remained in her seat and tried desperately to focus on the presentation.

It was futile, however. The speaker's voice was too soporific, his writing too dense and convoluted, and Hannah's mind was soon wandering again. This time her thoughts returned to the *Mail* article, and her jaw pulsated with renewed anger. Why would someone write an article like that? What was the point of making up all those lies? What angered her most of all was the feeling that Sofia's determination might be crushed. It had been Sofia—her anger, her humor, her willfulness—that had gotten the whole protest off the ground. It was Sofia, on the day of the protest, who had held everything together. Hannah hated to think that Milo's article would defeat Sofia. Without her, there would definitely be no hope for the garden.

Hannah scratched her pen furiously across her notepad until the lights dimmed and the room was plunged into darkness. Startled, she looked up. At the front of the room the projector screen glowed white, and after a loud click a photograph of a urinal flickered into focus.

"This, of course, is Duchamp's *Fountain*," the speaker was saying from somewhere in the gloom.

Hannah wanted to stay for the slides, but she knew this might be her one chance. Carefully pushing back her chair, she stood up, tiptoed to the door, and let herself out. She headed quickly along the corridor, and when she got to the bathroom and into a stall, she discovered she was right. At long last her period had arrived. Doing the pregnancy test had not just soothed her frantic mind; it had clearly relaxed her tightly wound body. Sitting on the toilet, she propped her head in her hands. She was overwhelmed with relief, and for a few minutes just sat there letting the feeling ripple over her.

A little later, as she plucked at her short red hair in the bathroom mirror, her phone vibrated in her pocket. She wiggled her cell free and saw in the glowing screen that it was Michael. She was about to answer but stopped short. Did she really want to talk to him? It occurred to her that she didn't. If she answered she'd have to make conversation, and that was often hard with Michael these days. Even if he was in the mood to talk, he'd no doubt go on about Stanford: the campus, his amazing colleagues, the "awesome" hardware, the "gigs," and the "RAM." Hannah couldn't stomach hearing all this, not now. She was resigned to the idea of moving to the West Coast for a year, but she still wasn't happy about it. Leaving New York, her MFA program, and her studio was so painful, and she was going to do it only for the sake of her marriage. A cloud of sorrow hung over her, though, and it made her unable to really imagine life in California or to start organizing for their move.

As Hannah slipped the phone away and headed out of the bathroom, she tried to tell herself it wouldn't be so bad and that she must be more positive. She tried to will herself to smile, but couldn't.

"Are you okay?"

The concerned voice was Patrick's. He was walking slowly along the corridor toward her.

"Yes, thanks, fine," she croaked, trying to calm herself. She was feeling the same rush of panic and excitement she'd felt when she'd seen him at the protest just a couple of days ago.

"I saw you leave." He waved toward the seminar room. "And I wanted to make sure everything was all right." He looked both concerned and slightly embarrassed as he spoke.

Hannah looked up into his green eyes and fought an overwhelming urge to throw her arms around him and sink her face into his chest.

"I'm fine," she repeated, her voice still strangled.

Patrick reached out and gently took her arm. He then guided her around the corner.

"You're not angry with me, are you?" Patrick asked when they came to a standstill and the open door to the seminar room was out of sight.

Hannah's arm tingled from where he had touched it. "No." She shook her head. "No, of course not."

Patrick looked relieved. "Good," he breathed quietly.

"Don't you need to be in there?" Hannah waved down the hallway and toward the seminar room.

"It's wrapping up," he reassured her, and then he added, "I wanted to say something to you. I wanted to say it to you the other day in the garden, but then your husband . . . well . . ."

Hannah shuddered a little at the memory of Patrick and Michael shaking hands.

"I don't want what happened between us . . ." Patrick went on. "I don't want to cause any problems for you."

The concern and intimacy in his voice made Hannah want to cry. The other day when she saw him, she'd thought all his caring had gone. Yet here it was again.

"I . . ." she began. But then, much to her own horror, it happened: She began to cry. Unable to stop them, she felt warm tears slide down her cheeks, and her chest began to convulse with silent sobs.

Patrick immediately put his hand up, held her face, and gently wiped at her tears with his thumb. His warm touch only made her cry more.

"I'm so sorry," he said, his face furrowed and panicked.

"No." She gulped through her tears. "No, it isn't your fault."

Patrick was shaking his head and still holding her cheek. "I've never done anything like that," he whispered. "I feel ashamed. I shouldn't have let it happen. But you . . ." He shook his head again, and he closed his eyes. "It's just . . . you get it."

Hannah blinked back her tears and looked up at Patrick quizzically. "Get it?"

"I've never met someone who thinks like I do." He gave a little laugh. "From Picasso to Karl Marx to Freud, you just get it. Or should I say, you get it the way I get it."

It was Hannah's turn to give a little laugh. "But don't all your students get it? I mean, you're such a great teacher, you make it all make sense."

"I wish that were the case." Patrick took his hand from Hannah's face and ran it through his thick hair. "It's hard to find a soul mate, even amongst my academic brethren." He smiled.

For a moment the two of them simply looked at each other. The sound of voices nearby soon broke their trance, however, and Hannah found herself backing away from Patrick and urgently dabbing at her red eyes. Patrick stared over at her with regret and then, clearly remembering something, reached around and pulled a card from his back pocket.

"Try to make it, if you can," he said as he handed her the glossy postcard.

But before Hannah could ask him what it was, a group of grad students rounded the corner, spotted Patrick, and were firing questions at him about the seminar that had just ended. Hannah took a few more paces back and let the students encircle Patrick. Over their heads he gave her an apologetic smile.

Pressed against the opposite wall, Hannah looked at the postcard. On the front was a beautiful abstract painting in vibrant reds and yellows with a backwash of pale pink. She flipped the card over. In small print the card announced an opening for an exhibition titled Articulations. Below the title, in an even smaller font, Hannah read the words, *Paintings by Patrick O'Hare.*

She flipped the card back over and stared at the painting. This was Patrick's? she wondered in surprise. Patrick painted? He was an artist with an upcoming exhibition? And not just any exhibition: an exhibition at the prestigious Manya Boyd Gallery in Chelsea. She looked from the postcard up at Patrick. She tried to catch his eye, but he was preoccupied with the students.

As Hannah looked back at the painting she felt light-headed. He'd never told her he was an artist. All that stuff he said earlier about her "getting him," when the truth was she hardly even knew him. What other secrets did he have? she wondered. Once again she looked over and watched him push back his ruffled hair. There was no ring on his left hand, but that meant nothing. Perhaps there was a wife and kids, a dog and a family home back in England.

A sudden vibration from her cell phone made Hannah jump, and, feeling discombobulated, she snatched the phone out of her pocket. She peered at the screen and discovered that Michael had now sent her a text. She pressed the receive button and scanned the message.

Hey, my beauty, it read, *I'm in CA. I'm online and waiting. M.*

Hannah stared down at the message. *My beauty.* She read the words again. Michael hadn't called her that in years. It used to be his pet name for her, but now he just used plain old *honey* or, most often, *Hann.* She had no idea why he was telling her he was in California and waiting online. Was he expecting her to e-mail him?

Talking to Michael wasn't what she needed right now, but this message was disconcerting. Perhaps there was something she was supposed to have done for him, she wondered as she slunk off down the corridor and called his number.

After a couple of rings Michael picked up and said immediately, "Hann? I can't talk now. I'm going into a meeting."

"But," Hannah began, her forehead crinkling in confusion, "your text?"

"What text?" Michael said, sounding distracted and harried.

"The one you just sent me."

There was a silence on the line, and then Michael gave a quick laugh. "Ignore it. Something's come up now and I have to go."

"Did you want me to e-mail something?" Hannah asked.

But Michael didn't reply; he'd already hung up. Pulling the phone from her ear, Hannah looked at it, her brow still lined with bewilderment. After a few seconds she pinched the cell between her thumb and forefinger and slapped it shut.

"Men," she muttered under her breath.

Her own husband was proving to be as mysterious as Patrick. She was probably better off without any of them.

Sixteen

Ashleigh

"Waffles or pancakes?" Gina peeked in the door, her face already made up and her smile wide and sparkling.

"Sorry?" Ashleigh croaked, and then blinked her heavy eyes.

Gina pushed the door open and wiggled in. She was wearing an incredibly tight pencil skirt, a spotless white blouse, and a pair of three-inch heels. "You're a sleepyhead this morning." She giggled, pulling back the soft pink drapes behind Ashleigh's bed.

Ashleigh squinted and groaned as daylight blasted into the room. "What time is it?"

"Time we were getting up. It's a beautiful Saturday morning out there." Gina wagged her finger. "Now, which is it? Waffles or pancakes?"

Propping herself on her elbows, Ashleigh looked up at her smiling cousin. Panic gripped her chest as she wondered whether this was how every morning was going to be: a chipper wake-up call followed by a home-cooked breakfast? It wasn't exactly how Ashleigh wanted her days to begin. She'd never been a morning person. Sam had always understood that about her, and always gave Ashleigh a wide berth in the morning as she tumbled into the shower, threw on a suit, and then headed out to work—via the Italian coffee shop on Bleecker Street. Sam understood that Ashleigh was not one for conversation or hearty breakfasts, not until she'd knocked back her first espresso of the day.

"Thanks, Gina." Ashleigh's parched mouth attempted to work itself into a smile. "Please don't put yourself out. Perhaps we can go out for brunch later," she offered, hoping to secure herself some more sleep. "My treat, of course. To say thanks for putting me up like this."

Gina laughed. "Don't be silly, Ashey. It won't take a second." She patted the comforter covering Ashleigh's knees. "Anyhow, having you stay is *so* fun," she added as she tottered back out of the room.

Ashleigh watched her leave and then slumped back on her pillow and considered whether she'd just made a huge mistake in taking up Gina's offer to come stay. Perhaps she should have stayed with Sam just until she'd found herself a new place. But Ashleigh also knew she had to make the break straightaway, otherwise she would never do it. And Gina had been so sweet and excited when offering Ashleigh her spare room, it had been hard to refuse. The arrangement was only meant to be temporary, of course. Ashleigh got back from DC yesterday morning and then had moved her belongings to Gina's on the Upper West Side by yesterday evening. She was determined to leave Gina's apartment as soon as possible, though, and already she'd spoken to a broker and scheduled a couple of appointments to see apartments in Brooklyn this afternoon.

Remembering the busy day ahead, Ashleigh pushed herself up to sit and swung her legs out of bed. She turned to look out of the window before getting up, though. Under a cloudless blue sky, Central Park was a vast patchwork of green leaves and even greener grass. She could see just a corner of the boating lake in the distance, twinkling in the early morning sun. Of course, this was one of the good points about taking up Gina's offer to stay: the breathtaking view of the park. As soon as she moved out of here, no doubt Ashleigh's windows would overlook some drab alleyway or straight into her neighbor's apartment. Not only that, she wouldn't be sleeping in a proper bedroom on a spacious queen-size bed. More likely she'd be sleeping on a lumpy futon tucked between a bathtub and set of rickety bookshelves.

Blinking out at the view again, Ashleigh thought about Gina and the fact that her cousin woke up to this view every day, even though she'd never worked a day in her life. Whereas Ashleigh's parents believed in careers, hard work, and proving oneself, Gina's parents had always been the opposite. Since she was tiny Aunt Gaynor and Uncle Ray had lavished everything on their beloved daughter, and with her vast trust fund—a gift passed down from Aunt Gaynor's wealthy New England family—Gina never needed to work. Instead she spent her days flitting from fund-raiser to charity ball to film premiere and back again.

Ashleigh wasn't jealous of her cousin's life, though. Neither was she jealous of the apartment. It was vast and its views incredible, but it wasn't where Ashleigh wanted to be. It wasn't home. Instead of walls lined with books and vibrant paintings, Gina's walls were bare except for the occasional pastel print or a murky collage of a ballet dancer. There were no interesting knickknacks brought back by Sam from Ghana or Pakistan or Romania. Instead bowls containing pebbles of colored glass or unlit scented candles lurked on Gina's sparse coffee tables and dressers.

Most of all, it wasn't home because there was no Sam. Ashleigh had moved out only yesterday morning, but it felt like an eternity. She'd already endured nearly two weeks away from Sam while she was with her father in DC, and now an unknown stretch of time lay ahead when she would no longer come home to Sam. She wouldn't see the books, knickknacks, and disarray of their apartment, or smell the familiar smells of brewing coffee, cinnamon, and Sam's rose-mint shampoo, or hear Sam's sweet voice singing in the shower. Ashleigh experienced a weird vertigo feeling and a nagging pull in her stomach when she thought about having to live without all those things.

Sam had tried to persuade her to stay, but Ashleigh was resolved, and so yesterday, blinded with tears, she'd packed her bags, kissed Sam gently on the forehead, and headed out of the apartment. Although Sam was dismayed at Ashleigh's decision to move out, she wasn't angry, and true to her loving and eminently patient self, she'd agreed to hang in there and wait for the day when Ashleigh would be ready to come back home. At least, that was what she'd said when Ashleigh left.

Sam had also agreed to meet Ashleigh for dinner tonight.

"It will be like we're dating again," Ashleigh said as they discussed the idea in the minutes before she left Sam's apartment.

Sam simply smiled. "Maybe so."

Thinking back to Sam's words and to her beautiful smiling face, Ashleigh sensed the weird dropping feeling again, coupled with a pull in her stomach. She stood up and grabbed her bathrobe. When she glimpsed the clock on the dresser—nearly nine o'clock, it read—her spirits buoyed a little as she calculated that in just ten hours she and Sam would be sitting side by side at their favorite Mexican restaurant in the East Village, sipping frozen margaritas. She carried this thought with her into the shower, and by the time Ashleigh was washed and dressed, the nagging feeling in her belly was almost gone and she was ready to face breakfast with her cousin.

In the kitchen Gina was standing by the griddle with a long silver spatula in her hand.

"I decided on pancakes," she called out as she heard Ashleigh come into the room. "Hope that sounds good."

Ashleigh scooted up onto one of the stools at the huge granite-topped island. A myriad of stainless-steel pots hung above her from an ornate wooden rack. Gina had already set out pristine cloth napkins, silverware, and a small glass of orange juice for each of them.

"You don't have to do all this." Ashleigh waved toward the place settings and then the griddle. "Really, Gina, I mean it."

"I enjoy it." Gina beamed. "And I need the practice for when I'm married. Davey loves a cooked breakfast."

Ashleigh was about to laugh, thinking Gina was joking. But of course Gina wasn't joking. She had every intention of becoming a full-fledged Stepford wife. She and Davey were already looking for a house in Westchester, not far from where Gina grew up. Only last week they put a down payment on a Mercedes SUV. Watching Gina gaily flipping the pancakes, Ashleigh felt her old antipathy for Gina rising in her chest. But then, as her cousin turned toward her, smiled her wide and honest smile, and slid a stack of pancakes onto Ashleigh's plate, the bad feelings instantly melted away. *Who cares, if that's what Gina wants?* Ashleigh told herself. It was Gina's life, and if she wanted to be a stay-at-home wife in the suburbs, that was her choice.

As Ashleigh took her first bite of the delicious and perfectly griddled pancakes, she began to feel guilty. Over recent years she'd been so hard on her cousin: never returning her calls, always trying to avoid her at family functions, bitching about Gina to friends. Yet all the while she had never stopped to consider that Gina was just trying to be friends, and that, unlike Ashleigh, Gina held no judgments about her cousin's life.

Ashleigh looked over at Gina, who now sat at the opposite end of the island, popping tiny bites of pancake between her cherry red lips. "So, how are the wedding plans?" Ashleigh asked. It was long overdue, but it was now her turn to make the effort, she decided.

Gina wiggled on her stool. "Well," she said with an excited puff, "today I'm picking out my bouquet and the flowers for the church."

"Yeah?"

Gina nodded. Then, with her arms waving and her eyes flashing, she went on to describe every flower and shrub, every color and tone, every ribbon and corsage, and how all this would complement her dress, and the bridesmaids' ribbons, and Davey's cummerbund. Ashleigh nodded and smiled as Gina spoke. There was something so soothing and captivating about listening to her and watching her. Whatever Ashleigh thought about Davey or their lavish wedding plans, Gina was happy. And seeing her like this was entrancing.

When Gina had run out of breath and began clearing the dishes, she suddenly slapped her forehead and groaned. "Oh, darn it, I nearly forgot: Daddy called this morning. He says he spoke to your dad."

Ashleigh had been about to move toward the hallway and collect her coat, but at Gina's words she froze. A spasm of panic clenched her throat. "Is everything okay?" she squeaked.

"Yes. Oh, I'm sorry, yes." Gina dashed over to Ashleigh's side and patted her arm. "Everything is fine. In fact, it's more than fine. Your dad's feeling much better. He's coming to New York today."

"*What?*" Ashleigh's incredulous shout echoed around the spacious kitchen.

Gina blushed and stammered, "Th-that's what Daddy said. He said Uncle Chad had to meet someone in the city."

Ashleigh shook her head. "He just had a heart attack. He's supposed to be resting. When I left him in DC, he was still sitting in his armchair, gray-faced, with a blanket over his knees. He *can't* be coming to New York today. He can't be."

This time Gina was silent, and she just looked at Ashleigh with big, sympathetic eyes.

"I don't believe this." Ashleigh shook her head again, realizing Gina was telling the truth. "The man is crazy. He's going to wind up giving himself another heart attack."

Gina gave a small smile and said, "He's a tough cookie, your dad. He'll be fine." Then, turning back toward the sink, she said, "Anyway, he and Daddy want to take us both for dinner at the Algonquin. Won't that be fun?" She added with a tinkle of laughter, "I adore the Algonquin."

"When?" Ashleigh asked, once again frozen in panic.

"Tonight."

Ashleigh felt a little sick. "Tonight?"

"Uh-huh," Gina singsonged over the sound of clinking plates.

"Oh," Ashleigh murmured with a sigh, already thinking about the phone call she was going to have to make to Sam, calling off their date tonight.

The broker was late. She was supposed to meet Ashleigh at one, and it was already a quarter after. While she waited, Ashleigh sat on the steps of the unfamiliar building in Brooklyn where she would soon be viewing an apartment and fiddled with her cell phone. She didn't really care about the broker's tardiness. She had too many things on her mind to be bothered. Plus, from the dreary exterior of the building behind her, she was pretty sure the apartment would be a pea-sized hovel. This would be the first place she would see in her apartment hunt, and already she was sick of the whole process.

In her hands her cell was hot and clammy. Ostensibly she was using these spare minutes to erase some old texts and to tidy up her contact list—something she'd been meaning to do for a long time—but her mind wasn't really on the job. Instead she was thinking about Sam and the phone conversation they'd had an hour ago, when Ashleigh rang to cancel tonight's date.

As ever, Sam was kind and claimed she understood. "Do what you have to do," she told Ashleigh, her tone upbeat.

But not being able to see Sam's hazel eyes, which always spoke volumes, Ashleigh feared that Sam was bluffing and she really was getting exasperated.

"I promise this is the last time," Ashleigh responded. "It's just . . . with his heart and everything. . . . And Uncle Ray will be there too," she blathered on. "I think I really should go."

"It's fine, hon, honestly," was Sam's response.

But Ashleigh kept on talking. "I'll stand up to him one day, Sam. My dad, I mean. I'll stand up to him. I won't jump when he says jump." She gave a quick laugh. "I'll be tough with him, like I am with my clients. And I'll tell him about us. I really will."

There was a silence on the other end of the line, and as Ashleigh held her breath, wondering what Sam might say next, she heard Sam breathe out a small, light sigh, and the words "I miss you" followed.

Now, while Ashleigh sat on the stoop with her phone in hand, Sam's three short words played over and over in her mind. They were perhaps the saddest and the happiest words she'd ever heard. They held within them all Sam's love for her; all the love Ashleigh was so honored and happy to be given. But the words also encapsulated all their shared sadness too. The sadness that, because of Ashleigh's own cowardice, meant they weren't together on this beautiful spring afternoon, and instead Ashleigh was starting out on what would no doubt be a wretched hunt for a miserable place of her own.

Tears pricked at her eyes, and she had to blink hard to stop them from flowing. Before Ashleigh's mood could turn even more dour, though, her phone jumped and jingled in her hands and Sofia's name flashed up on the small screen. In spite of everything, Ashleigh smiled and immediately hit receive.

Before either of the women said hello, Sofia barked down the line, "What's all this about you moving out?"

Ashleigh was stunned. "How—" she began.

But Sofia was talking again. "I just stopped by your apartment and Sam told me," she explained. "What's going on? Have you broken up? I refuse to believe it if you say you have. You two are meant to be together."

Ashleigh found herself chuckling at Sofia's breathless rant. "No," she insisted, "no, we haven't broken up."

"What, then?" Sofia demanded. "What's going on?"

"It's just for a while," Ashleigh explained. "Just until Dad gets better. I want to . . . I don't know . . . I want to come out to them more gradually."

Sofia was silent for a second. "But that makes no sense," she said, and then she asked, "So you haven't told them yet?"

"No. How could I?" Ashleigh's mouth twisted into a sad smile. "It would give him another heart attack."

"But is moving out really the solution?" Sofia sounded exasperated.

Ashleigh paused for a moment. "Yes. No. I don't know. Sam clearly thinks it's dumb."

"It *is* dumb," Sofia blurted out. "You guys are so good together. You don't want to risk that, do you?" Sofia then shifted to a softer tone. "Look, all I'm saying is, don't make yourself unhappy for your parents' sake. All a parent wants—or should want—is for their kids to be happy."

"I know," Ashleigh said, defeated. "I know."

"In the meantime"—Sofia chuckled—"if you do go ahead with your plan, promise me you won't move to Brooklyn or some other far-off land!"

Ashleigh's eyes wandered up and down the street where she was sitting. "Oops." She laughed, crinkling her eyes in amusement. Before Sofia could ask what she was doing and she'd have to explain where she was, Ashleigh added, "I heard you were the Martin Luther King Junior of the garden protest last week."

"Or the ringleader of a club of vengeful professors' wives." Sofia sighed. "Depending on what you read."

Ashleigh cringed. "I heard about the *Mail* article too." She paused and then asked, "Why would the reporter write such trash?"

Sofia sighed again. "I have no idea. Although, you know what? The more I think about it, the more I think Jack Havemeyer had something to do with it. He's got his fingers in so many pies at the moment. What with the parking lot and now this new Poe Research Institute—which, of course, my dear husband is beside himself with excitement about," she added with a snort.

"But why would he have anything to do with the news story? After all, it doesn't exactly paint him in a good light. Didn't it call him 'the penny-pinching dean'?"

"It did." Sofia half laughed. "But it made Mary and her band of wife friends sound a lot worse."

Ashleigh thought about it for a second and then said, "Maybe he was trying to throw the press off the scent. You know, cover up the fact that he's ruthlessly digging up a beautiful garden in the middle of New York City to replace it with some ugly parking garage."

"Exactly my thoughts," exclaimed Sofia. "Havemeyer must know this Milo character. That's what I think. Perhaps he paid him off."

Both women were silent for a few beats until Ashleigh blurted out, "That reminds me."

"Reminds you of what?"

Ashleigh went on to tell Sofia about the conversation she over-heard in her parents' living room just last week, and how it turned out her very own law firm was responsible for the contract be-tween Wilkins Construction and Manhattan U.

"They were? They did?" Sofia cried. "Why didn't you tell me before?"

"I've been kind of busy," Ashleigh replied in a guilty whisper, "what with my dad and Sam and moving out. I—"

"Shit, yes, of course," Sofia interrupted. "Sorry, Ashleigh. I un-derstand. But listen, did you hear your uncle or your dad say any-thing else?"

"What do you mean, anything else?"

Sofia's voice started to sound a little raspy and excited. "I'm not sure really. It's just . . . the other day I heard that Wilkins Con-struction was the company Manhattan U used to pull down the old Poe house on Third Street. Apparently Wilkins was a night-mare. There were lots of delays, and they went way over budget."

Ashleigh brow furrowed. "And Manhattan U is using them again?"

"Yep," Sofia responded. "Weird, don't you think?"

"Weird," agreed Ashleigh.

She was then quiet again, and before she could say anything more Sofia asked, "Are you thinking what I'm thinking?"

With a smile, Ashleigh replied, "If you're thinking that maybe I could sneak into my office and take a quick peek at some of the paperwork between Manhattan U and Wilkins, we may well be thinking the same thing."

"Good girl!" shouted Sofia down the line, and then, without paus-ing for breath, she asked, "When do you think you could do it?"

Ashleigh looked up and down the street again. A woman in a neat suit with a clipboard tucked under her arm was heading down the sidewalk in Ashleigh's direction. She had to be the broker Ash-leigh was waiting for.

"How about now?" Ashleigh giggled, standing up and striding off in the opposite direction from the approaching woman.

Seventeen

Sofia

Just two hours after their phone conversation, Ashleigh was standing at Sofia's door holding a large manila envelope in her hands. Her cheeks were pink, and wisps of hair had fallen from her barrette and were scattered over her damp face. She looked exhausted but animated. She was also soaking wet. The beautiful spring day of a couple of hours ago had suddenly been replaced by heavy, dark clouds and torrents of rain, and it was clear Ashleigh had been caught without an umbrella.

"What took you so long?" teased Sofia as she shifted Edgar in her arms and pulled Ashleigh into her apartment. "A whole two hours. What kind of lawyer are you?"

Ashleigh laughed. "I'm sorry to keep you waiting, Mrs. Hysterical Professor's Wife."

"Touché." Sofia chuckled, leading Ashleigh into the tiny hallway and helping her shed her wet jacket and soaking shoes.

Once they'd discussed the abrupt change in weather, the two women moved into the living room and Ashleigh headed toward the couch. Along the way Ashleigh said hi to Gracie, who was lying on her belly watching *Dora the Explorer* and shoveling Goldfish into her mouth. Gracie was too absorbed in the TV and her snack to notice that someone new was in the room, let alone that it was her favorite babysitter.

While Ashleigh got seated Sofia lowered Edgar into his bouncy seat, where he immediately started to kick his legs and blow wet, contented bubbles. Sofia smiled down at him for a second and then looked up at Ashleigh, about to quiz her about what she'd found. Instead she noticed the clutter and disarray of her apartment. Ashleigh had barely managed to find a clear spot amid the toys on the couch to sit down. Gracie's books were in a jumbled mess all over the floor. Worst of all, an overflowing basket of dirty laundry was skulking in the doorway. Sofia's apartment was never particularly tidy, but this week she'd completely let it slide.

She'd done it on purpose to get back at Tom. Not that Tom was one to care about a tidy home, but she'd done it anyway as a silent payback for the other night at the Poe party and his little whispered exchange with that hot-pants grad student. Sofia hadn't confronted Tom about it. For one, she was preoccupied with the *Mail* article and her anger at the reporter for making a fool of her and her friends. Hayden, too, was binding a lot of her thoughts. Although she hadn't talked to Hayden since the party, the memory of Norman Watts's script in her hands kept coming back to her. She hated to admit it, but she was desperate to get her hands on it again—on any script, in fact.

And so, as the last few days passed and her mind swirled with other matters, Sofia began to wonder if she'd imagined the whole thing between Tom and the grad student, and she felt too unsure and a little embarrassed to admit her jealousy to her husband. Sofia's suspicions didn't entirely evaporate, however; they still lurked at the back of her mind. Hence the payback. Although letting her home descend into a pigsty was a lame payback, she realized now as she looked around at the cluttered room. She'd always thought she would be the kind of wife who would be totally honest with her husband. She'd be the kind of wife who'd lay it on the line, instead of skulking around doing little dirty revenge tricks behind his cheating back. After all, she was straight-talking, no-nonsense Sofia. That was how she used to be known back in Hollywood. So why was she being so gutless and pathetic now? she wondered.

Sofia was shaken from her thoughts by a loud squeak. Ashleigh had leaned back against the couch and squished one of Edgar's squeaky crib toys in the process.

"I'm sorry this place is a dump," Sofia said, jumping up and pushing all the toys from the couch with one decisive sweep of her arm.

Ashleigh waved. "I love clutter." She sighed. "My cousin's place, where I'm staying, is the antithesis of clutter."

Sofia plopped down next to Ashleigh and patted her knee. "That's why you need to go home." She waved toward the front door and toward the hallway she and Ashleigh had shared up until yesterday. She then added, "Back to Sam."

Ashleigh's face crumpled slightly. "I know," she said. "But I can't. Not yet."

Sofia didn't push her. She could see that Ashleigh was torn up and confused about everything that was going on. She didn't need Sofia nagging her too. Instead Sofia laughed and said, "Okay, out with it. Stop keeping me in suspense. What did you find?"

With a grin, Ashleigh raised the envelope she'd been carrying in her arms and said, "Ta-da!" But then, clearly having a moment of doubt, she let her eyes dart toward the doorway. "Is Tom around?" she whispered.

Sofia shook her head. "Fat chance," she huffed. "Thanks to Dean Jack and this new Poe institute, Tom's been working day and night submitting a whole bunch of scholarship proposals. The only way the institute will garner respect in academic circles is to win some big-deal grants. The deadlines for most of these proposals happens to be next week," she added with a frown.

At first Sofia had been pleased for Tom about the research institute. But she wasn't so happy now that it was sucking up all his time. He'd stayed in his office late all week trying to get the proposals ready for submission. At least, that was what he'd said he was doing. Sofia's throat clutched a little as she tried to banish the thought that Tom might be up to something very different from proposal writing—something very different that involved some sexy little grad student in tight jeans.

Tom would never do that to her, she attempted to reassure herself as she reached over to take the envelope that Ashleigh was passing her. Never.

"Here you go," Ashleigh was saying. "I suppose it doesn't matter if Tom knows that I'm showing this to you. It's not like he would run to Manhattan U management and tell them, is it?"

"Of course not." Sofia knew that much for certain about her husband.

Sofia pulled from the envelope a thick document, stapled at its corner.

"It's a copy of the construction contract," Ashleigh explained, "for the demolition of the garden and the building of the parking lot."

Sofia's fingers flicked through the pages. "Is there anything suspicious about it?" she murmured as her eyes scanned the dense legal jargon.

Ashleigh moved closer to Sofia and took the contract back into her hands. "There's nothing out of the ordinary, except this," she said, turning to the contract's very last page. "Read this clause."

Sofia followed Ashleigh's pointing finger and began to read. Under the heading Right of Access, the clause stated, *Dean Jack Havemeyer will be granted full access to the site during excavation and foundation construction and will oversee excavation and foundation disposal.*

Sofia read and reread the clause several times. She knew nothing about the construction business, but she knew this was weird.

"Weird, don't you think?" Ashleigh said, reading Sofia's mind.

Sofia looked at Ashleigh. "Have you ever seen anything like this before? In a construction contract?"

Ashleigh shook her head.

"Why does Jack want to nose around in all the mud and trash?" Sofia blurted out.

"Exactly what I wondered."

"What's he hoping to find?" Sofia asked, her eyes narrowing and her head shaking again. "He must be looking for something; he must be. Why else would he want to root around in all the debris?"

"I agree." Ashleigh nodded.

Sofia slumped back against the couch and fell silent for a moment as her mind raced. The dean had to be up to something, perhaps searching for something. If only she could figure out what.

As Ashleigh leaned over and cooed at Edgar, who was still kicking happily in his seat, Sofia's smile crept to the corners of her mouth. For the first time this week, she realized, she felt motivated again. After the article came out she'd flipped back and forth between an unquenchable rage and a feeling of utter defeat. Sofia was furious with the reporter and knew she should stand up to him and his story. At the same time she felt completely beaten. Hannah was totally right: Who would support the campaign after Milo's article made them sound like a coven of meddlesome witches? Sofia had no idea how they could counter this image. She'd called the *New York Mail* to get Jerry Milo's number, but they blew her off with an e-mail address. Sofia wanted to bawl out this Milo character; she didn't want to send some lame e-mail that he'd no doubt ignore. Being denied his phone number served to make Sofia even more frustrated and then despondent. In Hollywood she knew everyone. If this had happened there, if some movie magazine had written something bad about her or one of her clients, she could have pulled all kinds of strings. She could have unleashed a counterattack. But here in New York she didn't know the right people; she had no foot in. She was just a whining nobody.

But now that this contract had surfaced, Sofia could feel the old fires rekindling.

"We need to get more dirt on him," she said, clapping her hands and leaning forward.

Ashleigh peered at her. "And how will we do that?"

Sofia drummed her fingers on her lips and said, "I'm not sure yet. But there must be a way."

"What about Mary? Do you think she would help out?"

Sofia sighed. "I still haven't heard from her. It's so weird. One minute she's on board, bringing the keys to the garden, joining the protest. Next minute she goes AWOL. Tom said he saw her in the

English department early in the week, but she's not returned any of my calls."

"We could try going up there." Ashleigh pointed over her head. "To her apartment. They live on the thirtieth floor of building B, just above Hannah."

"And run into Jack himself?" scoffed Sofia. "I don't think so." She paused for a second. "He must have so much control over that woman. It must be why she's disappeared. Can you imagine how mad he was when she got back from the protest?"

Ashleigh grimaced and then drew in a breath. "You know what? The first time I ever met her, that night when Hannah and I were out in the garden, she was wearing these big sunglasses—in the middle of the night. And when she sat down I thought I saw a bruise, right there." Ashleigh pointed at her own cheek. "I thought it might be the light, a shadow or something."

"You think he did it?" Sofia looked appalled. "Shit. I thought about it once, but . . ." She trailed off.

"I don't know. It could have been nothing."

"But it could have been something." Sofia wagged her finger.

While the two women contemplated this, the front door clicked and banged open.

"Hey, there!" was Tom's jovial call from the hallway.

At the sound of her dad's voice, Gracie sprang to her feet and ran out to greet him. Meanwhile Sofia's face immediately sank into a frown. What was he doing home? she wondered. He said he'd be tied up until tonight with his proposal writing. He couldn't be home to see them. She'd arranged to go to the kids' art museum in SoHo with a mom friend. But when Ashleigh had promised to come around with her findings, Sofia had canceled. Tom didn't know that, though, which begged the question, Why was he here?

"You guys are still here?" Tom said as he ambled into the room with Gracie in his arms. "I thought you were going over to the art museum. . . . Oh, hey, Ashleigh." He smiled, spotting Ashleigh on the couch.

Before Ashleigh could reply, Sofia cut in. "I thought you were going to be at the office all afternoon." She couldn't disguise the edge of suspicion in her voice.

Tom's eyebrows rose and he cocked his head. "I am. I will."

"Then why are you back so soon?"

"What's the matter, Sofe?" Tom's face flickered between amusement and vague worry. "You're not happy to see me or something?"

Out of the corner of her eye Sofia could see Ashleigh shifting uncomfortably in her seat, but she couldn't stop herself. "Why are you back?" she demanded again.

"I forgot my wallet," he said defensively. Then, shaking his head and plopping Gracie back on the floor, he paced toward the bookshelf, where, on the second shelf, sat his wallet. As he slipped it into his pocket, he looked back over at Sofia and said with an edge of bitterness, "I'll get back to the office, then. I can tell when I'm not wanted."

Sofia didn't say anything; she simply narrowed her eyes and watched him leave the room.

When the front door slammed shut, Ashleigh said in a tentative whisper, "Is everything okay, Sofia?"

Sofia was silent for a beat, and then she turned to Ashleigh. "Do you think he would cheat on me?" She gestured to the doorway where Tom had just left.

"Tom?" Ashleigh almost shrieked. "You have to be kidding me."

Sofia shook her head. "He might look all innocent with those big blue eyes and nerdy glasses . . ." She trailed off.

"He wouldn't. The guy is so in love with you, with your kids, he just wouldn't," Ashleigh insisted. But, clearly noticing the frown still lingering on Sofia's face, she asked, "Why? Do you really think it's possible? Have you heard something?"

"No. It's just that things have been off lately between us. We never used to argue, but we've been fighting a lot lately. He's slept on the couch too many nights. And I haven't let him get near me, you know, in the bedroom," she said with a weak smile.

"You just had a baby, Sofia," Ashleigh blurted out with an incredulous puff of laughter. "You're tired. You're fragile. You have a lot on your plate."

"I know, I know." Sofia waved a hand. "But I've been a bitch. I know I have. And then there was this grad student the other day. Tom kept whispering in her ear, and they giggled together," she muttered. "And she was wearing these dangerously low, butt-grabbing jeans. I hated her," she added with a snort.

Ashleigh let out another laugh. "A whisper and a chuckle with a grad student in sexy jeans isn't exactly cheating." Clearly sensing that Sofia was serious, however, she asked, "Have you said anything to him about it?"

"Nope," Sofia sighed, waggling her head.

She then went on to tell Ashleigh that she couldn't bring herself to confront Tom because she was too scared he would confess and it would destroy her.

"I don't know," Sofia said finally. "I'm probably being postpartum and hormonal and ridiculous."

Ashleigh patted Sofia's knee as Sofia had done to her earlier. "You probably are," Ashleigh said with a teasing but gentle chuckle. Leaning in and nudging Sofia, she said, "Just to be sure, though, perhaps you could search his laundry." She winked over at the laundry basket near the doorway. "Perhaps there are some grad-student thongs lurking!"

Sofia's first thought was to be mortified that Ashleigh had spotted the laundry. But this was quickly followed by the thought that Ashleigh, although joking, might be onto something. "Not a bad idea," she exclaimed.

"I was kidding," protested Ashleigh.

But Sofia was already on her feet. "I need to get some laundry done anyway," she said, with excitement and a hint of trepidation rising in her chest. "Would you watch these two while I go to the basement and put this in the machine?"

"Sure." Ashleigh gave a weak smile. "And, Sofia?" she called as Sofia grabbed the heavy basket and headed out of the room. "I'm sure you won't find a thing. Or a thong, for that matter."

"We'll see." Sofia grunted as she heaved the basket onto her hip.

Down in the basement, Sofia was feeling ludicrous. She'd been through every one of Tom's pockets and sniffed every collar. She'd even taken a quick sniff at his underwear, appalling herself in the process. After all of this she'd discovered nothing untoward, and as she stuffed Edgar's drool-covered onesies into a machine, she muttered under her breath, "For God's sake, Sofia, what *are* you doing?"

While she set about filling a second machine with dirty clothes, Sofia heard voices behind her. She turned and squinted across the laundry room, with its glaring naked lightbulbs and cold cement floors, to see two middle-aged women coming through the door. They were speaking quietly to each other in fast, lilting Spanish.

Their conversation stopped, however, as they spotted Sofia. *"Hola,"* they called with big smiles on their faces.

"Hola." Sofia waved back. Then, as she got a better look at the women, she realized she knew the smaller of the two. It was Juanita, one of the nannies from the Washington Square playground whom Sofia would often chat with when she was out with Gracie.

"Juanita. *Hola!"* Sofia exclaimed. *"Qué tal?"*

Juanita looked again at Sofia and then dropped her heavy laundry bag to the floor and clapped her hands to her cheeks. "Sof-ee-aahh," she cried happily.

With big smiles, the two women moved toward each other, kissed cheeks, and embraced. In the same faltering and hand-waving Spanish Sofia always used when she talked to Juanita, she asked what on earth Juanita was doing in the dusty laundry room of Manhattan U's housing. Juanita chuckled and introduced her sister, Sandra, who apparently cleaned for some of the faculty who lived in the two buildings. Juanita had come along today to help her sister out.

"Hermana buena," Sandra called out, as she waved over at

Juanita with one hand and continued loading the washing machine with the other.

"You are a great sister," Sofia agreed.

Sofia and Juanita then went on to talk about Gracie, and Edgar's birth, and how Tom was doing at work. They talked about Sandra's family back home in Mexico and how she was now a grandmother.

Sofia shook her head, smiling. *"Abuela? Usted es demasiado joven!"* she managed in her slow and uncertain Spanish, as she tried to remember the correct way to offer the compliment, "You seem too young to be a grandma."

When Sofia was a child her Spanish had been fluent. Her dad, who was also from Mexico and came to the States when he was ten, spoke nothing but Spanish to Sofia at home. But as she got older and ended up at a whiter-than-white high school in San Diego, she'd tried to hide her Latina roots. At home, as a surly teenager, she insisted her father speak to her only in English. After he died a few years later, when Sofia was at college, just hearing Spanish filled her with sadness and regret. In recent years, however, she'd made some sort of peace with the language, and now she loved to try her Spanish out from time to time.

When Sofia and Juanita were finished up, Juanita waved toward her bag of laundry and told Sofia she must get on. They kissed once again on both cheeks and turned back toward their separate machines. Sofia resumed filling hers and then jingled her loose quarters into the slots.

Across the room she heard Juanita asking her sister, *"Dónde están ellos?"*

Where are they? Sofia smiled to herself as she translated the words in her head.

"Upstate," the other replied, her accent clinging, rich and deep, to the English word.

"Para el fin de semana?"

"Sí."

As Sofia listened, she realized they were talking about Sandra's clients and how they were away for the weekend. Sofia snorted quietly to herself. No doubt Dean Havemeyer had a team of cleaners, like these two, whom he underpaid to launder his Egyptian-cotton sheets and linen napkins.

Just as she thought this, Sofia heard the words *Señora Mary,* pass between the sisters, and she snapped her head up in surprise. The women noticed, and Juanita looked over at Sofia, gave a smile, and then turned back to her sister. They resumed their conversation in hushed whispers, and as hard as Sofia tried, she couldn't make out another word.

Disappointed, she turned back to her laundry, and as she prodded at the start buttons on both machines, she wondered whether "Señora Mary" could be Mary Havemeyer. It was possible, wasn't it? The Havemeyers lived in the building opposite, but the machines over there were notorious for breaking down, which meant the laundry room in Sofia's building was always overused. Sofia glanced at Sandra out of the corner of her eye. A wry smile inched across her face as she considered how much she'd love to be Sandra just for a day and go poking through the Havemeyers' apartment.

It was only when she picked up her empty basket and was about to head to the elevator that her last thought led to an idea. It was a crazy idea that probably would fail at the first hurdle. But if it did work, she might be able to get some of that dirt on Jack Havemeyer she was itching to find.

Sofia turned back toward the two sisters. "Juanita? Sandra?" she called out.

Eighteen

Mary

Mary shook the last raindrops from her umbrella, lifted her key to the lock, but then stopped. For the first time it occurred to her that perhaps Jack was home too. He had presented his paper yesterday, and even though he was meant to fly home tomorrow morning, there was a chance he could have flown back from Michigan today. It was unlikely, of course. Jack loved conferences. He adored the schmoozing, the dinners with colleagues, the fancy hotels. Mostly he loved to attend a myriad of panels and lambaste unsuspecting young history scholars who held different theoretical and methodological positions to his own. She'd seen him do it, and it wasn't pretty.

Raising her hand again, Mary shook her head. He wouldn't be here, she told herself; she was being paranoid. Yet, as the cold metal of her key slid into the lock, doubt kicked again in her stomach. If she'd come home early, maybe he had too. Mary had been away at her own writing conference in Beacon for a few days. While she attended workshops, hooked up with old friends, and cruised art galleries in the small upstate town, she convinced herself that her new plan was watertight. She'd return home early, Jack would be out of town, and she would do what she had to do.

Mary had been living in a time bomb before she left for her trip. Jack and she moved around their apartment like strangers in a subway station, neither of them acknowledging the other, neither of them making eye contact. They were existing in a tense, mute limbo. In spite of this eerie calm, Mary was sure that the explosion would happen at any moment. Jack would grab her and demand to know what she was doing, if she was leaving, and he'd chastise her for ever considering leaving him in the first place. Mary fluctuated between fear of this explosion and spine-tingling anger.

One thing Mary knew for certain was that she had to go. What was the point of staying another moment with such a man? The news that Sarah was pregnant with twins meant that Mary's San Francisco plans were up in the air, but that didn't mean she should stay with Jack. She could still leave the apartment and find a new place to live in the city. Knowing Jack as she knew Jack, however, she realized she had to be careful. If he realized Mary really was going to move out, if he knew that Sarah's news wasn't going to make his wife stay, he was capable of anything. He might destroy her precious books or sabotage her computer. Also, there was her mother's antique jewelry, which they kept in a safe-deposit box at the bank. It wasn't worth millions, but it meant so much to Mary, and Jack knew that. Mary would put nothing past him.

And that was why she'd returned two days early from her conference. While Jack thought she was upstate, safely ensconced in her bed-and-breakfast in Beacon, she would actually be clearing out the closets, dressers, and drawers and moving everything she owned out of their miserable, toxic apartment. She planned to do it all *and* find a place to live before Jack returned.

Confidence welled in Mary's chest once again as she thought of this plan, and she turned the key in the lock with a purposeful click. She pushed the door open and stepped into the hallway. She thought she heard a sound, perhaps a rustling of paper, but as she stopped and listened she heard only the ticking of a nearby clock. After plopping down her small suitcase and umbrella by the door, she began to walk toward Jack's study. She wasn't going to waste any time. Resting, getting herself a glass of water for her parched mouth, sorting through the mail—it could all wait. She must get the important things done first.

The door to Jack's study was ajar, and fear instantly fluttered in her stomach. Could he be here? she began asking herself. She tiptoed toward the door and nudged it very gently with her finger, all the while holding her breath. Mary opened the door far enough to see into the room, and immediately her hand dropped to her side.

"Wh-what the . . . ?" she stammered in shock.

In front of her, down on their knees, Sofia, Hannah, and Ashleigh were on the floor. All three of them looked up at her with eyes wide in surprise. They were holding stacks of folders and papers in their hands.

"Mary!" Sofia exclaimed. "What are you doing back?" Then, clearly realizing the incongruity of her question, she blushed.

"I came home early from my conf . . ." Mary began, looking in confusion from Sofia to Hannah to Ashleigh and then the papers they were clutching. "*Why* are you three here?" she demanded. "*How* did you get in here?"

Sofia looked alarmed. Carefully placing the papers she'd been holding onto the floor, she pulled herself to her feet and moved toward Mary. "I'm so sorry, Mary," Sofia said. "I know this must look bad." She waved around at Hannah, Ashleigh, and the documents. "But, well, we needed to . . ." Sofia paused for a second and then shook her head and started again. "Look, I won't lie and make up some lame excuse for why we're here. I like you, Mary, and you're a smart woman, and I don't want to do that." She took a breath and explained. "I ran into your cleaner in the laundry, and I told her I'd promised to mail a few documents you'd left in Jack's office. But please, Mary, don't blame Sandra," Sofia added, and with a nervous laugh said, "I can be very persuasive, even in my terrible Spanish."

"But why?" Mary asked. Her tone was still tinged with anger and confusion. What on earth did these women think they were doing, stealing their way into her apartment and leafing through Jack's documents? Yet something about Sofia's candor stopped her from bawling them out completely. "Why?" she then repeated in a quieter voice.

Sofia's cheeks flushed once again, but her gaze remained steady. "We wanted to find out something on your husband," she replied, but then, looking over at Hannah and Ashleigh, she made the correction: "Well, no, it was really *me* who wanted to find out something. I roped Ashleigh in earlier, and we just ran into Hannah in the elevator and she agreed to help out."

Mary felt a kick of nerves. "What kind of things are you looking for?"

Ashleigh was now on her feet too. She looked from Sofia down at Hannah and then at Mary. "We *all* want to know what he's up to with the garden."

"He wants it gone, doesn't he?" Mary said, unable to disguise the contempt and bitterness that always washed over her whenever she thought of Jack these days. "He's going to build his 'highly lucrative' "—she waggled her fingers in quotation marks—"his highly lucrative parking lot."

Sofia gave a wry smile at Mary's words and then said, "But we think there might be more to it."

Mary was silent for a few beats. She looked again at the women in front of her. They were looking back at her, anticipation fizzling in their eyes. They wanted to know where they stood; Mary could tell. Would she listen to them or would she shut down, tell them to leave Jack alone, and herd them out of the apartment?

A smile crept over Mary's face. She realized that, as ludicrous as it might sound, she'd rather have these three women sneaking into her home and rifling through Jack's things than find her own husband here.

"Okay," Mary said finally, as she looked in turn at Sofia, Hannah, and Ashleigh. "Tell me what he's up to now."

Ashleigh leaned over and from the floor picked up the manila envelope carrying the construction contract. "Perhaps you should look at this first."

Mary thought she'd never been angrier than the night Jack had smiled that awful smug smile of his and revealed that he knew of her San Francisco plans. On Monday, though, just two days later, she read Jerry Milo's article about the protest in the *Mail*, and she found herself even more enraged. A friend had tipped her off about the piece, and she'd grabbed a copy of the newspaper at lunchtime between classes. In her office she'd spread the paper on her desk, and while biting into her rye-bread sandwich she read every awful word. Straightaway rage detonated inside her. She tore the newspaper into pieces and threw a cup of steaming coffee at the wall. "How dare he?" she'd yelled.

It was Milo's article that Mary, Hannah, Ashleigh, and Sofia were discussing just half an hour after Mary's arrival home and the discovery of her unexpected guests. The three women were now all sitting on the floor of Jack's study, each of them with a steaming mug of herbal tea by their sides and a pile of papers on their laps. As yet, they had found nothing suspicious, just endless articles related to Jack's research, numerous student evaluation reports, tax forms, and minutes from history department meetings going back to the early eighties.

"I still can't believe it." Sofia was shaking her head. "I always thought I was such a good judge of character. Back in Hollywood I could pick out the rats a hundred feet away. But that Milo guy really had me duped."

"Sam said she spoke to him at the protest too." Ashleigh picked up her warm mug of tea and hugged it to her chest. "She said he seemed like a nice guy. She's usually spot-on about these things."

"I was fooled too," Hannah agreed. She then looked over at Mary, and a pink flush flickered on her high cheekbones. "There's something I should tell you, Mary," she began, her eyes wide and guilty. "I think I might have been the one who prompted the whole 'dean and wife do battle' stuff. I let slip that Jack was spearhead-ing the parking lot development. I didn't tell him you were at the protest or that you brought the garden keys, but he must have put two and two together."

"And come up with eighteen." Mary half laughed and waved a hand. "It's not your fault, Hannah. Milo would have found all that out eventually. If he is a halfway decent reporter, that is." Mary paused, sipped her tea, and then said, "He's tried to call me, you know."

"Really?" Sofia's eyebrows shot up. "After the article came out? What did he say?"

"I listened to one message where he claimed he was sorry and asked if we could talk. After that I deleted every message."

Sofia snorted. "I would have called the son of a bitch back and told him where to stick his article and just how far up he should shove it."

Everyone chuckled softly until Ashleigh turned to Mary and asked in a concerned tone, "But how did he get your number?"

"I have no idea," Mary spat out, "and I don't care."

Of course, she did care. After the article had run last Monday she'd spent far too much time thinking about and fuming over Jerry Milo. Almost more time, in fact, than she'd spent thinking about and being mad at Jack. Even at night, in her dreams, Jerry's face and those gray, seemingly honest eyes kept visiting her. And just yesterday, when Mary was still upstate, she had sought out one of his old books in a local bookstore and sat for an hour scanning the pages and wondering how someone so eloquent and interesting had turned so cheap and cruel.

Jerry's phone messages only made things worse. He'd left nearly ten during the course of the week. Part of Mary was desperate to know what he wanted to say and whether he really was sorry. Another part of her believed that the only reason he wanted to get in touch was to dig for more dirt or do some follow-up. "What kind of fool does he take me for?" she would hiss, as her embittered side would prevail and she would punch the delete button on her phone.

"What's that?" Hannah's voice suddenly chimed out, breaking the silence that had descended over Jack's study.

The other three women all looked over at Hannah, who was now on all fours, peering under the desk.

"Let's see!" Sofia cried out, getting down on her knees to join Hannah.

Hannah was already pulling out a hard black box that had been tucked under the drawers of Jack's desk. As she gave the box a last tug and it flew out from its cramped hiding place, every woman in the room spotted the label: WILKINS CONSTRUCTION.

Straightaway Hannah opened the box without saying anything and shimmied its contents onto the floor. The four women closed in and, still in silence, they began to peruse what was in front of them. Mostly it was paperwork to do with the demolition of the old Poe house, as well as newer documents concerning the garden and the parking lot—including a copy of the same construction contract Ashleigh had found at her law firm, and which she'd shown to Mary just a short while earlier.

One curious item included in the box was a Xeroxed copy of a very old map of downtown Manhattan. Amongst the faded lines and ornately written street names typical of old maps, someone had marked a cross with a blue marker.

"Isn't that the garden?" Mary said when the map was passed on to her. "The cross marks where the garden is."

Everyone stopped looking at the papers in their hands and stared over at the map in Mary's.

Sofia nodded and said, "You're right. Look, there's Bleecker." She pointed to the road north of the cross. "And there's Houston Street." She pointed south of the cross. Then her finger traced the road that ran from Bleecker to Houston, under the blue cross. "Greene Street," she murmured.

Mary nodded as Sofia's finger glided across the map. "It looks like Greene Street used to run farther north, doesn't it? Instead of stopping at Houston, as it does now, it used to run here." She pointed at the map and the hand-drawn cross north of Houston Street.

"So the garden and the faculty towers were built on what used to be Greene Street?" Hannah asked.

Mary nodded again. "It looks like it."

"Why's the garden been marked on this old map, anyway?" Ashleigh peered over the shoulders of the others and asked, "Why not on a contemporary one?"

Everyone shrugged and pondered this for a few seconds.

"And what's this all about?" Hannah said, waving another sheet of paper and breaking their thoughtful silence.

The other unusual item in the box was a piece of Wilkins Construction letterhead upon which Alan Wilkins had handwritten a note to Jack. The note read, *Here it is, Jack. May it bring you academic fame and riches! Best, Alan W.*

"What do you think it means?" Hannah went on.

The other three women had all read the note by now, but had quickly passed it on, hoping to find whatever it was Alan Wilkins was referring to. So far, none of them had.

"Perhaps it just refers to one of these contracts," Hannah suggested, waggling a document in her hand. "Maybe he was just sending Jack a copy."

"But what would that have to do with academic fame and riches?" Sofia said, her brow crumpling with frustration. "What could any of this"—she waved around at the documents in front of her—"have to do with academic fame and riches?"

Mary was wondering the very same thing. More precisely, she'd wondered the same thing a few moments ago and was now on to pondering Jack and Alan Wilkins and the night, just a few weeks ago, when the two men celebrated the signing of the garden contract right here in her apartment. Jack and Alan had boisterously finished off a bottle of Veuve Clicquot while Mary stood on the sidelines drinking water and saying little. Feigning a headache, she'd managed to slip to her bedroom before they opened the second bottle. She hadn't thought about it much since that night, but when she met Alan Wilkins, he had seemed a little familiar. Thinking back, hadn't Jack said something about knowing him at Princeton?

With this vague memory in mind, Mary jumped up and scuttled out of Jack's study, leaving the other three women exchanging curious glances behind her. "Where's she going?" Mary heard one of them whisper.

Within a few minutes she was back in the room brandishing a large photograph in her hands.

"Look at this." She grinned, holding the picture for Sofia, Hannah, and Ashleigh to see.

Three confused pairs of eyes scanned the myriad of faces in Jack's old graduation photograph.

"I don't get it," Sofia said, looking up at Mary with a baffled smile.

Mary crouched down in front of everyone and pointed at the tiny printed names under the photo. " 'Jack Havemeyer,' " she read, and, moving her finger down the list, she added, "And 'Alan Wilkins.' " She then pointed out a very young Jack and an equally young Alan Wilkins among the throng of gowned and grinning young men. Each of the three women took it in turn to stare, frown, then shake her head.

Hannah was the first to speak. "This explains what you heard, Sofia," she said, looking up, "about Manhattan U using Wilkins again, even though they did a bad job last time."

Sofia retorted, "Yep. The old-boys' club strikes again." She paused and frowned. "But it's not exactly incriminating, is it? Everyone does it. It's hardly going to put Jack behind bars." She chuckled and then, looking at Ashleigh, asked, "Is it?"

"Probably not." Ashleigh shook her head and smiled. "The dean has probably broken some of Manhattan U's own governance rules. But, as you said, everyone does it. They find ways around rules about nepotism or favoritism. CEOs and presidents and deans all know how to tweak the system so they can do an old friend a favor."

"Like handing their friend's company a million-dollar construction contract," huffed Sofia.

"Exactly," Ashleigh replied. "It's usually reciprocal. A favor for a favor. I suspect Alan Wilkins has done Jack a few favors in his time to get this one in return." She then waggled the handwritten note, which was still in her hands. "Perhaps this is the favor."

"Whatever it's referring to," Hannah said.

The four women were silent for a moment. Mary's eyes moved from the note in Hannah's hands and began roving Jack's study.

Not for the first time her eyes settled on the poster above his desk, the one of Edgar Allan Poe and the raven. It looked incongruous and out of place. Usually Jack's prints and paintings were expensively framed and carefully hung. This one, however, had been hastily tacked up with tape, and its corners curled and fluttered. Mary studied the poster some more as a thought started to form in her mind.

"You don't think all this has anything to do with Jack's new obsession with Poe, do you?" she said finally.

Sofia, Hannah, and Ashleigh all followed Mary's gaze up to the poster.

Sofia snorted. "The man's definitely obsessed. The new institute, this poster, and look, all those books on Poe," she said, pointing to Jack's bustling desk. "He's getting as bad as Tom." She chuckled and then asked Mary, "Has he always been interested in Poe?"

"Not at all. It started just a couple of months ago," she replied. "And let's not forget, it was my dear husband who pulled down Poe's old house in the Village. Not exactly the behavior of the world's biggest Poe fan . . ."

A thudding noise coming from the front door suddenly interrupted Mary, and she and the three women beside her froze. They looked at one another, panic visible in all their eyes. Was it Jack? Mary wondered. Had he come home from his conference early, after all?

Without uttering a word the women flew into action, tucking papers into drawers, throwing folders onto shelves, and kicking the box back under the desk where they'd found it. Amid their flurry of activity, they heard the front door open and footsteps along the hallway.

"Señora Mary?" came a quiet and uncertain voice.

Mary let out the breath she'd been holding. It was Sandra, her cleaner. *Thank God,* she thought, *thank God*. She jumped to her feet and headed into the hallway.

"Sandra." She smiled. *"Hola."*

Sandra looked confused and clearly surprised to see Mary home. Then, nodding down at the stack of sheets in her arms, she explained in her broken English that she was returning the sheets that she'd laundered. Mary stepped forward and took the sheets and then asked if Sandra had found the money she'd left out for her on the kitchen counter. Sandra nodded and smiled. After a little more conversation about Sandra's kids and Mary's trip upstate, Sandra hoisted her heavy purse onto her shoulder and left.

"That was too close." Sofia shook her head and whistled when Mary returned to the study.

"Too close." Mary grimaced, a trace of panic still waning in her chest.

"We should get out of here," Sofia went on. "Just in case *he* does show. Also"—she jerked her head toward the others—"we all have places to be. I'm already half an hour late for my babysitter, who kindly dropped everything to swing by my place at the last minute," she added with a laugh.

"Of course." Mary nodded.

After straightening up Jack's office and carefully returning papers to their folders and the folders to their drawers, the four women then arranged to meet again the following day.

"Surely, if we put our heads together, the Professors' Wives' Club can figure out what your husband is up to," Sofia said with a wink as they all said their good-byes at Mary's front door.

A little while later, everyone was gone and Mary was in the bedroom packing clothes, books, photo albums, and an array of knick-knacks into two large suitcases. It wasn't taking her long to collect everything she wanted to take. Most of her clothes and a lot of the paintings and ornaments in the apartment reminded her too much of Jack. She needed a fresh start, and that meant new clothes, new paintings, and new memories.

Mary moved over to her dresser, opened the top drawer, and scooped out her underwear in big handfuls. When she was nearly finished transferring her underwear to the suitcase and there were

just a few briefs and bras left, her fingers stumbled upon the apartment lease and air tickets that she'd hidden there two months
ago. She picked them up straightaway and stared long and hard at
them. Although Mary was resigned that she must stay in the city,
she still hadn't canceled the lease or the flights. She just couldn't
bring herself to do it. Now, holding them in her hand, she felt a
wave of yearning and disappointment. She wanted so badly to start
her new life in San Francisco, but she couldn't leave Sarah and the
twins. She just couldn't.

As Mary turned to place the beloved documents into her bag,
a thought suddenly struck her. She'd been wondering a lot over
the last week how Jack found out about her plans. She came to
the conclusion in the end that he must have heard about her appointment at Golden Gate through the academic grapevine. Even
though she'd sworn her new department to secrecy, these things
always had a habit of getting out.

Mary now wondered if Jack had simply found the tickets and
lease in her drawer. Over the past couple months, she'd told herself she should make a trip to the bank and hide the documents
in her safe-deposit box. But she never quite got around to it. Plus,
she figured they were secure enough in her underwear drawer,
where it was very unlikely Jack would poke around.

The only reason he might search this drawer, she now realized,
was if he wanted to get his hands on the safe-deposit key that
Mary had hidden there for years. Mary wasn't sure if Jack would
even remember that the drawer was the key's hiding spot. After
all, he didn't have much business going to her safe-deposit box at
the bank, because all it contained was Mary's mother's jewelry. But
perhaps he had remembered the hiding spot. And if he had, why
was he looking for the key?

Mary hurried back to the dresser while a panicked thought
began to form in her mind. Had Jack sold off her heirlooms to
fund some golfing trip or a new car? Or simply to get back at her?
The old Jack would have never done something so reprehensible.
But the old Jack would never have hit her either. Peering into the

drawer and pushing back the last items of underwear, Mary found
the yellowing piece of Scotch tape that for years had fixed the
small key to the bottom of the drawer. The key itself was gone.

"Jack," Mary hissed, her fists clenching, "what have you
done?"

Without hesitation she flew to his study. No one had stumbled
across a key earlier when they'd looked though Jack's things, but
no one had been looking for a key then. Mary rifled through Jack's
drawers and filing cabinet, this time not caring if she left the place
in disarray. Jack had trespassed in her space; it was her turn to
trespass in his.

After five minutes Mary had shaken out every folder, checked
a myriad of envelopes, hunted through every shelf, and still found
nothing. She was about to give up and was biting her lip to stifle
her frustrated and angry tears. The key, she figured, must be on his
key chain, and his key chain would be with him at his conference
in Michigan. Mary slowly turned toward the door. But as she did
so, she noticed that the hardback cover of a book on Jack's desk—
the topmost one in his stack of new Poe books—was slightly open.
Mary reached over and flicked the cover back. She gasped, utterly
surprised. She'd found the key. There it was taped to the inside
cover of a book titled *Poe's "The Raven."*

Mary unpeeled the tape, pocketed the key, and glared down
at the book, wondering why on earth Jack would hide their safe-
deposit box key in a book on Poe. Out of the corner of her eye,
Mary then noticed the black box they'd found earlier: the same
Wilkins Construction file that had been pushed under his desk.
She leaned down, swept it up, and, with her mind beginning to
whir, she opened up the box and flicked through to find the handwritten note. When she found it, Mary held it up and read Alan
Wilkins's words once again.

All of a sudden it occurred to Mary that perhaps Jack hadn't
wanted to get something *out* of the safe-deposit box. On the contrary: Perhaps he wanted to put something in it. Something he
wanted to keep safe. Something he wanted to keep a secret. And

perhaps something that his old college buddy had given him, and which he hoped would bring him academic fame and riches.

"I have to go to the bank," she muttered to herself.

Mary wasn't finished packing. If she left now she'd also take the risk of Jack returning home and finding out what she'd been up to. But she didn't care. She had to find out what was in their safe-deposit box.

Rain was still beating hard on the windows. After grabbing her umbrella and raincoat in the hallway, Mary stuffed the note into her purse and scooted out of her apartment. She shut the door behind her with a decisive thud.

Nineteen

Ashleigh

Ashleigh had agreed to meet her father, Uncle Ray, and Gina at the Algonquin Hotel. Aunt Gaynor was attending some charity gala and wouldn't be joining them. The old Midtown hotel was where her father always stayed when he came to the city, and, even though she often felt like the youngest person in the lounge by at least twenty years, she loved the hotel's dark paneling, the small glowing lamps, and the low-slung armchairs and couches. She also loved to think of Dorothy Parker and the Algonquin Round Table gathering here all those years ago, sneaking sips of illegal liquor, exchanging witticisms, and talking endlessly about ideas and writing and life.

Tonight, though, as she walked into the busy lobby, she felt irritable. She was running late, plus she really didn't want to be here. Even the smell of oysters and the clink of champagne glasses didn't raise her spirits. It was Saturday night and she should have been with Sam, snuggled on adjacent bar stools, sharing chicken tacos and frozen margaritas at Benny's Burritos. Yet here she was, coming to see her father, who, in his current state of health, shouldn't even be out of the house, let alone four hours away in New York City.

While she scanned the lobby of the hotel looking for her family, Ashleigh reminded herself of the one good thing that tonight's dinner offered: a chance to ask Uncle Ray about Wilkins Construction and the contract their law firm had drawn up. When she, Hannah, and Sofia had left Mary's place just a short while ago, they'd chattered about what they'd found in Jack's study, and Ashleigh promised the others she'd try to find out more from her uncle. Perhaps he'd know something that might give them a clue to what the dean was up to.

Ashleigh weaved farther into the room and finally spotted Ray and her father sitting in wing-back armchairs near the hotel's fireplace. Ashleigh maneuvered past small tables, old gray-haired men in suits, and white-haired women in pearls, toward them. There was no sign of Gina.

"Hello, Dad."

"Ashleigh." He nodded and then tilted his cheek for her to kiss it. His face was still very sunken and gray. "Punctual as ever, I see," he added with a smile but reproaching eyes.

"It was hard to get a taxi," Ashleigh muttered, and waggled her sodden umbrella as proof. Shimmering droplets of water sprinkled on the carpet around her.

After greeting Ray and planting a kiss on his cheek too, Ashleigh sat down between the two men on a low banquette and shook off her jacket.

"How are you feeling, Dad?" she asked, noticing the tumbler of scotch on the table in front of him.

"It's medicinal," her father retorted, following his daughter's gaze. "And, yes," he added with a snap, "I'm feeling much, much better. I'll be back in the Senate within the month."

Clearly her father's health scare had done nothing to change his ambitious, stubborn, and workaholic ways. Nor his impatient and brusque manner. Ashleigh had hoped that he might come out of the whole ordeal a mellowed man, but it had just seemed to make him harder, more resolute, and sterner than ever. She wouldn't argue with him about going back to work. She could tell from the steely look in his eyes that it wasn't worth it.

The three of them sat in silence for a few beats until Ray leaned forward and, with his sweet, familiar smile, said to Ashleigh, "Unfortunately Gina can't make it. Some of Davey's family came into town unexpectedly, and so they've taken them out for dinner and a show."

"How nice." Ashleigh smiled.

Inside she was envious and a little bitter. She would never be able to blow off her father the way Gina did with Ray. It wouldn't matter if Ashleigh had a fiancé and a fiancé's family to entertain. Her father wouldn't tolerate being stood up. Never. But then, in the next thought, Ashleigh wondered whether it was entirely about her father. Perhaps it was about her own cowardice too, her inability to stand up to her dad. Maybe Gina was just a braver person than she.

Ashleigh looked over at her uncle and studied his wide, open face. He was the rounder, softer, paler version of Ashleigh's father, who was all angles, furrowed lines, and brooding dark eyes. It would be easier, far easier, to stand up to Ray. Perhaps if Gina had been brought up in Ashleigh's home she would be cowardly just the same.

While her father and Ray talked about politics and then the law firm, Ashleigh sat between them, watching the two brothers but not really listening. Every now and then she glanced up at the old grandfather clock in the corner behind her father. It had turned seven thirty, and she wondered whether she might be able to run by Sam's place later on, if she could just hurry this up a little. She felt like she'd been zigzagging the city all day—what with going to Brooklyn, then over to Sofia's, and now up to Midtown to see her father. But another zigzag to see Sam would be worth it. Indeed, it might save her relationship. All day, the nagging worry that Sam was getting sick of Ashleigh's flakiness kept returning. How long would Sam put up with her? she asked herself again and again.

"We don't want to keep you," her father said with a frown when he caught her glancing at the clock at one point. "Is there somewhere you have to be?" His question sounded like an accusation.

"No, no," Ashleigh countered in a whisper.

"Good," her dad barked back, and, after taking a sip of his scotch, he added, "I have some good news, Ashleigh."

Looking into her father's somber eyes, Ashleigh felt an unexpected flicker of scorn. No doubt this piece of "good news" was good news for him and him alone. He'd probably been selected for some big-deal committee, or asked to write his memoirs by an editor at Penguin. Who knew? Maybe he was going to run for president. This last thought made Ashleigh smirk bitterly to herself. Terrific, she thought. With her father as president she'd have to stay in the closet forever. There would be no holding hands with Sam and smiling for photographs on the White House lawn.

Ashleigh's father misread her expression. "Yes." He smiled and nodded at Ray. "*We* have very good news for you."

But he was interrupted as a waiter bustled up to the table to take their order. Ashleigh grabbed the menu and picked two expensive appetizers together with a vodka martini. If she had to be here, she'd at least make it worthwhile.

When they were finished ordering her father looked at Ashleigh again, wriggled higher in his chair, and said, "You are going to be made partner."

Ashleigh, who'd just been taking a sip of iced water, spit it unceremoniously onto the table. "*What?*" she exclaimed, as she wiped her mouth and the table with a napkin.

"The announcement will be made on Monday."

Ashleigh stared at her father and then at her uncle, who shifted in his seat and flashed an awkward smile. "It's true," he whispered.

Ashleigh had no idea what they were talking about. She wasn't being considered for partner. At least, not at the moment. She'd heard a partnership announcement was in the air, but she'd doubted it was going to be her. She'd suspected it would be Aidan, one of her colleagues, who'd been at the firm a year longer than Ashleigh.

"Don't you have anything to say?" her father prompted her, a small, satisfied smile twisting the corners of his mouth.

"I . . ." Ashleigh began, and then she shook her head. "What do you mean, I'm going to be made partner?" She narrowed her eyes. "Dad, I've always told you. I've always told Uncle Ray"—she nodded at her uncle—"I don't want preferential treatment just because I'm family. I want to be made partner when I've earned it."

Ashleigh had graduated top of her class at Georgetown Law and received a clutch of job offers from top New York and DC law firms. But ever since she'd decided to go to law school, Ashleigh always wanted to work at Rocksbury, Chatham, and Wise. She loved her uncle, the law firm had a great reputation, and the cases they worked on were challenging and intriguing. Her only condition on accepting the post at the family law firm was that she be treated like every other junior attorney. No perks, no shortcuts, no nods and winks. She wanted her colleagues to respect her, and for Ashleigh this meant she had to earn respect by being a great colleague and an even better attorney. She didn't ever want to overhear people whispering, "She's partner because her uncle and father founded the firm."

"You've earned it," her father snapped.

Ashleigh was speechless for a second, taken aback by her father's curt tone, and still dumbfounded by what he was telling her.

"You *have* earned it, Ashleigh," her uncle was now saying, as he leaned over and patted her knee. "You're a superb attorney and an asset to the firm." Ray's eyes twinkled with honesty, but there was embarrassment in his tone.

Ashleigh looked from Ray to her father. She stared into his hard eyes and found herself asking, "You didn't tell Uncle Ray and the other partners to do this, did you?"

"Don't be ridiculous, Ashleigh." Her father gave a dismissive wave. "As if I can decide who should or shouldn't make partner at the firm." He puffed a small laugh. "I'm not a partner anymore, as I'm sure you're aware."

Meanwhile, Uncle Ray said nothing and simply looked at his shoes.

Ashleigh was silent again as she watched her father and then her uncle. Their differences had always been obvious to her. But it occurred to her only now how much her father bullied his younger brother, and how much Ray was scared of her father—just as she was. She wondered if her uncle had ever in his life stood up to his older brother. Then she wondered if there would ever be a day when *she* would stand up to the fearsome Chad Rocksbury.

Her father was now flagging down a waiter and asking him to bring a bottle of champagne. "Make it your best. We have something to celebrate," he told a pink-cheeked young man in a pristine white shirt and bow tie.

Ashleigh didn't want to celebrate. She didn't want to be unfairly made partner either. But her tongue was frozen, and she couldn't bring herself to argue. She wanted to be a million miles away from here, a million miles from her father and his surly tones, and a million miles from his brother, who lived in fear of him, and who reminded her so much of her own pathetic self.

There was one thing she had to do before she made up some excuse to escape the miasma of this dinner date, though.

"Uncle Ray," she said, turning toward him, "when I saw you last, you mentioned you'd worked on the Wilkins Construction contract. The one with Manhattan U?" she prompted.

Her uncle nodded and smiled. He seemed relieved that the subject had changed. "I helped Jeremy out. Yes."

Ashleigh knew she had to be careful at this point. She couldn't give away that she'd been poking around in one of her colleagues' files—it just wasn't what was done—and so she quickly concocted a lie. "A call came to my desk by mistake the other day. It was Dean Havemeyer. He was very upset."

"He was?" Ray stiffened in his seat.

"He said that an important last clause had been omitted from the contract. I tried to put him through to Jeremy, but he was having none of it. He insisted I retrieve the contract and check the final clause."

"Did you do that?" Ray asked, his eyebrows knitted.

"I did. It turned out the clause he was worried about was there after all. His copy must have had a page missing or something."

Ray puffed a sigh of relief and said, "Did you send him a new copy?"

"Of course, I faxed it straightaway," Ashleigh replied, thankful that Ray seemed to be buying her story. As innocently as possible, she then asked, "So what was that clause all about, Uncle Ray? It said the dean should have access to the site during excavation, and that he would oversee all disposal of debris. Seems strange that a university dean would want to wallow about in the mud," she added with a light chuckle.

"Ah, yes," Ray said, leaning forward. "Dean Havemeyer was *very* insistent about that. I asked—"

Ray didn't finish. Ashleigh's father interrupted by booming out, "Stop all this work talk. We're here to celebrate, not chitchat about clauses in contracts."

Ashleigh's gaze jumped across to her father. He was holding up a crystal flute while the waiter, a white towel draped on his arm, filled it with fizzing champagne. Her father's eyes had begun to take on that glassy shine they always got when he'd had a few drinks. This was the only time her father didn't want to talk shop. Ordinarily he'd spend his life *chitchatting* about the most insignificant of clauses. But never after a few scotches and some forthcoming champagne.

Disappointment thudded in Ashleigh's stomach as she realized it was going to be impossible to quiz her uncle any further—at least, with her father getting slowly tipsy nearby. She could be patient and hope that her father would leave for the restroom, but that might take forever, and she wanted to be out of there as soon as possible.

Before she lost heart, though, Uncle Ray unwittingly—or perhaps wittingly—provided a solution.

"If you'll excuse me . . ." he said, getting up and pointing in the direction of the restrooms.

Ashleigh watched him go. Her father, meanwhile, was attempting to press some champagne into her hand. She waved it away, probably too impolitely, and said, "Excuse me," as she gave the same wave toward the restrooms her uncle had given a few seconds ago. Lifting herself from the banquette, she heard her father mutter something about weak bladders. Nevertheless, she kept on moving.

Just as she'd hoped and dared to expect, her uncle was waiting for her in the small hallway between the men's and women's restrooms. She noticed that his eyes had a mischievous sparkle—the mischievous sparkle of a younger brother doing something his bossy big brother really wouldn't like.

"Dean Havemeyer was insistent that he be present during the demolition of the garden," he whispered, launching straight in. "He believes something of historical interest could be buried under the garden."

Ashleigh's eyebrows shot up. "Really? What? What does he think is buried there?" Her questions tripped out like gunfire.

"I'm sorry, Ashleigh." Ray shook his head. "I don't know much more than that. He didn't give too much away. He said it was for personal research, and he'd appreciate our keeping his search confidential. Wilkins Construction didn't seem to have a problem with adding the clause to the contract." Ashleigh's uncle then chuckled and added, "Being a history professor of 'some repute'—that's how the dean described himself—we just assumed he knew what he was talking about."

"Did you talk to him much? The dean, I mean."

"A couple of times." Ray nodded. "He's a tough cookie." He then paused and jerked his thumb toward the hotel lobby. "Not so different from that one in there." He sighed.

Her uncle's comment reminded her of what had happened earlier.

"Ray," she said, reaching out and touching his elbow, "don't make me partner just because Dad insists on it, will you? I want to be made partner when I've paid my dues—not a moment before."

Ray looked sheepish. "He's not in the best of health, Ashleigh," he began. "I don't want to upset him."

"I don't want to upset him either," Ashleigh interjected. "But"—she looked up at her uncle—"we can't let him bully us forever, can we?"

Ray shook his head.

As Ashleigh gazed into her uncle's sad but understanding eyes, she felt a curious kick in her chest—a kick of defiance. All of a sudden she knew it was time to leave. She had to tell Sofia and the others what she'd learned about the dean. Then she had to see Sam. It was all clear to her now. Crystal clear.

"Thank you, Uncle Ray," she said, standing on tiptoe and kissing his cheek. "I'm sorry to leave like this, but there's something I have to do."

"Yes, go," she heard him whisper as she turned to leave.

Then, just as she was moving out of the hallway, her uncle called, "Ashleigh?" And when she swung back to face him, he said, "He may be a bully, but he means well. He only wants the best for you. For everyone." Ray went on, "If you and your, um"—he gave a small cough—"your *friend* are happy, he will be happy for you too. Once he gets his stubborn head around it, that is."

Ashleigh jolted in shock at her uncle's words. But then a calm, a surprising calm, overtook her. Whereas once she had thought the world would tumble around her if her uncle mentioned her *friend*, instead she found she was curiously tranquil—happy, almost. She smiled at Ray, mouthed a silent thank-you, and then ducked out into the Algonquin's plush lobby, where she weaved again through tables, chairs, and chattering diners toward her father.

When she reached him, she looked him straight in the eye and said, "Dad? I'm sorry, but I have to leave."

Her father's eyebrows slammed together. "What?" he demanded.

But Ashleigh had already swept up her coat and umbrella into her arms.

"Bye, Dad," she said. "I'll call you tomorrow."

Without looking back, she hurried out of the hotel. When one of the few empty taxis on the rain-sodden street finally stopped at her outstretched arm, she told the driver, "Downtown. Bleecker Street."

Twenty

Hannah

"What do you mean, you're not coming?" Michael's eyes were wide with anger. "We've been over this, Hann. I thought we'd agreed it's what we both want."

Hannah looked from Michael out at the dark evening and the rain pounding on the window. She said with a sigh, "It's what *you* want, not me."

"But you agreed." Michael's voice rose a few notes. "In the end, you agreed."

Michael, who'd been standing near the door, now slumped down onto the couch next to Hannah. She turned back to look at him. "I've changed my mind," she said quietly. But with a firmness that surprised even herself, she added, "I don't want to leave New York. I don't want to leave grad school."

Michael glanced over at her. "It's just for a year. I don't see the problem."

Michael had arrived home an hour ago, just a few minutes after Hannah got back from the Havemeyers' apartment. Since he'd gotten in they'd said very little. Michael was busy on his laptop, pounding away at some e-mails that he'd informed Hannah were "very urgent." Then, when the wireless connection in their apartment cut out, which it sometimes did, he slammed the laptop shut with a growl and tried to leave for his office in the department. But Hannah stopped him. It probably wasn't the best time, as he was clearly angry and frustrated, but she needed to get off her chest what she'd been agonizing about all week.

"I've made up my mind," she was now saying in a hushed but determined whisper.

"And," Michael continued, ignoring Hannah, "I think it might be good for you. You've been . . . I don't know . . . so serious since you started your MFA. California might lighten you up." He said these last words through a forced chuckle.

Hannah was almost too shocked to speak. "Lighten me up?" she finally managed in an incredulous hiss.

Once again Michael ignored her. "I was talking to one of the guys on the project, and his sister works at Rawls Two. You know, the big modeling agency for older models? Anyway, he says she could set you up. You could do some tests as soon as we get there." He then did a camera mime with his thumb and forefinger and a silly *click-click* noise with his tongue.

"Michael," Hannah snapped, turning to glare at him, "I'm not a model anymore. I never want to be a model again."

Michael cocked his head to one side, and his forehead crinkled into three distinct lines. "You should think seriously about it, Hann. You really should."

Hannah's mouth dropped open in shock. "I *have* thought seriously about it," she countered, trying hard to maintain her cool. "You know that, Michael. You've been with me the last few years, haven't you? I retired from modeling after a lot of thought." She shook her head and added, "And now my art is what I want to spend my life doing. Not standing in front of a camera for money."

"You can do your art anytime. You don't want to get old and wrinkly"—he screwed up his nose as he said *wrinkly*—"and then regret not taking advantage of your most beautiful years."

"But haven't we talked about this a million times, Michael? Haven't we discussed how tired I got of the crazy fashion world and all its crazy people?" she implored. "Didn't we discuss this and talk about how much more important it was for me to follow my art?"

Michael gave a dismissive wave, as if batting at an irritating fly. "I know all that. I'm just suggesting you should think again. Your beauty won't last forever. In fact"—his mouth twisted a little as he looked down at her belly—"you're letting yourself go already."

Hannah was shocked beyond words yet again. But as she glared over at her husband and took in his familiar brown eyes, something startling occurred to her: Talking to her husband, this man beside her, was impossible. For the past few years she'd started to think she wasn't expressing herself properly, or perhaps she was saying the wrong thing. All along, however, Michael just wasn't listening—or rather, he wasn't hearing her. She could tell him she didn't like sushi, or she didn't want to watch *The Sopranos,* or that she wanted to be an artist, not a model. But if Michael wanted her to want those things, that was what he heard. He lived in his own bubble these days. He thought he knew her, and he thought he was listening, but really he was hearing nothing of what she said. This realization made Hannah suddenly feel utterly lonely and sad. She felt as ripped out and alone, in fact, as that cold day nearly ten years ago when she found out her mother had died.

"Michael," she said finally, her tone quiet, unhappy, but determined, "I don't want to model. And I don't want to move to Stanford."

Michael was silent for a few beats, and then something flickered across his face. It wasn't a look of disappointment or heartbreak or sadness; it was something else. Disdain, perhaps. And while Hannah studied him, he snatched his eyes away from her and jumped to his feet.

"You're being ridiculous, Hannah," he blurted, his face now closed and hard. "No, in fact, you're being childish. It's just a year. You won't miss anything important." He waved his hand again. "You might miss this whole soap opera with the garden and your Professors' Wives' Club, but that's probably a good thing."

Hannah's jaw dropped again. "How dare you?" she began, but Michael held up his hand to stop her.

"Mom and Dad will be here in a few minutes," he said with an air of triumph. "They're in town for a reading, and they're going to swing by to say hi." Looking Hannah up and down, he added with a sneer, "You might want to clean up." He then turned on his heel and left the room.

With her pulse racing and her cheeks flushed with anger, Hannah looked from the doorway through which Michael had just left down at herself. She was wearing a rumpled T-shirt, her stained painting pants, and a pair of ragged tennis shoes. She reached up and touched her hair. It was greasy and clumpy. Before today, if she had known Diane and Bill were on their way, she'd have leaped up, straightened the apartment, teased her hair, changed her clothes. It wasn't that Michael's parents cared about those things; they lived in constant disarray themselves. But because she loved Diane and Bill so much, she would do anything to make them happy. She would tidy herself and her home, gather her face into a brilliant smile, and make them believe she was good enough for their son. She'd make them believe she and Michael were the perfect couple, if that would make them happy.

And that was exactly why Michael had looked so victorious when he left the room. He knew his parents were his winning card. He had only to mention their names and Hannah would always become more amenable, more forgiving, more likely to acquiesce to whatever it was that he wanted. It was only now, however, as she sat fuming on the couch, that she realized how much he'd used this over the years. If Michael wanted to eat at a restaurant on Broadway that Hannah thought was overpriced and stuffy, he would point out that his parents liked it too and they wanted to join them. If Hannah made plans to see some friends on an evening Michael wanted her to stay in, he would invite his parents. And if they were fighting, like tonight, he'd find a way to wiggle Diane's and Bill's names into the heated conversation.

"Not anymore," Hannah hissed to herself as she pushed herself up from the couch.

Anger still pulsed through her body, and the only thing she could think to do right now was to get out of the apartment. She couldn't face Michael again, and she definitely couldn't face his parents. But as she headed toward the front door, picking up her coat and umbrella on the way, the buzzer sounded. Her body went from tense and pulsing to weak and lifeless. How could she walk out now? How could she look at their smiling, familiar faces and not want to stay?

"Get that, Hann," Michael called from the bedroom. "It's them."

His voice was cheery and light. It was as if their earlier conversation had never happened, and immediately Hannah felt her anger rise up again. She paced the last few steps to the door and swung it open.

"Hey!" Bill and Diane said in unison. Their faces were beaming and happy, as usual.

Hannah smiled back. "Hey," she said quietly, and before either of them could move into the apartment, Hannah took Diane, then Bill into her arms. As she clasped them both, she whispered, "I love you, and I'm sorry."

Pulling away from them, she felt her eyes burning with imminent tears. Diane and Bill, their smiles ebbing from their faces, looked at Hannah with concerned gazes. She said nothing more. Instead she shuffled between them and then walked, with her head bent, around the corner and toward the elevator.

The rain hadn't stopped the Saturday-night crowds. Spring-semester classes had finished yesterday, and the bars, restaurants, and streets of Greenwich Village were packed with reveling Manhattan U students. Clutching her unwieldy golfing umbrella, Hannah had to step into the puddle-strewn gutters a number of times to maneuver around the lively throng. She had no idea where she was headed. She just had to keep walking. The image of Diane's and Bill's worried faces was burned into her mind, and if she stopped she would cry. But if she kept going, the stinging in her eyes would remain just stinging. The tears wouldn't come.

In her old tennis shoes her feet were soaked, and the water was beginning to creep up her pants and soak her calves too. The rain pounded down noisily on her umbrella, and Hannah had to squint at crosswalks to see the flashing walk signs. It was a miserable night, but she couldn't go home. Not now, and perhaps never again.

So she kept on walking.

"Hannah?"

When she heard the voice call her name, Hannah looked up and, glimpsing a street sign, realized she was no longer in the Village. She was now way over in Chelsea on Ninth Avenue. How had she walked so far without even noticing?

"Hannah?" the voice said again.

She turned and, through the drips and the fuzzy wet night, she saw a girl from her art theory class huddled under her own umbrella.

"Hi, Erika," Hannah called, pleased she'd remembered the girl's name.

"I thought it was you," Erika shouted over the wail of a passing fire truck. "Are you on your way?"

Hannah moved forward and tilted up her umbrella. "On my way?"

"Professor O'Hare's opening." Erika sounded surprised, and her heavy eyebrows shot up to meet the severe line of her dark bangs.

Patrick's opening, of course. She knew it was tonight. After all, she'd pored over the postcard all week since Patrick had given it to her. But she decided early on that she wouldn't go. The way Patrick had held her face after the seminar, the way he looked at her, and what he'd said, it was all too much. She didn't know if she was ready to see him again. She didn't know if she could stand being touched or looked at like that another time. On the other hand, would she survive *not* being touched and looked at like that again?

Yet, with rain beating down and with Hannah having no other destination on this dreary Saturday night, Patrick's opening was the only place she could imagine going.

She found herself nodding and saying, "Of course, yes, I'm headed there now."

Side by side with Erika, she then trudged through the puddles toward Tenth Avenue and the Manya Boyd Gallery.

Only five minutes later they arrived, and the gallery was teeming with the usual New York art crowd. Vintage dresses, linen scarves, black collarless shirts, chunky retro glasses, and asymmetrical haircuts jostled in the small, brightly lit space. Hannah scanned the room but couldn't see Patrick anywhere. The gallery was so crammed full she could barely see the paintings either.

"There's Ryan and the others," Erika said, waving her hand high in the air. "Come on."

Hannah weaved, bobbed, and followed Erika through the crowd to join a group of her art theory classmates hovering by the drinks table. Once they'd shouted their hellos over the noise, Hannah grabbed a plastic glass of red wine and pushed herself through a further myriad of elbows, waving hands, and chattering mouths toward one of Patrick's paintings.

She recognized the pink canvas straightaway. It was the painting from the postcard. But here, under the naked gallery lights, it was even more beautiful—stunning, in fact. Swirls and hardened splatters of red and yellow acrylic paint swooped across the pale canvas. In some places the thick paint almost folded and bubbled and looked as if it were teetering, ready to drip to the floor. Hannah moved back, nearly stepping on a woman's foot, and took in the whole thing, and then smiled to herself. It was like Jackson Pollock in drag, she thought. The splatters and splotches were Pollock-like, yet the palette was amusingly feminine. Patrick probably did this painting a long time ago, but Hannah couldn't help seeing it as a response to a conversation the two of them once had after class about Pollock and his macho artistic ways.

After staring at the piece for some time, she was finally disturbed by familiar voices nearby. It was two more students from her class. She couldn't remember their names.

"He's had one show in London," a guy in wire-rimmed specs was saying to his shorter friend, "but this is his first in New York."

"Too bad he's not going to be teaching here again next year. I'd like him as my adviser."

Out the corner of her eye Hannah could see the first guy nodding. "Yeah. I hear he's going back to London pretty soon. Like next week or something."

Hannah's stomach flipped. Next week? Patrick was leaving next week? Of course, she'd always known he was going back to England at the end of the semester. But now that the time had arrived, it seemed too soon—way too soon. Clutching her middle and trying to quell a sickening feeling growing there, she turned and started to move through the room. She had no idea what she would say, but she wanted to talk to Patrick. This might be the last time she would see him, and she needed to talk to him.

Finally, after squeezing and elbowing her way through the crowds, she spotted him. He was smiling and nodding, and his green eyes sparkled. He was surrounded by a group of students and a couple of other people Hannah didn't recognize. As she moved closer, she noticed an attractive woman, in a dark halter-neck dress with bare, tanned shoulders, tugging coyly on his shirt-sleeve.

Hannah stopped. The gnawing in her stomach was now a violent ache. She couldn't talk to him, not now. Tonight everyone wanted a piece of him, and he wouldn't have time for her. And she had no idea who this woman was. Perhaps she was his date.

"Excuse me." A man's voice spoke nearby, and a hand gently touched Hannah's arm.

She turned.

"It's Hannah, isn't it?" the bearded man asked as his hand dropped back to his side. "We met at the garden protest. At Manhattan U."

Hannah stared, and, through her fog of thoughts about Patrick, she realized he was right. She did know him.

"Jerry Milo," he said, offering his hand.

Every muscle in Hannah's body tensed. "You asshole," she hissed without missing a beat. "Who the hell do you think you are?" Jerry looked pained, but Hannah wasn't finished. It was as if the ache in her belly were now imploding with anger, and she couldn't stop. "The Professors' Wives' Club," she barked. "Where did you dream that one up? And all that crap about avenging the dean? You're despicable. Really despicable."

Before he could respond, she pushed past him and into the throng of people. Once she'd battled her way through and located her coat and umbrella by the door, she stumbled out of the gallery onto the wet street. There she puffed and panted with exhaustion and anger.

"Wait," Jerry called. He'd managed to keep up and was now standing behind her, rain pouring down on his thick gray hair and beard. "Please wait," he begged.

Hannah wanted to keep walking, but something in his voice made her stop. He sounded so desperate.

"Please," he went on. "Please hear me out."

"Why should I?" she spat.

He moved closer. "The article," he said, shaking his head, "it wasn't what I wrote. I swear to you."

Hannah glared. "What do you mean? It was your name on the byline, wasn't it?"

"I know." Jerry's eyes were imploring. "But I'm telling you, the article that ran was very, *very* different from the one I submitted. The editor took a lot of liberties."

"The editor took liberties?" Hannah's bitter laugh rang out. "Oh, yes, how convenient. Blame it on your editor."

Jerry shook his head and sighed. "If I really did write the story, I would have stayed a million miles from you tonight. I wouldn't have risked this confrontation." He sighed again. "But I didn't write it, not that version, and I wanted to apologize to you. To everyone. Sofia, Mary. Everyone."

In silence, Hannah simply stared at Jerry.

"I made the mistake of agreeing to do the job for an editor, a friend of my son's, who turned out to be an ambitious young guy. He thought my account of the protest too dull, not sensational enough for the *Mail,* and so he spiced it up without my approval."

As Jerry spoke, Hannah studied his face. It could be that she was being suckered again, but she couldn't help softening at his seemingly candid tone and honest eyes.

"How did he know all our names? How did he know about Mary's daughter getting married?" Hannah demanded, not letting him see that she was beginning to believe his tale.

"Your names he got from my original article," Jerry replied. Then, with his eyes downcast: "And I hate to admit it was me that gave him the lead on Mary." Jerry then went on to explain how he'd met Mary before the protest, when she was hurrying to buy her daughter's wedding gown. For some reason this meeting had come up when Jerry had spoken to his editor. "I mistakenly believed that my passing comments about Mary Havemeyer were extraneous and off the record. I was an idiot," he concluded with a frown.

Hannah was about to respond when Jerry spoke again. "Aside from apologizing, there's something I want to tell you. Something I found out about the garden."

Hannah lifted an eyebrow.

"It's important. I think you all should know."

"Really?" Hannah said, her eyes now narrowed.

"Really." He nodded.

For a few moments Hannah paused and continued to study Jerry's face. *What the hell?* she thought. It wouldn't hurt to hear him out.

She tilted her umbrella, nodded at Jerry, and beckoned him to join her underneath its blue-and-white expanse. "Let's go somewhere dry," she said.

Twenty-one

Sofia

With one hand, Sofia fingered her way through the folders in Tom's filing cabinet. Her other hand supported Edgar's head as he gently suckled at her breast, his tiny fist clenching and un-clenching the fabric of her T-shirt and his long lashes fluttering over his half-closed eyes. It was only nine thirty, but the apartment was dark and still. The only sounds were Edgar's nursing lips and Gracie's and Tom's deep, sleeping breaths coming from the nearby bedrooms. Tom had come home from his office a couple of hours ago, eaten dinner, and crashed out when Gracie had, a little after eight. He never usually missed their Saturday-night tradition of a bottle of wine, a snuggle on the couch, and a movie. So when he headed off to bed claiming he was beat, Sofia couldn't help won-dering what had made him so tired—or, perhaps, *who* had made him so tired.

But Sofia was trying to quell her worries about Tom. She had a mission this evening, and she couldn't get distracted. So now here she sat, as the rain poured down outside and Edgar nursed at her breast, in the glow of a desk lamp in Tom's study. It wasn't really a study. Not like the study she'd seen earlier in Jack and Mary's vast apartment, with its endless shelves, huge oak desk, and antique lamps. Tom's study was a joke in comparison. Between their two tiny bedrooms, where the wall dipped back a few feet, Sofia and Tom had built a desk, five shelves, and the space for a small filing cabinet. When Tom wasn't at his office on campus, this was where he read, graded, and wrote his lectures and papers.

Pulling out one of the folders from the top drawer, Sofia opened it on the desk in front of her. She switched Edgar to her other breast and then leafed through the pages. As she'd done with other folders in Tom's meticulously arranged drawers, she scanned for the name Jack Havemeyer. So far she hadn't found much except a few old memos about the demolition of Edgar Allan Poe's house on Third Street a few years ago. But Sofia was convinced that she was going to find something else, some clue as to what the dean might be up to.

When she'd left the Havemeyers' apartment earlier, her mind had fluttered and whirred all the way home. She was now convinced that Dean Jack's recent interest in Poe, all those questions he'd fired at Tom during the dinner party about "The Raven" and Poe's drinking, might have something to do with the garden. She also figured it had to be connected to the clause in the construction contract and the permission the dean was being granted to snoop around the excavation site. Did Jack expect to find something under the garden? Something linked to Poe? That might explain the cross on the old map, the obsession with Poe, his desire to dig around in the rubble.

Sofia was animated by these suspicions, and at dinner, even though Tom didn't seem in the mood for talking, Sofia asked him whether he thought Dean Jack might have ulterior motives with the garden, and whether these ulterior motives might have something to do with Poe. She was careful not to mention her trip to the Havemeyers' apartment, though, or what she and the others had found. Thanks to the new Poe institute, Tom and the dean had been spending a lot of time together over the past week discussing grant proposals, scholarships, and possible research positions. Tom would be livid if he found out what Sofia had been up to, and would no doubt think that what she'd done would jeopardize his relationship with the dean and his hopes for the director's position at the institute.

In response to Sofia's suggestions about Jack, Tom was dismissive. "What? Do you think he's looking for Poe's remains or something?" he scoffed.

"Perhaps," Sofia replied.

"Sofe"—he gave a small laugh—"you *know* Poe's buried in Baltimore. I took you to see his grave a few years ago. Don't you remember? We went on his birthday in January."

"How could I forget?" huffed Sofia. "I froze my ass off in that cemetery." She paused and then added, "But isn't there some controversy about where he's buried?"

Tom laughed raucously this time. "Take my word for it, hon. No one's going to be finding Poe bones buried in a garden in New York."

They sat in silence for a while, and Sofia pushed the food around on her plate. Finally she said, "So, you don't think there's anything to it, then?"

Chewing a mouthful of pasta, Tom shook his head. "If there were something under that garden, the Poe Foundation would have been onto it years ago." He then paused and added, "In the meantime, perhaps you should lighten up where the dean's concerned. Okay, he's not the sweetest person on campus, but I'm sure deep down he's a decent guy."

Although she was mad at Tom for so quickly dismissing her ideas and siding with Havemeyer, she didn't want another row. So she'd said nothing more, and when Tom passed out in the bedroom she'd quietly headed for his study. If he wouldn't help her, she would just take the matter into her own hands. After an hour of searching and finding nothing, Sofia felt her fervor beginning to wane, and as she closed up yet another folder and placed it back in the drawer, she sighed.

"What am I doing?" she muttered.

She looked down at Edgar, who'd finished nursing and was now asleep in the crook of her arm, and then carefully got to her feet. Holding him tight to her chest, she padded lightly through to the bedroom and laid him down in the small crib next to her bed and the sleeping Tom.

After checking that Edgar was settled, she headed back to the study and, having decided she might as well turn in herself, she busied herself straightening the papers she'd disturbed on Tom's desk. She was about to turn off the lamp when she noticed a large brown envelope stuffed between some books on the highest shelf. She quickly wiggled it free and saw on the front Tom's name written in large, loopy letters. Opening the already broken seal, she pulled out a clutch of papers and turned them over in her hand. She immediately spotted a yellow Post-it, and her heart skidded to a halt.

Thanks for the other night, Tom, it read in the same loopy writing. The note was signed, *Saw these and it made me think of you, Reyah,* followed by a smiley face.

Who was Reyah? What had Tom done for this Reyah the other night? And apart from thirteen-year-old girls, who drew that kind of cutesy face and wrote in such bubbly handwriting? The image of the grad student, the one at the Poe party with her tight jeans and impossibly small backside, popped into Sofia's mind. With panic rising in her chest, Sofia flipped through the papers under Reyah's note. Every page bore a *New Yorker*–style cartoon. Sofia's eyes idled on the last one, a picture of two talking men and a raven perched nearby. *He only knows one word,* read the speech bubble above the men's heads, and the caption underneath the cartoon said, *Edgar Allan Poe Returns a Christmas Gift.*

"Oh, ha-ha," Sofia hissed, not particularly amused by the humorous reference to Poe's most famous poem and his *nevermore*-cawing raven.

She snapped the papers shut and began fumbling them back inside the envelope. All the while she muttered and panicked. It *must* be that girl. Poe cartoons? The Poe party? It had to be her. What had they been doing together the other night? But before Sofia could whip herself into a complete frenzy, her mutterings were silenced by a gentle knock at the front door. The knock was so gentle, in fact, that Sofia wondered if it was a knock at all. Perhaps it was just the refrigerator and its usual nighttime rumblings. But the rapping sound came again, a little louder this time, and it was clear that someone was out there.

Darting across the hallway, Sofia set about fiddling with the sticky latch. Finally, with a wrench and a tug, the door opened, and in front of Sofia stood Mary.

Mary spoke first. "I didn't wake you or the kids, did I?" she asked in an urgent whisper. When Sofia waved her hand and shook her head, Mary went on: "It's just . . . well, I thought you might want to see this." She tapped a dark leather box clutched in her right hand.

Sofia stepped forward and stared curiously down at the box. "What is it?" she said with excitement. "Did you find something?"

Mary said nothing. Instead she set down her wet umbrella and opened the box in front of Sofia. Sofia moved closer and was just about to peer inside when a rumble of nearby footsteps and voices caused Mary to snap the box shut. Sofia looked first at Mary and then the two of them turned to look down the hallway. The footsteps and voices were getting closer.

Ashleigh was the first to round the corner in the hallway. Her cheeks were flushed and her hair twinkled with raindrops. Next followed Hannah, looking similarly flushed. Her bright red crop was plastered to her high forehead. Behind the two of them someone else followed. Glimpsing the man's gray hair and long raincoat, Sofia thought for a second it was the dean, and her blood froze in her veins. But then, as the man got closer, she recognized the pale eyes and gray beard and realized it wasn't Jack. It was Jerry Milo, the journalist from the *Mail*.

Anger snapped like a twig inside her, and as Jerry neared her doorway Sofia lunged toward him.

Twenty-two

Mary

Unlike Sofia, Mary recognized Jerry straightaway. A searing fury stabbed her chest as his unmistakable gray eyes rounded the corner in Sofia's hallway. How dared he come here? was all she could think. How dared he? Although, when Sofia sprang toward him with flaming eyes and a hand ready to slap, Mary was the first to pull her back. At that moment she would have loved nothing more than seeing Sofia's wrath enacted on Jerry, but the mother and professor in Mary made her intervene immediately.

"Sofia," she said, grabbing Sofia's shoulder and holding it firmly, "come on. It's not worth it. *He's* not worth it."

Sofia strained under Mary's grasp while Jerry stood a few feet away, waving his hands and looking anxious. Over Sofia's shoulder Mary glared at him, every muscle in her own body clenching with anger. *Pathetic,* she thought. *This guy is pathetic.*

"I—" he began, but he snapped his mouth shut and took a quick step back as Sofia attempted to lunge again.

This time it was Hannah's turn to get involved.

"Guys, guys," she said, springing in front of Sofia to protect Jerry. "Listen," she pleaded. "You have to listen to him."

"Why?" barked Sofia.

Mary said nothing but continued to glare into Jerry's pale eyes. He looked back at her, his brow furrowed with concern.

"The article wasn't his," Hannah continued, looking from Sofia to Mary and then over at Ashleigh, who stood nearby, her eyes wide and startled. "I mean, it was *his,* of course." Hannah waved back at Jerry. "But his editor meddled with it."

"Yeah, right," Sofia barked, while Mary shook her head in disbelief.

"It's true," Jerry said, his voice soft and tentative.

Clearly aware that Jerry's words weren't going to have much impact on the angry women in the hallway, Hannah spoke for Jerry again.

"Sofia, Mary," she said, "he's telling the truth. I'm sure of it." Hannah turned around, held out her hand, and Jerry gave her some soggy papers. "Look, here's the article *he* wrote."

Sofia snorted. "Which he concocted this afternoon, more like."

Hannah waggled her head furiously. "No, look, it's pasted to an e-mail. See?" She held out the paper. "The date's last Sunday. *Before* the article ran."

While Sofia eyed the papers in silence, Mary finally found her voice. "If this is true, why wasn't he"—she nodded vaguely toward Jerry, but intentionally avoided his gaze—"why didn't he object? Why did he let the article run with his name on it?" She couldn't curb the bitterness in her tone.

Jerry's voice was quiet but firm. "The first I knew about it was when I picked up the paper on Monday."

"Surely journalists at the *Mail* get to review their own articles before they're published," Mary spat out finally.

Jerry flinched at her angry tone and said with a sad frown, "It appears we don't." He then continued in his quiet, measured way to explain about his young and ambitious editor and the mistake he'd made by putting his trust in him. "Never again." He shook his head. "Never."

While Jerry spoke, fury bubbled in Mary's chest. She wasn't convinced by his story. It just seemed too convenient to blame some young editor for changing his article and claim he knew nothing about it. Sofia and Ashleigh were clearly thinking the same, as they exchanged silent and skeptical glances.

"And there's something else," Hannah said, interrupting their shared thoughts. "Jerry's found out something interesting about the garden."

Sofia's eyebrows shot up, and, clearly unable to stop herself, she barked out a curious, "What?"

"According to a contact of Jerry's at the department of buildings," Hannah began, "the garden isn't the only site Manhattan U has considered for the proposed parking lot. Initially the plans were drawn up for a site two blocks away."

Hannah looked over at Jerry, and he nodded back.

"The proposed site was over on LaGuardia Street, just below Bleecker," Jerry went on. "There's not much there except Manhattan U's security office and some storage units. I went to check it out a few days ago. It would have been the perfect place for new development." Jerry looked around at the women and continued, "Anyway, Manhattan U went as far as getting a construction permit for the site. But at the last minute they about-faced, tossed the permit they were granted, and reapplied for a building permit for the garden site."

Hannah carried on where Jerry left off. "And get this: It was none other than Dean Havemeyer who dealt with the department of buildings about the change of plans and who kept bugging them to hurry the whole process along."

Hannah raised her eyebrows expectantly and waited for the other women to respond.

"I knew it," Sofia exclaimed. "He wants the development to go ahead on the garden site because he's looking for something. Something old, I think, hence the cross on the old map."

Ashleigh then moved forward with her finger raised. "That's it," she blurted out. "He thinks there's something of some historical interest under the garden."

Everyone looked over at Ashleigh.

"My uncle," she began. "That's what my uncle just told me, and what I came here to tell you guys." She then recounted the meeting with her father and uncle at the Algonquin, and how she'd quizzed Ray about the clause in the contract. "He wasn't sure what the dean's looking for. Apparently he played it close to his chest."

Mary took this as her cue. This was the moment to show everyone what she'd found. Looking at the four people in front of her, she lifted up the large leather box that had been under her arm and held it with outstretched hands.

"I think you all need to see this," she said.

Everyone huddled around the box as Mary opened it and explained how she'd found the key in the Poe book and rushed to the bank to check the safe-deposit box. Once Mary's tale was told and the box was open, the five people in Sofia's hallway stared at its contents in awed and curious silence. Even Mary, who'd had more time than the others to study what was inside, continued staring.

Within the box was a smaller glass container that contained three fragments of old yellowing newspaper fixed with tiny pins to a sheet of green felt. One of these fragments was about five inches by five inches. The other two were a little smaller. The three pieces all bore old and fading printed text, but the larger piece also carried some handwritten notes in its margins and squiggly lines through some of the text. Just as Mary had done a few hours earlier, when she had opened the box in the safe-deposit room at the bank, the others recognized the text. The famous *nevermore* refrain of Poe's "The Raven" appeared on all three of the fragments, and the words *Evening Mirror* were visible at the top of the largest piece. It was clearly a very old newsprint version of Poe's most famous poem.

But the handwritten notes in the margins were much less distinct. The writing was blotchy and gray, obviously aged by time, and here and there water marks smudged the lettering completely. It was clear, though, that the notes and lines through the text were someone's edits to the poem.

"Is that Poe's handwriting?" Sofia whispered finally. "Are these his edits?"

It was what everyone else was thinking, but nobody replied because they were too busy watching as Mary lifted up the glass container and revealed a red cloth underneath. Mary then peeled back the cloth and uncovered another glass container the same size as the first. This time pinned to the same green felt was one yellowing fragment of paper that bore a few sentences of small, neat, and inky handwriting. It was the exact same handwriting they'd seen on the newsprint. Some of the text was smudged and worn with age. At the bottom, however, the words *Your friend, Poe* were as clear as day.

"A letter," Sofia exclaimed, leaning in and tapping on the glass. "He often signed his letters like this, just 'Poe.'" When Mary and Ashleigh looked up at Sofia with their eyebrows raised, Sofia waved a hand and said, "I suppose I've learned a thing or two living with a Poe fan."

Everyone chuckled briefly, and then Ashleigh craned her neck and asked, "So what does it say?"

Mary replied, "It's hard to make out every word, but this is what I think it says." She lifted the box closer and began to read.

"'Let me tell you, it was quite a night. First, my dear Thomas, I ripped my shirt on the stairs down to the tavern.'" Mary paused and squinted her eyes, trying to make out the blotchy text. "'The owner knew of my "Raven" and offered me a drink in exchange for a copy. I wrote one in my own hand and he secured it in a bottle—'" A bottle, how curious." Mary paused again and held the box closer. "'It seems "The Raven" will keep on running. I wrote it for the express purpose of running, as I told you before. Write immediately upon receiving this. Your friend, Poe.'"

When Mary was finished, there was a silence, until Jerry whistled and whispered, "Wow. Do you think it's real?"

It was the first thing he'd said in a while, and Mary found herself jerking her head up and staring over at him. She still wasn't sure whether she trusted Jerry, and she especially wasn't sure she should have let him see all this. Would he run off and write some other article for the *New York Mail* and expose what she'd found? Or worse, make up another vindictive-wife-versus-the-dean story? But as she carried on staring at Jerry, he returned her gaze, and a small, apologetic smile flickered across his face. His gray eyes seemed to plead for her forgiveness. She quickly looked away, but as she did so something inside her shifted a little. The edges to her anger softened. Maybe, just maybe, she thought, his story was true. Perhaps this editor person did meddle with what he wrote. That kind of thing wasn't unheard-of, after all.

"Clearly, Jack thinks it's real," Mary eventually responded, trying to avoid Jerry's gray eyes.

"So you think he's after the copy of 'The Raven'?" Ashleigh asked Mary. "The one Poe gave to the owner?"

Mary shrugged. "He must be."

"He has to be," Sofia cut in. Then, looking over at Mary, she went on. "You remember that night when you came for dinner, Jack asked all those questions about the poem? He wanted to know if finding an early manuscript would be the holy grail for Poe collectors."

"I remember." Mary nodded. "He also wanted to know about Poe's drinking habits while he lived in New York." She paused and added, "He must believe the garden lies on the site of the tavern Poe refers to."

"But the tavern could have been anywhere." Hannah shook her head. "And even if it was on the same site, what are the odds of Jack finding the bottle or the manuscript?"

"Negligible," Mary agreed. "But Jack must think it's worth a shot, especially if an early version of the poem is so rare and sought after." She looked down at the box again. "I think all these fragments came from Alan Wilkins, together with that note wishing Jack academic fame and riches. And if they came from Wilkins it probably means they were found at the old Poe house that Wilkins Construction pulled down."

"And if the fragments were found on Third Street," Sofia picked up and continued Mary's line of thought, "Poe would have written them there, and most likely the tavern he refers to would have been in this neighborhood."

Jerry nodded two or three times while Sofia spoke, and when she was finished, he added, "And it's not hard to find out where the old taverns used to be."

"It's not?" Sofia shot back.

"The dean wouldn't have gone far to find out that kind of information. Manhattan U's library has a whole room devoted to old maps and plans of New York. I've used the room many times in the past."

"Well!" exclaimed Sofia after a pause. "We clearly have work to do."

"Work?" Hannah asked.

"At the library," Sofia cried.

Ashleigh looked at her watch. "But it's nearly ten o'clock. On a Saturday. Will it even be open?"

Mary, who was already packing up the leather box and grabbing her umbrella, smiled and said, "It's finals week. The library's open all night."

When they exited Sofia's building en route to the library, everyone looked up in surprise. The rain had finally stopped, and now wispy clouds, lit by the glowing half-moon, dallied across the night sky. Mary smiled. With the rain gone and Sofia, Hannah, and Ashleigh with her, she felt invigorated. She felt on the cusp of something big, something that would finally turn her life around. Like Nancy Drew setting out on an adventure, Mary felt buoyant and plucky and ready to take on the world—even Jack.

Looking down from the stars, she glimpsed Jerry sidling up next to her. He was smiling too, and when he caught her eyes his smile grew wider.

"What a beautiful night," he whispered.

Mary nodded, and as she studied his face an unexpected jolt of desire shot through each nerve and muscle in her body. She couldn't believe it. Only twenty minutes ago she had hated every inch of him, and now, as much as she tried to quell it, her body was drawn to Jerry's. His gray eyes, his smile, his gentle manner, Mary knew she could sink so easily into all of that. Her body ached to be close to this man she barely knew and whom she barely trusted.

She shook her head and looked away. It had clearly been way too long since she'd been held tenderly by someone or truly loved by someone. She was just lonely; that was all. Now wasn't the time nor the place—nor the man, for that matter—for these feelings. *You have to keep on task,* she scolded herself. *You have to remain brave and feisty, not distracted by this man.*

Without another word or smile, Mary bustled in front of Jerry and quickly caught up with Sofia, who was leading the group across the forecourt in front of the Manhattan U housing and onward to the library. Mary fell in step with Sofia's purposeful strides and immediately began to feel invigorated once again.

"Sofia," she found herself saying, "I admire you."

Sofia gave a surprised laugh. "Why?"

"You're so courageous."

Sofia smiled, but then, with a small smile and an unreadable shake of her head, she said, "Not always."

A loud, monotonous beeping noise and the roar of large engines brought the two women to a halt on the curbside of Bleecker Street. Coming from the west, a procession of large construction vehicles dominated the street. A large bulldozer, with its orange lights flashing, led the way, followed by a dump truck and small digger. Mary, Sofia, and the others, who'd now caught up, stood on the sidewalk waiting for the vehicles to pass. Just before the noisy procession reached them, though, the bulldozer swung slowly into the forecourt. The dump truck and digger did the same.

Over the din, Hannah shouted, "Where are they going?"

The vehicles moved slowly around the forecourt and came to shuddering, groaning halts alongside the garden.

"Shit!" cried Sofia, as everyone looked at the machines and realized what was going on.

"We're too late." Hannah shook her head.

Ashleigh shook her head too. "This is insane," she exclaimed. "Surely they're not going to start tearing up the garden in the middle of the night."

Mary continued to stare at the menacing, flashing machines. "Jack," she spat out finally. "With Jack in charge, anything's possible." And then, after a pause, she added with a glint in her dark eyes, "We're not going to let this happen. We can't." She then looked at everyone in turn. "Who owns a flashlight?" she demanded.

After they exchanged glances and gave confused nods, Mary hitched the leather box tighter under her arm. "Okay. I'll meet you all in fifteen minutes." She waved toward the garden. "Bring your flashlights and warm clothes. I'll bring the key to the garden." She then added with a grin, "And a tent."

Twenty-three

Ashleigh

Ashleigh was the first to wake. Slowly pushing her arms out of the sleeping bag she'd borrowed from Mary, she sat up, rubbed her bleary eyes, and looked around her. The walls of the tent bagged out in two corners and were stretched tight in others. They had put up Mary's old family tent last night, with only the moonlight and a couple of small flashlights to guide them. Fortunately, the bad weather had moved on. Ashleigh could see that the poorly constructed tent would not have survived a gust of wind, let alone a gale or downpour.

Inside the now sunlit tent, Hannah and Mary were still sleeping amid an assortment of empty plastic glasses, chip bags, and bread crumbs. The spot where Sofia had sat until two a.m. was now empty. She'd left to go home and nurse Edgar, but vowed she'd be back first thing.

Ashleigh yawned and looked at her watch. It was just after seven thirty. Even though she was tired from the late night and her uncomfortable and fitful sleep, her body still insisted on waking at its usual hour. She smiled, though. Last night had been worth the groggy head and tired eyes.

When Ashleigh, Hannah, Sofia, and Jerry had all arrived back at the garden, they'd found Mary unfurling the large tent on the moonlit grass with a tiny flashlight in hand. The machines still loomed outside, but their engines were silent and their drivers gone. Under Mary's guidance the five of them got the tent up quickly, and by midnight they were all inside, huddled around a small lantern.

For a long time, as they drank wine and ate snacks, they talked about Jack, the garden, and the bulldozers waiting outside, and after some debate they agreed they would stay in the tent until the police, or whoever it might be, removed them. The conversation then returned to the contents of Jack's leather box. Although they had not yet confirmed whether the garden was on the site of the tavern, they were now pretty convinced that Jack was after the copy of "The Raven" mentioned in Poe's letter.

"He has to be crazy, though," Hannah said at one point, waggling her head. "Digging up a garden based on the slim chance he might find some old manuscript." She then looked over at Mary and her brow crinkled. "Not that I want to call your husband crazy."

"Feel free," Mary muttered. "He *is* crazy, and he's also ambitious. He'd love all the academic kudos that would come with such a find. And not just that. I read an article in *The New Yorker,* which had been lying around my apartment for a while, and had clearly been read by Jack. It was about an archive at the University of Texas that is home to all kinds of rare manuscripts, first editions, proofs of famous books, that kind of thing. The director pays a whole lot of money for new acquisitions, sometimes millions." Mary paused and then went on. "Not that he would be able to keep any of it personally. The manuscript, *if* he found one, would belong to the university. But Jack would sure love all the back patting and promotions he'd receive if he managed to bring in that kind of money." She frowned deeply as she said these last words, but then catching herself and giving a sheepish look in Jerry's direction, she trailed off.

It was at this point that Jerry took his cue.

"You know what?" he had said. "Perhaps I should get over to the library and see if I can find out a little more about this tavern." He started pulling on his plastic raincoat and added, "I also know a couple of people who might be able to help. I just hope they won't mind a late-night call," he added with a grin. And then he was out of the tent and gone.

As his footsteps crunched off across the wet grass, Mary let out a loud sigh, and her shoulders drooped with apparent relief.

Ashleigh looked over at her. "You're still not sure about him, are you?"

Mary shifted awkwardly. "I don't know—" she began, but Hannah interrupted her with a laugh.

"He's sure about *you,* though." She grinned. "I've never seen a man look so enamored!"

Mary swatted at Hannah. "Don't be ridiculous," she said with an embarrassed chuckle, and even though it was dark, it was clear she was blushing.

"He's one handsome guy," Sofia joined in, waggling her eyebrows. And then, in a more serious tone, she added, "And even if it's not *that* man"—she waved behind her—"it's time you found yourself *some* nice man, Mary."

In the glow of the lantern Ashleigh looked from Sofia to Mary. She held her breath, uncertain how Mary was going to react to what Sofia had just said. After a second of silence Mary began to smile.

"You're right," she said. "I deserve better."

There was no stopping her after that. It was as if Sofia had turned some invisible key. Sipping on her red wine, Mary told them everything she'd been through in the last few years with Jack. Ashleigh, Sofia, and Hannah listened, shaking their heads as she recounted every fight, every bruise, every plan to leave. Now and then one of the women would lean in and squeeze one of Mary's hands.

When Mary was finished, Hannah sat forward. "Mary's not the only one who's fed up with their marriage," she confessed, shaking her head. Then, in a long tearful monologue, she told the other women about her fight with Michael earlier that evening, and how she'd told him she wasn't going to Stanford, and how she'd hugged his parents and was scared she might not see them again, and how Patrick was leaving and she might never see him again either. Offering her Kleenex and hugs, the others reassured her that she was doing the right thing and that everything would turn out okay in the end. Maybe, they suggested, she should try to talk to Patrick before he left New York.

Next up was Sofia. She told them all her suspicions about Tom and Reyah, from their whispered exchange at the Poe party to the note she'd found earlier that evening in Tom's study.

"You should have seen the dumb little smiley face," she seethed. "It had to be her."

But the other women weren't buying it. Mary was especially insistent.

"He wouldn't." She shook her head. "I know him, Sofia, and he just wouldn't do that to you."

Sofia didn't look convinced, but she agreed she couldn't stay suspicious forever, and in the end she assured the others, "Okay, I'll ask him."

Ashleigh was the last to talk. After listening to the others, she realized she had little to say. Suddenly everything seemed very clear to Ashleigh, and so, when Sofia was finished and everyone's eyes turned automatically to Ashleigh, she simply waved her hands and laughed.

"I know, I know." She smiled. "I was dumb to move out. I miss Sam more than anything in the world. And I have to tell my father all about her."

Sofia, Hannah, and Mary all raised their eyebrows in surprise.

"You go, girl!" Sofia then shouted, slapping Ashleigh on the back, and everyone, including Ashleigh, laughed. They were still laughing when Sofia got up to leave and the others zipped them-selves into their sleeping bags and lay down to sleep.

Sitting in the tent the next morning, Ashleigh smiled again. She was terrified of what she had to do, but she knew she was going to do it. She'd messed around long enough with Sam, and it was time to make amends. She looked over at Hannah and Mary and wondered if she could just sneak out for a while and find Sam. But as she began struggling from her sleeping bag, the tent's zipper whizzed upward, and a tray of steaming take-out cups thrust its way through the flapping door.

"Good morning, campers," chirped Sofia as she maneuvered her way into the low tent with Edgar strapped to her chest, a cardboard box under her arm, and three coffees balanced on the tray in her outstretched hand. "Ready to take on the mighty machines?"

Hannah's gave out a tired and gravelly groan. But as she emerged from her sleeping bag, she grinned and said, "Of course we are."

Then Mary rolled over and said with a wry grin, "Look out, mighty machines!"

"Hot muffins, anyone?" Sofia said, plucking the box open in front of them. Four steaming muffins gleamed in the bluish light in the tent.

"Yum." Ashleigh grinned, reaching for one. "Where did you get these?"

Sofia laughed. "I just made them."

Everyone stared, and finally Hannah asked, "Do you ever sleep, Sofia?"

Chuckling again, Sofia took a bite of her blueberry muffin and replied, "Not when there are gardens to save or deans to do battle with."

Sofia was cut off by the tent suddenly beginning to shudder above them. The four women exchanged startled glances as the poles strained and the canvas flapped. It was as if a hurricane were engulfing them. They all looked up to see a large shadow, with long legs and extended arms, looming over the tent.

As suddenly as the juddering started, it stopped. Then the shadow retreated a little, and a man's voice boomed, "Mary?"

Mary sprang up in her sleeping bag, frowning with surprise and urgency. She mouthed the word *Jack* to the others, and then quickly wiggled the leather box, which she'd been carrying since last night, under her legs. Meanwhile, Sofia grabbed for the zipper and pulled it closed.

"Mary," Jack barked again, "I know you're in there."

The women remained quiet.

"Of course you're in there," he shouted. "This is *our* tent. How else would our tent be in this garden, if you weren't in there?" He paused and then added in a low growl, "Don't make me come in there and get you."

After a few beats of silence, Jack's shadow enlarged and one of his hands moved downward. He was clearly going to try to come into the tent. Once again, Sofia sat forward and grabbed for the zipper. She then held it with all her might as Jack tried to tug at it from the other side. Jack was strong, but Sofia was determined. With white knuckles, she managed to keep her hold on the zipper's small metal loop until Jack finally gave up with a loud, frustrated grunt. The four women looked at one another as Jack retreated for a moment or two. But before they could say anything, his shadow loomed forward again. He took the top of the flimsy tent in his hands and shook it ferociously. Every seam and stitch in the tent seemed to vibrate under Jack's rage. The four women continued to sit in silence, but now they had reached for one another's hands and were holding them in defiant and protective grasps.

Edgar suddenly let out an ear-piercing scream from inside the sling on Sofia's chest, which immediately caused Sofia to shout out, "Go away, Jack. Just go away. Leave us and this garden alone."

The baby's wail and Sofia's shout stopped Jack from shaking the tent. They didn't make him retreat, however, and outside the tent he started to cackle.

"You silly women." He guffawed. "I don't know what you are trying to achieve. No one supports your little 'save the garden' campaign, and you will *not* stop the demolition work. Take it from me: You are simply making fools of yourselves." He paused and then let out another loud cackle. "By the way, construction work doesn't start until Wednesday. Looks like you are going to have a nice, long camping trip."

Beside Ashleigh, Mary took a deep breath and then squeezed Ashleigh's hand. "Jack," she began in a firm, steady voice, "you are a mean, arrogant, and sad man." She took another deep breath and looked around at the other women in the tent. They nodded gravely, offering their silent support, and so she continued. "You've made my life miserable. You are going to make many more lives miserable if you carry on this way."

Jack started guffawing again, but Mary wasn't going to be stopped.

"I am leaving you. Soon your daughter will want nothing to do with you. And if you don't change and realize how mean and angry you've become, you will die lonely and bitter like your father did."

The shadow loomed large again as Jack made another lunge for the tent. As the poles began to vibrate, Mary raised her voice.

"We know what you are up to, Jack. We know about Poe. We know why you're digging up the garden."

The tent ceased vibrating, and Jack's shadow froze above it. There was a long, agonizing pause. All four women looked at the flimsy door to the tent. Only a small zipper stood between them and the furious man outside. Expecting him to burst in and make a grab for his wife, Sofia, Hannah, Ashleigh, and Mary tensed every muscle in their bodies, huddled closer, and squeezed hold of one another's hands.

But the zipper remained closed, and after a few moments Jack retreated a few paces. The women slowly began to breathe again as Jack spoke.

"I have no idea what you are talking about, Mary," he snapped, and then he added, "I trust you will be out of this tent soon. As of Wednesday this site will be considered a construction zone. If you're still here, you will be trespassing. I will not hesitate to call the police department."

With that he made a triumphant huffing noise, and his footsteps could be heard padding across the grass and away from the tent. It was not until the gate clanged open and then shut that the women began to speak.

"Jesus," Hannah half moaned and half laughed. "That man is *mean*."

Ashleigh nodded. "Really mean."

Sofia looked at Mary and said simply, "You rocked."

Mary's cheeks were flushed. "Thank you," she replied, and

then with a smile she looked at the women in front of her and said, "It felt *so* good. And you know what? I couldn't have done it without you three."

After a short silence, Ashleigh wondered aloud, "What do you think he's going to do now?"

Hannah picked up her coffee from the tray, took a sip, and looked at Mary. "And will he find out that you have the box?"

Mary shrugged. "I replaced the key and straightened his office, but he's sure to figure it out sooner or later."

Hannah then looked around at everyone. "What's our plan? Do we stay here till Wednesday?"

"Of course," Sofia exclaimed, but Mary held up her hand to stop her.

"No," she said with a determined shake of her head. "You three"—she eyed them all in turn—"have important things to do, and you need to go do them. Ashleigh, go home to Sam. Hannah, speak with Michael and *make* him listen. And Sofia"—she gave a small laugh—"please, *please* talk to your husband."

"What about you?" Ashleigh blurted out. "We can't leave you here. What if Jack comes back?"

Sofia nodded. "And there's still so much to do. We need to find out exactly what Jack's up to."

"All in good time," Mary said.

The others were about to protest some more when the zipper to the tent shook. There was a collective gasp and they all turned toward the door. But the tension quickly passed as the flaps were pushed back, the morning sun streamed in, and Jerry's tired but smiling face peered into the tent.

"Hi," he said, looking a little bemused at the sight of four women huddled together, staring wide-eyed at him. "I don't mean to interrupt." His tone was cautious. "But I wanted to tell you what I found out."

After a few beats during which everyone was still too shocked and blinded by the sun to say anything, Mary finally let out a deep, relieved laugh and said, "The cavalry has arrived."

*   *   *

Half an hour later Ashleigh stood in the hallway outside Sam's apartment. In one hand she held her cell, in the other a plastic grocery bag from the deli. She looked at them both for a second. Then she looped the plastic bag farther up her arm and used her free hand to flip open her phone. She scrolled down to her father's number, and with her heart quickening in her chest, hit send.

"Dad," she said, after he'd barked a terse greeting, "I have to see you."

Her father made an inaudible grunting noise.

"There's something I need to talk to you about." As she spoke the words her heart continued to kick and tumble in her chest, but at the same time she felt strong, determined. "So," she carried on, "can we meet?"

"I am very busy, Ashleigh," her father snapped.

But Ashleigh, for the first time ever, didn't buckle under his chastising tone. Instead she persisted. "It's important," she said, making her voice as steely as his.

Finally and begrudgingly he agreed. They would meet tonight for dinner.

Ashleigh hung up, slid the cell into her pocket, and moved toward Sam's door. She pressed the buzzer and, as she waited, pulled a cardboard tub from the bag hanging on her arm. The door finally clicked and began to open. Ashleigh held the cold container high up in her hands.

Sam's beautiful green eyes, still heavy with sleep, peeked around the door. She looked from Ashleigh to what Ashleigh was offering and then asked with a growing smile, "Cherry Garcia for breakfast?"

"How about it?" Ashleigh grinned.

Twenty-four

Sofia

When Sofia got back to her apartment from the garden, she was surprised to find Hayden in the living room, dancing to music from the booming stereo. Next to him Gracie was twirling around and around dressed in a pink sequined tutu, her red Converse high-tops, and a yogurt-stained I LOVE THE SAN DIEGO ZOO sweatshirt. Sofia looked at her daughter and realized this was the price she paid for leaving Tom to get Gracie up in the morning. Tom generally let Gracie decide on whatever she wanted to wear, and thus practicality, cleanliness, and the weather outside never factored into her day's outfit.

In spite of everything, Sofia smiled. She might be about to learn that her husband was cheating on her, but she couldn't help loving his scattered yet endearing fatherly ways.

"Want to be a backup dancer?" called Hayden as he spotted Sofia in the doorway. "I'm afraid this one's the lead singer, though." He waved at Gracie. "So it's backup dancer or audience. Take your pick."

Sofia laughed and wiggled toward the two of them to the music. After swaying happily for a few minutes, with Edgar still slung on her chest, she asked Hayden, "Where's Tom?"

Hayden stopped dancing and looked at her, his eyebrows raised. "I thought you knew."

Instantly something snapped in Sofia, and all her turbulent feelings about Tom returned. "Knew *what*?" she spat.

"He had to go do something," he said, waving his hands defensively and looking troubled by Sofia's apparent anger. "He said something important came up at the office. That's why he called and asked me to watch Gracie."

With her hands shaking, Sofia started to furiously undo Edgar's sling.

"Important? What can be so important on a Sunday morning? He's an English professor, not a brain surgeon, for God's sake," she muttered, remembering how Tom had looked to be in no hurry to go anywhere just an hour ago, when she headed out to the garden. "I'll show him *important*."

When Edgar was free she said to Hayden, "Can you watch Edgar too?" Hayden nodded, and she thrust the baby into his open arms. "I'll be back soon," she said tersely, before scooting out of the room.

On the way over to the English department, Sofia mumbled and fumed and shook her head. She knew she must look like a madwoman, with her unkempt hair, her pink blouse covered in the remnants of this morning's muffin baking, and her whispered rantings. But she didn't care. She had more important things to worry about.

Earlier, on the way back from the garden, and spurred on by Mary and the others, Sofia had hoped that her confrontation with Tom would be a civilized and short-lived affair. She'd ask if he was cheating, he'd say, "Of course not," and she would fall into his arms and chuckle with relief. But this fantasy was ebbing away fast. Now things looked a whole lot worse. She was going to catch him in the act. And if she didn't catch him in the act, if he and Reyah had chosen to go off to some seedy hotel somewhere, Sofia would no doubt find Tom's office empty and thus be confronted with the glaring evidence of his lies and deceit. It was a terrifying thought. Nonetheless, Sofia knew she had to go through with it. She wasn't going to be an ignorant, cuckolded fool any longer, and so she stomped onward.

The elevator in Tom's building wasn't working, so Sofia flew up a whole twelve flights of stairs. It was the most exercise she'd done since before she was pregnant with Edgar, and as she barged through the fire doors toward the English department, she was sweating and wheezing. She didn't stop, however. She kept on moving down the corridor and toward Tom's office.

When she reached his door she found it closed. She knocked a few times, but no one answered. Then she angrily waggled the metal handle while pressing her ear to the door, listening for any whispers or hurried movements. She heard neither, and so she paced angrily back to the English department's common area near the elevator. She had no idea what to do next. She could sit and wait for him, but he might never turn up. He might have slunk straight to a hotel or to Reyah's apartment—no doubt some East Village student hovel—never having contemplated coming by his office.

Sofia was about to slump down onto one of the common area's boxy sofas when a flash of red caught her eye. Slung over a nearby chair was Tom's favorite red sweater, and poking out from underneath it was a battered strap from his old leather backpack. Sofia lunged toward them and pulled both the sweater and the bag tight into her arms. She shook her head from left to right and found herself expecting to see Tom and Reyah emerging from some nearby seminar room or stationery closet, all ruffled and flushed.

They didn't emerge, but as Sofia's eyes darted around she remembered the grad-student office next to the faculty lounge. If Reyah was a grad student in the department, as Sofia suspected, perhaps that was where she would find them. Sofia dropped Tom's bag and sweater and raced back down the hallway, past Tom's office, and onward. When she rounded the first corner and passed the door to the faculty lounge, she came to a grinding halt. Just a few feet away a strip of daylight glowed across the corridor. The door to the grad-student office was ajar. Sofia held her breath and then tiptoed slowly, very slowly, toward the light.

With her first glimpse into the room Sofia's stomach somersaulted, and she was overwhelmed with an urge to retch. Obscured by the partially open door, she could see a woman on her knees and leaning forward. Even though she could see only part of the lower back, feet, and a ponytail, Sofia knew it was her. There was no mistaking that velvet hair, tanned skin, and lacy thong protruding seductively from her skintight jeans.

For a second Sofia froze. She wasn't sure if she could go in. The thought of finding some hot young grad student blowing her husband was too much to bear. From where she was standing, that was sure as hell what it looked like. She'd never be able to erase such an image from her mind, and so it might be better just to leave now, pretend she'd never seen anything. But the thought of Tom not getting caught and being let off the hook reignited Sofia's fury. He couldn't get away with this.

Flinging out her right arm, she punched the door wide open and was instantly confronted with two pairs of startled eyes: Tom's and the grad student's. Instead of being in the compromising position Sofia had expected, however, they were fully dressed, both of them kneeling over a number of large boxes. Tom was clutching a stack of papers, and his glasses were perched on his head—something he did when he was studying small print, and not generally something he did when he was having sex.

"Sofia?" Tom squinted up in surprise. "Hi."

Sofia was instantly relieved to find they weren't doing what she thought they'd been doing. Yet she couldn't quite dampen the anger still boiling in her chest—anger that was now coupled with confusion and embarrassment.

"Can I talk to you, Tom?" she blurted, and then, eyeing the student, she added, "Alone."

The girl's fair eyebrows fluttered in surprise and panic as she scrambled to her feet.

"Of course," she whispered, scooting around Sofia and out the door.

"What's wrong, hon?" Tom said after she was gone.

Sofia stepped toward him and then dropped to her knees. She wasn't sure if she wanted to shout or cry, she was so confused. She hadn't found Tom doing anything untoward, but what was

he doing here? With that girl? The girl from the Poe party? It was
Sunday morning and he was supposed to be watching Gracie.

In a strained whisper Sofia finally asked, "What's going on?"

Pushing his glasses back onto his nose, Tom then searched
his wife's face, his eyes wide and confused. "I'm—" he began, but
Sofia's rambling cut him off.

"Is something going on between you and her?" She jerked her
head toward the door. "Between you and Reyah? I presume she's
Reyah. Because if anything is going on, I want to know now. I don't
want to be made a fool of, Tom."

Tom let out a loud puff of laughter and shook his head.

"Don't laugh at me!" Sofia snapped.

Tom searched Sofia's face again and then, apparently realizing
she was serious, asked, "Does this look like the scene of some hot
affair?" He waved around at the boxes, colored folders, and piles
of paper.

Sofia simply snorted.

"Sofia," Tom persisted, taking her shoulders with his hands and
looking straight into her eyes, "is that really what you think is going
on?"

Under his gaze Sofia felt her certainty begin to waver. She
looked down, past Tom's arms at the papers. It just didn't make
sense. "But why *are* you here?" she said, her tone deflated and
meek.

"Because," Tom said, "Reyah called me this morning. She
needed some help. A friend of hers—or, rather, a friend of her
dad's—called late last night and needed some information on Poe.
It's a long story, but it looks like your hunch was right. Our dear-
est Edgar Allan might have something to do with the garden and
Havemeyer's plans to bulldoze it."

"How do you know all this?" Sofia demanded. She and the
others had figured all this out only yesterday, and she'd told Tom
nothing.

"Like I said, a friend of Reyah's dad called her. He knew she was the secretary of the Poe Foundation and he wondered if she could help out." Tom paused and then added, "And Reyah called me this morning. She was having trouble deciphering some of my old notes about the demolition of Poe's house on Third Street." Sofia was still eyeing Tom suspiciously, so he added, "You know, notes I made when I was chairperson."

"I realize that," Sofia snapped, and then she was silent for a few beats. She was desperate to ask what they'd found, but then something occurred to her. "So, Reyah's the secretary of the Poe Foundation? I thought your student Christian was the secretary?" Sofia asked, finding it hard not to sound bitter and accusing,

"Reyah took over the job at the beginning of the year," Tom explained. "Christian had too much on his plate."

Sofia was still frowning. "But what about the note?" she said in a small voice.

"What note?" Tom retorted. He was beginning to look frustrated.

"The note Reyah sent you with those cartoons."

"Cartoons?" Tom looked utterly bemused. But then, after a second or two, something clicked. "You mean those old *New Yorker* cartoons? Where . . . I mean, how did you know about them?"

"I saw them in your study," Sofia shot back. "And on the note Reyah said, 'Thanks for the other night.' " Sofia's voice was tinged with renewed panic as she thought again about the note. "What was she thanking you for, Tom?"

Once again Tom looked baffled. He thought hard and then said, "I remember. We ran into each other one evening a while back. I was on my way home, she was heading into the library, and she asked a question about a citation she was looking for. I popped into the library to help her find it."

Sofia was about to say something more, but Tom put a finger to his lips. He then stood up and held out a hand for Sofia. When she was on her feet he took her by the elbow and guided her toward the door.

"Do you know Reyah's last name, by the way?"

Sofia looked up at her husband, confused. He was already looking at the door to the office and pointing. Sofia followed his finger. On the nameplate, which she hadn't thought to check when she'd barged in earlier, were the words GRAD STUDENT OFFICE. Under that were two names Sofia didn't recognize, followed by a third: Reyah Poe.

"Oh," was all Sofia could say.

Tom pulled her around and held her cheek in his hand. He smiled, looking deep into her eyes, and said, "Not 'oh,' honey, Poe." He then gave her a long, tender kiss, and when he finally pulled away, he added with a seriousness and honesty that made Sofia want to cry, "I would never cheat on you, Sofe. You are my life."

Sofia felt pretty foolish. Not only had she missed Reyah's name on the door, she'd also missed a framed photograph on a nearby desk that showed Reyah happily snuggled with her boyfriend. Reyah, who'd obviously figured out Sofia's suspicions for herself, quickly pointed the photo out when Sofia summoned her back into the room and apologized for her earlier rudeness. Reyah also quickly pointed out that she was a distant descendant of Edgar Allan Poe, and since she was a kid had been a "self-confessed Poe junkie."

But Sofia didn't dwell too long on her mistake and the fool she'd made of herself. There was work to be done. Straightaway she told Tom and Reyah everything she and the others had found out about Jack, Wilkins Construction, and the fragments in the box. She hadn't told Tom last night because he'd been asleep when she returned from the tent, and he was still asleep when she'd left again this morning. There was also a part of her that hadn't wanted to tell him. She was still mad at him for siding with Jack and laughing off her suspicions. Now, however, they needed Tom; they needed his expert eyes to confirm whether the fragments were real.

Tom and Reyah jiggled with excitement when they heard about the contents of the leather box, and quickly abandoned their fruitless search amid the Poe Foundation paperwork. Soon all three of them were hurrying out of the English department, along Bleecker

Street, and toward the garden. By the time they reached Mary's tent, Sofia was panting and wheezing once again.

"Oh, my God!" Tom and Reyah exclaimed in unison as soon as Mary opened the box and handed over the two glass containers.

For the next couple of minutes they both studied the fragments in a pregnant and industrious silence. Meanwhile, Mary, Jerry, and Sofia, who were all squeezed into the tent beside them, exchanged excited and silent glances.

"I think these might be the real thing," Tom said finally in a hushed and astonished whisper. "I really do."

"I agree." Reyah nodded. "The handwriting is Poe's, without a doubt."

Tom prodded the container holding the letter, "This looks like part of a letter to Poe's friend F. W. Thomas. The two exchanged numerous letters over the years, and Poe often referred to him as 'My dear Thomas.'" Tom pushed his glasses onto his head and stared harder at the document. "And if my memory serves me correctly, there's a letter on record where Poe talks to Thomas about the success of 'The Raven.'"

Sofia and everyone else in the tent peered over at the letter, but Tom's attention had now switched to the other box containing the fragments of newsprint.

"But this . . ." He whistled, tapping at the container. "*This* is really exciting. I think these are from the very first printing of 'The Raven' in New York's *Evening Mirror*." As he said this he pointed to the larger fragment upon which the words *Evening Mirror* were written. His finger then moved to a smaller fragment. "And you see there. You see that number four?" Everyone huddled in and nodded, so Tom went on. "The poem was printed on page four on its first run."

Letting out a snort of laughter, Sofia said, "You even know the page number? You're an even bigger geek than I thought."

Tom looked up and winked. "But you love me anyway, right?"

"Of course." Sofia winked back.

Sofia then sat back and listened as Tom grinned and talked,

with his hands waving, about how exciting it was to see Poe's own edits on this very first publication of the poem. Sofia couldn't help smiling. Her worries about Tom now seemed a distant memory, and all she could think was how much she loved him—her smart and geeky man—and how dumb she'd been to ever doubt him.

When Mary redirected Tom's attention to the letter and asked if he thought it was possible Jack would find the copy of "The Raven" that Poe spoke of, Tom shrugged.

"I suppose it might be worth a try," he said. "If the letter is real and Poe did leave a copy with the tavern owner, it wouldn't be an original manuscript of the poem, but it would probably be one of the earliest versions in circulation. Although"—Tom shook his head—"I'm not sure if it's worth digging up a whole garden in the hope of finding something that probably disappeared years ago.

"But this," he went on, again tapping the container with the newsprint, "this is quite a find. This, if it is the real deal, will cause a big stir in the Poe world. The emendations marked here"—he nodded down at the box—"could explain a lot about the evolution of the poem."

As Tom spoke, an unexpected idea popped into Sofia's mind. Her heart began to thump in her chest.

"I have to go," she blurted out, causing everyone to look up. "I have a plan."

But before anyone could ask what she was talking about, she was gone.

When Sofia got home she didn't go straight into her living room, where she could hear Gracie chattering and Hayden laughing. Instead she opened the doors to the closet in the hallway and stepped up on a couple of boxes full of old books. Balancing precariously, she reached high above her head and fished around on the cluttered top shelf. Her fingers worked blindly amid the junk, but finally, after pushing back what felt like beach towels and old pillowcases, she found what she was looking for. She grabbed the handle of a canvas bag and jerked it free. Unfortunately, as she did so, she wobbled on her cardboard perch and clattered with a thud to the floor.

"What are you doing?" Hayden asked from the doorway of the living room, a smirk creeping across his face.

From where she lay, crumpled on the floor and clutching the canvas bag to her chest, Sofia laughed. "Hayden," she said, "do you want to be a movie star?"

"I am, aren't I?"

"Do you want to be an even bigger movie star?"

"Why?" Hayden beamed. "Are you going to be my agent?"

Sofia sat up and unzipped the bag in her lap. "Nope," she said as she pulled out an aging video camera, held it up to her eye, and pointed it in Hayden's direction. "You are going to be the star of a groundbreaking new movie by a talented, up-and-coming director named"—she dropped the camera from her face and grinned—"Sofia Muñoz."

Twenty-five

Hannah

Hannah had no idea where Michael was. She'd gotten back from the garden a few hours ago to an empty apartment. Michael had left no note, and his cell was going straight to voice mail. Hannah was determined, however. If it meant waiting here all day, that was what she would do. Like Mary had said, she had to make him listen. She had to tell him that she wasn't coming to Stanford, and he had to hear her this time.

And so Hannah sat on the couch, twizzling between her fingers a piece of cotton frayed from her sweatshirt, waiting for his arrival. She eyed the front door from time to time. Michael was sure to be in a foul mood when he returned. After all, she'd disappeared all night without so much as a call or an explanation. Not only that, she'd walked out on him when his parents had come to visit. Michael hated having intimate discussions with Diane and Bill, and Hannah's disappearance was sure to have prompted all kinds of concerned and probing questions.

Hannah began to look back toward the door once again, but her gaze faltered. Stretching from an electricity socket below the bookshelf to the foot of Michael's favorite armchair, there was a curling black wire she'd never seen before. She sprang up from the couch, moved closer, and found Michael's laptop on the floor beside the chair. She stared at it for a moment. Michael rarely sat here with his computer, she realized; he usually scurried away to his study or his office on campus if he wanted to work.

Feeling a little bored and also somewhat curious about what Michael might have been working on, Hannah flopped down into the armchair and pulled the small computer onto her lap. She then flipped open the laptop, and, because Michael had left it on standby, the screen glowed instantly to life. Hannah couldn't access the desktop straightaway, though, as Michael had enabled some sort of lock. On the vivid blue screen a small gray box demanded a password. Looking up, Hannah pondered this for a second. Then, smiling to herself, she tapped out the letters A-T-H-E-N-A. The blue screen quickly disappeared and the desktop popped up.

Hannah was so busy congratulating herself on figuring out Michael's password, she didn't immediately take in what was in front of her. When her eyes settled on the two open programs, however, her head jerked back in shock. In one window, under the banner *Russia with Love, No. 23: Anastasia,* was a photograph of a high-cheekboned, flawless-skinned, green-eyed beauty who had to be no more than twenty-one. In the second window—an instant messange window—there was the tail end of a typed exchange between "Stasia" and "Mikey44."

After blinking a few times, Hannah slowly moved her fingers to the touch pad, and she scrolled to the top of the message window. Her eyes widened and her breath quickened as she began reading. Throughout the exchange, Mikey44 told Stasia how beautiful she was, and how her cheekbones were "extraordinary," and how she should really consider sending shots of herself to modeling agencies in the States. In one line he even wrote, *Send some to me; I know people in the fashion business.* Stasia's replies were short and sweet and written in broken English peppered with typos and clichés. *You my kind man, Mikey,* read one line near the end. *You rock my worlds.*

When Hannah had scrolled as far as she could scroll, her heart hammered in her chest and she was about to snap the laptop shut. She stopped, though, when she noticed a series of programs minimized at the bottom of the screen, and her fingers returned to the touch pad. Soon Tatiana, Svetlana, and Natalya were all staring out at Hannah, with their beautiful young faces posed and plucked and perfectly photographed. Then, as Hannah tapped on the remaining minimized programs, she was confronted with yet more instant message windows. Although the interlocutor was different in each one, the screen name Mikey44 glowed in every window, and in each typed conversation Mikey44 praised the girls' beauty and talked at length about their possible careers in modeling. Every exchange was relatively innocent. There was no talk of sex or hooking up. But there was a deep familiarity and intimacy in the way Mikey44 and these girls spoke to one another, and it was clear they'd spoken before—and that they would speak again.

Worst of all, in the final window, which held one of the longest conversations, Mikey44 repeatedly called Natalya "my beauty." It was the same pet name, in other words, that Michael had once used for Hannah, and the same pet name he'd unexpectedly used in the text he'd sent to Hannah last week. With a wrenching feeling in her gut, Hannah realized Michael's text was never meant for her. It was meant for Natalya. When he'd said in his message that he was going online, it was because he wanted to exchange sweet words with Natalya and tell her how beautiful she was. Hannah, with her paint-splashed pants, her cropped hair, and her pooching belly, was probably the last person he'd wanted to speak to at that moment.

Hannah slowly pulled the laptop closed and placed her hands on top of the warm machine. She let her head flop back against the armchair and sighed a deep, mournful sigh. What she'd seen made her feel queasy. What she'd figured out about the text made her angry, but most of all she felt sad—gut-wrenchingly sad. Hannah wasn't really surprised that Michael would yearn for these Russian beauties. After all, fifteen years ago she was so much like them herself, with her high cheekbones, her doleful eyes, her flawless skin, and her plump lips. She could have easily passed as a Tatiana or a Natalya.

What made Hannah truly sad, though, was that Michael hadn't moved on. He still wanted the twentysomething Hannah he'd first met on that red velvet couch at a West Village party, with her flowing locks and coltish body. He didn't want the thirty-three-year-old art student she now was. Hannah had known this for a long time, of course, but seeing these pictures, finding Michael's online flirtations, just confirmed it all in glorious Technicolor. Hannah had always been determined to marry a man who would love her in every way: love every part of her, love her and never leave her, like her father had left her heartbroken mother. Michael hadn't left her physically, but he'd left her in another way. He was still in love with the girl he married. But he'd checked out on the woman Hannah had now become.

This realization left her winded and startled and deeply sad. She didn't feel like crying, though. She didn't feel like yelling or screaming either. She was just shocked and numb and disappointed that her marriage had come to this. When she'd married Michael, he'd saved her from a loneliness that she'd never quite acknowledged. He gave her a family and love and security, where before all she had was a passport with many stamps, her portfolio, and the promise of the next photo shoot. But Michael's love for her was now outdated. His parents' love for her was still strong, but that wasn't enough to go on with. Hannah wanted a husband who loved her in all her complexities and passions. She wanted a husband who listened and understood and loved her in all her changes and growth. She wanted a husband who was happy too, and not channeling his passions into images on a computer screen and yearning for the kind of woman his wife no longer was.

Hannah now understood, as she sat in the familiar old armchair with Michael's computer in her lap, that her marriage was over. It wasn't just Stanford. She was going to move out as well. She was going to say good-bye to Michael—and his parents. Hannah's heart thudded fearfully as she realized all this, but she felt a spark of invigoration too. For the first time in a long time she felt certain about something. One hundred percent certain. Her eyes flashed open, and she scooted the laptop onto the arm of the chair and made toward the bedroom. Once there, she began gathering clothes and shoes from the closet and precious knickknacks and photographs from the drawers in the dresser. She made a pile on the bed and then carefully began to fold and prod everything into a large backpack. Hannah had no clue where she would go when her bag was packed. But it was time to go, she was certain.

Fastening the backpack, Hannah was about to move it into the hallway when she heard the front door bang open. She froze for a second as the old wavering, uncertain Hannah tried to resurface. But then she sucked in a determined breath and moved, backpack in hand, out into the hallway.

"Hannah?" Michael called, his voice sounding angry and strained. When he caught sight of her, he glared. "Where have you been?" he demanded, and as his eyes slipped down to the bag, he barked, "What *are* you doing?"

Hannah moved slowly toward him. "I'm leaving, Michael."

For a few beats Michael did nothing. He simply stared at the backpack. Then he let out a long, bitter laugh and said, "Don't be ridiculous, Hann."

This, of course, was what he always said. This was the patronizing tone he often took, and usually Hannah would crumple beneath it. Today, however, she stepped closer, caught his gaze in her own, and repeated very calmly, "I'm leaving, Michael. I'm not coming to Stanford, and I'm moving out."

Michael waved his hand and shook his head. "If this is about the modeling, okay, I hear you."

"It's not just the modeling—" Hannah began, but Michael kept talking.

"If you don't want to do it, fine. Although I think you're missing out on a great opportunity."

"It's—" she tried again.

"Hann, Stanford will be awesome. I'm telling you. You can sunbathe every day." He laughed. "Swim. Take day trips to San Francisco and go shopping."

Hannah sighed. Not only wasn't he listening; he was just proving, once again, how little he knew her. She hadn't sunbathed or shopped in years. It was clear that this wasn't going to work. Even with her bag packed in front of him, he still wasn't going to hear what she had to say.

But Hannah had an idea. Dropping the backpack where she stood, she pushed her way past Michael and then beckoned him to follow. Back in the living room she plopped down into the armchair and pulled Michael's computer back into her lap.

As Michael looked on, the blood drained instantly from his face. "What are you doing?" he demanded, his voice urgent and shrill. He tried to grab for the laptop, but Hannah moved it quickly away from him.

Then, after she'd opened it up and quickly tapped in the password, she called up one of the instant message windows.

Michael ranted angrily nearby. "Hannah, that's my computer. You have no right. Hannah? What are you doing?"

But Hannah didn't look up. Instead she began to type.

Dear Michael, she wrote. And then, with her fingers flying across the keys, everything poured out. She told him she wasn't going to Stanford, and all the reasons why she was leaving. She explained that they were strangers with very different loves and very different dreams. And after thanking him for all the beautiful times, she wrote that it was time to say good-bye. As she typed, Michael jiggled restlessly beside her and demanded to know *what the hell* she was doing. Every now and again, he'd even make a grab for the computer. But Hannah twisted away each time his hand got close and continued typing. In the end, Michael, clearly not wanting a tussle over his precious laptop, reluctantly let her go on with her task.

When she was finished, Hannah typed her name and handed the open laptop to Michael. Without looking, however, he slammed the computer shut and glared. "What else did you see?" he asked. "On this," he added, prodding the laptop.

Hannah said nothing. She simply got up from the chair and moved into the hallway. There, she slung her backpack onto her back, picked up her easel and duffel bag by the door, and let herself out of the apartment. She walked slowly down the corridor to the elevators. If Michael chased her out and wanted to talk, of course she would. She didn't want to run from him. She was happy to talk and listen and cry about the end of their marriage, but only when he was ready to do that.

She looked back toward the apartment as she waited for the elevator. The door remained closed. Two elevators came and went and still the door stayed shut, and so, in the end, when the elevator opened a third time, Hannah got in.

Out in the garden, the sun was hot on Hannah's back. Beside her the tent was still quiet. When she'd peeked in earlier and dropped her heavy backpack inside the tent, Mary was curled up asleep, her long hair splayed out majestically on her pillow. Beside her lay Jerry, fully clothed and also fast asleep. One of his hands lay lightly but protectively on Mary's shoulder. The two of them looked peaceful and curiously happy in their sleep. Hannah smiled when she saw them. They were on the verge of something joyful and new, she could tell, and it gave her hope.

A breeze was now gently shaking the canvas in front of Hannah, and she stepped forward and held it with her paint-stained fingers while she scanned her work. She'd started painting only twenty minutes ago, but already the canvas was bursting with color and light, lines and shades. After weeks lost in her worries about Michael and Patrick and being pregnant, at last Hannah felt loose and free and inspired. The painting was spilling out of her.

From the canvas Hannah looked up at the sky. It was that impossible blue she loved so much, but had never been able to capture. Hannah stared up for a few minutes and then reached into her duffel for three tubes of paint. Squeezing them onto her busy palette, she began to mix. When she was through mixing, Hannah took up a fresh brush, dabbed it into the blueness she'd just created, and painted it onto the canvas in wide, looping arcs.

Twenty-six

Mary

Mary and Hannah spent three nights in the tent, until Ashleigh, with the aid of her uncle, managed to get the work on the garden stalled for a short while. Mary then moved to her daughter's place. She'd arrived on Sarah's doorstep a week ago. Within an hour she'd explained to her daughter everything that had happened between her and Jack. Sarah was shocked and tearful and enraged, and quickly offered Mary their couch. Mary had been there ever since.

Now, ten days after their camping adventure, Mary and Hannah were reunited once again. Lurking in the shadows just inside the doorway to Manhattan U's largest auditorium, the two of them watched as hundreds of students filed past with their long graduation gowns flowing and their square caps perched precariously on their excited, bobbing heads. A hum of chatter and anticipation floated in the air, and parents looked down with wide, proud smiles from the auditorium's upper tiers. Mary spotted a couple of her students as they passed, but she didn't call out to them. For now she had to remain in the darkness. If Jack caught sight of her he might suspect something, and it could ruin their whole carefully choreographed plan. And if that happened, by the end of the week the bulldozers could be all over the garden.

In the gloom Hannah sidled a little closer to Mary and whispered, "I hope everything is going okay upstairs."

By "upstairs" Hannah meant the projector room. That was where they hoped Sofia and Ashleigh were. They'd left Mary and Hannah just five minutes ago, saying they would have everything under control in no time.

"I'm sure it's fine," Mary assured Hannah.

But Hannah still looked panicked. "And where's Hayden? He was meant to be here twenty minutes ago."

Mary gently patted Hannah's arm and smiled. "He'll be here."

Since they'd spent those nights together, a special bond had formed between the two women. Mary and Hannah stayed up late every night in the tent dissecting their failed marriages. But also, while clinking small mugs filled with wine, they toasted their futures. Even though there were twenty years between them, and their husbands were very different men, they seemed to share so much. In many ways Mary recognized her younger self in Hannah—the sensitivities, the insecurities, but also the burning passion to be creative. Mary was pleased that Hannah wasn't going to follow the path she'd taken, though. Unlike Mary, Hannah wasn't going to waste years in a marriage that would hold her back. Hannah had realized in time that she had to put herself and her dreams first.

While Mary was enjoying spending time with Sarah, cramped though they were in Sarah and Greg's small one-bedroom in Tribeca, she missed Hannah and those nights in the tent, and it pleased her to find out Hannah felt the same.

"I miss our tent." Hannah was giggling close to Mary's ear as the final students walked into the auditorium. "It was fun, wasn't it? Plus, I slept so damn well. Ashleigh and Sam's couch is *very* lumpy. Not that I'm complaining, of course. It was totally sweet of them to take me in."

"How's the apartment search going?" Mary asked.

Hannah's eyes sparkled. "I think I might have found somewhere. The place is in Brooklyn, way out on the F line, Mary, you should see it. It has these big windows, cool old floors, and I think I can use the bedroom as a studio. It's not very big, but it will be fine."

As she said the last words, the sparkle in her eyes dulled for a second. Mary knew that, just a few days ago Hannah had moved all her painting gear from the studio in her in-laws' attic. It had been a painful time, but Hannah was brave. She'd seen it through.

"But at least it will be *all* yours," Mary said, squeezing Hannah's arm again.

Hannah nodded, the glimmer returning to her eyes. "Yes," she whispered. "All mine."

Mary opened her mouth to say something else, but a crackling and squealing noise from the auditorium's speakers made them both look toward the stage. While the hum and buzz among the students and audience began to trickle into silence, Manhattan U's vice provost stepped up to the lectern and began his opening address. Mary didn't really listen to what he said until the vice provost opened up his arms and invited the faculty and the dean of humanities onto the stage.

Mary found she was holding her breath. This would be the first time in nearly two weeks she'd seen Jack. She watched as the faculty traipsed from where they'd been standing in a side aisle up the small flight of stairs and toward the chairs set out for them at the back of the stage. They looked like colorful canaries, Mary thought, in their rainbow of different gowns. Jack was last. He walked with his chin high and his orange and black Princeton gown billowing from his broad shoulders. He took his seat close to the lectern and scanned the auditorium with that smug smile Mary knew so well.

Watching him, Mary felt surprisingly calm. She didn't feel angry or sad; she just hoped that by the end of today that smile would be wiped from his face. If everything went according to plan, hopefully it would be. Once the faculty were seated, the graduation ceremony began in earnest. The valedictorian and salutatorian gave their speeches, followed by a poet who'd graduated from Manhattan U ten years ago. Mary and Hannah stood together, half listening but also, now and again, looking at their watches and then toward the door.

"What will we do if Hayden doesn't get here?" Hannah whispered amid the applause for the last speaker.

"He will," Mary said, but her earlier confidence was beginning to wane a little, and she couldn't resist flicking another glance toward the door.

Just as she was silently beginning to pray for Hayden's arrival, the door next to them eased open. It wasn't Hayden, however. Instead, it was Ashleigh's smiling face that peeked through the door, and she was flashing them a thumbs-up.

"It worked?" Hannah blurted out, and then as some students in the chairs in front of them turned to see who'd spoken, she slapped her hand over her mouth and shrank back against the wall.

Luckily, the vice provost announced the beginning of the commencement, and soon all eyes were back on the stage as the first group of students filed up. Meanwhile, Ashleigh made her way through the doors and sidled up next to Hannah and Mary. The vice provost began to call names, and as students crossed the stage and collected their certificates, applause, whoops, and cheers ebbed and flowed throughout the auditorium. Still hiding in the shadows, Mary and the others felt it safe to have a whispered conversation.

Hannah spoke first. "Is everything ready?" she demanded.

Ashleigh nodded and said, "Piece of cake. You know Sofia. She wooed the projector-room guys with her usual charms."

"And what about Hayden?" Mary asked the question that she knew was on the tip of Hannah's tongue too. "Is he on his way?"

"He's on his way," Ashleigh whispered.

"But will he be here in time?" Hannah pressed. "Sofia says he's always late."

Ashleigh grinned. "Sofia told him that if he's late she'll go to every gossip rag in the country and divulge all the dirt she has on him."

Mary could sense Hannah still panicking beside her. "This is going to go on forever," she assured her with a wave. "Look how many students are graduating. Jack's speech isn't until the end. We've got plenty of time."

Mary then looked over at Ashleigh and muttered, "Good job

getting the construction delayed." Mary had seen Ashleigh earlier, but in the excitement and bustle this was the first time she'd gotten to congratulate her.

"My uncle is the star." Ashleigh gave a modest wave. "He stuck his neck out, pretending our firm made some errors on the construction contract. Wilkins was mad as hell." She rolled her eyes. "I owe Uncle Ray, big-time."

"You must have done some sweet talking." Hannah giggled.

Ashleigh smiled. "I did." But then her mouth descended into a frown and she added, "Wilkins ended up going to another law firm, and if their attorneys work fast, which I'm sure they are being paid to do, construction could start by the end of the week."

Hannah smiled a tight smile. "We have to pull this off then," she murmured.

Another rumble of applause echoed around the auditorium, and Mary looked at Ashleigh and said, "Whatever happens, you and your uncle did a great job."

Before anyone could say anything more, the lights in the auditorium suddenly flickered on and off. The applause and calling of names stopped as everyone looked up and wondered what was going on. Mary froze. The lights weren't supposed to go out now. She hoped Sofia was okay.

After a few seconds, though, the flickering stopped and the ceremony resumed. Mary, Hannah, and Ashleigh all gasped with relief.

"Do you think Sofia has everything under control up there?" Hannah asked, as the applause started up again.

"Perhaps. I'll go back up and check," Ashleigh whispered before slipping back out the door.

Watching her go, Mary crossed her fingers behind her back.

Twenty minutes later the row of students in front of Mary and the others stood up, scooted out into the aisle, and started moving toward the front of the auditorium. This was Hannah and Mary's cue. The commencement was nearly finished, and it was time to get ready. Mary bent down and started hauling two large bags from behind the heavy curtain, where they'd hidden them earlier. Hannah dragged another two bags from the same spot. Then they unzipped the bags and started scooping out the contents. Soon over two hundred T-shirts and a stack of brightly colored flyers sat in piles around them.

Mary picked one of the T-shirts up and flapped it open.

"Hannah." She whistled. "It's amazing."

She held it closer to take a better look. Under a banner that read, *Save the Garden,* a painting of Hannah's was reprinted on the center of the T-shirt. It was breathtaking. Even in the gloomy light at the back of the auditorium, its vivid blues and misty grays shone out against the T-shirt's white fabric. Mary had looked at this painting a hundred times already, but still she couldn't get over how incredible it was. With playful flourishes, Hannah had reproduced Gustave Doré's *The Raven.* The original painting, which Hannah had shown Mary just a few days ago, was one of the illustrations used in an old edition of Poe's famous poem, and depicted a skeletal Grim Reaper perched on top of a glowing world. In Hannah's interpretation the Grim Reaper wasn't a skeleton. Its face was a little more familiar.

"You really captured him." Mary huffed a laugh and nodded toward the Reaper.

Hannah smiled and flicked a glance up at Jack, sitting on the stage. "You think he'll recognize himself?"

"If he doesn't, he's in denial," Mary muttered.

Hannah took the T-shirt from Mary's hands and said, "Did you see what we had printed on the back?" She flicked the T-shirt around so Mary could see a word emblazoned in black across the back. " 'Nevermore,' " Hannah then quoted in a portentous growl.

"Excellent!" Mary exclaimed with a light clap of her hands.

Thunderous applause from the auditorium halted their ensuing chuckles, however, and signaled the end of commencement. As the last student walked from the stage, Jack stood up, unfolded some papers in his hand, and moved toward the lectern. Mary grabbed Hannah's hand and squeezed it.

Hannah squeezed back and then asked in a fraught whisper, "Where's Hayden?"

"He's coming." Mary grimaced. "I *hope* he's coming."

At the lectern Jack pulled out his glasses and perched them on the end of his long nose. He coughed a few times and began. He congratulated the students and thanked the audience, but just as he launched into his prepared speech his microphone suddenly squealed and promptly cut out. Perplexed, he looked up. At that same moment the lights in the auditorium dimmed to a dull glow, and a huge white cloth unfurled from the rafters at the back of the stage.

Sofia was doing it, Mary thought as excitement bubbled in her throat. She was doing it!

As the audience hissed and murmured and Jack made panicked gesticulations to the people around him, the white cloth began to glow, and the words *Edgar Allan Poe at Manhattan U* flickered into focus on the giant makeshift screen. The film's title was quickly replaced with Hayden's smiling face. He was wearing a casual denim shirt, open at the neck, and as ever he looked handsome and at ease. From the gasps and whispers Mary heard in front of her, it was clear the students recognized who it was immediately.

With a sparkle in his movie-star eyes, Hayden spoke straight to the camera.

"Before you trip off out of here with your brand-new degrees, there's something you ought to know," he began. "I want to tell you a little story about Edgar Allan Poe and your university. Yes, your very own Manhattan U."

The mention of their school set off a tidal wave of excited whispers, whoops, and applause among the students. These noises only got louder as the camera panned back to show Hayden walking along Third Street and then coming to a stop outside the new business school building.

Mary could hear Jack's voice amid the chatter and clapping.

"What the hell is this?" he was barking to someone at the side of the stage.

Up on the vast white sheet the movie played on. Hayden was now explaining about the demolition of the Poe house a few years ago, and his commentary was intercut with old drawings and photos of the town house. As Hayden went on to talk about "The Raven" and how it was believed that Poe did important revisions to the famous poem while living on Third Street, Mary smiled to herself. These were the words she had written just last week. She'd had so much fun staying up into the night with Sofia and Tom and Hayden, hammering out ideas, and then going back to Sarah and Greg's apartment and working on the script. The film was just a short documentary, not exactly Mary's genre, but writing the script felt good. It was like blowing the cobwebs off some twinkling chandelier she'd kept hidden for way too long. She knew now, after writing the script, that new stories, new voices, new fictional worlds, and even new novels were waiting for her. Indeed, they itched to spring out of her.

"Turn this crap off," Jack's voice bellowed out once again, causing Mary's eyes to snap downward and watch him.

He was pacing the stage, his cheeks flushed and his brow furrowed. A flurry of activity was happening at the side of the stage, and graduation officials were racing up and down the aisles. But still the movie continued to roll, and the audience, clearly baffled but nonetheless intrigued, murmured as they watched Hayden walking around the garden and explaining its imminent demolition.

"Poe," he was saying, "once frequented a tavern on this very spot."

Mary's eyes were still on Jack, however. She could tell by the way he was raking his fingers through his hair that he was mad as hell. He always raked his hair like this in the moments before he would lash out at her. The memory gave her an instant chill. But she quickly reminded herself that today—only today—Jack's anger was a good thing. It was what they'd hoped for, what they'd planned for.

Mary looked from Jack over at Hannah. Hannah's eyes weren't on the movie either. Instead they flickered anxiously toward the door. She caught Mary's eye.

"I thought he'd be here by now," she hissed. "If he doesn't get here soon, the dean's going to shut this off and carry on with his speech like nothing happened."

Now it was Mary's turn to give a worried glance over at the door. Hannah was right: If Hayden didn't show, their plan might not work. The movie by itself wasn't enough to get Jack really mad. After all, the movie didn't make any accusations about Jack, and didn't mention the artifacts Jack had hidden in the safe-deposit box. That was all supposed to come with Hayden's arrival.

As Mary's chest began to flutter in panic, her attention was soon brought back to the stage. The lights in the auditorium had snapped on, and the audience started to boo as the movie began to fade into the cloth under the glaring lights. But no sooner had the lights come on than they flashed off. The audience immediately cheered as Hayden's face stared out at the auditorium once again.

Under the white cloth Jack was pacing up and down and is-suing violent orders to people at the side of the stage. His hands were now flying through his thick gray hair.

"What do you mean, you can't get in?" he was barking at an usher in a blue blazer. "Please, will you get this crap off?"

Jack was bellying up to the terrified young man when the lights snapped on again and the movie completely disappeared from the screen. Jack backed away from the usher, and the usher, visibly relieved, scuttled offstage. Meanwhile, Mary and Hannah looked up at the auditorium's dazzling lights and then exchanged pan-icked glances.

"Someone must have gotten into the projector room and stopped them," Hannah said.

Jack was back at the lectern, putting on his glasses and tapping the microphone. Within a few seconds his voice boomed out from the speakers.

"I'm very sorry about that, ladies and gentlemen," he began.

The audience was still bustling and murmuring, and a few students shouted, "Show the movie, Dean Havemeyer." But he ignored them and instead reopened his papers and started to read. His voice quavered a little at first, but soon he found his stride. Mary's heart began to sink as he blustered on. Perhaps they should have named him and shamed him in the movie, after all. Now the students would just think the film was some stunt pulled by a bunch of nutty Poe fans. They wouldn't think it had anything to do with Jack.

However, as Mary considered this with her heart sinking further, the doors beside them swung open and Hayden burst in.

"Thank God," Mary and Hannah exclaimed, and as they took in the costume he was wearing they both chuckled.

Hayden beamed at them from under his dark, flowing wig, his heavy fake eyebrows, and his matching mustache.

"Hello, ladies," he whispered, before straightening his ornate white neck scarf, tugging on his dark velvet jacket, and moving off with a purposeful stride down the aisle.

Jack didn't see him at first. But when Hayden was on the stage just a few paces away, Jack sensed his presence and looked up. His brow furrowed in confusion for a second, but then he turned back to his paper and tried to carry on.

"Jack Havemeyer?" Hayden asked when he was just a few feet from the dean.

Irritated and confused, Jack snapped off his glasses and glared at Hayden. "Yes," he barked.

Hayden held out a hand. "Edgar Allan Poe," Hayden said. "Pleased to meet you."

Jack didn't move. He continued glowering at Hayden, and after a few beats he asked, "Hayden? Is that you?"

The audience let out a crescendo of animated murmurs. Students and parents were beginning to figure out that it was indeed Hayden Burgess under the dark wig and comic eyebrows.

Up onstage, Hayden let his hand drop and gave the dean a cool smile. "As I said, my name's Edgar Allan Poe, and I have a question I want to ask you, Dean Havemeyer."

Jack's cheeks flushed with confusion and then with renewed fury. But he attempted to keep his cool and said with a wry grin and a wave at the audience, "As you can see, *Mr. Poe,* I'm rather busy. Could this wait?"

There were a few muffled laughs in the auditorium. Mostly there was silence. Everyone was transfixed as Hayden inched closer to Jack.

This time Jack backed away, held his hands up, and hissed, "Good God, man. What are you playing at?"

"Dean Havemeyer, I believe you're in possession of something that rightfully belongs to me." Hayden's face was perfectly deadpan as he spoke.

"What are you talking about?" Jack barked, as one of his hands moved toward his hair and his enraged raking began.

"A letter I was writing," Hayden went on, still with a smile. "And a copy of a poem I was editing."

The color ran from Jack's face, and his hand froze midrake. After a pause, he said in a strangled shout, "Please get off this stage."

Hayden didn't move an inch. "I would like my documents back first. I believe you—or perhaps a friend of yours—found them at my old residence on Third Street, and I'd really like them returned."

"Get off this stage," Jack boomed. The veins in his neck were now visible and pulsating, and his forehead was furrowed into a thousand lines.

As Mary watched from her hideout at the back of the auditorium, every pore and every muscle in her body could feel Jack's fury, and even though he was a long way away and his anger was directed at someone else, her throat tightened with a fear she knew all too well.

"Wilkins." Hayden stood his ground, unfazed by Jack's anger. "I believe your friend is called Wilkins. I hear he runs a construction company. . . ."

But Hayden didn't finish, because Jack had lunged forward and snatched Hayden's velvety lapels in his shaking hands.

"Get off this stage," Jack repeated in a raging bellow just inches from Hayden's face. His knuckles were turning white and his face crimson.

The auditorium was silent, utterly and completely silent. Even the excited whispers that had accompanied Hayden's arrival had died out.

"Dean Havemeyer," Hayden said, still managing to stay composed under Jack's fearsome grip, "in exchange for my documents, I'll happily give you this."

Hayden then fished in his pocket and pulled out a piece of yellowing paper. Jack, meanwhile, dropped his hands from Hayden's jacket, stepped back a little, and then swiped the paper out of Hayden's hand.

"It's 'The Raven.'" Hayden smiled, his fake mustache twitching. "I heard you were after a copy."

Jack looked down at the paper and then up at Hayden. Mary, although far away, caught the almost imperceptible flicker. She knew that flicker too well. She knew Jack had been pushed to his limit and he was about to erupt.

She was right.

"Get off this stage," Jack roared one last time before throwing his fist toward Hayden.

Luckily Hayden sensed the punch coming and dodged effortlessly out of the way. Jack's fist flew through empty air and landed with a thud on the lectern. As Jack let out a shocked grunt, the audience gasped and Mary winced, remembering the force of that fist on her own body.

"Cool it, Dean," Mary heard Hayden saying.

But Jack wasn't listening. He was already pushing past Hayden, his face still flushed with anger and now embarrassment too, and he stalked off the stage. He then thundered up the aisle with hundreds of students' eyes watching him. As Mary saw him get closer and closer, her blood pulsed in every vein and her knees began to shake. He was about ten feet away when he saw her. His angry hazel eyes locked on hers and he began to move faster toward her, like a heat-seeking missile. But before he reached Mary, Hannah moved quickly in front of her, and at the same moment the lights in the auditorium snapped off and the movie began to play once again.

The noise and sudden darkness threw Jack off course. Instead of grabbing for Mary, as she thought he might, he swerved away and grabbed the door handle. Pulling open the heavy door, he turned and gave her the most withering stare.

"You'll pay for this," he hissed.

When the door banged shut behind him, Mary let out a long, low sigh.

"Are you okay?" Hannah asked, touching her arm gently.

Mary nodded and smiled. "He's gone," she murmured. "I'm okay."

Just a short while later, the credits to the movie rolled and the provost followed with a hasty, confused, and slightly ruffled farewell speech. The students were soon bustling out, chattering about all that had happened during the ceremony. As they left, Mary and Hannah thrust flyers and T-shirts into every passing hand, and Hayden, who'd quickly recovered from his scrape with the dean, scampered back to help them. Still excited by his presence, students bustled around Hayden, clogging the doorway and begging him to autograph their flyers, their graduation programs, even their shirtsleeves under their gowns.

When the auditorium was finally empty, Mary, Hannah, and Hayden slumped against the wall.

"I'm sorry he went for you," Mary said, looking over at Hayden. "I thought he'd get mad, but I didn't think he'd actually try to hit you, not in front of all the students."

Hayden was pulling off his wig. "But he didn't hit me, did he?" He grinned.

The doors beside them thumped open before Mary could respond.

"We did it!" Sofia shouted excitedly as she strode in. Ashleigh followed, waving her hands goofily in the air.

"We did it!" whooped Ashleigh.

When the hugs and high fives were done, Hannah asked, "What was going on up there?"

Sofia smirked and winked at Ashleigh. "Some small hitches, which we soon straightened out."

Ashleigh looked at the others and jerked her thumb at Sofia. "She placated the security guards with promises of minor parts in major motion pictures."

"And when that didn't work anymore"—Sofia laughed, now jerking her thumb toward Ashleigh—"she threatened legal action and they ran from the building."

Mary laughed. "Whatever you did, it worked."

"We can't keep dallying around congratulating ourselves. The show ain't over yet," Sofia interjected, and then, looking at Ashleigh, she asked, "How are the party preparations going?"

"I spoke to Sam earlier," Ashleigh replied. "She's in the garden with Gina, Tom, and the kids. All the decorations are up and the food's been delivered."

"Great." Sofia clapped her hands. "So off to the president we go!"

"President?" Hayden piped up, looking confused.

Mary patted his shoulder. "The president of Manhattan U. Not the one in the White House." She raised her eyebrows and added, "Unfortunately."

As they all filed out, Mary looked down at one last flyer still in her hand. *Save the Garden from the Grim Reaper,* it read in bold print, and then underneath it explained about Poe, the tavern, and how the garden should be preserved as a site of historical and literary importance. Then it invited the students to a postgraduation party at the garden that same afternoon. Jack's name was nowhere in the text.

But it didn't matter. The glory of some great Poe find would no longer be his. If a manuscript was ever found, it would be rather incongruous for Jack to take all the credit while also having to admit where he'd gotten the clues from in the first place and how he didn't declare them to the university when Wilkins had passed them along. He would be disgraced, and if the women played their cards right with the president, perhaps his beloved parking lot would never happen, either.

Mary smiled to herself as she followed the others out of the building's large glass doors and into the bright sunshine.

Epilogue

Three Weeks Later

It was a beautiful summer afternoon: hot but not sticky; breezy but not windy. The grass in the garden was a vivid, flawless green, not yet parched by the July temperatures that awaited it. Hannah was the last to arrive, and as she pushed her way through the gate, she spotted the others sitting on a sprawling blanket near the maple tree. With the sun sparkling through leaves, the scene was idyllic. Sofia sat with her eyes closed, her dark curls tossed back and her face turned happily to the sky. Ashleigh was opposite with her legs crossed. She was wearing a billowing gypsy shirt, and her fine blond hair was set free from its usual barrette. Between the two of them Mary was laughing as her long hair flittered across her face.

Hannah hadn't visited the garden since the party three weeks ago because she'd been too busy settling into her new place in Brooklyn. That day, graduation day, the entire lawn had been covered with people. Students were dancing with *Save the Garden* T-shirts pulled haphazardly over their graduation gowns. Parents milled around by the buffet table, some of them also sporting T-shirts over their suits and floral dresses. Everywhere she turned, Hannah's painting glinted and shimmered out at her. The garden was filled with balloons, streamers, chatter, music, and laughter. And with no sign of the dean or the police, the party went on long into the evening.

Now the garden seemed like another place entirely, so quiet and still. Looking around, though, Hannah noticed that she and her friends weren't alone. A couple sat on a nearby bench, huddled close, looking at a newspaper together. At the opposite end of the garden, near where a blue tarpaulin was stretched around the excavation site, a woman in a flowing linen dress ran in circles with her small white dog.

Sofia was the first to see Hannah. She shaded her eyes from the bright sunshine and flashed a wide smile.

"Hannah!" she cried. She then pointed to a bottle of champagne sitting in the middle of the blanket and added, "It's about time you got here. That baby is itching to be opened."

Hannah circled the group, squatting to give them warm hugs, and then plopped herself down on the blanket.

"They've started," she said, pointing toward the tarpaulin at the end of the garden.

Mary nodded. "They started on Monday."

"And have they found anything yet?"

Sofia laughed. "If they have, they're not letting anyone know about it. Although I was out here a couple of days ago with the kids and there was a lot of excitement. All these bespectacled archaeologists looking animated—or as animated as a group of bespectacled archaeologists can look. They were darting in and out behind the tarpaulin and lugging in all kinds of weird equipment and boxes."

Hannah looked over at the dig site again. "We'll find out one day, I suppose." She thought for a moment and then said with her mouth twisting into a smile, "I wonder if the dean has been past to take a look."

Mary chuckled. "Now that accolades and academic superstardom no longer await him, he won't give a damn. Anyway, my soon-to-be-ex-husband is not a dean anymore," she added with a sparkle in her eye.

"Really?" Hannah clapped her hands.

Sofia nodded. "The announcement was made yesterday. The president 'accepted Jack's resignation.'" She flicked her fingers to make quotes. "In other words, he kicked his sorry ass out the door."

"I knew that president was a good guy." Hannah laughed.

After the graduation ceremony, the four women had gone

straight to Manhattan U's presidential office. On the president's huge oak desk they spread out maps of Manhattan, copies of contracts with Wilkins Construction, Polaroids of Poe's letter and the old newsprint fragments, and a letter from the Poe museum confirming these items as authentic. Mary had even brought the photograph of Jack and his old Princeton classmate Alan Wilkins. The president, after looking it all over and hearing their case, was shocked and furious. By the end of day, just hours after graduation had ended, the president had construction work on the garden halted and ordered an immediate investigation. A week later the president agreed to allow an archaeological team, funded by the Poe Foundation, to start digging in the garden, but only with the proviso that after the work was done, the garden would be returned to normal and preserved as the university's "Poe Garden."

"He *is* a good guy," Mary muttered.

The four women were silent for a few moments as they smiled to themselves. Then, remembering something, Hannah turned to Mary and said, "I picked up *The New Yorker* yesterday. Your story was awesome. Really awesome. I loved it."

Mary thanked Hannah while giving a modest wave.

Sofia cut in. "Did you know it took her three days to write it? Three days! Then, when she sent it off, they agreed to run it *that* week. Can you believe that? *The New Yorker* agreeing to publish a short story that very week! Writers eat their own laptops, chop off their testicles, do all kinds of crazy shit for a slot in *The New Yorker*. And Mary over here waltzes in with her three-day-old story and they're like, 'Hey, let's run it tomorrow.'"

Everyone laughed while Mary shook her head. "Mostly I have Jerry to thank. He knew someone who knew someone—"

Ashleigh interrupted. "And, of course, the facts that you won the Pulitzer and that this new story is incredible have nothing to do with it."

They all laughed again, and this time Mary joined them.

"What a perfect segue," Sofia said, reaching for the champagne. "I do believe we are all gathered here to celebrate. The first toast," she added, grimacing as she tweaked the bottle's cork, "goes to Mary and her fine story!"

There was a loud pop, and fizzing champagne gushed from the bottle. Luckily Ashleigh was already holding a plastic cup and lunged forward to catch the flow. When they all had cups in their hands, they held them up, tapped them together, and Hannah said, "To Mary and *The New Yorker!*"

"To Mary and *The New Yorker!*" Sofia and Ashleigh repeated with wide grins.

After taking a sip of her champagne, Mary waved her hand and said, "But we have more to celebrate than just my silly story. Ashleigh, Sofia." She turned from one to the other. "You said you both have big news. Come on, out with it."

Ashleigh and Sofia argued about who should go first. "No, you." "No, you," they squabbled.

With a laugh, Ashleigh finally opened up her purse, pulled out a stack of business cards, and passed them around. Hannah looked down at the small card in her hand. In large embossed writing it read, *Ashleigh Rocksbury, Attorney-at-Law,* and gave her details and an address in Tribeca.

Hannah whooped. "You did it!"

Ashleigh nodded and beamed. "Yup. My office opens next month."

Everyone cheered, kissed Ashleigh, and tapped their glasses in another toast. When they were done, Sofia asked, "So what did Senator Daddy have to say about you turning down the partnership at his old firm?"

"I have no idea." Ashleigh grinned. "He hasn't spoken to me since I told him about Sam."

Sofia shook her head and looked concerned.

"It's fine." Ashleigh continued to smile. "For the first time in my life I don't care what he thinks, and it feels great. I'm positive that one day he'll get over himself and accept me and Sam. My mom has already broken rank and started calling me. It's only a matter of time before he follows suit."

"And what about your uncle?" Hannah asked. "Was he mad about you leaving?"

Ashleigh shook her head. "Not at all. He was sad to see me go, but he's a good man. He understood."

As Ashleigh spoke, Sofia suddenly reached out, tugged on Hannah's arm, and pointed. "Sorry to interrupt, Ashleigh," she said, "but I think I'm having déjà vu."

Everyone swiveled to look where Sofia was pointing.

"If I'm not mistaken, I'm sure I've seen that sexy art professor standing there once before," Sofia added, tweaking Hannah's arm playfully.

Sofia was right, of course; it was Patrick. He was standing outside the garden, smiling in through the high fence. Hannah immediately felt herself blush. She wasn't sure if it was because of Sofia's teasing or because, just fifteen feet away, with twinkling green eyes and a broad smile, stood Patrick.

"Excuse me," she murmured, pushing herself to her feet.

"Take as long as you need." Sofia chortled. "As *long* as you need."

Hannah moved toward the fence. Instead of feeling heavy with guilt and fear, as she had on that cold, dreary day only a couple of months ago when she'd poured her heart out to Sofia, she now felt giddy and joyful. Her steps felt light, her heartbeats even lighter.

"Hello," Patrick said as she reached the fence.

"Hey," she replied, reaching out to touch his fingers, which, in between the honeysuckle, were grasping the fence's steel struts.

"I didn't mean to interrupt," he said. "I just saw you and wanted to say hi."

Hannah smiled, and as he laced his fingers in hers she whispered, "Hi."

They remained like that for a few moments, just smiling and staring, until Patrick finally said, "Oh, and I wanted to give you this." He pulled a small package wrapped in tissue from his pocket.

Hannah grinned as she took the square package into her hands and began unwrapping it. "A present? For me?" She giggled.

As the last piece of delicate paper fell away, she gasped and then giggled. In a small cardboard box with a clear front window there stood a toy figurine of Sigmund Freud. *He remembered,* Hannah thought, her heart skipping. Patrick remembered that night and the saucy joke she had made about her big, hard copy of Freud's *Interpretation of Dreams.*

"I thought he might like to sit on the windowsill in your new studio," Patrick said in a whisper as Hannah continued to stare at the box and the small bearded man. "You know, watching over you, making sure you're okay."

Hannah felt a lump rising in her throat. Patrick knew how hard it had been for her to say good-bye to the old studio—and mostly how hard it had been to say good-bye to Bill and Diane. Traipsing down the familiar stairs lugging easels and boxes, with Bill and Diane looking on with sad eyes, was one of the hardest things Hannah had ever done. But she'd done it, and she'd survived. And now her small studio in her new apartment was her sanctuary, full of light and possibility.

"Thank you, Patrick," she whispered finally, as she reached out to touch his hand again.

"My pleasure." He smiled and then, after a pause, he said, "Okay, I must leave you to it."

"You don't want to join us?" Hannah suddenly felt an ache in her stomach. The same ache she got whenever she said good-bye to him.

He shook his head. "Oh, my, no," he said with an impish grin. "I couldn't intrude upon you and your ladies."

Hannah rolled her eyes and then tried to pinch at his middle through the fence but Patrick jumped away before she could reach him. As he backed across the sidewalk, he blew a small kiss and mouthed, *See you later.*

"See you later," she whispered back.

When Hannah returned to the blanket, plopped down, and took her plastic glass back into her hands, the others looked at her with smiles, mischievous and expectant.

"Well?" Sofia demanded.

"We . . ." Hannah began as the heat returned to her cheeks, "we've been on a couple of dates."

"Dates." Sofia winked. "I see. The guy postpones his trip back home to England for some *dates*. Makes perfect sense to me."

Hannah shook her head, smiled, and covered her burning cheeks. "It's true," she pleaded.

It was true. A few days after moving out from Michael's, Hannah went to find Patrick at the gallery. She knew that if she didn't go, she would always regret it. She wasn't expecting anything big; she wasn't even sure she wanted anything big. The wounds from her broken marriage were still too sore, and they needed to heal before she threw herself into anything new. But when she saw Patrick and they went from the gallery to a cozy nearby pub, Hannah had talked late into the night and Patrick had listened. When closing time came, they didn't go home together; Hannah wasn't ready for that. But Patrick offered to stay. Perhaps, he suggested, if he spent the summer in New York he could take her out on a few dates. "I could court you like a gentleman," he offered with a coy smile.

"We've been on four dates so far," she said, looking at her friends. "It's been nice. Really nice."

Mary held up her glass. "To you and Patrick and many more dates."

"And to you and Jerry too," Hannah responded, grinning and pleased to shift the attention elsewhere.

Sofia's ears pricked at Jerry's name. "And what *is* happening with you and our lovely Mr. Milo?"

It was now Mary's turn to look bashful. She looked from Sofia to Hannah, and Hannah could see in her eyes all the same excitements and fears. On the one hand the possibility of a new love was exciting and magical, but it was frightening and fragile and overwhelming all at the same time.

"We went on some dates too." Mary gave a soft laugh. "But now he's back home in San Francisco." She then paused and took a deep breath. "Perhaps we'll go on a few more when I get there next month."

Hannah, Sofia, and Ashleigh all dropped their glasses from their lips.

"You're going?" Hannah barked in surprise.

Mary shrugged and nodded. "Sarah persuaded me it was the right thing to do. She was insistent, in fact. She took me aside at her wedding last week and told me that I had to live my own life, and that she and the twins could not hold me back. Those were her words." Mary laughed again. "My daughter told *me* that; can you believe it?" She shook her head.

Sofia reached across and squeezed Mary's hand. "We're going to miss you. But Sarah's right; you have to go. The West Coast needs you. Golden Gate College needs you. And Mr. Milo probably won't complain either!"

The women then toasted new loves.

"And old loves," Ashleigh added, while she and Sofia exchanged knowing nods.

The four of them sat back to enjoy the sweet-tasting champagne. The sun was now beginning to dip behind the tall buildings and trees, but the breeze was still warm, and a golden light hung across the garden. A few tiny birds floated and danced in the sky above the maple tree.

Finally Hannah looked at Sofia. "Come on, Sofia. Enough about us. What's your big news?"

"Thank God, a chance to talk about *me*!" Sofia joked, slapping her hand to her forehead. After they'd all laughed, she sat back and pointed to herself, "Ladies, you are looking at the newly appointed president of Muñoz Films."

Sofia went on to tell them that, with some help from Hayden, she was setting up her own film production company.

"Unfortunately, I'll be forced to cast my dear brother-in-law in lead roles." She grinned. "Perhaps that's not so bad. After all, his pretty face pulls in the punters."

"No more stay-at-home mom, then?" Mary asked.

"I'm going to be more of a stay-at-home-but-be-on-the-cell-phone-a-lot-and-sometimes-racing-out-the-door mom." She laughed.

Ashleigh then sat forward, tapped Sofia's knee, and asked, "And what's going to be your first movie?"

"I haven't thought too much about it yet. Hayden and I have some artistic differences." She chuckled. "He wants to make interesting, edgy, art house films. I, on the other hand, want to make action movies with lots of cool women running around kicking ass." Then, leaning back on her elbows, Sofia scanned the group and said, "You know what? That gives me an idea. Perhaps my first movie will be . . ." She paused, her eyes darting playfully from side to side, and said with a growl, *"Revenge of the Professors' Wives' Club."*

There was a beat of silence, and then the group erupted in loud, irrepressible laughter. When their giggles finally abated, they raised their glasses once more.

"To *Revenge of the Professors' Wives' Club,*" they sang out in unison.

Photo by Adrianna Glaviano

Joanne Rendell was born and raised in the United Kingdom. She has a PhD in literature and is married to a professor at New York University. She currently lives in faculty housing in New York City with her family. *The Professors' Wives' Club* is her first novel. Visit her Web site at www.joannerendell.com.

THE PROFESSORS' WIVES' CLUB

Joanne Rendell

This Conversation Guide is intended to enrich the
individual reading experience, as well as encourage us
to explore these topics together—because books,
and life, are meant for sharing.

A CONVERSATION WITH JOANNE RENDELL

Q. Why did you write a novel about professors' wives?

A. The initial inspiration came amid a rather giggly, wine-soaked evening with one of my girlfriends, who, like me, is a professor's wife. After our usual catch-up, the cabernet began to flow and we found ourselves gossiping about other faculty wives. We talked about a wife planning a boob job, another pregnant with her fifth child. The best piece of gossip came last, however: a professor's wife who'd just run off with one of her husband's grad students.

The next morning I started to hammer out my first ideas for the novel. As I typed, the more I realized what intriguing characters professors' wives would make. Even if they aren't professors themselves (which many are), most professors' wives are deeply connected and invested in the university where their husband or partner works. Like my friend and me, they live in faculty housing, they go to the campus gym, often their kids go to the same day care.

Yet, these women—women like my friend and me—have little power when it comes to university decisions. They don't get much say if the university decides its budget cannot stretch to child care anymore, or it wants to close its faculty housing.

Q. Speaking of which, where did you come up with the idea about professors' wives doing battle with a ruthless dean to save a faculty garden from demolition?

A. The idea came to me at the NYU children's playground. Although situated on busy Bleecker Street amidst towering faculty housing buildings, the university playground is a serene little oasis in the heart of downtown Manhattan. It has delightful amounts of shade, two vast sandpits, and a heavy gate that even the nimblest of little Houdini fingers can't undo.

Not long after I'd started working on ideas for the book, I was playing with my son at this playground and suddenly had a gripping panic. Wouldn't it be awful if the playground were shut down and demolished? Would NYU ever decide to use the space for a new lecture hall or, worse, a parking garage?

I looked around at the park and the other moms with their kids, and it then occurred to me how all the moms I knew there would put up a tenacious fight if the university ever tried such a thing.

The book flooded out after that day. In fact, over the next few months I could often be found typing furiously away on the book, sitting on a bench in the university playground with my son playing in the nearby sandpit.

Q. Your book portrays not only a unique story about professors' wives, but also a story about the power and strength of female friendships. Why did you choose to write such a story?

A. Relationships between women frequently get a bad rap, in my opinion. Women are too often portrayed in film, TV, and books as bitchy, competitive, and at odds with one another. We constantly see the bitchy woman boss mistreating the young female employee, or the woman who treats her nanny like a slave, or the sisters who hate each other, or the mother and daughter who constantly fight, or the "friends" who bitch behind each other's back or betray each other over a guy.

Granted, in real life, women can be like this. But not *all* the time. Women, in my experience, also have wonderful, supportive, and nurturing relationships with other women.

I wrote *The Professors' Wives' Club* to echo what *Sex and the City, Steel Magnolias,* and books like Kate Jacobs's *The Friday Night Knitting Club* have done a wonderful job showing us. In other words, how joyful, fun, powerful, and sometimes life-sustaining female relationships and friendships can be.

Q. Which character is most like you?

A. Probably Sofia. She's a mom living in downtown Manhattan with a nice husband who's a professor . . . which sounds a lot like me. Also, I gave birth watching *Terminator* movies just as Sofia does in the book (it really is true!). However, Sofia has a feistiness that I can only fantasize about having. She's fearless yet also fun and loving. I love that about her.

Q. Your book is set at the fictional Manhattan U, which bears more than a passing resemblance to NYU. How much of the book is true?

A. Well, my husband is a professor at NYU; we live in university housing, so that's the world I know, and so, of course, real life sneaks into the novel here and there. But I'm not telling exactly where. My husband likes his job at the university too much!

Q. Edgar Allan Poe and his poem "The Raven" play an important role in The Professors' Wives' Club. *What were your reasons for this?*

A. I always wanted *The Professors' Wives' Club* to have some kind of literary subplot running through it—I have a PhD in English literature, after all! I chose Edgar Allan Poe and "The Raven" for three reasons. First, I just love Poe's work, and particularly "The Raven." Second, Poe wrote and published the poem when living in Greenwich Village, where I live and where my book is set. Finally, Manhattan U is loosely based on NYU, and NYU and Edgar Allan Poe have a history. During the time he lived in the Village, Poe was meant to deliver a reading at the university but was too drunk to show up! Also, a few years ago, NYU caused a furor by pulling down the old house on Third Street where Edgar Allan Poe lived for six months, to make way for a new law school building. Both these stories show up in the novel.

Q. One of your characters, Mary Havemeyer, is in a physically abusive relationship. What were your reasons for including such a character?

A. When people hear the title *The Professors' Wives' Club,* the last thing they would probably expect is a story about a professor's wife and her abusive husband. After all, aren't male professors a smart and gentlemanly crew who would never abuse their wives? For the most part, of course, they are.

But domestic violence goes on in all walks of life—including behind the closed doors of faculty marriages—and I wanted to show this. I wanted to show that smart women, strong women, and accomplished women can be abused by their supposedly smart and accomplished husbands.

There aren't many portrayals of domestic violence in popular culture—especially few in middle- or upper-class settings. Yet, in spite of this, the Family Violence Prevention Fund reports that nearly one-third of American women report being physically or sexually abused by a husband or boyfriend at some point in their lives. This statistic is staggering, and thus, it seems to me, we need to represent, talk about, and deal with the issue of domestic violence much, *much* more often.

Q. You have a second book coming out in 2009. What's it about?

A. The book tells the story of two female professors working in the English department at Manhattan U (the same university featured in *The Professors' Wives' Club*). I had a lot of fun writing about professors' wives, but I always knew I wanted to write a novel that explored the campus in more detail. I wanted to show what life is like in the classroom, in faculty meetings, in the library, on study-abroad programs. I know a lot about this world from my own years in academia, and I had a lot of fun spinning all the gossip, competition, jealousies, even forbidden romantic liaisons into my new novel.

Q. You have a PhD in literature, but you decided not to stay in academia. What is it like being a novelist instead?

A. It's a lot of fun. Creating my own fictional worlds is proving just as fun, perhaps more fun, than studying and analyzing the fictional worlds created by other people. I'm glad I decided not to stay in academia. Being a writer instead of a professor means no faculty meetings, no teaching prep, no tenure worries, no never-ending reading lists, and no hours fretting over a lost citation. However, I do acknowledge the rich foundation that my academic studies gave me for my current writing life. It taught me how to read books with a keen and studious eye. It taught me the power of words and the tools of research. It gave me great training for executing projects and working for hours on my own with only my laptop and a steaming cup of tea for company! Plus, I can still enjoy the best parts of the academic world through my husband. Together we are faculty fellows in residence in one of NYU's dorms, which means we have a lot of interaction with students, and I get to organize and attend all kinds of interesting discussions and events.

Oh, and there's also the not-so-small fact that the intriguing and gossip-ridden world of academia has given me great fodder for my novels!

QUESTIONS
FOR DISCUSSION

1. Who was your favorite character, and why?

2. Jack Havemeyer is an ambitious dean, and a mean and sometimes violent husband. If you were in Mary Havemeyer's position, how would you have dealt with Jack? Can you understand why she stayed in their marriage so long?

3. Look again at chapter six and compare Mary, the fearless and confident teacher, with Mary at home, frightened and silenced by her husband. Do you see her as a strong or a weak woman? Is it possible to be both?

4. Hannah has a one-night stand with her professor Patrick, even though she's married to Michael. Did you feel sympathetic toward her character despite the fact that she cheats? Could you ever see yourself in her position?

5. Why do you think Hannah married Michael? She talks about her loneliness, her love of his parents, and how he was different from men she met in the fashion world. Do you think the way she treats Michael in the end is selfish or for the best?

6. Sofia gave up a fast-paced and exciting career to be a stay-at-home mother. What are her reasons for doing this, and do you think you would have done the same in her position?

7. After the birth of a baby, relationships can often be fraught, given the lack of sleep, new responsibility, recovery period, and sometimes postpartum depression or baby blues. Tom seems to be a loving, fun, and loyal husband. Nevertheless, after the birth of Edgar, Sofia starts having suspicions about him. Is this a realistic depiction of the insecurities women face after they've given birth? And can you think of instances where you've seen similar behavior?

8. Ashleigh has been living with her girlfriend, Sam, for some time, but still hasn't told her parents. What do you think about the way Ashleigh handles her girlfriend and her parents in the novel? How difficult do you think it would be for someone like Ashleigh to come out to parents like Chad and Thelma Rocksbury?

9. Coming to understand and appreciate her cousin Gina is an important transitional moment in Ashleigh's story. Why?

10. The faculty garden is central to the novel's plot. Why and how does it become so important to the four women? Why do you think they fight so hard to save it?

11. The author tells the story through alternating points of view. Did this affect your reading of the story?

12. How did the author use setting—and, in particular, the

garden—to reflect the moods of the characters and the tensions in the plot?

13. Jack wasn't always a ruthless and ambitious man. Mary observes that his anger started after the death of his father. Why do you think his father's death changed him in this way? Has grief dramatically changed anyone you know?

14. What would the story look like if it were told from Jack's point of view?

15. The tone of *The Professors' Wives' Club* is generally light and upbeat. However, there are a number of poignant scenes, and the novel deals with some serious issues, such as domestic violence. Did this mix of light and more emotionally intense moments and themes work for you? Did any scene or issue touch you? Did it resonate with your own life?

16. What did you make of the Edgar Allan Poe subplot? Did it add something unique or interesting to the novel? What did you learn about Poe and his poem "The Raven"?

17. The importance and power of female friendships is a central theme of the novel. Relationships between women frequently get a bad rap in popular culture. Women are often portrayed in film, TV, and books as bitchy, competitive, and at odds with one another. However, *The Professors' Wives' Club* paints a very positive picture of women supporting and enjoying one another and enabling one another to stand up for their lives, their dreams, and their dignity. Is this realistic?

18. How do you think this novel compares to other books, TV shows, and movies that deal with female friendships, such as *Sex and the City, Desperate Housewives, Steel Magnolias,* and *The Friday Night Knitting Club?* Does it do anything new or different?